A Year at The Cosy Cottage Café

The Cosy Cottage Café

Rachel Griffiths

Cosy Cottage Books

For my family with love always
xxx

Cover Art by Stunning Book Covers

Copyright © by RachelA.Griffiths 2018

All rights reserved. This book or any portion thereof may not be reproduced or used in any manner whatsoever without the express written permission of the author, except for the use of brief quotations in a book review.

❦ Created with Vellum

Contents

Summer at The Cosy Cottage Café

Summer at The Cosy Cottage Café	11
Chapter 1	13
Chapter 2	24
Chapter 3	36
Chapter 4	46
Chapter 5	57
Chapter 6	62
Chapter 7	72
Chapter 8	84
Chapter 9	94
Chapter 10	103
Chapter 11	108
Chapter 12	115

Autumn at The Cosy Cottage Café

Autumn at The Cosy Cottage Café	125
Chapter 1	127
Chapter 2	138
Chapter 3	146
Chapter 4	155
Chapter 5	161
Chapter 6	173
Chapter 7	183
Chapter 8	194
Chapter 9	204
Chapter 10	217
Chapter 11	228

Winter at the Cosy Cottage Café

Winter at The Cosy Cottage Café	241
Chapter 1	243
Chapter 2	250
Chapter 3	255
Chapter 4	262
Chapter 5	268
Chapter 6	274
Chapter 7	285
Chapter 8	294
Chapter 9	302
Chapter 10	309
Chapter 11	317
Chapter 12	326
Chapter 13	338
Chapter 14	348
Chapter 15	355
Chapter 16	360
Chapter 17	366
Chapter 18	372

Spring at The Cosy Cottage Café

Spring at The Cosy Cottage Café	381
Chapter 1	383
Chapter 2	389
Chapter 3	393
Chapter 4	399
Chapter 5	405
Chapter 6	412
Chapter 7	416
Chapter 8	421
Chapter 9	430
Chapter 10	436

Chapter 11	441
Chapter 12	447
Chapter 13	453
Chapter 14	458
Chapter 15	463
Chapter 16	467
Chapter 17	473
Chapter 18	479
Chapter 19	485
Spring Spritzer Cocktail	501

A Wedding at The Cosy Cottage Café

A Wedding at The Cosy Cottage Café	505
1. Allie	507
2. Dawn	511
3. Camilla	515
4. Honey	520
5. Allie	523
6. Dawn	528
7. Camilla	530
8. Allie	534
9. Dawn	537
10. Camilla	543
11. Honey	546
12. Allie	550
13. Dawn	556
14. Camilla	559
15. Honey	564
16. Allie	567
17. Dawn	569
18. Camilla	573
19. Honey	576
20. Allie	579
21. Dawn	582
22. Camilla	585
23. Honey	587

24. Allie	590
25. Dawn	599
26. Camilla	603
EPILOGUE - ONE SATURDAY IN JULY	613
Dear Reader,	623
Acknowledgments	625
About the Author	627
Also by Rachel Griffiths	629

Summer at The Cosy Cottage Café

Summer at The Cosy Cottage Café

Allie Jones loves her cosy cottage café in the picturesque village of Heatherlea. Author Chris Monroe has it all - critical success, a luxurious apartment, and a jet-set lifestyle. When a family bereavement throws these two old friends together, love is in the air, but do they have room in their busy lives for more than a summer fling?

Chapter One

'Such a terrible loss, Mrs Burnley. I really am sorry.'
Allie Jones nodded solemnly as the elderly woman dabbed at her eyes with a tissue.
'She was a good friend... all these years.' Judith Burnley's watery eyes burned into Allie's. 'Since school you know? Even though she was a few years older than me, we were still so close.'
'I can't imagine how you must be feeling.'
'Dreadful. *Dreadful.*' Mrs Burnley's emphasis caused a tiny bead of saliva to land on her chin. 'I still can't believe she's gone. Although it was a lovely service.'
'Oh good. I would have gone myself but I had to be here to get everything ready.'
'Of course you did. Her son said some very nice things about her. He's a good lad that Chris Monroe.'
'Yes, indeed.'
Allie chewed her bottom lip, wondering how long she was supposed to stand with the older woman. After all, what length of time did social etiquette demand? Plus, she really didn't want to discuss Chris right now and had been trying not to think about him too much.

'I hope someone says positive things about me at my funeral. At my age, I probably don't have much time left...'
Time!
The word made Allie think about the miniature quiches in the oven. She needed to rescue them. Five more minutes would mean perfect pastry but any longer and they'd be ruined.
'I'm sorry, but I need to get back to the kitchen. I have a thousand things to do before everyone arrives.'
Mrs Burnley's grey eyebrows shot up her heavily powdered forehead. 'I have quiches in the oven that will burn,' Allie added, in case the urgency of the situation was in any doubt. She placed a hand on the older woman's arm. 'Again, I'm sorry.'
Mrs Burnley seemed placated. She gave a sharp sniff then headed across the café to a group of women standing near the log burner. Their uniform of black skirts and jackets paired with flesh-coloured tights, made Allie think of a nature documentary she'd once seen about crows, especially as they took it in turns to cast inquisitive glances around the café.
Allie picked up two used cups from a table near the counter then went through to the kitchen. The quiches should have been ready before the funeral party started arriving. She was sure the service had been scheduled for eleven o'clock and hadn't expected anyone to turn up at the café until around noon. But the group of women had arrived promptly at eleven thirty-five, so Allie guessed they had left the small village church as soon as the final hymn had been sung.
Poor Chris!
Allie hadn't seen Chris Monroe in years. After he'd left the village, he rarely returned. Allie thought she had an idea why, having known his mother – the rather harsh Mrs Monroe – since she was a child, but there could be other reasons she knew nothing about. Whenever she'd asked Mrs Monroe how Chris was getting on, her stock response had been 'he's travelling with his writing' and that was as much as Allie had known. Until a week ago, when she'd received a phone call out of the blue, from Chris himself.

The call had been polite and brief, not allowing for more detailed pleasantries or a potted history. In fact, if Allie was being honest, Chris had been a bit rude and rather cold. But business was business and she wasn't going to turn down a job. Besides, where else would they have held the wake? At one of the village pubs? Allie knew that Mrs Monroe would never have been happy with that. The old woman had seen the local pubs as dens of iniquity and would, no doubt, have turned in her new grave had her son chosen to hold her wake surrounded by locals enjoying a lunchtime pint.

Allie shivered. All this thinking about graves and funerals summoned her own dark clouds to the horizon and the old sadness tugged at her heart. She didn't have time for this today, so she'd have to pin her knickers to her vest and get on with things.

She opened the oven door and the comforting aromas of grilled cheese and caramelised onion greeted her. *Just in time!* She removed the trays from the oven then set them on the worktop to cool.

'Hey, Mum!'

Allie turned to find Jordan had joined her in the kitchen.

'Oh thank goodness! I thought you'd forgotten you were working this morning.'

He shook his head and his floppy fringe fell over his left eye.

'Of course not. Would I let you down?' He gave her a cheeky grin then pulled an apron from a drawer and hooped it over his head. Allie knew she could tell her son that he had let her down in the past, and that, yes, he did sometimes oversleep and forget about his Saturday morning shifts at the café too, but she didn't. He was here now and that was what mattered.

'Where do you want me?'

'You oversee things out front. I'll get everything finished up in here then come and help you. Just keep the tea and coffee going.'

Jordan paused then rubbed the back of his neck as he inhaled deeply, a sign that he was worrying about something.

'What is it, love?'

'Mum... Are you, uh, OK?'

'Why, Jordan?'
He met her eyes and she watched as he chewed his lower lip.
'Well, you know, with this being a wake.'
Allie nodded. 'Honestly, I'm fine. This isn't the first wake we've done since your dad...' She swallowed the end of her sentence.
'Well I'm here for you.'
'I know and I'm here for you too. I love you, Jordan.'
He smiled. 'I know.'
'Now go and make some hot beverages.'
'Yes ma'am!'
He gave her a mock salute then disappeared.

Allie knew why he was concerned about her and she worried about him for the same reason. Funerals always reminded them of Roger's and although she had been strong in front of her children at the time, it had been truly awful.

She turned her attention back to the quiches and removed them from the trays, then deposited them onto foil serving platters before adding sprigs of decorative parsley. The pastry was light and crisp and the cheese on top had a rich golden hue. She might have got some things wrong in her life but she did know how to bake, and opening the café had been, perhaps, the best decision she'd ever made. Of course, it had been a lifelong ambition too, one she'd harboured since her days at secondary school when she'd excelled at food technology. She'd always enjoyed baking with her mother as a child and an enthusiastic cookery teacher had encouraged her to consider baking as a career. However, she'd fallen in love after while sitting her A Levels and an unexpected pregnancy had led her to sideline her ambitions. She'd still baked regularly and taken cakes and savoury delights to birthday parties, village fetes and church celebrations, but thought her café dreams would never be realised. Some things brought out a wave of yearning in her, like occasional trips to Bath when they'd visit the delightful tearooms for refreshments, but she'd told herself she was lucky to be a wife and mother and tucked her old ambitions firmly away.

Until her life had changed dramatically and she'd had to make some big decisions.

Allie shook the sadness away; she couldn't afford to think about all that right now. She had to focus on the positives. She'd had another good spring, and early summer was looking good so far – in part because the medieval Surrey village of Heatherlea was a tourist attraction, which meant plenty of business for the café—and she was seeing some pleasing profits. Her situation was looking better by the minute and she was hoping that August would bring plenty of customers. She had her own business, two wonderful grown-up children, two funny cats and her grief was not as sharp as it once was.

She crossed her fingers instinctively as superstition shrouded her. The future looked bright but she'd never take anything for granted. Everything could change within minutes.

She lifted two of the serving platters of quiches and turned round to take them through to the café, then let out a screech as she hit a wall of chest. Quiches and parsley went flying into the air and the platters crashed to the floor. Allie was only saved from face planting into cheesy pastry by two strong hands that caught her, just in time.

'Allie, I'm so sorry!'

She shook her head and a chunk of quiche dropped onto her shoulder then bounced off and landed on the tiles.

'Chris?'

'Yes.'

His dark eyes roamed her face, familiar yet different. Older. Wiser. 'What on earth were you doing sneaking around like that?'

She realised that he was still supporting her, so she took a step backwards and slipped out of his grasp.

He looked at his hands, as if surprised that they'd been wedged under her armpits, then back at her face.

'The um... the young man out front told me you were in here and I came to check that everything was OK.'

'Yes, everything's fine. Well, it was fine until you just...' She swallowed the rest of her sentence, not wanting to accuse him of quiche destruction on what must be a very difficult day. Then she realised he was staring hard at her. Heat rushed into her cheeks, so she broke eye contact and picked at a bit of onion that was stuck to the neckline of her good white blouse – the one she wore for funerals and wakes.

'And that was my son, Jordan.'

Chris ran a hand through his salt-and-pepper hair and sighed as if exhausted. His face was still handsome but he had tiny lines engraved around his eyes, suggesting that he frowned or squinted a lot. The last time Allie had seen him, his hair had been black as a raven's wing, but that had been about ten years ago. And then she'd only seen him in passing. Apart from the recent phone call, she hadn't spoken to him in over twenty years – not since her wedding reception. When she'd returned from her honeymoon in Tenby, Chris had already left Heatherlea, leaving no details for her or Roger to contact him. She'd tried to talk to her husband about it but he'd always found a way to avoid the conversation, as if the friendship they'd once had with Chris was something she'd imagined. And she hadn't liked to keep pushing, because even Chris's name seemed to irritate Roger and she'd hated to upset him. His moods had been so unpredictable.

'Again, I am sorry. I'm running a bit later than expected because I went to the cemetery, but then everything got a bit delayed because the vicar got his foot stuck in the freshly dug earth at the graveside and lost his shoe. It took three people to pull it out and by that time he'd stumbled and got his sock all wet and it was just...' He rubbed his eyes. 'Anyway, I came to say hello and it was so weird when I saw you stood there. You look exactly the same as you did at eighteen.'

Allie laughed. 'I doubt that.' She swallowed her retort about a fatter bottom and thicker waistline. 'But thank you. You don't look that different either.'

'Except for the rugged grooves on my face and the George Clooney hair, right?'

'Mum!' Jordan interrupted as he appeared in the doorway. 'They're all arriving.'

'OK, I'll be there in a moment.' She scanned the floor with dismay; it was clear that none of the mini quiches she'd dropped were salvageable. Thankfully, she had two more foil platters on the work surface and another batch in the freezer that she could pop in the oven.

'Is there anything I can do to help?' Chris gestured at the quiche carnage.

'No. Thank you. You have to be out there with the… uh… guests. I'll sort this out.'

'Thanks. Catch up later?' He looked at her from under his dark lashes, as if suddenly shy.

'Yes. Sure. That would be nice.'

Chris left the kitchen and Allie located the dustpan and brush. As she started to sweep up the mess, she wondered at the way her heart was thumping behind her ribs. Had Chris really startled her that much, or was there something else about seeing him that had made her heart beat faster?

Allie stood behind the counter and surveyed the funeral party in her café. The crows had taken themselves to a table by the window and were tucking into sandwiches and fruitcake. She watched as Jordan approached them with the large stainless steel teapot, and filled each cup in turn. The elderly women were certainly making the most of Mrs Monroe's wake and Mrs Burnley had a big smile on her face, as if her sadness about her friend had already receded. But perhaps she was just reminiscing. It was better to try to remember the good times when you lost someone you cared about; Allie knew that better than most. And she also knew that keeping busy was the best way to avoid dwelling on the past.

She carried a tray of vanilla-frosted cupcakes around, offering them to people she knew and strangers alike, until the tray was empty and her face ached from maintaining a polite smile and repeating words of condolence.

Every time Allie attended a funeral and a wake, she had to battle her own demons, but she suspected it was that way for most people. The grief of others was bound to remind you of your own. Although it was true, the old adage, that time did help with the healing process. The pain would never completely disappear, but it wasn't quite as sharp, except for those odd occasions when it took her by surprise. But that was to be expected; she had lost her husband, after all, and when he was so young.

She swallowed hard. Roger had been gone six years and she had kept going by putting one foot in front of the other. That was how it was done. Some days were harder than others and she couldn't deny that she sometimes indulged in daydreams about what might have been had things worked out differently, but she had become quite adept at giving herself a firm shake and donning the good old stiff upper lip. Besides, her version of *differently* was more complicated than she cared to admit to herself.

It wasn't until after everyone had gone and she was filling the dishwasher that she realised she hadn't seen Chris again.

'Jordan?'

Her son paused in covering sausage rolls with cling film. 'Yeah?'

'Did you see Mr Monroe at all?'

'Why, Mum? Has he done a runner without paying you?' He waggled his eyebrows at her.

'No. Uh... I don't think so anyway.'

Chris had paid a deposit over the phone when he'd booked the café but she hadn't seen him to take the balance. Although in circumstances like these, she often didn't expect the rest on the actual day because people were generally too upset to think about money. Her daughter, Mandy, told her she was too soft and that she let people take advantage, but Allie saw it as part of what The Cosy Cottage Café represented for her and for the locals. It wasn't all about the money and she could trust most people to pay her within a few days. Chris would likely do the same.

'I just didn't see him again after he... popped into the kitchen to say hello and I wondered if he was OK.'

Jordan scrunched up his nose then flicked his head to clear his fringe out of his eyes. He had, thankfully, worn a clip in it for most of the day – to avoid adding his blond hairs to the food he was serving – but it seemed that he'd removed it since the café had emptied. Which meant the leftover sausage rolls would now have to be eaten by Allie, Jordan and the cats. *Just in case.*

'He's probably just upset, Mum. He has lost his mother. Perhaps he went out for some fresh air. I'm sure he'll be back tomorrow.'

'Yes. I'm sure you're right.'

Allie closed the dishwasher then switched it on and went to the sink to wash her hands. She gazed out of the latticed kitchen window at the pergola she'd had built in the spring, where the fragrant pink flowers of the climbing honeysuckle now bloomed in abundance. As well as being good at baking, she'd discovered that she had green fingers, and everything she'd planted within the café garden was thriving. There was a definite satisfaction to be found in gardening and enjoying the fruits of that pastime.

She went through to the café and made a mug of tea, then took it over to the comfy leather sofa in the corner by the window. She put the mug on the small wooden table then slumped onto the sofa and smiled as it squished up around her. It was an old one that she'd found in a charity shop and it was exactly what she'd imagined having in her own café. Behind it, and on the opposite wall, were shelves full of books all genres. Her regulars often brought in books they'd read and donated them to her shelves then took ones that they wanted to read. On quieter days, and sometimes after closing, Allie liked to curl up on the sofa with a warm drink and a book and to lose herself in another world.

The café was, in her eyes, perfect. Inside and out. The exterior was chocolate-box pretty with a thatched roof and shuttered windows. Roses climbed around the door and ivy climbed the walls. A café sign in the shape of a teapot hung from the side of the building. She had sown wildflower seeds for the bees and butterflies in pots and raised beds, and as it was summer, everything in the garden was in full bloom. She'd even managed to find some colourful milk-urn planters that she'd filled with trailing nasturtiums and their bright orange, red and gold flowers made her heart lift every time she saw them.

Inside, she'd had the two front rooms of the cottage converted into one big room, with the counter in the far right corner from the door and the café kitchen behind that. Allie had gone for the shabby-chic look, using reclaimed wood and second-hand furniture that she found online and in antique shops, and tables in a variety of colours and shapes took up most of the floor space. She often wondered if it was a reaction to the life she'd shared with Roger, when everything from their house to their carpets to their towels had to be brand new, spick and span. After he had died, Allie had gone out of her way to find the perfect old cottage to convert into a café, as well as searching for the loveliest second-hand furniture, fixtures and fittings. Roger had wanted everything in his home to tell people how successful he was and how well he was doing. And for a while, Allie had gone along with that, but when she'd lost the first flush of youth and Roger had expressed his disappointment with that, Allie had been devastated. So yes, perhaps her rebellion against all things new was deliberate.

A large log burner was centred on the back wall, directly opposite the front door. It wasn't currently lit but had logs piled up inside it with sprigs of dried lavender and rosemary tucked in around them. On cold winter days, the log burner kept the café warm and the table nearest to it was very popular.

The ceiling was white with exposed wooden beams that gave the café the cosy cottage atmosphere Allie had envisioned. She'd hung salvaged 1920s raspberry glass pendant lights from between the beams and they created a relaxing ambience in the darker afternoons that came with autumn and winter.

As she sipped her tea, the strains of being on her feet all day slipped away, and her thoughts strayed once more to Chris. It wasn't the money she was worried about, and she had no doubts that he would pay his bill. She just really wanted to see him again. He was one of her oldest friends and she'd like to catch up and find out how he'd been all these years. Everyone of her own age in the village seemed to be married or remarried, and lots of her old school friends had moved away a long time ago.

At one point Allie, Roger and Chris had been inseparable. A wave of nostalgia washed over her and she shuddered with surprise. Chris's return to Heatherlea was having quite an impact on her.

She did have some good friends in the village now; they just weren't ones she'd grown up with. So it would be nice if she got the chance to chat to Chris about old times. And there was nothing wrong in wanting to do that with an old friend now, was there?

Chapter Two

Allie peered at the red digital display of the clock on the bedside table and groaned. It was six o'clock but her room was still quite dark and that never inspired her to get out of bed.
She rolled over and was greeted by a terrible stench.
'Eurgh!' She reached out and her hand met soft warm fur. 'Is that you, Ebony?'
The cat purred in response.
'Where's your sister?'
As if summoned, silver grey Luna pushed open Allie's bedroom door and entered, bringing a warm glow from the hallway. Jordan must have forgotten to turn the light off again before he went to sleep.
Allie sat up and swung her legs over the edge of the bed. The double bed that she usually shared with a cat. While Luna was quite an independent feline, preferring to spend her nights going in and out of the cat flap on the backdoor, Ebony liked to spend her nights cuddled up to her mistress. Although Allie had originally tried to discourage the cat from sleeping with her, she now welcomed the presence of another living being at night. It could get lonely and Ebony offered the sweet, unassuming company that Allie appreciated.

Luna let out a meow then began circling Allie's legs.

'I know, I know. Time for some breakfast.'

Both cats shot out of the bedroom door and Allie followed them, pulling on her dressing gown as she descended the stairs.

After she bought the cottage, she'd had a ground-floor extension built at the rear. The building maintained its original façade but out back was an L shape, with her kitchen and lounge overlooking the back garden. When she'd had the property renovated, turning the ground floor into The Cosy Cottage Café, she'd kept the first floor as it was, with three bedrooms. Two of the bedrooms were small but the master bedroom was an adequate double. The bathroom, however, was the size of a phone box with just a shower, sink and toilet, and Allie did sometimes miss soaking in a bubble bath. But she couldn't deny that it was cosy and she was perfectly comfortable there.

The cottage offered the security she'd craved following the loss of her husband, and Allie, Jordan and the cats managed just fine. She did miss Mandy, who had moved away to attend university just before Roger died, and only ever returned for a few days at a time. However, she understood that her daughter was following her dream career in publishing and that she had to be at the heart of it all in London. Besides, Allie knew that Mandy had struggled terribly with the loss of her father, and that coming back to Heatherlea was painful for her. So she kept a room ready for Mandy, in case she ever wanted to come home, but she suspected that her daughter never would, at least not on a permanent basis.

Allie switched the kettle on then poured cat kibble into two bowls under the breakfast bar. As the cats crunched contentedly, she made herself a mug of tea and drank it gazing out of the long windows that overlooked her lush green garden and the fields beyond, watching as the sky changed from indigo to rose. The old saying *red sky at morning, shepherd's warning...* popped into her mind. She really hoped it wouldn't rain today because she had washing to peg on the line, including the tablecloths from the wake yesterday, and she wanted to try to get out for a walk. It was all very well owning a café and being able to bake delicious delights for her customers, but Allie sometimes enjoyed a few too many of those delights herself, from leftover cupcakes with rich fondant icing to buttery croissants that melted in the mouth, to tasty savoury quiches. So she tried to walk every day to keep the wobbles at bay.

Chris certainly hadn't looked like he had any extra pounds to spare, even though he must be forty-four now, at two years older than Allie. In fact, he looked pretty good with his salt-and-pepper hair and lean jaw, as if time had improved him like a fine wine. And his chocolate-brown eyes were still gorgeous. She recalled how they used to twinkle mischievously, suggesting that he knew far more about what she was thinking than she could ever imagine. But that had been before everything had changed.

'Mum!' Allie jumped and spilt tea down her fluffy dressing gown.

'Where are the frosted flakes?'

'When did you get up, Jordan?'

'Just now.'

'But it's not even seven o'clock yet.' He wasn't an early riser, even as a child at Christmas time when Allie had been up hours before him and Mandy, waiting for them to wake up and open their presents. And waiting for Roger to wake up, of course, because Christmas Eve often saw him enjoying a few drinks at the pub then not wanting to rise too early the following day.

'My rumbling stomach woke me.'

'Oh.' Allie grabbed a tea towel and tried to use it to mop some of the tea from her front. 'Didn't you eat enough yesterday?'

He shrugged.

'Maybe not. Anyway, what's got you gazing into the distance?'

'What?'

He produced a box of cereal from the cupboard then shook it.

'Your face was all dreamy like you were thinking about what you'd do with a lottery win.'

'Was it?' Allie shook her head then pointed at the fridge where a magnetic notepad held the weekly shopping list. 'Write frosted flakes on there.'

He nodded then peered into the cereal box. 'Not sure these bran flakes are still good. They look a bit grey.'

'Toast?'

'Please.'

Allie opened the bread bin and pulled out a wholemeal loaf then popped a few slices into the toaster. Thank goodness Jordan thought she was daydreaming about the lottery. If he knew the truth, she suspected he'd be horrified. Allie was way past the stage where she fantasised about handsome men and way past the stage where she could imagine being with anyone again.

Besides, Chris was just an old friend and she doubted he'd be hanging around in Heatherlea for long. So she'd have to make sure she didn't allow her fantasies to get too carried away.

'Ooh! What's happened to you?' Camilla Dix leaned on the counter and stared hard.

Heat rushed into Allie's cheeks at the sudden scrutiny.

'What do you mean?'

'Well,' Camilla narrowed her eyes, 'you look different.'

'Do I?' Allie turned to the counter behind her and picked up a plate laden with sandwiches.

She pretended to arrange the triangular slices of bread for a moment, so her colour would have time to fade. When she turned back to her friend, Camilla had her hands on her hips and was chewing her bottom lip. 'I know what it is!'

'Oh?' Allie came from behind the counter and carried the plate of sandwiches to the table in front of the log burner. She put it down then busied herself setting four places with cutlery and wine glasses.

Camilla clapped her hands. 'You're wearing makeup!'
Allie frowned. 'So? I always wear makeup.'
'No you don't.'
'I do, just not much.'
'It's the mascara and flicky eyeliner.' Camilla gestured with her hands in a manner that suggested Allie had wings either side of her nose.
Allie shrugged. 'Just trying something new.'
'It looks nice.'
'Thanks.'
The door to the café opened and two women entered.
'Hello!' Camilla's younger sister, Dawn Dix-Beaumont crossed to Allie and hugged her then did the same to Camilla. 'Feels like a year since we last got together. It has been *such* a long week.' She pulled out a chair and sat down.
'Allie, it smells incredible in here. Have you made lemon drizzle cake?' Honey Blackwell sniffed the air dramatically and Allie smiled. Honey was currently enthused about an amateur dramatics class that she was taking and everything she did was exaggerated, as if to show how good she was at acting.
'I know it's your favourite, Honey.' Allie said. 'I'll just get the wine.'
She went through to the kitchen and got two bottles of white from the wine cooler. When she returned to the café, she paused for a moment by the counter and smiled. Six years ago, her life was very different; she had a husband and two children and lived in what was then a new-build on the other side of the village. Her daily routine had involved household chores and a certain amount of daytime TV. She'd been plodding along, even though she'd sensed that something wasn't quite right, possibly that something was missing. Of course, her daughter had gone off to university, leaving her with the beginnings of empty-nest syndrome. But at least she'd still had Jordan at home – leaving his dirty socks lying around, as well as plenty of dirty dishes in the sink and muddy shoes in the hallway.
Then everything had changed.
She'd lost Roger, twice in one day. *Out of the blue.* Well, she'd told

herself it had been out of the blue but she sometimes suspected that she'd known more than she'd cared to admit to herself. The accident had been fast and fatal, tearing Roger from his family forever. Allie had been left to pick up the pieces.

And now...

She'd used his significant life insurance to invest in a fresh start. It had been hard at first, because she'd found that she didn't want to touch the money, almost as if it was tainted. But necessity had driven her to see a financial adviser and to consider her future, as well as that of her children.

She had never really liked the new-build, preferring the quirks and idiosyncrasies of older cottages, as well as having her view of it distorted by Roger's obsession with everything new – including women, it later emerged – so selling the family home hadn't been that hard. Then she'd put an offer in on the rather run-down cottage and with the help of a good local builder, had transformed it into The Cosy Cottage Café. The necessary food hygiene qualifications had been acquired while the building work was being done, and Allie had worked hard to bring everything together.

With the passing of time, had come new friendships. The raven-haired, green-eyed sisters Camilla and Dawn had always lived in the village, but with them being younger than Allie, at seven and nine years respectively, she'd only ever known them to say hello to in passing. Then one day they'd come into the café together on a quiet day, and Allie had ended up joining them for a coffee. And that had been that. As for hippy Honey, as Allie affectionately thought of her sweet-natured friend, the twenty-six year old artist had inherited her aunt's cottage in Heatherlea two years ago, and soon settled into a routine as one of their group. With her light-brown eyes and green and blue hair that made Allie think of a mermaid, she always brought a smile to Allie's face. She was only two years older than Mandy, but very different to Allie's serious daughter, and Allie sometimes wondered if the young women would get on should they meet.

She suspected that Mandy's grief had affected her deeply and added to her serious nature, but also knew that growing up with a father like Roger would have had an impact upon her. He had loved his children and provided for them, but he'd been so stern and such a perfectionist, and it had been hard to live up to what he'd expected from his family. Allie knew she could have made the move to leave him when Mandy and Jordan were younger but she hadn't been able to bring herself to do it. Roger's parents had both died when he was at university – his mother first then his father two years later – so she'd worried about him being alone. Her own parents had always been so happy and united, and Allie believed in marriage and commitment. As soon as she'd known she was carrying Mandy, she'd felt that she had only one course open to her: marriage to Roger, and he had agreed wholeheartedly. She didn't want her parents to see her as a failure, as being incapable of finding the love they shared. Even though she knew they'd never express it outwardly, the idea that they might think it made her sad, especially as she felt she'd let them down by not going on to higher education as she'd planned. She hadn't wanted to fail at that, then at her marriage. So she'd stuck with Roger in spite of her misgivings.

But times had changed. Allie didn't know how she'd manage without her Tuesday evenings at the café. They were her weekly highlight. She'd shut up shop at five-thirty, then Camilla, Dawn and Honey would arrive and they'd put the world to rights over wine, sandwiches, savoury pastries and cake. And often more wine. They could have gone through to her personal kitchen and lounge, but the café was so cosy, especially on chilly autumnal evenings, that they had automatically gathered around the log burner instead.

'What do you think?' Camilla asked loudly, dragging Allie back to the present, and all three turned to look at her.

'Ooh, suits you!' Honey said. 'Very pretty.'

Dawn nodded.

'I like it. What's the occasion?'

Allie took the wine to the table and opened a bottle then filled their glasses in turn.

'There's no occasion, I just wanted to try wearing my makeup differently.'

When all glasses were filled, Allie sat down next to Camilla then raised her wine.

'To Tuesday evenings!'

Her friends raised their glasses and clinked them against Allie's. Suddenly, Dawn coughed and spat a mouthful of wine back into her glass.

'God what's wrong?' Allie asked. 'Don't you like it?'

Dawn shook her head.

'You want red?' Camilla asked.

Dawn shook her head again then her face crumpled.

'Oh, sweetheart.' Allie got up and went round the table to hug her friend. 'It's OK if you don't like it. Not everyone's a fan of Pinot Grigio.'

Dawn waved a hand.

'It's not that. I do like the wine and I wish I could drink it but I can't...' A tear trickled down her face, so Allie rubbed her back in the same way she used to do the children's when they had fallen over and hurt themselves.

Camilla shook her head and mouthed *no idea* at Allie and Honey. When Dawn finally stopped sobbing, Allie smoothed her friend's dark hair back from her forehead and handed her a tissue.

'You want to talk about it? Then we're here. You don't? At least get some food into you. You're probably just exhausted running round after two kids and a husband. I know what it's like; I've been there remember.'

Camilla shuddered.

'Can't think of anything worse.' Then she held up her hands. 'Not that I don't adore my niece and nephew but it's a lot to deal with on a daily basis. I'm full of admiration for you, little sister.'

'It's not that either. I am tired, yes, but it's something else.'

Allie looked around the table at her friends then gave Dawn another hug.

'Ah... I think I know.'
'You do?'
'Well I don't think you're crying because you've got a water infection and are on antibiotics and can't drink alcohol. So are you—'
'Yes.' Dawn sniffed. 'Somehow, in spite of using bloody condoms and being on the pill, we've managed to get pregnant again. Just when I was starting to feel normal. When I've finally got James sleeping through at night.' She blew her nose loudly.
Camilla took a gulp of wine then raised her glass.
'I guess here's where we say congratulations.'
'You just said you couldn't imagine anything worse than having children.' Dawn scrunched the tissue up as she stared at her sister.
'Yes but you're a great mum and one more won't make a massive difference will it?'
'I guess not. I hope not.'
'And we'll all be here for you,' Allie added.
'Sorry am I intruding?'
Allie turned to see Chris standing in the doorway. She hadn't even heard him come in. Her heart skipped as she took in his faded jeans, navy hoodie and scuffed brown boots. The shadow of stubble on his chin matched his hair colour and somehow his eyes seemed darker than yesterday.
'No!' She released Dawn then smoothed her hair. 'Not at all.'
'Hi.' Chris waved at the other women then came closer. 'I need to pay for the wake. I meant to do it yesterday but the day got away from me, then I had a few things to deal with this morning and before I knew it...' He held out his hands.
'Better late than never,' Allie said, offering what she hoped was a warm smile.
They crossed to the counter and she went behind it to locate the bill.
'Here you are.' She waited as he perused it. 'Is it OK? No nasty surprises?' Behind him, Camilla was grinning at her and Honey was making heart signs with her thumbs and forefingers. None of them

had attended the funeral, as they hadn't known Mrs Monroe very well, and as far as Allie knew, they hadn't met Chris before.

'No problem at all. It's very reasonable.' He glanced behind him and Honey and Camilla quickly stopped what they were doing and feigned interest in their food. 'I just... uh... I wondered if you might like to catch up sometime.' He raised his eyebrows then pulled a credit card from his wallet and handed it to her.

'Oh!' She held the card for a minute then realised she was supposed to put it through the card machine. 'If you'll just input your pin, please.'

Chris typed in four numbers and the machine beeped. 'You can take your card back now.' Allie handed him a receipt then put the transaction through the till.

'So what do you think?'

'About catching up?' Her chest had tightened and her neck felt stiff and twitchy. This was ridiculous. He was an old friend asking her if she wanted to catch up, not if she wanted to jump into bed with him. But he was so handsome and Allie didn't have much interaction with the opposite sex, except to serve them food and drink in the café and even then a lot of them were over sixty and accompanied by their wives.

'Yes. We could go for a drink. Perhaps Friday? I would've suggested tomorrow but you're probably busy.'

Allie wasn't busy but rational thought seemed to have deserted her. Besides, she realised that she needed some time to mentally prepare herself before 'catching up' with Chris.

'Friday would be lovely. We could go to The Red Fox, if you like? They serve great bar meals.'

'Brilliant. Shall I pick you up or meet you there?'

Allie imagined Jordan's reaction if she was collected by a man from their home. Her son might be twenty-three but he was still so young in some ways and she didn't want to worry him. Better if he didn't know too much about this. She was just going for a meal with an old friend, after all.

'Meet me there? I'll have to tidy up after closing anyway and sort out Jordan's tea.' Jordan was capable of making his own meals but she didn't want to have to rush to get ready.
'OK, no problem. See you there about seven-thirty then?'
'Great.'
Chris paused for moment as if wanting to say more, but he glanced at the three women again, then gave a small shake of his head. 'Bye then, Allie.'
'Bye.'
'Bye ladies.'
'Byeeee!' they cooed.
Allie watched as the door closed behind him then returned to her seat.
'*Who* was that?' Camilla demanded.
'Just an old friend.' Allie took a sip of her wine.
'He seems familiar.'
'He's an author. You've probably seen his picture on the back of a book cover or something. He's in Heatherlea because his mother passed away and I catered the wake yesterday.'
'Ahhhh.' Camilla nodded.
'Anyway, how're you feeling now, Dawn?'
Dawn shook her head. 'Never mind me, Allie Jones. Did I hear you agree to go out on a date?'
'She did!' Camilla said. 'In all the time we've been friends, no men around. Not one. Then out of the blue, George Clooney's double appears.'
Allie laughed. 'Hardly. He's at least ten years younger.'
'Even better!' Dawn said, rubbing her hands together. 'Now then, how about you tell us all about Mr Clooney-come-author?' She picked up her wine glass and raised it to her lips then slammed it back down on the table again. 'Dammit!'
'I'll get you some orange juice.' Allie got up and went to the fridge behind the counter.

'And when you sit back down you're telling us everything.' Camilla thumped the table.

Allie knew she had no choice but to give her friends some background information. She'd never spoken about Chris because it was… complicated, and not the type of thing you randomly threw into conversation. It was almost as if she'd separated her life into two sections: before and after the café.

Camilla topped up her glass. 'I think you're going to need this.'

'I think you're right,' Allie said. She took a big swig of wine then swallowed it. 'So, to begin at the beginning…'

Chapter Three

The following three days passed in a blur of opening the café, baking, exchanging pleasantries with customers and cleaning up after closing. But when Friday morning arrived, Allie was a bag of nerves. Which was ridiculous really, seeing as how she wasn't even going on a date, just meeting an old friend for a drink.
At four-thirty, she was browsing cake recipes on her tablet, trying not to think about how she would feel being alone with Chris again, when the door to the café opened and Camilla sashayed in.
'What are you doing here? Shouldn't you be working?'
Camilla smiled. 'It's a beautifully sunny Friday afternoon, so I finished a bit early. I had a lunchtime appointment with a client in London then I deliberately kept the rest of the day free.'
'Why? Are you going somewhere?' Allie asked the question though she already had her suspicions about why Camilla might have come to see her.
'Yes. I'm going to ensure that you're ready for your date.'
'Oh Camilla, it's not a date! How many times?' Allie sighed with exasperation. Her three friends had bombarded her with texts and social media messages about her so called 'date' since Tuesday. At

first, it had amused her and she'd glanced at them then got on with what she was doing, but by this morning, it had started to add to her anxiety about the evening.

Camilla placed her bag on the counter and shrugged out of her olive-green linen jacket. 'Allie, we only want to see you happy.'

'I am happy.'

'You are... I guess... but we want to see you happier.'

'Why do I need a man to be *happier*?' Allie realised she'd raised her voice when the two women sat at the window table turned to look at her. She smiled at them. 'You're single, Camilla and I don't see you looking for love.'

Camilla shook her head. 'I'm not looking for anything, darling. But I do have male *friends*.'

'Your one night stands that Dawn's always fretting about?'

'Look, none of the men I see are unvetted and they're all in the same boat as me; they don't want a committed relationship and neither do I. So we, you know... enjoy each other's company. And just because Dawnie is happily married, doesn't mean I have to be.'

Allie bit back her reply. Camilla had never been in a relationship that she knew of but she seemed at peace with that. And Allie could understand why she was happy with life being that way: Camilla was a freelance accountant, she had plenty of clients – including Allie – and when she wanted some male company, she had no shortage of admirers. It was just that the way Camilla hopped from one man to another seemed to be a rather lonely way of life. Didn't she ever want to spend more than one night at a time with one of her *friends*? Allie didn't think she could have lived quite so carefree. If that's what it was, because she sometimes wondered if Camilla's carefree attitude towards sex and men was hiding something deeper, some fear of being hurt, perhaps.

'And neither do I.' Allie closed the cover of her tablet and tucked it under the counter.

'But you can have some fun, can't you? And what's-his-name—'

'Chris.'

'Yes, *Chris,* is rather gorgeous!'
Allie nodded. She had a feeling that the more she protested, the harder Camilla would dig her heels in.
The café door opened and Jenny Talbot, the local beautician, strutted in.
'Hi Jenny, thanks for coming.' Camilla waved her over to the counter.
'No problem at all. What're we looking for today, ladies?'
Allie straightened up and pushed the strands of hair that had fallen out of her bun behind her ears. Something about glamorous women made her feel a bit inadequate. Possibly because Roger had always pointed out that they looked much better than she did. Allie had felt that way around the delicate-featured Camilla during the early days of their friendship but Camilla had proved to be so down to earth and so funny, that Allie had soon been able to relax around her. But here was the very gorgeous and surgically enhanced Jenny, and Allie couldn't help feeling a bit...
Plain. Underdressed. And awkward.
'Nothing for me, Jenny, thanks, but I want you to give Allie the works!'
'What?' Allie went cold all over. The only time she had any form of beauty treatment was when she'd received one of those gift vouchers for a day spa – which hadn't happened since Mother's Day 2013 – or when she was really desperate for a haircut. And come to think of it, she hadn't had her hair done properly for well over a year. She made do with trimming it herself, usually with a nail scissors, over the bathroom sink. As for any other self-care, well, she might run a razor over the bottom half of her legs if it was hot out and she was wearing a skirt. Although the last time she'd done that in a hurry, she'd used a blunt razor and ended up with red-raw shins. Sometimes personal maintenance was more trouble than it was worth.
Had she let herself go then? In another rebellion against Roger? A man who was no longer here to pass judgement on her looks.
'The works, eh? Be my pleasure. Shall I go up and get everything

ready?' Jenny raised her rather large carpetbag in the air and Allie swallowed hard, imagining it contained a range of torture devices.

'Yes, you carry on. I'll help Allie close the café then make sure she finds her way up to you.'

Jenny went past the counter and through the short corridor that led off the kitchen. Allie heard her clomping up the stairs in her shiny black platform boots.

'Camilla, this is very kind of you but I don't need any treatments.'

Camilla came round the counter and released Allie's hair from its bun, then lifted some strands to the light. 'You have lovely hair, Allie, but it's gone a bit brassy. You've been using those home dye kits from the pound shop again haven't you?'

Allie's cheeks warmed. 'Well they're a bargain.'

'They're OK... but why not have your hair done properly? If anyone can sort out your colour, it's Jenny. She'll be able to have your tresses back to best in no time, I'm sure.'

It would be nice to have her hair lightened a bit. She had noticed that the blonde had turned more yellow after the last home colour and the old washing-up liquid trick hadn't managed to strip the brassy tones away. Sitting in the sunshine with lemon juice on her hair hadn't worked either. It had just led to a burnt scalp followed by weeks of peeling, as what looked like thick flakes of dandruff got stuck in her locks. It was not a good look for anyone, especially not for someone who served food for a living. So she kept her hair clipped back most of the time, hoping the dye would fade.

'OK. I'll agree to my hair being done. But nothing else.'

Camilla lowered into a crouch.

'What're you doing?'

'Checking your legs.' Camilla grabbed the hem of one leg of Allie's jeans and pulled it up then ran a finger over her shin. 'Yikes!'

'What is it?'

'Yeti.'

'No I'm not! It's not that bad.' Allie bent over and rolled down the leg of her jeans.

'It really is, you know. When did you last shave? 2002?'
Allie frowned at Camilla. 'It doesn't matter because no one is going to see my legs anyway. Besides, it's acceptable now to be hairy.'
'One flash of those babies and Chris will run a mile. Nope, sorry, you're being waxed too.'
'Oh, Camilla, Chris won't be seeing my legs.'
Camilla pouted and Allie sensed she was going to lose this battle.
'Right. I'll have my legs waxed and my hair done and *that is it*!'
Camilla gave her a cheeky wink.
'You know I love you.'
Allie couldn't help smiling, but as she took the money from her final customers of the day, then loaded the dishwasher, she had to admit to feeling uneasy. Because Camilla's idea of Allie's best, would probably differ significantly from her own.

'Ouch!' Allie reached out to rub her top lip but Camilla grabbed her hand and stopped her.
'Let it cool down.'
'But it stings.'
'Don't be such a baby. You've had two kids so doesn't that mean you can handle pain?'
Camilla tutted but Jenny smiled.
'It does hurt like hell but it'll be worth it.'
'Will it?' Allie blinked hard to clear the tears. She couldn't believe what Jenny and Camilla had done to her. And although Camilla hadn't actually done anything physically to hurt her, she'd been there every step of the way, encouraging Jenny to *do whatever it takes* and to *ignore Allie's pleas, she'll be grateful afterwards*.
Allie allowed Jenny to direct her from the bed where she'd lain as Jenny stripped her body of hair – except for her bikini line, she'd

drawn the line at that. Now she was pushed down the stairs and onto a kitchen chair in the extension, as Jenny wrapped her in a black cape. Allie took a deep breath as Jenny raised her scissors; this was a good thing, but it made her nervous handing over so much power. Over the next fifteen minutes, she watched as brassy locks fell away to the regular *snip snip* of Jenny's sharp scissors, then gratefully accepted a coffee from Camilla while Jenny mixed up a foul smelling paste in a small black bowl.

'This will get rid of that brassy tone. It will be a bit lighter at first but I can always add in some foils in a week or two if you want some warmer tones.'

Allie nodded then Jenny spread the paste onto her hair and scalp, impressed at how efficiently she worked. Jenny's hair fell to her waist in several different shades of grey. The colour would have made Allie look ten years older but on the twenty-seven-year-old Jenny, it was trendy and chic. Allie wondered if it was real and if so, how much belonged to another woman, or man, who'd had it cut away to make some money. She'd recently read a magazine article about how there was money to be made in growing your hair then selling it. Allie wouldn't fancy having someone else's hair woven into her own; she didn't even like touching her own hair once it had been cut, but she could understand how others wouldn't mind. Especially if it made them look as glamorous as Jenny.

'OK. We need to leave that for a bit, so you can relax. Oooh!' Jenny stepped back and frowned.

Allie watched her carefully; panic flooding her belly like a freezing cold drink.

'Oh dear.' Camilla grimaced.

'Some ice will help. Probably just a bit of a reaction to the wax. Don't worry!' Jenny went to the freezer, located the ice cube tray then pressed a few cubes onto a piece of kitchen roll. 'Here, hold this above your top lip.'

'What's happened?' Allie asked, trying not to breathe too deeply as the smell of the bleach on her hair was making her throat ache.

'Just a bit of swelling.' Camilla waved a hand. 'It'll go down.'
'How much swelling?' Allie asked, pushing to her feet.
Camilla stared at her feet, so Allie went into the downstairs cloakroom that led off the kitchen.
'Argh!' She stared at her reflection. Her hair was pasted to her head making her look like she was wearing a bald cap and the area above her top lip – which used to be quite flat – was now bulging like a magenta moustache. 'I can't go anywhere like this!'
'Don't worry. You have an hour or so yet,' Jenny called from the kitchen. 'It's perfectly normal.'
'Normal?' Allie asked. 'I look like I've done that stupid lip-enhancing challenge that Jordan got involved in a few years ago.'
Camilla appeared in the doorway.
'Oh, yeah. I remember that. His lip was swollen for about two weeks, wasn't it?'
Allie nodded.
'He was in agony. I worried he'd end up with permanent nerve damage. And all to show off to his mates from college when one of them dared him to try for a trout pout.'
'In all fairness, Allie, he'd had a few drinks.'
'He'd have regretted it if the results had been permanent. Thankfully, it went down.'
She prodded her own face tender face and winced.
'Get the ice on it and give it time to work.'
'I'm not going if it doesn't.'
'You can always wear a scarf.' Camilla suggested.
'What all night?' Allie had images of speaking to Chris from behind her silk scarf printed with tiny cupcakes. 'How will I eat and drink?'
'You'll manage.' Camilla flashed her a guilty smile.
'If this doesn't go down, I will hold you personally responsible.'
Camilla grabbed her hand. 'Come and have a glass of wine and you'll feel better about it.'
'I doubt that but it certainly can't get any worse.'

An hour later, Allie was ready. Well, almost. She stood in front of the full-length mirror in her bedroom and surveyed her makeover.
'In all fairness, Jenny, you have worked miracles.'
Jenny sat on the edge of the bed and crossed her endless legs. 'A job well done, I believe.'
'You're gorgeous. Chris'll be all over you.'
Allie scowled at her friend.
'Camilla, I do not want him to be all over me. Besides, although the swelling has gone down now, my lip is still very sore.'
Allie turned back to the mirror. Her skinny black jeans went well with the sheer grey thigh-length blouse Mandy had bought her for Christmas. Allie had never worn it; not wanting to ruin it after seeing the price tag her daughter had accidentally-on-purpose left attached. But tonight, seemed like a good time to give the blouse an airing. Underneath, she wore the matching grey camisole that clung to her curves and reached just below the hem of the blouse. The layering seemed to help disguise some of her lumps and bumps. She had teamed her outfit with a pair of silver-grey pumps.
Jenny had done her makeup as natural looking as possible, except for smoky eyes that really brought out their blue, and her hair was now a shiny golden mane. When Jenny was cutting it, Allie had thought she was taking lots off, but in reality, she'd merely trimmed the ends and given it some layers. The colour made it appear gently sun kissed and made her think of beaches with palm trees and soft white sand.
'Thank you so much, Jenny.'
'My pleasure, Allie. Don't leave it so long next time though. You're an attractive woman and you should pamper yourself.'
Camilla let Jenny out then returned to the bedroom, where Allie had now slumped onto the edge of the bed.
'Hey what is it?'

Allie shook her head, unable to speak as Camilla wrapped an arm around her shoulders.

'Tell me.'

'It's just... you doing that for me. It's so kind.'

'You're one of my best friends. Of course I'd do that for you. I'd do anything for you.'

'Thank you.' Allie smiled as Camilla squeezed her. 'You know, some days I can't believe this is me. That this is my life.'

'Why, sweetie?'

Allie met Camilla's bright green eyes.

'Well, I was married with two children. I thought I knew where my life was heading until six years ago.'

'Things can change very quickly. None of us know what will happen in an hour let alone in six years.'

'I know. Losing Roger so suddenly was such a shock.'

'Of course it was.'

'I thought he'd always be around.'

Camilla nodded. 'You were together a long time. And now, here's Chris, back on the scene. But from what you told us the other day, he could have been in Roger's place.'

'Perhaps. But it never got that far between us. I mean, a few kisses hardly qualify as a promise of eternal commitment do they?' Allie had told her friends about the way she'd been close to Roger and Chris growing up, and that at one point, it had seemed like she was closer to Chris. But in the end, life had taken an unexpected turn, and she'd ended up as Mrs Jones, not Mrs Monroe. Then Roger's quirks had become exaggerated as he'd grown older and more disappointed with life and other people, and things that had initially drawn Allie to him were no longer so endearing.

'Maybe it meant more to him than you know.' Camilla stood up and took Allie's hands then pulled her up.

'Maybe. But I don't think so.'

'Well now you have the chance to find out, right?'

Allie gave a brief smile then opened her wardrobe to locate her small black handbag.

'I guess I do.'

But after everything that had happened, she couldn't help wondering if she even wanted to know, and if it would be too painful raking up the past.

Chapter Four

Allie gave Camilla a quick hug then opened the car door. She could have walked the five minutes to the pub but Camilla had been worried the breeze would mess up Allie's hair and insisted on driving her.

'Have fun, won't you?' Camilla leaned over and squeezed Allie's hand.

'I hope so. I'm really nervous now.'

'Don't be. There's nothing to worry about. But be careful.'

'Careful? I've known this man most of my life. He's hardly got serial killer potential.'

Camilla laughed. 'I didn't mean that kind of careful but you never know someone inside out. So just take care.'

'I will.'

'Oh!' Camilla rummaged in her pocket. 'Before you go, I have something for you.'

'You do?' Allie frowned.

'This...' Camilla held out a small square foil packet.

'What's that?'

'Oh come on, Allie, don't tell me you've never seen one before.'

'A condom?' Allie's cheeks burned. 'I don't need that. I won't be getting up to anything that requires protection tonight.'

'Humour me. If you don't take it and the moment arises, you'll be disappointed you didn't. Especially if he's not carrying any.'

Allie stared at the offending square of foil and thought about what it meant if she accepted it. But what if she didn't and Camilla was right? She shook her head. There was no way she was sleeping with Chris, gorgeous as he might be. She hadn't slept with a man since Roger – or before for that matter – and couldn't quite imagine that kind of intimacy after so long. Yes, people on movies said it was like riding a bike and that you never forgot, but perhaps you did. Perhaps, for this woman on the brink of middle age, sex was a thing of the past.

'Hey Mum.'

'Shit, it's Jordan!'

Camilla snorted then threw the condom at Allie. It landed on her lap just as he stuck his head around the car door, so she quickly stuffed it into her bag.

'Hi, love. Everything OK?'

'Yeah. Just popping home for a shower then I'm off to see Max.'

'Oh right?' Allie willed the heat to recede from her cheeks but she was worried that he'd seen the condom. 'What're you two going to be doing this evening then?' She'd been so flustered earlier with worrying about meeting up with Chris, that she couldn't remember if Jordan had already told her. During her makeover, he'd been out on his bike, and he hadn't returned before she left.

'Oh, we, um... we're going to be gaming.' Was it her imagination or had Jordan's cheeks darkened? But perhaps she was projecting her own discomfort onto her son.

Pull yourself together...

Jordan pushed his hair back from his sweaty forehead and frowned. 'You look really nice, Mum.'

'Do I?' Allie sank into her seat.

'Why are you all dressed up?'

'We're off to the pub.' Camilla nodded. 'Girls' night out.'

'Right. Well have fun. I'll see you later.' Jordan tapped the car roof then cycled away.
'Camilla.' Allie grimaced. 'He could have seen that.'
'I take it you didn't tell him about your date then?'
'It's not a date—'
Camilla held up a hand. 'Whatever. But if it's not, why didn't you tell him you were meeting Chris?'
'I just don't want to worry him. He's been through a lot, you know?'
'We all lose loved ones, Allie. I know Jordan lost his dad but he is all grown up now. You can't protect him from everything forever and surely it's better to be honest. This is hardly a big village and he'll soon hear about your da... *evening out* with Chris from someone.'
'I'll tell him later. That I met up with Chris for a meal just to catch up on old times.'
'Probably best to be honest with him.'
'Right, I'm off.'
'Text me later. Unless you're... you know, busy. And if that happens, don't video call me whatever you do.' Camilla giggled and Allie shut the car door with a bit more force than was necessary.
Then she hooked her bag over her shoulder, crossed the road and entered the small garden of The Red Fox. Her heart was pounding, her palms were clammy and her stomach was full of butterflies. But in spite of all this, she was also a teeny bit excited.

When Allie entered the pub, the aroma of beer and chips greeted her and her stomach rumbled. She hadn't felt hungry all day, but she now realised she needed to eat something.
She scanned the room and spotted Chris at a table in the corner. He raised his pint in greeting.
Damn he looks good.

She tried to push the thought away but it lingered as she took in his salt-and-pepper hair and freshly shaven face. As she approached him, the warmth in his dark eyes made her skin tingle, and when she leaned in to kiss his cheek, her legs weakened at his delicious spicy scent.

'Allie, you look beautiful.'

'Thank you. You look pretty good yourself.'

He smiled and the corners of his eyes crinkled adorably. The plain black jumper he wore with grey jeans and black boots suggested self-confidence; he didn't feel the need to overdress. She wondered if he'd fretted about what to wear this evening then squashed the idea. Of course he hadn't, he probably hadn't given it any thought at all.

'Well thank *you*. You know,' he said as he pulled out a chair for her, 'I was actually quite nervous. I had no idea what to put on. I didn't want to look like I hadn't tried yet I didn't want to look like I'd tried too hard.'

Allie coughed. Her mouth and throat had dried up. 'No way!'

'Yes, way.'

She coughed again. Damn her throat was dry.

'Let me get you a drink. I didn't order you one because I wasn't sure what you like these days.'

'Pinot Grigio, please.'

She hung her bag on the back of her chair and looked around. There were a few regulars and a few unfamiliar faces but The Red Fox offered a delicious menu and cosy atmosphere, so she wasn't surprised to see people she didn't know. Chris had chosen a good table; fairly private and far enough from the bar to avoid being jostled by people carrying trays of drinks.

He returned with a large glass of white and handed it to Allie.

'Thank you.'

'My pleasure.'

She took a sip of the wine, enjoying the delicate peach fragrance and crisp finish, then placed the glass on the table. She noticed that Chris hadn't bought himself another drink but he still had half a pint left.

So he was taking his time, as she intended doing. She'd prefer to stay relatively sober and in control because she didn't know how she'd react to being with him again if alcohol lowered her emotional defences. Although being around him made a defiant part of her feel as if she wouldn't mind losing control, just for once.

'Shall we check the menu?' he asked.

'Yes, please. I'm quite hungry, actually, so I wouldn't mind eating soon.' Allie took the menu he proffered and opened it. But the small black print was blurry and even when she squinted, she couldn't decipher it. She peered over the top of the menu at Chris and he seemed to be reading his with no trouble at all. She couldn't remember him wearing glasses when they were younger but then didn't most people need them at some stage? The optician had told her that it was common to need glasses for reading once you hit forty.

Chris caught her watching him. 'Everything OK?'

'Yes. Uh... no. I can't see without my glasses these days.'

'Thank goodness for that!' He laughed. 'Me neither but I didn't want to put mine on. Vanity, eh?'

'After three?' She swung her bag around and unzipped it.

'I will if you will.'

He pulled a small case from the pocket of the suede jacket that hung on the back of his chair, then opened it and held out a pair of square dark-rimmed glasses. 'With writing, there's no way I can cope without these. I try not to wear them but it's a losing battle. I might only be forty-four but things start to slide.'

Allie rummaged in her tiny bag. When her fingers found her glasses case, she tugged at it, but it was lodged beneath her purse. She tugged again and it loosened and shot out, but as it did, a shiny square of foil came flying out too. Allie watched in horror as it soared through the air then landed in Chris's pint.

He stared at his glass.

Allie stared at his glass.

Then they both started to laugh.

'Oh my god, I'm so sorry.'
His face had turned red and he held his stomach as if it hurt. Allie grew hot all over as mortification mingled with amusement.
Bloody Camilla!
'Well,' Chris said, when he finally caught his breath, 'I didn't expect that to happen.'
'Blame my friend, Camilla. She forced it on me in the car earlier and wouldn't take no for an answer.' She took hold of his glass and fished out the condom then dried it with a napkin and stuffed it back in her bag.
'I have to admit, I'm disappointed now. I thought my luck was in.'
Allie shook her head and removed her glasses from the case then put them on.
'I'm not that kind of girl.'
He put his glasses on then gazed at her from behind the lenses, his dark eyes twinkling. 'No you're not, Allie. You're a woman now.'
Allie raised her menu to hide her face.
What was happening here? What was this strange sensation coursing through her body, making her feel so vibrant and alive?
Whatever it was, she liked it.

An hour and a half later, Allie was thoroughly relaxed. She sat back in her chair and fingered the stem of her wine glass. She'd enjoyed her dinner of vegetarian lasagne and chunky beer-battered chips and was waiting for dessert to arrive. Chris was good company and he made her laugh as he told her stories about people he'd met over the years and about his experience with an overly zealous fan. The woman had followed him everywhere for six months, attending every book signing and reading, before finally deserting him for the next bestseller, a reality TV celebrity who had his autobiography published at twenty-two.

'So you've done well with your books then?'

'I'm no Stephen King but I do all right. My books are a kind of hybrid genre of thriller and horror.'

'Are you with just one publisher?'

'Tied in for the next three books because of a rather generous advance but who knows then? This business is a rollercoaster. One day you're number one, the next...' He shrugged. 'It's not for the faint-hearted, that's for sure.'

'Have you met lots of famous people?' Allie asked, thinking about her own sheltered existence within the confines of Heatherlea. Yes, she'd had holidays and headed to London for the odd show or night out with the girls, but apart from that, she was either in the café or in bed alone. It didn't bother her at all normally, but she realised that her life probably seemed a bit sheltered and possibly even boring to Chris.

'Some. At book signings and events like the London Book Fair. But at the end of the day, celebs are just people like you and me.'

Allie watched as he took a sip of his second pint. His full lips were still so kissable and with his movie star looks, he probably fitted in around beautiful people with ease.

'What about you though, Allie? I noticed how you've deflected my questions so far tonight. Very cleverly but you've done it all the same. What's life been like for you?'

'Oh...' Allie swallowed hard. 'There's not much to tell.'

Chris leaned forwards and covered her hand with his. His skin was warm and smooth and goosebumps rose on Allie's arms. She met his gaze and her mind went blank.

'Allie, you've been through a hell of a lot. Don't underestimate that. You lost your husband and brought your kids up alone. I know they're older but you still had to be there for them. You renovated an old cottage and turned it into a successful business. I know I haven't been around but I heard how you were doing from my mother. She said you coped admirably with it all.'

'She did?' Allie fought back her surprise. All she'd ever known of Mrs Monroe was as an acid-tongued woman who never seemed to have a good word to say about anyone.

'She did. Mum always told me good things about you, although the rest of the village didn't enjoy such leniency. She said you did yourself proud and encouraged me to come back and see how you were doing. On more than one occasion.'

Allie sipped her wine.

'That's not exactly how she came across.' She thought of the woman who'd cast icy stares across the post office and been painfully blunt when she'd come into the café.

'My mother was a harsh old bat at times, I know.' He sighed.

'Chris, are you OK?'

'I still can't believe she's gone. I mean, I didn't come back all that often but I knew she was here. Harsh as she could be, she was still my mum.'

'I know. I'm sorry.'

He shrugged then nodded.

'Thanks. I guess it'll just take time to come to terms with it. Like everything in life, right?'

'It's still early days.' Allie fought the urge to jump up and hug him. She hated to see his pain.

'She thought very highly of you, Allie. She wanted...' He shook his head.

She realised he was still holding her hand.

'She wanted what?' she asked gently.

'It doesn't matter now.'

'It does. Tell me.'

'OK. She wanted me to... for us to... she always thought we should have been together. If she ever seemed at all resentful, it was because of that.'

'But why would she have thought that we could have been a couple?'

'She knew how I felt about you.'

'How you felt about me?'

He inclined his head.

'After all, that was why I left.'

'Oh Chris. I didn't know.'

Allie turned her hand over and squeezed his fingers. He'd had feelings for her? All these years had passed and she'd seen Mrs Monroe around the village, completely unaware that Chris's mother had known something she hadn't. As a mother, Allie could understand how Mrs Monroe must have worried about her son. No one wanted their child to be sad and Allie thought she'd struggle to hold back if anyone ever hurt Mandy or Jordan.

But now she wondered. If Mrs Monroe had spoken to her about it, could things have worked out differently? Would it have changed anything?

'It's all in the past now.' Chris smiled then gently pulled his hand back. 'But tell me more about you and your children. How are they getting on?'

'Mandy's twenty-four now. I can't believe that I have a daughter six years off thirty. That's when you know how quickly time has passed. She's working in London as a publishing intern.'

'Brilliant career ahead of her, no doubt.'

'I hope so. She's very driven and motivated. Not at all like I was at her age.'

'Don't be so down on yourself. You were full of ambition but life kind of got in the way. Besides, I'm full of admiration for you and what you've achieved, especially in light of the circumstances. And things were different when we were young.'

'I guess so. I just couldn't envisage leaving Heatherlea after I got pregnant. The world suddenly seemed far too big and scary. Motherhood creates a vulnerability in you that wasn't there before; everything takes on a different slant as you realise what could hold potential danger for your child.'

'I didn't really have any intention of leaving myself until... well, things changed.'

Allie nodded, suddenly nervous about hearing more and feeling a need to fill the space between them with innocuous conversation. 'Then there's Jordan. He's twenty-three now and still living with me. He does some shifts at the café and some odd jobs around the village. He's a good lad.'

'Does he have any ambitions?'

Allie scanned Chris's face, wondering for a moment if he thought Jordan should be out in the world by now, following a career in a city office perhaps, but all she found in his eyes was interest.

'Not that I know of. I've tried since he was about fourteen to get him to consider different careers and qualifications but he was never interested. He hated school and couldn't wait to leave. He says he doesn't care about earning lots and that he'll be fine as long as he earns enough to put food in his belly and a roof over his head. Of course, at the moment, he doesn't have to worry about a mortgage or rent, but I like having him around. It would be too quiet without him there. And too tidy.' She laughed. 'I suppose I could have pushed him harder but I think kids these days have it tough enough. They're all competing to climb the ladder or to be famous and I'm sure it's why depression is on the increase. Pressure makes people miserable and I just want my children to be happy, whatever they're doing. If Jordan is content being so laid-back, then that's fine with me. Perhaps he'll take over the café once I'm too old. Who knows?'

In all honesty, she was glad Jordan was so relaxed about life. If he'd been more like Roger, she'd have been worried about him. The quest for perfection was one that often ended in disappointment.

'Sounds like you're all doing well.' Chris smiled. 'I'm sorry I wasn't around after Roger...'

'It's OK. Don't worry about it. I completely understand. You're a busy man.'

'I should have come back for the funeral but I just knew how awful it would be.'

'It *was* awful. But it's been six years since he passed away and so much has happened since then. He'd have understood why you weren't there.' She took another sip of wine, gazing into her glass to

avoid meeting Chris's eyes. 'I read the newspaper stories about your success and watched that TV interview a few years back.'
'Sorry about that.' Chris finished his pint.
'Hey it was interesting.'
He shook his head.
'I was so uncomfortable in front of the camera.'
'You couldn't tell. It's wonderful to see how successful you are. I mean, we went to the same school and were friends when we were younger and look how well you've done. I'm so proud of you.' Her breath caught in her throat. Did she have any right to say that?
Chris lowered his eyes and toyed with a cardboard beer mat. He turned it over and ran his finger over the logo at its core.
'I've done all right. I'm comfortable but I'm tired too. It's not easy travelling so many weeks of the year and living out of a suitcase. To be honest, Allie, I think as I get deeper into my forties that I'd like to put down roots.'
'Village life appealing to you now?'
'Something like that.' He met her eyes and her heart raced at the intensity of his gaze.
'Shall we have another drink? Something to wash our dessert down with?'
'Go on then. But only one more as I've got to be up early for work.'
'The burden of being self-employed, eh?'
'Tell me about it.'
When Chris went to the bar, Allie took the opportunity to check her mobile. No missed calls but a text from Camilla asking if she'd managed to get a kiss yet. She shook her head then stuffed her mobile back in her bag without replying. There'd be no kissing or any other shenanigans this evening.
Or any evening, for that matter.

Chapter Five

'So that's one latte, one pot of Earl Grey and two scones with cream and jam?' Allie hovered the pencil over her small notebook.
'Yes please.' The blonde woman nodded at Allie then resumed her conversation with the older woman, who Allie guessed was probably her mother. The resemblance between them was too strong for there to be no connection.
In the kitchen, she got two china plates from the cupboard then took two freshly baked lemonade scones from the wire rack. Next to each scone she put a small white ramekin full of thick clotted cream and an identical one full of homemade strawberry jam. Last year she'd had fabulous crops of strawberries and raspberries in her back garden and had enjoyed turning them into delicious preserves to use in the café.
She carried the plates to the counter then set about making the latte and the Earl Grey. Everything was automatic now; she'd developed her routines and enjoyed the comfort that came from them. From baking to serving to making conversation with the customers, running the café was everything Allie had hoped it would be and more. It kept

her busy, busier than she could have imagined, and that had filled the gap in her life.
Until now.
Seeing Chris again had made her realise that she used to have something that she no longer had. In fact, she hadn't had it in quite some time, and that thought gave her a sudden surge of disquiet. She had so much to be grateful for.
But...
She was lonely.
And not for just any company, but for the man she'd grown up with, a friend who knew her well and whom she shared so many memories with. She missed Roger in some ways, yes – it was inevitable, even with things being as they had at the end – but she couldn't get him back. However, Chris was here, alive and well, and he'd told her he left because of his feelings for her. Was it possible that he still had some of those feelings? Or was that too much to hope for? After all, she didn't even know if he was involved with someone. It was a question she'd been too afraid to ask last night, even when he'd walked her back to the cottage and insisted on seeing her inside. He hadn't come past the threshold, though, just watched as she'd shut the door then told her through the letterbox to make sure she locked it properly.
That had made her laugh, especially when he'd stuck his finger through and wiggled it as he said goodnight.
She'd gone to bed with a smile on her face and a sense of lightness in her heart. Feeling like a teenager all over again.
'Mum?'
She blinked, coming back to reality with a jolt.
'I asked if those scones are going to blondie younger and blondie older.'
'Yes they are. And Jordan please don't refer to our customers by their hair colour. They might be offended if they overhear you.'
'Well what else should I call them?'
'The two ladies? Or just use the table number.'
He grinned at her.

'But hair colour's much more fun.'
Allie shook her head.
'Yes, take the scones over then come back for the drinks.'
Jordan delivered the scones and drinks then joined her behind the counter.
'Did you have a good time last night, Mum?'
She met his blue eyes.
'Yes, I did.'
'I saw Camilla driving away.'
Allie froze. What should she do? Confess?
'She did go home early. She thought she had a migraine coming on.'
'Oh.' He shrugged. 'Shame. As long as you had fun.'
'I did.'
'Mum?'
'Yes, darling.'
'I need to tell you something and I never seem to be able to find the right time.'
'Right...' A thousand worries shot through Allie's mind. Was he ill? Was he leaving Heatherlea? Had he found out about his father – the thing she'd never wanted him to know? Was he in trouble or had he got someone else in trouble? She looked at his sun-kissed hair and the spattering of freckles over his nose and cheeks. He was a man now but in so many ways, he was still her baby boy and always would be.
'Don't look so worried, Mum. I haven't done anything wrong. It's about me and... and Max. See—'
'Allie!' Camilla bounded across the café.
'Hi Camilla, I didn't see you arrive.'
'I got my heel stuck in the welcome mat outside, so it took me a while to free myself. Anyway, Allie, I—'
'One moment.' Allie held up a hand to her friend. 'What was it you wanted to tell me, Jordan?'
He opened his mouth then closed it again and shook his head. 'It doesn't matter, Mum. We can talk about it tonight.'
'OK, sweetheart. As long as you're sure it can wait.'

'I'll just see if blondie... I mean the ladies at table number five want anything else.' As he went over to the table and turned on his youthful charm, Allie hoped he was all right; that whatever it was that he wanted to tell her could wait. She'd spent twenty-three years trying to protect and nurture him; keeping him safe as he crossed the road, as he used the internet, as he negotiated his way through life. She would do anything for him and Mandy, anything at all.

'Allie, I know you've been ignoring my calls and text messages but I want all the gossip from last night. Was it a passionate reunion? Did he have to purchase more... protection from the pub toilets? Did you rediscover your sex drive after—'

'Stop!'

'What?'

'That's enough. You are incorrigible, Camilla. Nothing happened.'

'What? Nothing?' Camilla's mouth sagged open.

'Well not *nothing*, because we had a really nice time.'

'Really *nice* time?' Camilla snorted. 'Nice?'

'Yes, nice. We chatted and enjoyed a delicious meal then he walked me home.'

'I'm disappointed.'

'Well don't be.'

'But I am. I had high hopes for you, darling.'

'I'm happy as I am.'

'Whatever!' Camilla waved a hand in the air, her red shellac nails flawless as always.

'Now what can I get you?'

'Some hope.'

'Hope?'

'Yes. The hope that you're going to see him again.'

'Ah.' Allie released a sigh. 'Well I am actually. Tomorrow, I'm going round to his mother's house to help him start clearing it out.'

'He's selling?'

'I would think so.'

'Shame.'

'Well that's up to him, isn't it?'
Allie turned away then, to make her friend a cappuccino and to hide her expression from prying eyes. If Chris did sell the house, she would be disappointed too. Because now that he'd returned to Heatherlea, she was starting to realise that she didn't want him to leave.

Chapter Six

Mrs Monroe's old stone cottage was picture-book pretty in the morning sun as Allie opened the garden gate and walked up the path. Ivy climbed the front of the cottage and primrose yellow roses grew around the front door. The shutters around the windows had recently been painted forget-me-not blue to match the small garden bench. The bushes in the garden had been pruned to perfection and Mrs Monroe could still have been there, alive and well. The wiry old woman had kept her path clear of weeds and washed it down at least three times a week and it showed.

Allie found it hard to accept that she was gone. Death was strange like that, taking people away, people who seemed to have plenty of time left ahead of them.

Just like Roger.

She pushed the thought away as she always did, refusing to allow it to cloud her day.

She used the heavy brass knocker and while she waited, she hoped that she looked OK. She didn't usually dress up on Sundays, unless attending church for a special service like a wedding or Christening, but today she felt particularly underdressed. She'd slung on jeans and an old Guns N' Roses t-shirt with trainers that had seen a few painting sprees. She'd pulled her hair into a bun and the only makeup she'd bothered with was a flick of powder just to take the shine off her nose.

But she wasn't here to look glamorous; she was here to help Chris sort through his mother's things.

The door opened and there he was. He looked at her, then at himself and laughed.

'Twins!' he was wearing a Guns N' Roses t-shirt with jeans too, but his feet were bare.

'How long have you had that t-shirt?' Allie asked as he stepped back to let her in.

'Probably the same length of time as you. I bet we even bought them at the same concert.'

'The old Wembley stadium.'

'When we all went on a minibus.'

'Wow! That was such a long time ago.'

'What would you have been? About sixteen?'

Allie nodded. 'Time flies, right?'

'Sure does.'

A memory of the hot, sticky summer day returned with a jolt. Allie had been so young, high on life and full of youthful anticipation. Her relationship with Roger had still been new and exciting in the way that only unconsummated teenage love can be. She'd been flattered that handsome, older Roger, already at university, had been interested in her when he could have chosen a girl of his own age. She'd also been so very naïve.

'Anyway, where do you want to start today?'

His face fell.

'What is it?'

'You are not going to believe how bad it is here.'

'I don't believe it. Your mother was a stickler for cleanliness.'

'Nope.'

'Nope?' Allie couldn't contain her shock.

'Outside maybe, and in the rooms people would see if they came here, but the front room and upstairs are bloody awful.'
'Messy?'
He shook his head.
'Dirty?'
He sighed. 'Try both and then some. It appears that my mother was a... hoarder.'
'She wasn't!' Allie swallowed back laughter. She didn't want to hurt Chris by seeming to mock his mother but she was so surprised. Mrs Monroe hadn't seemed the type of woman to hoard things. Then again, perhaps people never did. No one ever really knew what was behind closed doors, did they?
'I'll grab some black bags and cardboard boxes that I got from the supermarket and we can sort the rubbish from things that can go to charity.'
'Right.'
'Go and take a look if you like.' He gestured at the front room.
Allie nodded then pushed the door. It creaked open on its hinges and she was immediately overwhelmed by the smell of damp and something rotting. She covered her nose for a moment and swallowed hard. This was evidently not going to be as straightforward as she had first thought, and she was glad that she was here to help Chris. It wouldn't be something she'd want him to have to do alone.

Allie stood on the bare wooden boards and stared at the piles of books, papers, cards, blankets, and plastic bags that were stuffed with bottles and cans. The junk dominated the front room of Mrs Monroe's house. The sun shone through the front window, illuminating the dust motes that floated through the air, and the smell in there was so strong, sweet and cloying, that it was making her feel queasy.

'Pretty bad, huh?' Chris had joined her and he dropped a roll of black plastic bags and two boxes on the floor in front of him. 'I think there could be a field-mouse or a dead rat in here somewhere.'

She nodded. 'Mind if I open the window?'

'Be my guest.'

She pushed the window open as far as it would go and took a few gulps of fresh air before turning back to Chris.

'I'm just... stunned.'

'Me too. I mean, how didn't I notice how bad things had become?'

Her heart squeezed at the confusion on his face.

'How are you doing?'

'Up and down. I keep expecting her to walk in and offer me a cup of tea.'

'That will happen for a while.'

'You know, Allie, I've been so busy building my career and travelling from one place to another, immersing myself in my books, that I was oblivious to the fact that my mother was living like this. I'm just so annoyed with myself.'

'You weren't to know so don't blame yourself. '

'It's hard not to. Look at this mess... and upstairs is just as bad. Mum used to be so meticulous about everything, even OCD. At one point, this front room was her pride and joy and only ever used for best.' He rubbed his eyes and sighed. 'If I'm honest, when I did come back, I'd take her out for dinner then bring her home and rush off again, back to my London apartment, or to catch the next flight. I hadn't been in here for ages. Or upstairs. I just wonder how long this had been going on.'

'What are the other rooms like?'

'Not so bad. It's like she stuffed it all in here and the spare bedroom. My old room is pretty much the same as when I was living here. A bit like the room of a teenage boy.' He gave a wry laugh. 'Although her room isn't great. You should see under the bed and in her wardrobe.'

'In all honesty, I never noticed anything different about her. She was always well turned out when she came to the café and when I saw her around the village.'

'That's good to know. At least she held it together in that way. But knowing that she was saving all this stuff at home makes me sad. She must have been lonely.'

Allie chewed her bottom lip as she listened to him. She knew what he meant, because it was sad. Mrs Monroe had seemed outwardly fine, yet she'd been dealing with all this. What on earth had she been saving it for? And Judith Burnley hadn't said anything about it, so evidently hadn't been as good a friend to Chris's mother as she'd made out at the wake.

'Still,' Chris said, 'no point standing here staring at it. Let's get stuck in. If you want to that is. It stinks in here and I wouldn't blame you if you want to leave.'

'Of course I'm not going to leave. I'm happy to help.'

They took a bag each then got to work.

Two hours later, Chris stood up and arched his back. 'I don't know about you but I'm parched. Fancy a cuppa?'

'I'll make it.'

'Thanks. I'll take all this out to the back garden and pile it up. I think I'm going to need to hire a skip.'

Allie went through to the rear of the cottage and froze in the kitchen doorway. Beautiful solid oak units lined the walls on both sides, and under the window, which was adorned with a rectangular wooden box full of fresh growing herbs, was an apron-front sink with a vintage style rose-gold tap. Of course, she'd been in Mrs Monroe's house a few times when she was younger, but only in the hallway to wait for Chris, as his mother had once explained that she didn't like other people's children traipsing through her home.

Allie located the kettle then filled it and switched it on. She found mugs in the cupboard under the kettle – behind the bone-china cups and saucers that were evidently Mrs Monroe's preference – and tea bags in the cupboard above. As she waited for the water to boil, she gazed around. The units were good quality and built to last. The grey slate floor tiles were pretty with their uneven hues of orange and blue. The curtains on the window above the sink and the one to the left of the room, that overlooked the garage, were pale blue with tiny white daisies embroidered on them. It was clear that Mrs Monroe had loved her kitchen and kept it immaculate. Unlike other rooms in the house.

She poured water over the tea bags then went to the freestanding silver fridge. There was a fresh container of milk in there, a tub of spreadable butter and a bag of mixed salad leaves but nothing else. She wondered what Chris had eaten for breakfast.

When the tea was ready, she took it through to the front room.

'Just what I need.' Chris smiled as he accepted the steaming mug.

'You don't take sugar, do you? I didn't see any in the kitchen.'

'No, thanks. Sweet enough already.' He winked.

'Chris, did you have anything to eat this morning?'

He nodded. 'I had a piece of toast and an apple.'

'Aren't you hungry? It's gone eleven and you're quite a big guy.' Her cheeks coloured as she realised how that sounded. 'Oh. I didn't mean big as in fat. I meant big as in muscular and...' He was grinning at her now and her blush deepened.

'Nothing like a compliment or two to make a man feel good about himself.'

'I am such an idiot.'

'No you're not. You are as sweet as always. It was one of things I lo... liked so much about you.'

Allie swallowed a mouthful of tea. 'Look, we've done quite a bit now, so why don't we head over to the café and I can make us some pancakes.'

Chris frowned. 'Pancakes, eh?'

'With maple syrup.'

'And chocolate spread?'

'If you like.'

'Now you're talking. Not that I need distracting from this mess but I certainly can be persuaded to leave it for an hour if pancakes are involved. As you said, I have all these muscles and they need feeding.' He flexed his left arm and laughed. 'Well, not exactly up to bodybuilder standard, but I'm working on them. I mean, I work out when I can as it would be a shame to waste having access to all those hotel gyms.'

Allie drained her tea then reached for his mug. 'I'll put these in the kitchen and we can head over there.'

As she left the room, she hugged herself inwardly. Chris might not have muscles the size of a bodybuilder but he certainly had a very toned physique indeed, and Allie had to admit that she wouldn't have minded watching him work out.

Or helping him work out.

Or working out with him.

Or... she wasn't quite sure what she meant.

Allie ladled batter from the mixing bowl then carefully poured it into the frying pan. As the surface bubbled, she got two plates out of the cupboard then located the thicker maple syrup that she preferred. Chris had asked her what she wanted him to do to help, so she'd asked him to make some drinks.

When the pancake was browned on one side, Allie flipped it. She continued the process until all the batter had been used and each plate was heaped with thick fluffy pancakes, then she poured maple syrup over each pile.

She went through to the café and found Chris sitting on the leather sofa reading a magazine that he must have found on one of the bookshelves. On the table were two steaming mugs of hot chocolate, their surfaces were brimming with whipped cream and chocolate shavings.

'Very nice! You know how to use the machine then?'

'I've watched enough times in enough cafés to master it, yes.'
'The hot chocolates look delicious.'
'And so do those pancakes.'
Allie handed him a plate and watched as he lifted a heaped fork to his mouth. As he chewed, he widened his eyes and moaned.
'Sooooo good, Allie.'
'Thank you. And so easy to make.'
'You'd make someone a good wife…' He winced. 'What a stupid thing to say. God, I'm so sorry.'
Allie shook her head.
'Don't be. I was a good wife, I tried really hard to be what Roger wanted.'
She pushed a piece of pancake around her plate.
'What do you mean?' He put his fork down and covered her hand with his.
'Oh nothing.'
'It's not nothing, Allie. I know you, remember. We were best friends for a long time. You seemed happy with Roger though, and I assumed it would always be that way for you guys.'
Allie sipped her hot chocolate, enjoying the silky feel of the sweet drink in her mouth. It was comforting, like a hug in a mug.
'It was good between us for a while. Even after we had the two children, it was still OK. We enjoyed a lot of things together but I don't know… somewhere along the way, something changed. He…' Was she really going to tell someone the truth? If it was going to be anyone, she guessed it should be Chris. 'Roger liked things done a certain way. I think it might have had something to do with losing his parents when he did. He had no control over that and it emerged in other ways. The house had to be spotless, the garden had to be tidy, the children had to be well behaved and I had to be… perfect. He had a gardener in twice a week, so the roses were gorgeous and the lawn was up to bowling-green standard, and I did my best to keep the house the way he liked it. But I wasn't perfect and neither were the children. He never let on to them how he felt about their so called

imperfections, but he never failed to tell me.' She smiled to try to lighten the impact of what she'd just confessed. 'I don't know. Maybe my bum was too big or my roots were showing or perhaps he just found that he didn't really love me.' The old humiliation swept through her.

'Well that's crazy. I can't understand how he wouldn't have loved you. You're amazing and as for your bottom… well, let's just say I've sneaked a peek and it's looking good.'

'You're very kind. But things did change between us and Roger drifted away from me. Or rather, we drifted apart.' The full truth was on the tip of her tongue – the details about Roger's final day – and she was about to tell him when he spoke again.

'Some men find it hard with kids around, even their own kids. And with Roger being an only child, like you and me, perhaps he struggled with having more people in his space. Although I often thought that was why the three of us gelled, you know? We three were a bit lonely growing up and there was a kind of affinity between us. But I don't know. Perhaps he felt a bit left out because you were wrapped up in the children? I'm not excusing him. If that was the case, as an adult, he should have tried harder. Not that I should be judging anyone.' He gave her a shy smile. 'After all, I've shied away from commitment all these years. Never settled down, never moved in with anyone–'

'What? Never?' Allie was surprised by the hope that fluttered in her belly.

'Never.'

'But why?'

Chris shrugged.

'After I left, I never found anyone who made me want to get married or procreate. I'm not saying I've lived like a monk, because that would be a lie, but I've kept away from commitment like it was a disease.' He shook his head then started tucking into his pancakes.

'So you're not seeing anyone at the moment?'

He swallowed before replying.

'Haven't even dated for about six months.'

'Oh.' Allie raised her mug and hid her smile behind it. Not that it should matter, of course, whether Chris was dating or not, but she found that she was delighted that he was single. And that he thought her bum looked OK.

All the more reason to relax and enjoy her pancakes. Then she'd go back to Mrs Monroe's house and help Chris to carry on sorting through everything. Now that there was no other woman to worry about, she felt even better than she had done before.

Chapter Seven

The next day, Allie pulled into a parking space at the Meadowsweet Retirement Complex and cut the engine. The drive wasn't too onerous and today had only taken forty-five minutes. Sometimes she wished there was a similar complex closer to Heatherlea, even in the village itself, but at others she was glad of the distance. It meant that she could visit her mum and dad whenever she wished but also didn't feel obliged to visit them every day.

Her parents, both now in their early seventies, had lived in Heatherlea all their lives but following Roger's death, it was as if they'd been struck by a sudden urge to change something and moving out of the village had been their solution. Perhaps they'd even hung around there until they thought she was at the point where she could manage alone, as if they knew she'd do so better after Roger was gone. Meadowsweet was a modern complex with everything her parents had wanted. Small apartments were built into blocks that led out onto the vast rear lawns with luscious green grass that looked as though it had been painstakingly combed. Her parents had a ground floor apartment with one bedroom, one bathroom and an open plan lounge / kitchen. However, if they didn't feel like cooking, there was a food hall at the centre of the main building. There were also shops, a unisex hairdressers, a swimming pool and sauna, a bar and an onsite doctor and dentist. It was almost futuristic in its self-sufficiency. Outside were sprawling well-kept gardens, a golf course and tennis courts, so they had no excuse for not keeping fit. There were wardens on call at the complex at all times, so there was always help available should they need it. Allie knew her parents paid a high premium to live there but her father was fond of repeating that they couldn't take their money with them, so he intended to enjoy the good life while he could.

She entered the main building and headed through the warm sunlit hall – that strangely smelt of peaches – to the corridor that led out to the lawns. When she reached her parents' white PVC door, she knocked and waited.

The door swung inwards and her mother stood there in a flowing purple kaftan and green monster-head slippers, smiling broadly as she opened her arms.

'Allie, darling. So good to see you.'

'Hi, Mum.'

Allie breathed in her mother's familiar rose and patchouli perfume as they hugged.

'Come on in.'

Allie automatically followed her mother through to the kitchenette where the kettle was bubbling away. The aromas of freshly baked bread and chicken soup made her stomach grumble.

'Something smells good.'

'It's our lunch.'

'Wonderful. Where's Dad?'

'Oh he went out for a quick round as he put it. Quick often turns into three hours but who am I to complain? I'm just glad he's making the most of the facilities.'

'He does seem happy here.'

'He's getting plenty of exercise that's for sure and I'm reaping the rewards.' Her mother's hazel eyes sparkled as she giggled.
'Mum!' Allie shook her head. 'I don't want to know things like that.'
'Don't be such a prude, Allie. How'd you think we conceived you?'
'Yes but I only thought you did it once.' Allie winked at her mother.
'We're enjoying it even more now we're older, especially since he doesn't have to waste energy taking care of those ridiculously high-maintenance gardens, believe you me.'
Allie nodded, keen to move her mother on from the subject of her sex life. 'Yes it must be a huge relief.' She'd been sad to see her parents sell her childhood home, but knew it made sense for them.
'How are the new owners?'
Her mother always did this, asked about the people who'd bought her old home as if they moved in just yesterday even though in reality it was just over four years.
'Oh they're doing well, I think. I see them around the village and they sometimes come in the café.'
'Good. Such a pleasant couple and they have lovely children, don't they?'
'They do, although two of them are at comprehensive school now and the oldest girl is at university.
'Lovely.'
When her mother had made tea, they took their mugs to the square table in the small dining area and sat opposite each other.
'So what's on your mind, Allie?'
'What?'
'I know you, my darling, and I know there's something troubling you. I can almost hear the cogs whirring.'
Allie met her mother's curious eyes.
'You know Mrs Monroe died?'
'Yes.' Her mother nodded slowly. 'We did consider coming back for the funeral but she wasn't exactly a good friend, so we sent a card to the house instead, thinking Chris would pick it up.'
'He did and he asked me to pass on his thanks.'

Allie thought back to the previous day when she'd started to help Chris clear out the house. After pancakes at the café, they'd spent another four hours sorting Mrs Monroe's front room. They hadn't even managed to get upstairs.

'Well, I've been spending some time with Chris.'

'I see.' Allie's mother eyed her over her mug. 'And how do you feel about that?'

Allie's skin prickled. Sometimes it was as if her mother could see into her heart and mind.

'It's strange. We used to be so close – me, him and Roger – but that was such a long time ago.'

'Time is a matter of perspective, Allie. At my age you understand that more than ever. In my heart, I'm still a girl, but my body tells me otherwise, although yoga is really helping with my flexibility. You know, your father said—'

'OK, Mum!' Allie held up a hand, not wanting another insight into her parents' bedroom shenanigans.

'Anyway, as I was saying, the years fly by. You and Chris were close and you'll probably find you still have things in common.'

Allie gazed into her mug, wishing someone would tell her fortune. At least then she'd know if her recent thoughts and feelings were real, acceptable, normal.

'Allie,' her mum said as she took hold of her hand over the table. 'You are still young and life has so much to offer you. If you want Chris then go get him.'

'But how do I know if I do? I feel silly that I'm like a teenager with a crush whenever he's around, yet I also feel more alive than I have done in years. Since way before Roger died if I'm completely honest.'

Her mother nodded. 'I know things weren't right in your marriage and your father and I often talked about it. Dad always said you married the wrong one.'

'But he never said that to me. Neither did you.'

Her mother pressed her lips together.

'It wasn't our place to be quite that blunt. Although, we did try to

encourage you not to rush into marriage but you were so set on it. And you had to make your own decisions.'
'I just wanted to do the right thing. After I got pregnant and let you down by not becoming the amazing chef I'd said I would become, I didn't want to let you down again. And you and dad have always been so happy. I thought Roger and I could have that too. Roger seemed like the right choice.'
'Because he had prospects?'
'He did. He was so handsome and determined and he was the father of my child. I just didn't know that his determination and career drive was due to his desire for perfection in everything.'
'And none of us are perfect, Allie. Not me, nor your father, nor our relationship. Every marriage has ups and downs.'
'Really?'
'Of course. But if you're with the right person for you, then you weather the storms together. However, if someone makes you feel that you're lacking in some way, then they are wrong for you. Now though... Chris is back and you want him, don't you?'
Allie nodded.
'I'm afraid though. That what I'm feeling is just because we're old friends. And because he's... well, Mum, he's gorgeous.'
'Take some advice from me, sweetheart. Life is short; time is precious. If you and Chris got together and tried each other on for size, who would lose out?'
Allie took a deep breath then released it slowly.
'No one, I guess.'
'But if you don't try to see where this could go... who misses out?'
'I get your point.'
'That's my girl.'
'Thanks, Mum.'
Allie sat at the table, deep in thought, as her mother pottered about preparing dinner. She'd tried to help but her mother had muttered something about too many cooks and insisted that she sat down and relaxed. She mulled over the idea of a possible relationship, or even

just a fling with Chris, and both seemed scary, risky. But even scarier was the prospect of him leaving and never having the chance to see if there was still something between them.

An hour later, Allie sat at the table with her parents. As her mother ladled chicken soup into bowls, Allie's mouth watered at the delicious aroma.

'Help yourself.' Her mother gestured at a pile of shiny brown pretzels on a side plate.

'Thank you.'

'Well, you've done it again, Connie.' Allie's father smiled at his wife. 'Delicious.'

'Allie takes after me, don't you darling?' Her mother sprinkled pepper over her soup. 'That's why the café has been so successful.'

'I certainly inherited my cookery skills from one of you and I don't think it was Dad.' Allie winked at her father to show she was teasing.

'I'll have you know that I make a mean chilli.' Her father held out his hands. 'I'm just better with the ironing.'

'That's true. He can press creases into trousers that I could only dream of achieving.' Her mother gently touched his cheek.

'You two! You're still so in love.'

Her parents nodded simultaneously.

'Has she told you yet, Bruce?'

Her father raised his eyebrows in question. 'There's news?'

'Chris Monroe is back in Heatherlea and they've been spending some time together.'

'And how's that going, Allie?' Her father's keen blue eyes fixed on her and she realised what her mother had just done; she was making it impossible for Allie to leave without committing to something regarding Chris. There was no way Allie could lie, or even twist the truth, while under the scrutiny of her retired lawyer father. He could spot a fib or an evasion at twenty paces.

'It's going OK, I guess.'

'Now come on, tell him what you told me, Allie.'

She repeated the details she'd relayed to her mother earlier, and her father listened carefully.

'I see.' He dipped a pretzel into his soup then chewed it thoughtfully. 'Bruce, I think it's time to tell her.'

Her father inclined his head. 'Allie, we never told you this before because we didn't think there was much point. You made your choice and married Roger and gave us two lovely grandchildren. Mandy rang last night by the way and is full of the joys of her job. Lovely to hear her enthusiasm. Anyway, at your wedding reception, while you were busy with Roger attending to your guests, I went out for a cigar.' He took another bite of pretzel.

Allie nodded. Her father had given up cigars, as far as she knew, following a bit of a health scare about three years earlier, but she remembered him smoking throughout her childhood and teenage years. The aroma had been almost comforting, something akin to rich loamy soil or a sawmill in the rain, and was one she always associated with him. But she'd been glad when he'd quit because she'd worried about the dangers of smoking.

'Outside the hotel,' her father continued, 'I found Chris perched on the edge of the stone fountain. And he was in a right old state.'

'What was wrong?' Allie's stomach clenched at the thought of him being upset.

'At first, he wouldn't tell me. But after a while, the floodgates just opened. He was very drunk or I don't think he'd have told me at all.'

'What did he say?'

'That he was in love with you and that at one point he thought you would get together but something happened and it broke his heart.'

'Wow.' She stared at her soup, her appetite fading.

'I know he was young. You all were. But he loved you, Allie. And you know we liked Roger but Chris just seemed... more suitable for you. Now I'm not one to judge the romantic decisions of others, and I've been very lucky to have your mother, but I think you might have ended up with the wrong man.'

Allie stared at her father and felt her mouth drop slowly open.

'Allie!' He held up his hands so his palms were facing her. 'Don't look at me like that. You and Roger had fabulous kids and a long time together but we know something went wrong towards the… end.'
'We could tell it wasn't working between you, darling,' her mother added.
'How? I barely admitted it to myself until afterwards.' She'd never told her parents everything but now they were telling her they had suspicions. Not voicing the truth about Roger's idealism or his final moments had been a way of keeping it from becoming a painful reality. Or so she'd hoped. But the truth had a way of outing itself.
'Chris really loved you. I don't know how he feels now, Allie, but I'm sure he will always be a good friend. Possibly more if you rekindle that old spark. Who knows? At least you're both older and wiser, eh?' Her father squeezed her fingers. She gazed at the white hairs on his knuckles and the slight swelling of his joints. Her parents were getting older; she couldn't deny that and they wouldn't always be around. They were good people and like any loving parents, they just wanted to see her happy. Her life was good now; she had the café to focus on, and her children – although they had their own lives and so they should. She knew they'd always love her but they were adults and didn't need her as much as they once had.
It was time now to think about herself and what she wanted. She was entitled to have a fulfilling life of her own too. But did she need a man for that?
No.
Not just any man.
But it was possible that she needed Chris. That she had always needed him.
She covered her mouth and took a shaky breath.
'Allie, do you want to tell us what happened with Roger?' Her mother tilted her head to one side, inviting her to confide in her calm, reassuring way.
'I guess so.'
'We love you and are here to support you, whatever you tell us. And

we won't be judging anyone. Goodness knows we've been around long enough to know that most people have flaws.'
Allie steeled herself.
It was time to say the words she'd kept inside for so long.

In the café the next morning, Allie felt dazed. She went through the motions of making coffee and serving breakfasts then brunches then lunchtime orders, but it was all done on autopilot. Telling her parents about Roger had been difficult but cathartic. It was as if saying it out loud had made it real and when she'd finished she'd broken down, realising that she'd actually been ashamed about what had happened and blamed herself.
Hearing about Chris's drunken confession had also knocked her sideways. She was so fond of him, and knowing how much he'd been hurting all those years ago made her own heart ache. Why hadn't he said anything? Had he tried but she'd been too caught up in the dominant whirlwind that was Roger to listen?
'Penny for them.'
She jumped and sloshed coffee over the counter.
'Sorry, I seem to have developed a habit of startling you.' Chris smiled at her, holding her captive with his dark brown eyes. She had an urge to throw herself into his arms and apologise for the pain he'd felt at her wedding. For the pain he'd felt when she'd chosen Roger.
'I was miles away.' Allie felt the familiar heat creeping into her cheeks that his presence conjured. She wiped the coffee up then cleaned the bottom of the mug, silently thanking the patron saint of cafés that she hadn't spilt much. It had probably been too full anyway because she'd been so distracted. 'I just need to take these over to that couple.'
'Of course.'

As she passed him, she noticed that he held a carrier bag in one hand and it looked heavy. She gave her customers their drinks then turned back to Chris.

'Take a seat.' She gestured at the table nearest the counter. 'Can I get you anything?'

'A cold drink would be nice. I've been sorting through everything in Mum's room and it was quite dusty under the bed.'

Allie fetched two glasses of lemonade then joined him at the small square table for two.

'What did you find?' She had wanted to help him with clearing the rest of the cottage but she couldn't be there every day as she had the café to run. Jordan had watched it for a few hours when she'd gone to see her parents but she didn't like to leave him alone for too long, though what she thought might happen in her absence, she wasn't quite sure. She worried about a blockage in the coffee machine perhaps or a power cut though they were both things that would cause her problems too, and she suspected that laid-back Jordan would be far calmer in a crisis than she would be.

Chris lifted the carrier bag onto his lap then pulled out a pile of books.

'Are they yours?'

He nodded. 'All six of them are the same thriller.'

'She had six copies of the same book?'

He shook his head. 'They're in different languages. Translated versions.'

'She was very proud of you.'

His Adam's apple bobbed furiously.

'I... I always sent her copies of my novels but not foreign editions. There's not much point having those unless you speak Italian, Spanish and so on. But she must have ordered them from somewhere.'

'How many books did you find altogether?'

He sighed. 'Too many to count and I banged my head after pulling these out so I couldn't face carrying on.'

'I could come and help you later, or tomorrow, if you like.'
His eyes flickered. 'That would've been great but I have to catch the train to London this evening and I'll be gone until the weekend.'
'Oh.' Allie's stomach dropped to the floor.
'I will be back. I just have a few things to sort out at my apartment and with my solicitor.'
'OK.' Allie plastered on her brightest smile, determined not to make him feel guilty. 'Well if you need anymore help, you know where I am.'
'Thank you.' He moved his hand closer to hers and gently stroked her thumb. 'I know I came back for sad reasons but seeing you again has been amazing.'
Allie tried to swallow but there was a painful lump in her throat. Trying to fight how she felt about this man was proving to be a struggle, and finding out what she had yesterday had only made it harder. She'd cared about Chris so much but made a choice all those years ago because she'd thought she knew what she was doing. Roger had seemed to need her more than Chris did. She had also believed, at one point, that Roger loved her. She hadn't thought Chris felt that way about her, hadn't thought he could see her like that.
She'd been wrong.
But here he was, a forty-four-year-old man, with a successful career and a busy life. Time had moved on, and as much as there might be residual feelings between them, surely there was no chance of anything happening? So she needed to get a grip, and showing him that she was his friend would be the best way she could think of to achieve that.
'If you are back on Saturday, there'll be a party. It's a tradition I started when I opened the café, kind of a summer celebration.'
'Sounds great. What time?'
'From about seven.'
'I'll do my best to be here.'
'Now what else have you got in that bag?'
He rolled his eyes. 'Embarrassing newspaper clippings.'

'Come on then, let's have a look.'
'All right but no laughing. I'm just not photogenic at all.'
He spread the clippings on the table and they went through them together, laughing and joking in the comfortable way they used to do. And Allie was warmed inside, because even if there was nothing romantic blossoming here, then at least she was getting reacquainted with an old and very dear friend.

Chapter Eight

The rest of the week dragged for Allie, in spite of her efforts to keep busy. It was as if there was something missing from the village, and even though she told herself it was silly and self-indulgent, she couldn't shake the fresh sense of loneliness.
The day Chris left, she'd had her usual Tuesday evening with the girls and they'd soon worked out that something wasn't quite right with her. It had led to reassurances and wine, and by the end of the evening, she'd been smiling again. But it was hard to get him off her mind and part of her worried that he might not return, that being back in London would remind him of why he'd decided to leave Heatherlea in the first place. *That* being her and the fact that she had broken his heart.
Thankfully, Friday was a mad blur of getting everything ready for the party, as Allie confirmed that the local band were able to play, and that everyone who'd replied to the email would be bringing the food they'd selected from the list.
Saturday morning, Allie was up and about early. Jordan ran things out front in the café, while Allie baked and stirred, chopped and whisked, huffed and puffed.

Summer at The Cosy Cottage Café

The August morning was warm and dry, the air sweet and fragrant with the scents of the flowers in her garden. Allie had to wear sunglasses to set up the tables outside because it was so bright, and when she removed the covering from the barbeque, she felt a flip of anticipation in her belly. She loved this time of year and had always celebrated summer with her children, wanting them to appreciate the longer days and to enjoy being outdoors. Life was for living and summer was perfect for making the most of time with family and friends.

They shut up the café at three o'clock, then Allie finished off in the kitchen and checked her list one last time.

She had no idea what time Chris was due back. He'd sent her a text the previous evening just to say hello and to ask what she was doing, but although he'd said he was looking forward to seeing her again, he hadn't said what time he'd return. And she hadn't liked to ask.

Allie had enough time to shower and dress before people started arriving. She hoped Chris would turn up, but if he didn't, then so be it. She had a life to live and she intended to get on with it.

Allie strolled around the front lawn of the café, greeting friends and acquaintances, and encouraging them to help themselves to drinks. Jordan had helped her to set up trestle tables on the flat lawn at the one side of the path. There was a table for soft drinks, one for alcoholic beverages – which was manned by the vicar, who kept a watchful eye on the youngsters to ensure that none of them tried their luck – and one for food contributions.

The first year Allie had held a party like this, she'd done all the catering herself, but over the years, others had brought their own offerings and it was a relief, as it meant Allie didn't have to make quite as much. It was also lovely to enjoy the wonderful variety of food, such as this year's savoury delights including herb, feta and courgette risotto, chicken and ham pies, minted melon and prosciutto salad, stuffed wild mushrooms, lemon sunflower pesto pasta and olive and rosemary bread.

The desserts on offer this year were coconut panna cotta with strawberry gel, swirled meringues with blueberry sauce, orange and ginger ricotta tart and raspberry mojito cupcakes. Everything looked delicious and in spite of her apprehension that Chris might not make an appearance, Allie felt a flicker of hunger as she eyed the feast before her.

The local band set up in the corner of the garden close to the café, so that they had access to power cables. Jordan had laced fairy lights between the branches of the trees and looped them around the shutters on the café windows for when the afternoon light faded. The braziers were also ready to be lit and every table had a colourful glass tealight holder at the centre, which held a citronella candle to keep the bugs at bay.

Camilla appeared at Allie's side, wearing a white cotton maxi-dress printed with tiny rosebuds. Her black hair was freshly cut, her eyes were lined with black kohl and her lips painted a glossy red to match her nails. Allie noticed, as she always did, how stunning her friend actually was. Camilla pressed a glass of mimosa into Allie's hand.

'Here. This'll help you relax.'

'Thank you.'

'How're you feeling?'

'Good, actually. I love this party. It just makes the summer feel extra special.'

'It does. But I meant how're you feeling about Chris?'

Allie shrugged. 'Nothing to feel really.'

'Oh come on, Allie. That's not what you said on Tuesday.'

'I know. Sorry. I'm all right, I guess. Really hoping he'll turn up but resigned to the fact that he might not.'

Camilla rubbed Allie's shoulder.

'He'll come. I have a good feeling about it.'

Erica Connelly, the singer of the band, tapped the microphone. 'Hellooooo, Heatherlea! Great to be here and to see you all looking so well. As usual, big thanks go to the fabulous Allie Jones for organizing our celebration of summer bash!'

There were some cheers and whistles from the gathering. Allie waved a hand self-consciously, not wanting all the attention to be focused on her.

'And thanks, as well, to every one of you who brought food and drink. I cannot wait to try out the raspberry mojito cupcakes, so make sure you leave me one. Pretty please?' She smiled and offered a thumbs up. 'So let's kick this party off with a little number we wrote ourselves.'

The band launched into a song and some of the villagers were soon bopping around on the lawn.

'Coming for a dance?' Camilla asked.

'Not just yet. I want to say hello to a few people.'

'OK. But no mooning around waiting for you-know-who.' Camilla headed towards the dancers and Allie went to the table where Dawn sat with her husband, Rick. They were a handsome couple with two beautiful children who were currently running around with their friends, safe in the front garden of the café.

'Evening.' She took a seat next to Dawn.

'Hey you.' Dawn smiled at her but Allie noticed that she didn't look well.

'How're you feeling?'

'I've felt better.'

'Morning sickness?'

Dawn nodded.

'Since I found out, it's become a hundred times worse. I'm sure it wasn't this bad with the first two.'

'Perhaps it's because you're tired? I mean, you have got two young children to look after already, so you're probably not getting as much rest this time around.'

Dawn glanced at Rick and he shifted in his chair.

'It's difficult with Rick working such long hours.' She bit her bottom lip as if preventing herself from saying more.

'She'll be all right. It's just early days.' He slid an arm around Dawn's shoulders. 'The sickness usually disappears around fourteen weeks then she'll return to her usual superwoman self.'

Allie swallowed a response. She wondered if Rick was helping out enough at home, if he did his fair share? If he was working long hours, it meant that Dawn would be spending a lot of time home alone. Allie knew from personal experience that being a mum wasn't easy, especially when you felt under the weather.

'Excuse me a moment.' Rick got up.

'Look, Dawn, if there's anything I can do, just let me know. I can have the kids for you so you can get some rest or I'll come over and cook you all dinner.'

Dawn smiled.

'Thank you, Allie, you're a star. I'm sure I'll be fine. It's just a bit of a shock still. And Rick's right, I do get over the morning sickness after the three-month point, so not long to go!'

'You're that far along then?'

'About nine weeks.'

'Wow!'

'I know. I missed all the usual signs because I was so busy.' Dawn shook her head. 'But what can you do? It's happened, so now I just have to deal with it.'

'Well you both have to... deal with it. Not just you.'

Allie hoped that Dawn would soon feel more positive about the pregnancy and that it wasn't just something to *deal with*, or she'd have a difficult few months ahead.

'You're right. I think Rick's just a bit shocked too.'

Allie watched Dawn's husband as he accepted a bottle of beer from the vicar. Rick had a successful city career in investment banking. Dawn had met him at university in Northampton and when she'd returned to Heatherlea, he'd come along too. Dawn had conceived Laura, who was now eight, at twenty-five and James had followed two years later. Dawn had given up her teaching post when she was pregnant with James because she'd been struggling to juggle everything. She'd insisted she was happy with that. For a while. But now... Allie wondered if that was still the case. And she wondered if Rick was using his job as an excuse not to be around more.

But, she reminded herself, it wasn't her business. Dawn was her friend and she'd be there for her but she had no right to interfere.

'Isn't that Chris?' Dawn pointed at the gate to the café garden.

Allie's stomach flipped. 'So it is.'

'Well go on then.' Dawn grinned.

'Go on what?'

'Go say hello. I know you're desperate to see him.'

'There's some peppermint cordial inside. I'll get you a glass. It will help with the nausea.' Allie swallowed her desire to rush over to Chris. She had to stay calm and in control. She'd get Dawn a drink first. Otherwise, she was going to seem far too keen, and she was so glad he'd turned up that she might just wrap herself around him. And that would be way too embarrassing.

She headed into the café and located the peppermint cordial behind the counter. She poured some into a glass, annoyed that her hand was trembling, then topped it up with bottled water.

The doorway to the café darkened and when she looked up, she almost cheered.

'Allie!' Chris crossed the floor in three long strides.

'Oh hello...' Her heart fluttered.

'It's so good to see you.' He opened his arms then leaned over the counter and kissed her cheek. His spicy scent washed over her and she wobbled on her feet.

'Good to see you too. I wasn't sure what time you'd be back.'

'I missed the damned train I'd intended to catch but thankfully made the next one. Then there was a delay.' He shook his head as if shocked at his choice of transport. 'But I couldn't wait to get back.'

'You couldn't?' She gazed at his face, appreciating the familiar contours, the deep dark brown of his eyes and his kissable lips that were smiling at her right now.

'Of course not. It felt like weeks, not days, that I was away.' He paused as if realising how frank he'd just been. 'It looks amazing outside. Did you do all that?'

'I had some help. It's a community thing, most people who attend bring something to eat or drink, however small.'

'Great band too.'

'Yes, all locally grown.' Allie laughed. 'They do some of their own tunes but also some covers.'

Chris raised his eyebrows. 'Do they take requests?'

'I believe they do.'

He nodded. 'Good to know.' He looked at the glass of green liquid she was holding. 'What on earth is that?'

'Peppermint cordial. For nausea.'

He frowned. 'Aren't you feeling well?'

'I'm fine.' *Now you're back.* 'It's for my friend Dawn to help with her morning sickness.'

'Better get it out to her then.'

'Yes.'

'I'll come with you.'

They went outside and Allie took the drink to Dawn, then introduced Chris to Rick. The two men shook hands and exchanged pleasantries.

'So you're Chris Monroe, the author?' Rick asked.

'The one and only.' Chris winked at Allie to show he was teasing.

'Wow, great to meet you. I've read most of your books.'

'Really?' Chris asked.

'Absolutely brilliant stories. Um... while you're here, if you ever want some financial advice, about investment and so on, I'd be happy to have a chat. How about I give you my card?'

'Sure.' Chris accepted Rick's business card.

Dawn rolled her eyes at Allie. 'Always on duty.'

'Well I have a growing family to provide for.' Rick gently patted Dawn's belly.

'Thanks for this.' Dawn raised her glass to Allie. 'It's very refreshing, even if it does look like pond water.'

'There's plenty left inside if you want more. In fact, you can take the bottle home with you.'

'Thanks, Allie.'

The late afternoon turned into evening and time passed quickly, as food was eaten, song requests were played and the amber-streaked sky turned indigo. Jordan switched the fairy lights on, giving the garden a magical quality. Allie went inside to get her cardigan, and when she came back out, she saw Chris speaking to Jason Robins, the lead guitarist of the band. Jason was nodding, his long blond ponytail hanging over one shoulder and his round glasses – that always made Allie think of John Lennon – perched on his aquiline nose. Allie had known Jason since he was at primary school with Mandy, and although he was a year older than Jordan, the young men were good friends.

Allie stood back and watched the party of people in her café garden with a sense of pride. After she lost Roger, even before she lost him, she'd never have imagined she could organise something like this, let alone do it year after year. Her confidence had been so eroded that she'd barely believed she could iron a shirt to a satisfactory standard. But recent years had gradually strengthened her self-belief. Organising this party gave her a sense of achievement and she found great satisfaction in doing things for others and in bringing people together. With modern life being so busy and such a struggle at times, having a sense of community was important, and for her, The Cosy Cottage Café was the heart of that community. She knew it wouldn't be the same for everyone, but she hoped that the people of Heatherlea did see the café as somewhere they could go to relax, to seek comfort and enjoy good food, a drink and a warm welcome. Special occasions such as this one offered her the opportunity to cement friendships old and new and to bring new people into Heatherlea.

New-old people, even.
Like Chris.
Who was walking towards her right now, a smile playing on his handsome face as he held out his hands.
'Dance with me?'
'I don't dance.'
'Nonsense!'
'No, I don't. I'm not graceful enough and I have no sense of rhythm.'
It was true and one of the reasons she had avoided Camilla's invitation earlier.
'I don't care. You can step all over my toes if you like.'
'Oh, Chris, I don't like to be out in front of everyone making a display of myself.'
'But you're always in front of people. You run a café, remember.'
'That's different. I'm safe behind the counter then. Or hidden in the kitchen. They're roles I'm comfortable in. Dancing is different, it's like... letting go and I'm not very good at that.'
He took her hands and laced his fingers through them. 'You're a funny one, Allie Jones, that's for sure. Come with me.' He led her around the side of the café and beneath the pergola. Fairy lights sparkled amongst the delicate pink flowers of the honeysuckle and its sweet, heady fragrance permeated the air.
From the front lawn, the opening chords of a familiar song rang out.
'Dance with me here,' Chris whispered as he gently pulled her close. Allie's breath caught in her chest as Chris slid his arms around her and rested his hands on her waist. Her hands seemed to have a mind of their own, and they moved up Chris's arms to rest on his shoulders. They danced together slowly, and the years fell away.
Allie was eighteen again and Chris was twenty. She gazed into his deep, dark eyes and saw what she had seen all those years ago.
Love.
Her heart pounded and she gasped as his arms tightened around her.
'Allie.'
'Chris.'

'I should have come back before I did.'
'Perhaps it wasn't the right time.'
'But if I had come sooner, then we could have talked about things. I could have helped you with things after Roger died.'
'It doesn't matter now.'
'But I wish I had. I just wanted you to know that.'
'I'm glad you're here now. I had a journey to travel after losing Roger and I don't regret having to do it alone. I needed some space, to be honest. I've learnt a lot about myself and I know I can be strong, that I can do things I never dreamt of doing before.'
'You're wonderful and you've always been wonderful.'
He lifted a hand and stroked her cheek, sending heat coursing throughout her body.
Then he lowered his head and kissed her.
His lips were warm and soft.
His body was hard and strong as it pressed against hers.
Allie wrapped her arms tightly around his neck and pulled him closer.
The world spun around them and she became weightless as a long-buried passion flooded through her limbs, awakening sensations at her core that made her shiver with delight.
When Chris finally pulled away, his cheeks were flushed and his eyes sparkled.
'Welcome back,' Allie said as her heart filled with happiness.
'It's good to be home.'

Chapter Nine

Allie floated around the next morning. The sun warmed the floorboards of the cottage and the cats followed her as she moved from room to room. They took turns to rub against her legs and to purr when she stroked them. It was as if they could sense that something was different about their mistress, as if her sudden flush of happiness was something they could share in too.
She did a quick clean around then stripped her bed and put the linen in the washing machine in the small utility room just off the kitchen. She felt energised, renewed, full of anticipation, as if she'd removed her own dust sheets and was ready to face the world again.
When she went back upstairs, she remade the bed and stretched out on the sheets that smelt of strawberry and lily fabric softener. Her entire body tingled as she thought about the party the previous evening and about the kiss under the pergola.
It had been magical and she'd felt as exhilarated as she had all those years ago when he'd kissed her that first time, but without the guilt she'd been burdened with then. The guilt that she'd kissed someone other than Roger and that someone had been their mutual best friend. The first time had been sudden and they'd been slightly

drunk. They'd shared a bottle of wine in the pub garden then another before going for a walk to make the most of the warm evening. They'd ended up sitting on a bench in the park, watching as the sun changed the sky from orange to lilac to inky blue.

Made bold with alcohol, Allie had suddenly blurted out her suspicions that Roger was seeing someone else, suspicions that she'd been harbouring for a while. Chris had appeared surprised at first. Roger had been away for the late-summer weekend with friends from university and Allie had suspected he might be seeing a young woman on his course. She'd asked Chris if he knew anything, but he'd pleaded ignorance. Yet, he'd said, because he cared about Allie, if he had known anything, he'd have been compelled to tell her the truth.

Something had come over Allie and she'd turned on the bench and taken Chris's hands. She'd known deep down that things weren't right with Roger but with the naivety of youth and the optimism that burned through, she'd been hopeful that everything would turn out for the best.

But in that moment, as dusk fell, she'd leaned in close to Chris and kissed him. It had been clumsy at first, slightly awkward as the lines between friendship and romance blurred, but passion had soon carried them away and Allie had felt something she'd never felt before. That sense of coming home, yet being free, as if Chris held the answers to all the questions she'd ever wanted to ask.

The next day, following the kiss, Roger had come home to Heatherlea for the rest of the holidays. Somehow, Allie had omitted to tell him about what had happened with Chris, and life had just continued as before. But Roger had been so affectionate, so full of promises that he would give her a lifetime of happiness. He'd also told her that he needed her, that she was his whole world and he couldn't live without her. Looking back, she realised he must have been feeling guilty about something. But she'd been taken in, told herself that Chris was wilful and independent, that his dreams of being an author might not even be realised and that she wanted what Roger could offer. She'd convinced herself that Roger needed her more than Chris did.

How she regretted that now, but she also knew that if she'd changed the course of their lives back then, she'd have missed out on having Mandy and Jordan, and she would never, ever wish them away. Sometimes things happened as they were meant to, and if you were lucky, it all worked out right in the end.

After all, it seemed that life was giving her a second chance and she was fit to burst with delight.

'Morning Mum.' Jordan stood in her doorway, his t-shirt rumpled and his hair sticking out at odd angles.

Allie sat up.

'Morning, angel. How'd you sleep?'

He rubbed his eyes. 'Good yeah.'

'Where did you go after the party?'

Allie had noticed that her son hadn't come straight home. She'd been very aware of the fact that Chris had hung around long after everyone else had left – as he'd helped her to tidy up and to load the dishwasher – and she had worried that Jordan might have wondered why Chris was there for so long.

'I went to Max's.'

'That late?'

Jordan shrugged. 'I wasn't tired.'

'What time did you come home?' Allie had slept so soundly she hadn't even heard the key in the lock or her son's heavy tread as he crossed the landing.

'Around three.'

'I hope Max's mother and father don't mind you being there so late.'

'His parents are away at the moment. They're visiting his mother's sister in Birmingham.'

'I see. You want some breakfast?'

He nodded.

Twenty minutes later, as they sat in the sunny kitchen eating scrambled eggs, Jordan put down his fork and sighed.

'What is it, love?'
'I need to tell you something.'
Allie put her own fork down and wiped her mouth with a napkin. She'd been wondering when he'd tell her what was on his mind but hadn't pushed him in case he wasn't ready.
'I've been trying to tell you for a while now but we always get interrupted by other people or I lose my nerve.'
'Jordan, you can tell me anything. You know how much I love you and I'll always support you.'
'Well, see, Mum, the thing is…' He took a deep breath. 'I'm in love.'
Allie's throat tightened and she took his hand.
'That's wonderful. Fabulous news.' *And so close to my own!* 'But you haven't been seeing anyone. Have you?' Allie thought back over recent weeks, trying to put a face to what Jordan had just told her, but she drew a blank.
'Mum, I'm in love with Max.'
Allie thought of the handsome young man who her son spent so much time with. He could have been a model with his tightly curled black hair, smooth dark skin and dazzling amber eyes. He took after his father in that respect and Allie had to admit to having a slight crush on Jerome Wilson when they'd first met. His mother was also beautiful and reminded her of Halle Berry with her effortless elegance and style.
'You love Max?'
'Yes.' Jordan watched her carefully and her heart cracked a little.
'And you were worried that this would be difficult to tell me?'
'Well, yes.' He bit his lower lip.
'Oh my darling!' She jumped up and went around the table, leaned over and hugged him. 'Jordan, I love you so much.'
'So you're all right with it?'
'Why on earth wouldn't I be?' She kissed the top of his head. Things that had previously crossed her mind about her son now fell into place – like he hadn't had a girlfriend since primary school, although she'd just assumed he was shy or hiding his flings from her.

'I'm glad you told me. I have never been anything other than proud of you and Mandy and all I've ever wanted is to see you both happy. If you love Max and he's the one you want, then I am over-the-moon for you.'

'I want you to be happy too, Mum,' he said, as he looked up at her. 'I wish you could find someone to love.'

Allie nodded.

'I know, sweetheart. I know.'

She would tell him about Chris and soon. But first she needed to know exactly what was happening, because until she knew herself, how could she explain it to her son?

Allie was buttering a toasted teacake in the café the next morning when the door opened and Judith Burnley walked in. Her brown cardigan was buttoned up to the neck and she wore a scarf around her head, in spite of the heat. She closed the door behind her then removed her scarf as she approached the counter.

'Good morning, Allie.'

'Morning, Mrs Burnley. And how are you today?' Allie forced the question out, knowing that it would be greeted with a list of at least eight ailments, some of which would undoubtedly make her cringe. Why the older woman thought Allie would want to know about her piles or ingrowing hairs in certain crevices that never saw the light of day, she had no idea.

'I'm not too bad, thank you.'

Allie swallowed her surprise.

'Good, glad to hear it. I just need to take this teacake over to table three then I'll be right with you.'

Mrs Burnley nodded.

Allie gave her customer, eighty-seven-year-old Fred Bennett, his teacake.

'Would you like anything else, Fred?'

He raised watery grey eyes to meet hers.

'No thank you, my darling. This is just perfect. Unless you're ready to accept my proposal yet?'

'Ah get on with you, Fred. And break the hearts of all the women of Heatherlea? I just couldn't live with myself.' She placed a hand over her heart and sighed dramatically.

'There is that, I guess. Maybe next week then.' He chuckled at their familiar exchange.

Allie smiled then returned to the counter. Fred was a Monday-morning regular and he always had the same thing: a toasted teacake spread with real butter and a pot of Earl Grey tea. He'd sit at the same table and read the Sunday Times – that he'd saved from the previous day – from cover to cover, before paying and leaving to take his stroll around the village. Allie admired his energy.

'Right Mrs Burnley, what'll you have?' Allie pulled her small notebook out of her apron pocket and took the pencil from behind her ear.

'One of those frothy coffees and an iced bun, please.'

'Of course. If you'd like to take seat, I'll bring them over when they're ready.'

'Thank you, dear.'

Allie hummed as she made the cappuccino then dusted the top with chocolate. She wondered what coffee Chris liked. Years ago, there hadn't been so much choice available, so it wasn't something she knew about him. It made her realise how much they had to learn about each other, which was exciting but also made her stomach flutter. Would they still like each other as much when they got to know more?

She hadn't seen him yesterday, wanting to spend quality time with Jordan after he'd told her about his feelings for Max, but she'd sent him a text to let him know that she would see him in the week. She was still apprehensive about taking up his time, still aware that he might have other things to do and other people to see. His reply had been sweet and relaxed and he'd told her not to worry, that he was still sorting through his mother's things, and that he'd look forward to seeing her soon. He'd even ended the text with a kiss, so that had to be a good sign, right?

Allie used the tongs to pick up an iced bun that she placed on a small plate then she took it with the coffee over to Mrs Burnley.

'Thank you, Allie, this looks lovely.'

'You're very welcome. Let me know if you need anything else.'

Allie was about to turn away when Mrs Burnley put a hand on her arm.

'Allie, I just have to tell someone.'

Allie met the woman's small hard eyes.

'Tell someone?'

'Yes! What I've seen this morning.'

'OK...' Allie pushed a few stray hairs behind her ears and glanced around the café. Apart from Fred, the only other customers were two delivery-men tucking into cooked breakfasts before heading out to spend the day driving around. She could spare Mrs Burnley five minutes. She pulled out a chair and sat down.

Mrs Burnley took a bite of her iced bun then chewed slowly. Allie waited, fighting the urge to tell her to get a move on.

'This morning, as I was making my way here, a very fancy car shot through the village.'

'A fancy car?'

'Yes, dear. It was bright red and very sporty looking.'

'Nice.' Allie took a deep breath and released it slowly. What on earth this had to do with her or Mrs Burnley, she had no idea.

'It stopped outside the Monroe cottage.' She paused and watched Allie, clearly waiting for a reaction.

'Outside Mrs Monroe's place, you say?'

'Well, I guess we should say Chris Monroe's place now, shouldn't we? Seeing as how my dear friend has passed, god rest her soul.'

Allie nodded, wondering what was coming next.

'And… the woman who got out of it was just…' Mrs Burnley held out her hands and wiggled her fingers. 'A vision of perfection.'

Allie's world lurched and she gripped her chair to steady herself. A woman had gone to Chris's house? A woman who was a vision of perfection?

'Of course, I'm not one to gossip.' Mrs Burnley shook her head.

'No, of course not.' Allie forced the words out through gritted teeth.

'But this woman knocked on the door and when Chris opened it, he scooped her up in what I can only describe as a passionate embrace.'

'Oh.' Acid churned in Allie's stomach. Chris had said he wasn't seeing anyone and that he hadn't even had a date in six months but perhaps he'd lied. Men did lie, she knew that from what had happened with Roger and he'd been her husband. Allie had no claim on Chris at all. They'd shared a kiss and some memories, but she didn't even know that much about him anymore. In fact, she only knew the version of him that he'd presented to her.

Dammit! She was a grown woman and she should have known better.

Mrs Burnley finished her bun then took a sip of her coffee before asking, 'Who do you think she is?'

Allie wondered if the older woman was torturing her by divulging this information. But why would she? No one knew that Allie and Chris had become close again, except for Allie and Chris. Mrs Burnley was just sharing gossip, as she was wont to do.

'I have no idea. What did…' She knew she shouldn't ask but morbid curiosity overwhelmed her. 'What did she look like?'

'Tall and very slim. She was wearing some tight little dress with shiny black heels. Must have been about six foot, I'd say. Flowing dark hair and a tan that couldn't possibly have been real unless she's just come back from the Caribbean. Bet she didn't have any white bits either. Chris was so glad to see her that I predict there'll be a wedding there. Probably on a beach somewhere hot with the sea lapping at their toes.' Mrs Burnley smacked her lips then drained her coffee, which left her with a frothy moustache.

'How lovely.'

Allie forced herself to get up. She knew she should tell Mrs Burnley about the froth on her top lip but she couldn't summon the energy.
'Can I get you anything else?'
'No thank you, dear. I'm off to the post office next.'
No doubt to share your gossip there too.
Allie nodded then took the plate and cup from the table and went to the counter. She rang Mrs Burnley's order through the till then went through to the kitchen and leaned over the sink. Her stomach was rolling so badly, she was afraid she'd throw up and her head throbbed with tension. She took a few steadying breaths, in and out, to the count of ten.
She had been a stupid, stupid fool and let her heart run away with her. Chris was a best-selling author now and she was just Allie Jones, owner of The Cosy Cottage Café – a dumpy, widowed mother on the wrong side of forty. Why would Chris come back and want her when he could have a vision of perfection? Hadn't Roger shown her that perfection was what all men wanted?
She ran the tap then splashed cold water over her face.
Well that was that.
Enough!
Time to get on with the life she'd made for herself. She had no time to waste fantasising about what might have been. She'd shared a kiss with an old friend and it had been nice, very nice in fact, but it meant nothing.
At least not to him.

Chapter Ten

Allie turned the sign on the door to closed, then locked it. She walked to the window by the sofa to close the blinds and looked out at the garden. The past few weeks had been eventful, and she'd been on a rollercoaster of emotions as well as a journey of self-discovery.
Quite frankly, she was exhausted.
She rested her head against the cool glass for a moment and closed her eyes.
Following Mrs Burnley's news about the vision of perfection in the red sports car, the rest of Allie's day had seen her yoyo between being stern with herself about staying strong and moving on, and fighting a deep sadness that made her cold to her bones and created an ache in her chest that wouldn't go away.
It was all so silly, really. Allie had jumped the gun and allowed herself to feel things about Chris that she had no right feeling. She'd been swept up in nostalgia and what-ifs, and it had ended badly. For her, at least. Apparently, Chris was making plans with a gorgeous raven-haired model.
She exhaled slowly then opened her eyes.
And screeched then staggered backwards.

On the other side of the glass, was a white face, its eyes wide and dark, its mouth stretched in a grin.

'Chris.' She covered her chest with her hands and willed her heartbeat to slow down.

What was he doing here?

He pointed at the door.

She unlocked it with trembling hands, wishing she had a valid reason to refuse that wouldn't make her seem completely insane.

'Hey, Allie,' he said, as he came inside. 'I've been meaning to pop over all day but I didn't expect to find you sleeping against the window.'

Allie offered a brief smile. 'I just have a headache.'

'Poor love.' He reached out and placed his palm against her forehead. 'You are quite warm. Hope you're not cooking something up.'

Allie moved away from his hand. 'I'm fine. I'll be fine.'

'Okaaayyy.'

He followed her to the counter.

'What do you want, Chris?' Her tone was so icy it surprised her.

'I came to see you.'

'But why?' She met his brown eyes and saw them fill with confusion.

'Because I wanted to see you. Because I like seeing you.'

Allie swallowed a retort about him seeing enough of a six-foot model that he shouldn't need to see her.

'Well you've seen me now.'

'Allie, what's wrong? Have I done something?' He ran a hand through his hair and frowned at her. 'I'm a bit confused. I thought we were... well, you know.' He shrugged.

'I guess we both thought wrong.'

She folded her arms over her chest.

Chris shook his head. 'I came to tell you that I've got some news. A plan, that is. Can I tell you about it?'

Anger fizzed inside Allie. This man had come back to the village, to her home, and toyed with her affections. He had hurt her pride and wounded her confidence. And he *still* wanted her to be his friend.

'You have a bloody cheek, you know that?' She spat the words at him and he flinched.

'I do?'

'Yes, you do. You come here and make me remember how it used to be and make all these damned feelings resurface then you… you're shagging some black-haired, long-legged…' Allie tried to think of an appropriate term that would convey her anger without making her sound jealous, but nothing came to mind. 'Thing!'

'Wait a minute…' He held up his hands. 'I'm shagging a black-haired, long-legged what?'

'You know what I mean.' Her voice came out strangled. 'You were seen this morning. *Snogging* on your doorstep.'

She choked on a sob.

The emotions swirling around inside puzzled her. She hadn't felt such anger, fire or need for reassurance in years. Chris might have hurt her but she had to credit him with burning away the numb haze she'd been wading through since Roger died, at least.

'I think someone has misunderstood what they've seen, Allie. That's the problem with village gossip. Can we sit down and talk, please? I feel terribly awkward standing here like this.'

Allie watched him carefully. Was it possible that he wasn't seeing another woman and that Mrs Burnley had been mistaken?

'I guess so.' Her voice sounded as if it had come from the bottom of a well. She should give him a chance to explain; she owed him that much.

They sat opposite each other at the table in front of the log burner, and Allie folded her hands on the tabletop.

'Allie, the woman who came to my house today was my literary agent, Audrey Harper.'

'Do you always kiss your agent?'

Chris laughed. 'She's very tactile but she's like it with everyone. What your source – whoever that was – saw, was probably just her kissing my cheeks in greeting.'

'Oh.' Allie's cheeks flamed. She'd let herself believe what Mrs

Burnley had told her and now she felt like a complete idiot. Not only that, she seemed jealous and irrational, and she had never wanted to be either of those things.

'Yes, *oh*. Audrey came with some good news and that's what I wanted to tell you.'

She bit the inside of her cheek, the physical pain nothing compared to the ache deep inside.

'Allie?' He took her hands.

'Yes.'

'Can I share my news?'

She nodded.

'Audrey is not just my agent but also a good friend. I told her I want to move back to Heatherlea and that I needed to either sell or rent out my place in London. The mortgage is extortionate and it would be ludicrous to leave it empty. Anyway, she knows someone who wants a city location and is prepared to pay cash for a quick no-chain sale.'

'You're selling your apartment? Isn't that a big move to make?'

He squeezed her hands. 'It's a move I'm prepared to make because I don't want to risk losing you for a second time. I mean, what if I don't stay in the village, and when I turn my back, someone else comes along and swoops you up? How would I feel then?'

'So you're telling me you're prepared to do all of this because of me?'

'No other reason.' He held her gaze, his brown eyes warm and sincere, and she felt him drawing her in, encouraging her to place her trust in him.

Something in her chest shifted a fraction.

'I can't ask you to do that. What if...?' She bit her lip, not wanting to cast doubt on the situation, yet afraid not to voice her fears.

'If it doesn't work between us?'

'Yes,' she whispered.

'Why wouldn't it?'

'It's been such a long time and I know I have feelings for you but we've both been through so much and time has passed and we're more set in our ways and—'

'Tell me.' He cut her off.

'What?'

'Tell me what's holding you back.'

Allie scanned his face, wanting to believe that she could do this; that it would be all right.

'Really?'

'I know something's stopping you letting go, so tell me what it is and we'll put it right together.'

Allie took a deep breath then exhaled slowly, clearing her lungs and giving herself a moment to collect her thoughts.

'It's not pleasant to hear and to be honest, I'm afraid it might alter the way you see me.'

'Nothing could ever do that.' He leaned over and pressed a kiss to each of her palms.

Allie hoped he was right but she wouldn't know until she shared the truth.

Chapter Eleven

Divulging the whole truth about Roger was difficult. Allie had never told anyone the truth about the day he died, apart from her parents. It was like admitting to being a failure and she didn't want to see the pity and possibly the understanding in people's eyes.
She wriggled on her chair and pressed her nails into her palms but Chris took her hands again and held them tight. His touch was reassuring, anchoring her to the moment.
'Right. Here goes.' She swallowed hard. 'Roger and I... well, things weren't as perfect as they might have seemed to an outsider. I told you before that we'd drifted apart and that things weren't that good between us, but I suppose I didn't admit exactly how far.'
She scanned his face.
'Anyway, he uh—' Her voice wobbled.
'You can tell me.' He squeezed her hands.
'The night he died...' The room swayed and Allie was hit by a wave of nausea. 'Look, Chris, I don't want the children to ever find out about this. They lost their dad once and I don't want them to lose him again. Perhaps with them being the age they were, they wouldn't have

been that bothered about us splitting up, but I didn't want to risk hurting them.'

He shook his head. 'This is between you and me. I promise I won't tell a soul.'

Allie nodded. 'Roger was leaving. I sometimes wonder if he waited until Mandy and Jordan were a bit older, or if he just got to the point where he couldn't take any more. Jordan was at a friend's house and Mandy was already away at university. After he got home from work, he got his bags out of his wardrobe – he'd already packed them you see, something I hadn't known at the time. We'd had a bit of a row that morning but I thought we'd sort it out or ignore it as we usually did. You know, we never cleared the air properly after an argument; it was always left to simmer and nothing was ever really resolved. But when he got his bags out, I was distraught. I begged him to stay. Which was stupid and ridiculous, in light of how things were between us, but I was so afraid.' Her cheeks burned with humiliation. 'I'm sorry.'

'Not so much about being alone as wondering how I would provide for Mandy and Jordan. How would Mandy manage with university fees and how would I keep a roof over Jordan's head? How could I give them a good life when I didn't have a job? Hadn't had one for years because I'd given up work to keep house. And according to Roger I didn't do that very well. My confidence was shattered.'

'Didn't he reassure you at all?'

'He said he'd sort out some money soon, that there was enough in the bank account to cover the month's bills then he'd make sure he put more in. He said he'd see Mandy right, but I didn't know whether to believe him. About any of it. ' Her stomach churned. 'I said I'd do anything if he stayed but he just looked disgusted. I grabbed hold of his arm and he shook me off. Then he delivered the ultimate blow.'

Chris shook his head. 'He didn't hit you, did he?' A muscle in his jaw twitched as if he was holding back his anger.

'No. He wasn't physically violent. But he told me he couldn't bear to spend another night under the same roof as me, that I repulsed him with my... my saggy body and hideous clothes. That I never made an effort anymore, and he hadn't even wanted me that much in the first place. I was horrified, Chris. I didn't realise the full extent of his animosity towards me. Then he told me about her, the woman he was leaving me for. Younger. Slimmer. More suitable for his lifestyle than I'd become. He said she was perfect.'

'What an utter bastard. That's totally unforgiveable and if he was around I'd happily give him a piece of my mind.'

Allie sighed then rolled her shoulders; keen to dislodge the tension that was building there. She'd managed to keep all this inside for so long by pushing it away and pretending it was all a bad dream.

'So I let go and went back into the house. I heard his tyres screeching as he drove away and that was the last time I saw him. Until... after...'

Chris nodded. 'I read the newspaper reports and saw the pictures on the news.'

'It was terrible. A horrific motorway pile up. He didn't stand a chance.'

'Bloody hell!'

'I assume he was on his way to meet her.' She waved a hand dismissively. 'Probably off to a hotel or a night out. Whatever. It doesn't matter really.'

'So you never told Mandy and Jordan that Roger was having an affair.'

'Nothing at all about it. I just said he was meeting some colleagues that night and that's why he was on the motorway at that time. I guess I hoped they wouldn't find out by any other means. Seeing as how he was dead, there was no point making it even harder for them.'

Allie lowered her eyes and gazed at her hands, enveloped within Chris's.

'I think it's amazing that you didn't tell them, that you protected them like that.'

Allie shrugged.

'I'm their mum. I'm all they had left. Why would I hurt them?'

'You wouldn't. You have a heart of gold, woman.'

'I don't know about that. I've cursed him so many times and burnt a few cakes as I've lost myself in daydreams where I walked out the door before he could. My favourite was one where I didn't cling to his arm and beg him to stay. If I'd only been stronger and not so afraid of failing. My parents have such a happy marriage and I wanted that too. After I got pregnant and I thought I couldn't pursue the career I'd always wanted to, the only thing I could do was try to make a go of it. And I hate that memory of me clinging to him; it's like, why didn't I have any pride?'

'I don't think you did anything that most people wouldn't do. Your world was falling apart and you tried to hold it together. Out of fear for what it meant for your children more than anything. There's no shame in being afraid of change and of losing the life you've had for so long. It's a pretty scary prospect.'

'Thank you. I saw her afterwards… the other woman. At the funeral.'

'That must have been awkward.'

'To say the least. I knew it was her because she was broken. She sobbed all the way through the service then couldn't meet my eye at the graveside. She was beautiful, exactly the type of woman he would have wanted. She's probably gone on to live a very nice life, maybe even has a family now. Hopefully, it's a better life than she'd have had with Roger.' She shook her head. 'I guess we all have regrets, right?'

'I know I do. But why did you think this would change how I saw you?'

'Well your former best friend was leaving me because I no longer pleased him. It's hardly an advert for how attractive I am, is it? Then there was the total loss of dignity with the clinging to him and the begging.'

Chris smiled then and some of the tension in Allie's shoulders loosened. His smile was like the sun when it appeared from behind a cloud: warming, reassuring and extremely welcome.

'You have to give yourself a break. This is all in the past and you are an amazing woman. Look at this business you built all on your own. Look at what a great job you did bringing up your two children. And look at me. I'm back here, still as crazy about you as I was all those years ago.'

His expression became serious then and Allie's heart skipped a beat.

'What is it?'

'There's something you should know too. I don't think I ever would have told you but hearing what a bastard Roger was, I think I can share.'

'I'm listening.'

'You know when we... when we had that time together. That weekend when Roger was away.'

'Yes.'

'When we—'

'Kissed.'

'Yes.'

He stroked her hands with his thumbs; it was gentle and soothing.

'Well when Roger came back, I had a word with him.'

'You told him?'

'I told him I was concerned about how he was treating you. That I was disgusted with how he had left you worried that he was cheating, that I thought it seemed like he was trying to control you by keeping you feeling insecure. I said that he should let you go if he didn't really want to be with you, and allow you to be happy with a man who could love you as you deserved to be loved.'

'Wow...' Allie shifted on her chair. No wonder Roger had turned against Chris if he'd given him a piece of his mind. Roger never liked being told the truth if it went against his own version of himself.

'He accused me of being in love with you and wanting you for myself. At first, I denied it, but he'd been my friend for a long time. He could read me well. So finally, I admitted it.'

'You were in love with me?'

He nodded.

'Truly. Madly. Deeply.'

'How did he take it?'

'He laughed.'

'He laughed?'
'Then he asked me if I thought I was good enough for you. If I thought I stood a chance. I didn't tell him I'd kissed you, I knew that would tip him over the edge.'
'He did have a terrible temper.'
'When I didn't answer, he leaned in close and told me I would never have you. He said that you were his and he'd make sure you had to marry him.'
'Oh god!' Allie gasped as realisation washed over her. 'He got me pregnant.'
'I don't think it was an accident.'
'Nor do I. He told me that night when we... you know... that he'd be careful and I believed him. Stupidly and naively. I should have known better.'
'Roger could be very convincing when he wanted to be. And the thing is... growing up, Roger was my friend. But he was always extremely competitive. If I had something, he had to have better. He did want you, I'm not denying that, but knowing that I cared about you made him want you even more.'
'And over the years, because you weren't around, that competition wasn't there anymore, which meant that his desire to keep me faded.'
'I'm sorry, Allie.'
'What do you have to be sorry for?'
'I should have told you sooner or put up a fight for you.'
'Things worked out as they did. We can't go back and change anything and regret is a waste of energy.'
'Well I'm here now.'
'Me too.'
'And I don't want to go away again. I want to be with you as I believe I always should have done.'
He got up and came around to her then pulled her to her feet.
'I'm afraid, Chris.'
He cupped her chin. 'Of what?'
'That I'm not very good at this relationship business.'

He gazed into her eyes and warmth flooded through her as he gently rubbed his thumb over her lips before kissing her.

'Don't be afraid. We can do this together.'

'Really?'

He nodded. 'You should have been with me from the start. Now... do you want to try this together? See if we can get it right second-time around?'

She pulled him close and kissed him, letting her answer come from deep within.

Chapter Twelve

Allie stood on the lawn and surveyed the exterior of the café.
'What do you think, Mum?' Jordan held out his hands. 'Pretty good job, huh?'
'It's fantastic. Just perfect for our end-of-summer party.'
The trees in the garden and the pergola were draped with strings of fairy lights in the shape of apples and pears and they'd hung colourful bunting from the shutters on the cafe windows.
'Time to get changed, Mum. Before the little guests arrive.'
'Come on then.' Allie followed Jordan and Max through the café and into the cottage.
Fifteen minutes later, she emerged from her bedroom to find Jordan and Max squashed in the tiny bathroom giggling. She stood in the doorway and smiled as she took in their matching costumes. They both wore Hawaiian shirts and cut off denim shorts and had big moustaches stuck above their mouths.
'You'll terrify the children looking like that.'
'I think we look cool, Mum. Kind of like Miami detectives from the 1980s.'

'You look pretty cool too, Allie,' Max said as he leaned back to look at her better.

'Thanks. I feel a bit daft but it's all for a good cause, right?'

In keeping with the summer theme, Allie was dressed as a bumblebee. Her costume consisted of a black-and-yellow striped dress with a flared black skirt that came to her knees, black cropped leggings and a pair of delicate black wings strapped to her back. She'd pinned her hair up and completed the outfit with a headband complete with antennae.

When they went downstairs, Allie headed into the café kitchen.

'Hello, my busy little bee.' Chris smiled at her from behind the kitchen island.

'Ha ha!'

He dusted his hands off on his apron then opened his arms.

'Kiss for the chef?'

Allie melted against him as he pressed his lips to hers.

'We'd better stop,' she said as she gently pulled away. 'Don't want to crush my wings.'

'That would never do. I need my honey.' He smiled. 'Too cheesy?'

'A bit.' She grinned.

'I'm just about done here. What do you think?'

'You've done a fabulous job.'

Allie eyed the delights that Chris had insisted on making that afternoon. He'd told her to leave him in the kitchen to get on with it, and sent her to get her nails done at Jenny's salon. And she couldn't deny that he had done well. Extremely well. The counters were filled with foil platters of treats including freshly baked finger rolls with a variety of fillings to suit everyone's requirements, cheese and bacon scones, sweet potato, avocado and feta muffins, cupcakes that had been iced so they resembled ladybirds and bees, and mini mixed-berry cheesecakes.

Suddenly her vision blurred.

'Allie, what's wrong?' Chris enveloped her in a hug before the first tear fell.

'It's just... the effort you've gone to. I know you've been practising these recipes for weeks just to get them right and I'm overwhelmed. No one has ever done anything like this for me before. And I know you have a deadline for your next book.'

He wiped away the tear with his thumb then kissed her gently.

'I work better under pressure.' He smiled. 'And perhaps no one has ever done this for you before because no one ever loved you like I do. The past five weeks have been the best of my life. Being back in Heatherlea with you and getting to know you all over again has been incredible.'

She shook her head. 'I still can't believe it.'

'No more doubts or worries, my love. I'm here and I'm here to stay. Now help me get these out to the trestle tables because the children will be arriving soon and I still haven't finished the drinks.'

An hour later, Allie stood watching as Jordan and Max guided children – dressed as surfers, princesses, dragons, superheroes and insects – around the garden as they searched for clues as part of the treasure hunt. Her son and his boyfriend had set up a variety of games including bowling – which involved knocking down tins painted with monster faces – and a homemade dragon piñata, which the children would take turns to hit with sticks until the dragon surrendered its sweet treats.

Chris had insisted on being the barman, which meant standing behind the trestle table in his pirate costume. Allie thought his costume of black trousers cut jagged at the knee, white t-shirt, stripy waistcoat, and red bandana perched above a long black wig with a black eyepatch – that he kept lifting up as he served soft drinks to the children and their parents – was fantastic. The most popular drink he'd created was his bloodthirsty pirate punch, a combination of cranberry juice, orange juice and cherryade.

'Hello, Allie.' Camilla sauntered along the path, a grin on her pretty face. Just behind her were Dawn and Honey. 'What a pretty little bee you are.'

Allie accepted her friends' hugs.

'This all looks delightful.'
'It's been fabulous so far. The children seem to be having a great time.'
'They certainly are burning off a lot of energy and should sleep well tonight,' Dawn added as she crossed her fingers and grinned.
'Laura and James are attacking the piñata. Rick's watching them so don't worry.' Allie pointed at the tree where Rick was shouting encouragement at James, who was waving a stick at the papier-mâché dragon while his father looked on.
'I was lucky enough to have an afternoon nap. Rick's been making the effort to get home early a few nights a week, so I can rest before dinner.' Dawn yawned. 'And although I wouldn't have minded another hour, I feel a lot better.'
'Yes but that's partly psychological too, isn't it?' Camilla asked her sister. 'Now you know everything's OK with the baby.'
'The scan went well?' Allie asked.
Dawn nodded then pulled a small card from her bag. She opened it and inside was a grainy image of a tiny baby.
'Perfect,' Allie said. 'I'm so happy for you. Do you know if it's a boy or girl?'
'No. We thought we'd wait and enjoy the surprise. I'm just glad it's only one and that it's healthy.' She cupped her belly and her expression softened.
'And how are you feeling now?' Honey asked Allie. 'Everything seems to be going well with Chris.'
Allie nodded. 'It is, thank you. Very well.'
They'd had to forgo their usual Tuesday evening get-together because of the party. This meant they hadn't had their opportunity to talk yet this week, which was why Allie hadn't seen Dawn's most recent scan picture. However, she had kept them updated about how things with Chris were going. *Slowly* being the word she kept repeating, although deep down, her heart was refusing to listen to reason.

Summer at The Cosy Cottage Café

When the grateful parents had taken the children home, and Jordan, Max and Chris had helped Allie to tidy up, she sat at one of the outdoor tables with a glass of red wine and sighed with contentment. Jordan and Max had taken themselves off to the pub, so she was left alone with Chris.
'It's a beautiful evening,' he said.
'It is and I had a great time. I put on a goodbye-summer party last year, but it wasn't as much fun.'
'Allie, nothing was as much fun for me until I came back to Heatherlea. You are everything I ever wanted.'
Allie sipped her wine, enjoying the spicy finish of the good quality Shiraz.
'So where do we go from here?' she asked. 'Not that I want to rush things. I mean, you haven't been back long and—'
'I've been wanting to talk to you about that.'
'You have?'
'Well now that the cottage has been emptied of my mother's collection, for want of a better word, and had a fresh coat of paint, it's looking pretty good there.'
Allie nodded. She'd been round to see how the decorators were getting on and encouraged Chris to keep the kitchen exactly as it was, although she had suggested he put in an island to match the rest of the units. He'd done so with the help of a local carpenter and had proudly shown her just yesterday.
'I was considering selling and buying something else local but I'd like to keep the cottage. It's a good size and with some new furniture upstairs and in the lounge, I think it'll make a great home to spend my twilight years.'
Allie snorted. 'You're not in your twilight years.'
'Not yet but always best to prepare.'

'Always.'
'There's something missing though.' He sipped his wine thoughtfully and gazed upwards as if considering his wording.
'There is?'
'Most definitely.'
'What is it?'
'A cat flap.'
'A cat flap? Why'd you want one of those you haven't got any ca... oh.' Allie bit her lip.
'Exactly.' He took her hands. 'I want your cats to come and live with me.'
She burst into laughter.
'My cats?'
He nodded.
'And you can come along too if you like.'
'Chris, that is not the most romantic way to ask me. Although I am glad you removed the eye patch first.'
He shook his head then toyed with a few strands from his long black wig.
'This is itching like mad.' He pulled it off and rubbed his head.
'That's better. I'm teasing about the cats. I just got all embarrassed for a moment there. It's the author in me; I'm terrified of using clichés. Anyway...' He took a deep breath. 'I have something for you.'
He stood up and pulled something from his trouser pocket.
'Open your hand.'
'Why? What is it? Not one of those pirate hooks is it? Or a bottle of rum.'
'It's not.' He hadn't laughed at her jokes and she realised his expression was serious, earnest.
'OK then.'
She opened her hand and Chris placed something warm and solid onto her palm.
She looked from the silver key to Chris, then back again.

'Allie, I don't feel I'm rushing anything because I've waited my whole life to be with you.'

Her heart pounded and blood whooshed through her ears as emotion surged in her chest.

'My home is your home, Allie. I don't want to be without you any longer. I don't want to spend another night away from you. Ever.'

'Well we haven't spent many nights apart this past fortnight.' Allie flushed as she thought about the times Chris had stayed over when they knew Jordan would be at Max's. Even though Jordan knew about Chris now, she still felt a bit awkward when they were all together. It was as if part of her believed that she shouldn't be dating anyone, let alone a man who'd known his father. But Jordan had insisted when she'd told him, then about thirty times more, that he was happy for her to see Chris, and always would be as long as she was happy. When she'd told Mandy on the phone, unable to get her daughter to commit to a trip home because of what she described as a very busy schedule – including a conference in Brighton for authors and agents – Mandy had gone quiet. Allie's heart had stopped as she waited for her daughter to say something. And she had. Eventually. She'd told Allie that it was great news and asked if Chris was thinking of changing publisher any time soon, which had been her way of letting Allie know that everything was all right between them.

'So let's not spend any more apart then.'

Allie turned the key over in her fingers, feeling its weight. It wasn't just a key; it was a symbol of the life she could embark upon now with the man she'd always loved. This was the start of something special. At her age, she'd thought all that was behind her, but here she was with a wonderful second chance. She was still young. Her children were happy, her parents were happy – and delighted that she'd started seeing Chris – and her friends were happy. Everything seemed to be going right for once.

She held the key tight, feeling its reassuring weight.

'OK.'

'OK?' Chris's eyebrows rose.

'Let's do it. I guess Jordan will be happy to have the extra space above the café now that he has Max. They were talking about finding somewhere together just yesterday, so this will work out well for them too.'
Chris pulled her to her feet then swung her round. 'You won't regret this, I promise. I'll do everything I can, every day of my life, to make you happy. I love you, Allie Jones.'
'And I love you too, Chris.'
As he squeezed her tight, Allie peered over his shoulder at The Cosy Cottage Café and smiled. Her life had started over when she'd taken on the café. Chris had returned at a time when she was doing well, when she felt good about herself. And that was important. She'd proved something by setting up her own business; that she was a strong woman with a good head on her shoulders and a good heart. She'd created a small corner of the community where people could go when they needed a break, some sustenance or even just a friendly face.
And now that Chris was here, life would just be even better.
'I think we'd better go tell the cats,' Allie said as Chris released her.
'Probably for the best. Wouldn't want those wily sisters finding out from someone else now would we?'
'And one more thing.'
He raised his eyebrows.
'When you said you wanted to get some new furniture, you meant old, right?'
'Whatever you want is just perfect. Like you.'
Allie held out her hand and Chris took it, then they entered The Cosy Cottage Café together, neither of them ever intending on letting go again.

The End

Autumn at The Cosy Cottage Café

Autumn at The Cosy Cottage Café

Mum Dawn Dix-Beaumont's plans to return to teaching are thwarted by a surprise from Mother Nature. Rick Beaumont loves his family but there's a lot to juggle. When the pressure mounts, will their marriage become stronger than ever, or will it be time to make some difficult decisions?

Chapter One

Dawn Dix-Beaumont dropped the Lego bricks into the large plastic bucket and leaned against the wall. The colour scheme of the playroom had been chosen to create a fun and lively space for their children, but right now, in the early October afternoon sunshine, it was giving her a headache. The yellow walls, the red and blue buckets for toys, the turquoise and purple beanbags, and the green shelves, all seemed to be growing larger as she stood there. Swaying.
Swaying?
She slid down the wall to the floor and pressed her head into her hands. It must be low blood pressure again. She'd suffered with it in both of her previous pregnancies and it had made her feel faint and lethargic. Only it hadn't come on quite so quickly before. This time, however, even though she was only thirty-three, it seemed that her body was not going to take pregnancy lightly.
Thank goodness it was Friday and Rick would be home for the weekend. Since finding out about the pregnancy, she'd tried to rest whenever she could, but it was difficult with two children and a house to run. As well as a rabbit and a guinea pig to take care of.
Shit!

She needed to clean the hutch out before it was time to pick the children up from school. She loved the animals probably more than Laura and James did. It had been Rick's father's idea to get the children pets. He'd said it would encourage them to be responsible and he'd insisted on choosing the rabbit and guinea pig and paying for them. In typical Paul Beaumont fashion, he'd turned up one day with the animals, a hutch, a garden run and all the necessary paraphernalia for looking after the pets.

Dawn had agreed with the concept of pets making the children more responsible, but her initial suspicion that Laura and James would soon tire of the day-to-day care of Wallace and Lulu had been correct, and now it was all down to her. But she didn't mind. She liked coaxing the rabbit and the guinea pig from their hutch, as it gave her a chance to cuddle them both before letting them loose in their run.

Of course, Laura and James did love Wallace and Lulu, although Laura was more interested in maintaining their social media profile than her younger brother was. She regularly took photographs of them on Dawn's mobile phone, which Dawn then helped her to post to the Instagram page that Paul had set up. *Wallace and Lulu's Adventures* was quite popular and received lots of likes, but Dawn also knew that it was a way for Paul to connect with his grandchildren. He was a busy man – even since his retirement – but the convenience of social media meant that he could check in with his grandchildren from the golf course, or the club at the docks where he kept his boat.

Dawn got up slowly, stood still for a moment to ensure that her head was clear, then went through the hallway to the kitchen. She picked up the shed keys and headed out through the back door and into the garden.

The sun was hot. Forecasters had predicted an Indian summer for England, but Dawn suspected that it would probably last a few days then they'd be plunged into Arctic conditions. The good old British weather never failed to keep people on their toes. Gone were the days where she used to pack her summer wardrobe away by September then her winter woollies by April. There was no point now; it was far more sensible to have a range of clothing to hand throughout the year. She opened the shed and retrieved her box of hutch cleaning supplies, as well as a bag of straw, then carried them across the garden. Lulu, the two-year-old floppy-eared rabbit hopped to the front of the hutch.

'Hello, sweeting.' Dawn knelt down and opened the front of the hutch then held out her hand. Lulu's nose twitched as Dawn smoothed her soft smoky-grey fur. 'Do you want to stretch your legs?' She lifted the rabbit carefully out then let her into the large square pen made of wood and wire netting. Lulu hopped about, clearly enjoying the freedom to nibble on the lush green grass of the lawn. Dawn peered back into the hutch, but guinea pig Wallace had not made an appearance from the sleeping compartment, which wasn't like him. Wallace was quite a greedy little thing and usually greeted Dawn with excited wheeking, especially if she had a carrot for him. She lifted the latch then gently opened the front of the sleeping compartment.

And there, curled up on the straw, was Wallace.

'Hey little man, don't you want to go for a run?'

He didn't move.

Dawn reached out and stroked his silky white fur carefully, expecting him to jump awake and to see his little nose and whiskers twitching as he greeted her. She gently touched his small brown paws, which made him look like he was wearing socks, then his matching brown ears. There was no response.

His tiny body was cold and stiff.

'Oh no!'

She covered her mouth with her hands as tears blurred her vision. Poor little Wallace, just two years old like his companion Lulu, had died.

And Dawn had no idea how she was going to break the news to her children.

Or how she would break the news to their grandfather and Wallace's Instagram following.

Dawn opened the door to The Cosy Cottage Café and closed it behind her, making sure that her tote bag was firmly hooked over her arm.
'Hello, Dawnie!' From behind the counter, her close friend Allie Jones, smiled warmly at her.
'Hi.' Dawn gave a half-hearted wave then hurried over.
'What's wrong? Are you still feeling queasy, love? I'm sure I have another bottle of peppermint cordial here somewhere. Let me get you a glass.'
Dawn shook her head. 'No. No time. I have to pick the children up in an hour and something terrible has happened.'
'What is it?' Allie took Dawn's hand and squeezed it. 'Not the baby?'
'No. The baby's fine. At least I think it is. I mean...' She took a deep breath as a wave of nausea washed over her. 'I'm feeling really bad, so I guess that's a sign that the pregnancy hormones are strong.'
She instinctively cupped her rounded stomach. She was around seventeen weeks along now, and she felt huge. In fact, Dawn was certain that she hadn't been this size until she was about twenty-five weeks pregnant with her first two. It was getting harder and harder to hide her bump.
'So why are you... upset?' Allie peered at her. 'Looks like you need a drink. Sit down and I'll get you one.'
'Oh, OK then. Just a quick one. Something cold would be lovely, thanks.'
Dawn took a seat on the squishy couch in the corner by the front window and placed her bag on the seat next to her. As she sank into the soft leather, she sighed. If only she could just put her feet up and

have a nap. Although it was cool inside the café, the afternoon was hot outside, and her t-shirt was clinging to her back following her short walk to the café.

Allie brought her a glass of bright green liquid.

'Peppermint cordial?'

Allie nodded. 'Drink it. You look like you need it.'

Dawn nodded and accepted the tall glass. Ice cubes clinked against the side as she raised it to her lips and took a sip.

'That's so good, thank you.'

'You're welcome. Now are you going to tell me what's worrying you?' Allie took a seat on the sofa.

Dawn placed her glass on the coffee table in front of them and watched as a bead of condensation trickled down the side.

'I don't know what to do, Allie.'

'About what? Is it Rick? Are you two doing OK now?'

Dawn met Allie's bright blue eyes and a lump lodged in her throat. She shook her head.

'No, it's not about us.'

Although, if she had the time to talk about it, she would tell Allie that, yes, there were some problems with Rick. Things had improved slightly for a while but over the past week – possibly even longer – for some reason, they seemed to have deteriorated again. But perhaps it was just her. She was, after all, pregnant and exhausted, and it was possible that her imagination was finding issues where in fact there were none.

Perhaps...

'Not really. Things are fine with Rick. I mean... well... they're...' She bit her lip. She didn't have time to air her marital woes right now. 'There's something more pressing to deal with.' She patted her black tote bag with the white writing *#babyonboard*. Her sister, Camilla, had bought it for her when she'd been pregnant with Laura and Dawn had kept it ever since, using it as a makeshift handbag when the lining of her old one was too sticky with old sweet wrappers and snotty tissues from the children. Rick had bought her new bags for birthdays and Christmases, but they were always designer labels and far too nice to fill with dummies, nappies, wet wipes and all the bits and bobs she'd acquired over the years as a mum of two.

Allie nodded. 'And...' She raised her eyebrows.

Dawn opened the bag and stuck her hand inside. She pulled out a small parcel and laid it on her lap.

'You've brought me a gift?' Allie smiled.

'Not exactly.'

'Then what is it?'

Dawn passed the parcel to her friend. Allie touched the pink tissue paper then peeled away the Sellotape that held the wrapping together.

'Oh my god! What on earth is that?' Allie grimaced.

'It's Wallace.'

'Wallace?'

'Our guinea pig. He's dead.'

'I can see that. If he wasn't, I'd be asking you why you've turned him into a bizarre pass-the-parcel.'

The door to the café opened and Allie quickly covered her lap with her apron.

'Good afternoon, ladies.'

It was Chris, Allie's boyfriend. He came over to their table, pecked Allie on the lips, then sat down on the reclaimed wooden chair opposite them.

'Hi Dawn.'

'Hi, Chris.'

'You OK there, Allie?' he asked.

'What?' Allie frowned, so Chris gestured at her lap where her apron bulged over Wallace.

'Oh... no.' Allie's cheeks flushed. 'Dawn brought something to show me.'

In spite of the current circumstances, Dawn had to admit that Allie looked really well. Successful author Chris Monroe had returned to the village of Heatherlea that summer for his mother's funeral and decided to stay. His main reason being because he was head-over-heels in love with café owner Allie Jones. Dawn was delighted to see her friend so happy. She'd known Allie for a long time but only become good friends with her in recent years after getting to know her in the café. Allie had been widowed six years ago when her husband was killed in a car accident. But she'd proved to be a strong, resilient woman and had used the life insurance money to set up The Cosy Cottage Café, which was now a very successful business in the pretty Surrey village.

'Something nice?' Chris asked.

'Oh no! Not at all.'

Sweat prickled on Dawn's forehead.

'I see. Shall I leave you two alone for a bit?' Chris made to get up but Allie shook her head.

'No, Chris, it's OK. Dawn's guinea pig died and she brought it to show me. Dawn, you need to get it out of here. If anyone sees it... I mean him... I'll have health and safety inspectors all over me.' Allie moved her apron then handed the parcel to Dawn.

'Yes, of course.'

'How did he die?' Chris asked.

'I don't know.' Dawn's lip wobbled.

Allie slid an arm around her and squeezed. 'Come on, love, it'll be all right.'

'But the children will be devastated. And my father-in-law will be too. I'm sure that Rick's parents already think I don't do a good enough job as a wife and mother and this will just be something else I've failed at.'

'I'm sure that's not true, Dawn, especially not where Paul's concerned. Although I know Fenella can be... challenging at times.'

Dawn nodded, thinking of how her mother-in-law made her feel.

'Is this the guinea pig with an Instagram page? As in *Wallace and Lulu's Adventures*?' Chris pulled a face.

'Shhhh!' Dawn and Allie shook their heads at him.

'Oh dear... and Allie's right; you can't have a dead animal in here.' He glanced around at the customers enjoying their afternoon tea and cakes.

'I know. That's what I just said to her.'

'What am I going to do?' Dawn stared at the bundle wrapped in pink tissue paper. 'Poor Wallace.'

'I have an idea,' Allie said as she stood up and beckoned to Chris. 'Put him back in your bag for now and let's see what we can do.'

Dawn slipped Wallace gently into her tote, then leaned back on the sofa and closed her eyes. She was so, so tired. If she could just have a short nap, then she was sure she'd feel better and everything would fall into place.

Then she'd know what she needed to do...

'Dawn?'

She floated through the warm water, weightless and completely relaxed. It was so nice to be light and free and...

'Dawn, wake up!'

'What?' She shot up through the water to the surface where bubbles popped.

'Dawn, it's three o'clock. Don't you need to get the children from school?'

Allie was leaning over her, with a hand on her arm, and Dawn realised where she was: on the sofa, in the café. She must have fallen asleep.

She rubbed her eyes. 'How long was I out?'

'About forty minutes.'

'Wow! Sorry.'

'Don't worry about it. Do you want me to go and pick Laura and James up?'

'Oh... they won't let you.'

'Why not?'

'They've really clamped down on who's allowed to collect the children and I had to list two authorised people, so I could only include me and Rick. My Mum couldn't even be on the list unless I add her as an alternative, and for that I needed to ask special permission from the head teacher.'

'Things have really changed since Mandy and Jordan were at school.' Allie frowned. 'But it's probably a good thing. Shall I come with you, though?'

'No, you have the café to run, and it's Friday, so you'll probably have a teatime rush.'

'Chris will help out.'

'Where's Jordan today?'

'He's gone to London to spend the weekend with Mandy. She got them theatre tickets and a dinner reservation at a swanky restaurant. Max has gone too.'

'How lovely.' It would be really nice to get away for the weekend, to enjoy a show and a meal that wasn't interrupted by a child refusing to eat their vegetables or by the other one needing a poo.

'Well as long as you're sure you'll be OK. Anyway, I think I've sorted something out regarding… Wallace.'

'Oh!' It all came flooding back then. Poor Wallace. She reached out for her bag and realised it wasn't on the sofa next to her, so she leaned over and spotted it under the coffee table. She pulled it towards her then reached inside but couldn't find the small parcel.

'He's gone!'

'What?' Allie's eyes widened. 'How can he be gone?'

Dawn emptied the bag over the seat next to her: tissues, Tampax – that she currently had no need of – two lip balms, half a biscuit, her purse and an old dummy covered in fluff. But no parcel wrapped in pink tissue paper. No Wallace…

She peered under the table again.

But there was no sign of him.

'What am I going to do?'

Dawn watched as Allie tucked her blonde hair behind her ears and looked around the café. There were two customers sitting at the table by the log burner – they hadn't been there when Dawn had arrived – and the table by the other window was now empty, so the elderly women who'd been there earlier had obviously left. But they wouldn't have taken Wallace. Why would they?
'Oh no!' Allie smacked her forehead.
'Oh no?'
'I bet this has something to do with Luna.'
'But she moved to Chris's with you, didn't she?' Allie had moved in with her boyfriend recently, taking her two cats Luna and Ebony with her.
'Yes... but she keeps finding her way back here. You know I don't let the cats into the café but Luna has followed Chris back a few times and she did sneak in earlier when the door was open. What if she—'
'Luna has stolen Wallace?' Dawn's heart pounded against her ribs. 'What will she do with him?'
Allie grimaced. 'She has a strong prey drive. She even toyed with a dead frog that she found on the road once. It was completely flat. I wrestled it off her and threw it over the back fence, a bit like a Frisbee, but she went and found it. *Four times.* So in the end I stuffed it in the bin.'
'But this is Wallace!'
'I know. I'm so sorry. However, Chris has popped out to see a man about a guinea pig, so you go and pick the children up and I'll meet you back at yours. And don't say a word about Wallace passing away to Laura and James. As far as they know, he's still alive and well.'
Dawn nodded. 'Thank you.'
'Don't be daft. What're friends for?'
She put her belongings back in her bag, even the fluff covered dummy, then finished her drink and got up. Allie was right; she needed to head over to the school. She hated being late for the children and rarely ever was. The thought of them waiting for her as

others went home with their parents and grandparents was too much to bear.

But as she stepped out into the sunshine, her heart jumped, as a piece of pink tissue paper rolled past her on the café lawn like tumbleweed in the Wild West.

Taunting her.

Reminding her that tiny Wallace was missing.

And that the weekend she'd been looking forward to, was not going to work out quite the way she'd planned.

Chapter Two

Dawn ushered the children towards home, glad that the school run was over until Monday. It was only a short walk to the village primary school but she was finding it tiring, especially in the heat. The heat that seemed incongruous when the remaining leaves still clinging to the trees were the rich reds, golds and browns of autumn.
'Mummy, can I have an ice cream, please?' Laura's big smile revealed her pearly white teeth.
'I'm sure we can find something in the freezer,' Dawn replied, mentally scanning her last shop to check if she had bought some ice creams.
'Me too?' James asked. 'Please?'
'Of course.'
Right now, Dawn felt so guilty she probably would have consented to two ice creams apiece. Anything to divert them from discovering Wallace's demise.
As they turned onto the driveway, she was relieved to see Allie waiting by the front door.
'Auntie Allie!' Laura flew at her, wrapping her arms around her middle.

'Hello, Laura. Had a good day?'

'Yes! I wrote a story and I'm going to read it on a YouTube channel and make lots and lots of money.'

'I see...' Allie raised her eyebrows and Dawn discretely shook her head.

'It's all about Lulu and Wallace and their adventures at the zoo and I'm going to post photos on Instagram to encourage people to view it.'

'Lovely. Well I'd really like it if you'd read it to me in person too.'

'Yes, come and have ice cream and I will read it to you right now.' Laura tugged at Allie's hand.

'Hold on!' Dawn unlocked the door then stood back. 'You two need to get changed out of your uniforms. Make sure you put them in the washing basket and put on the shorts and t-shirts that I've laid out on your beds.'

Laura nodded.

'Laura, no fancy dress this afternoon. It's too hot.'

'But Mummy...'

Dawn shook her head.

'Oh all right then. Come on, James.'

Laura took James by the hand and led him into the house.

'Did you manage to find a... uh... a replacement?' Dawn asked Allie.

'I did. Well, Chris did. I hid it round the side behind the recycling bins so the children wouldn't see it.'

'Brilliant. If we can just get it out to the back garden then they might never have to know.' Her stomach rolled. 'I hate to deceive them but they love those animals and I just don't think I can face seeing them upset right now.'

'Of course not.'

Five minutes later, Dawn and Allie were standing in the back garden gazing at the rabbit run.

'He looks right at home.' Allie smiled. 'They'll never guess.'

'I hope not. Come on, I'll get you a drink.'

Dawn didn't like to say anything, after Allie and Chris had gone to so much trouble to help, but although the guinea pig was white with brown paws, ears and nose, it was about twice the size of Wallace. Perhaps the children wouldn't notice, and if they did, she could say that he'd put on weight. Although there was something else about him that was different too, but she couldn't quite put her finger on it. Back inside, she opened the freezer and located two ice creams then she handed them to Laura and James when they entered the kitchen, thankfully wearing the clothes she'd put out for them.

'Thank you!' they chorused.

'Why don't you go and eat your ice creams in the garden?' Dawn asked.

They ran outside so Dawn stood still and listened, wondering if they'd spot the difference in their guinea pig. There were no immediate cries of shock or horror, so she released the breath she'd been holding.

'Shall we sit out in the shade?'

She poured two glasses of lemonade.

'Yes, lovely. I can't stay long though as Chris is covering for me.'

'Oh, I'm sorry, Allie, I wasn't thinking. You head back now, go on.'

Allie shook her head. 'He'll be fine for half an hour. I'll keep you company for a bit.'

'Thank you.'

They sat on the wooden chairs on the decking just outside the French doors and watched as Laura and James giggled together as they ate, sitting side by side on the root bench that Dawn had bought Rick for his last birthday. She'd looked online for weeks to find the perfect one. He'd hinted enough times when they'd visited garden centres and she'd finally found one that she thought he'd like. Her heart clenched. They'd been happy then hadn't they? And that was only in the spring. Before they'd got pregnant again. Before Dawn's hopes of returning to teaching had been replaced with thoughts of impending motherhood and how she'd manage with three children instead of two. Before Wallace had departed...

'Mummy!'

Laura was staring at the rabbit run.

Dawn pulled a face at Allie.
'Yes, love.'
'What's happened to Wallace?'
'Uh... why?'
'He's HUGE.'
'Is he?'
Dawn turned to Allie again and her friend pretended to stuff food into her mouth then waddled from side to side.
'Yes, Mummy, he's so fat.' James was next to his sister now, peering at their pet.
'Well... he has been eating a lot recently.'
'But he wasn't that big yesterday.'
Laura turned her intelligent gaze on her mother and a small frown furrowed her brow, then she put her hands on her hips. Dawn had to fight the urge to tell her not to get sticky hands on her clean clothes.
'No?' She asked her daughter.
'Perhaps he grew overnight.' Allie shrugged, as if guinea pigs doubled in size all the time.
'Hmmm.' Laura tapped a finger on her chin and Dawn held her breath. Her daughter was very bright and it was something that usually made Dawn's heart swell with pride, but right now, she'd have been delighted if Laura had just accepted what she was told as the truth. 'Perhaps.'
Dawn glanced at Allie who winked in return.
For now, it seemed that Wallace's replacement had been accepted, although for how long, she had no idea.
And she couldn't help wondering, and worrying, about what had happened to Wallace the first.

Dawn kissed James's forehead then padded out of his room, making

sure that she left the door ajar. She went into Laura's room and found her daughter staring out of the window that overlooked the back garden.
'Laura? What's wrong?'
'I'm just checking that Wallace and Lulu are OK.'
'Of course they are. We tucked them in after you had dinner.'
Laura shook her head. 'Lulu won't have much room now because Wallace is so fat.'
'They'll be fine, angel. Don't worry now.'
Laura allowed herself to be led to her bed.
'Why didn't you want to listen to the story with James tonight?'
Laura shrugged.
'I thought you liked the Big Book of Fairy-Tales.'
'I like it when Daddy reads to us.'
'I know you do and I like that too.'
Since the summer, Rick had made the effort to be home in time most nights to read to the children. But more recently, he seemed to be getting later and later each night.
'When will he be home?'
Dawn smoothed her daughter's soft hair back from her face. Her heart ached for her children when they missed Rick.
'He sent me a text to say he'll be back soon.'
'When is soon?'
Dawn sighed. 'In about an hour. The trains were delayed.'
'Again?' Laura scowled. 'I hate the train men.'
'Do you want to read your story to me again?' Dawn asked, hoping to distract her daughter.
'No, I want to go to sleep now.'
'OK then. Goodnight sweetheart.'
She tucked the covers around Laura then got up and crossed the room, switching off the light at the doorway.
'Night Mummy. I love you.'
'I love you too.'
Dawn turned away, the lump in her throat threatening to choke her.

Damn Rick and his delayed trains. No, damn the delayed trains. It wasn't Rick's fault, she was sure of it. He was trying to provide for his family and she knew he couldn't rush out of the office before his colleagues. The world of investment banking that he worked in was a tough one and she knew that competition amongst employees was fierce.

But she did wish that he could try a bit harder to get home before nine, at least a few times a week. Surely that wouldn't be too much to ask?

'Rick? What was that noise?'
Dawn reached out to pat her husband but his side of the bed was empty.
'Rick?'
Her heart raced as she tried to fight the sleep fog.
There it was again. A clinking sound coming from downstairs. She'd have to go and investigate, as it seemed that she was alone with the children. Rick hadn't come home by ten and she was exhausted, so she'd gone up to bed, telling herself she'd read until he returned but she must have fallen asleep as soon as she lay down.
She pulled her dressing gown over her pyjamas then scanned the room, hoping to find a weapon. The only thing she could see was a coat hanger dangling over the door handle, so she grabbed it.
'Ready or not... death by Debenhams size 12-14 hanger.'
She padded down the stairs, her bare feet sinking into the plush fibres of the carpet, and made her way across the hallway and through to the kitchen and the source of the noise.
She raised the coat hanger above her head and took a deep breath, ready to scream if need be, then launched herself into the kitchen.

'Who the hell do you think you are?' she screeched, as she spotted the intruder in front of the fridge with the door open and his back to her.

'Wha...' He turned around and as he did, she realised that it was Rick.

'Shit, Rick, you scared the hell out of me.'

Her heart thudded and nausea flooded through her, filling her mouth with saliva and bringing her hand automatically to her mouth.

'Who were you expecting?'

She lowered her hand slowly. 'I thought we'd had a break-in.'

He shook his head. 'Don't be daft. In this neighbourhood?'

In the blue light from the fridge, his lean physique was shown to advantage in his expensive shirt and suit trousers. His jacket had been slung onto the kitchen island, as if he'd been in a rush to get something to eat.

'It could happen,' she replied, feeling foolish at her sleep-fuddled reaction, then turned the light on.

'Hopefully not.'

He closed the fridge then opened his arms.

'Anyway, how's my beautiful wife?'

'Tired. Sleepy. Recovering from the fright of thinking we had an intruder.'

'Got a hug for me?'

She nodded then walked into his embrace.

As he wrapped his arms around her, she sighed against his chest. She loved him so much but sometimes he irritated the hell out of her. Yes, she was pregnant and her hormones were all over the place, but that didn't mean that she was an idiot. Not that Rick was suggesting that she was, but she felt that way when he came over all cool-headed and in control.

'Sorry I'm late. Between trying to get out of the office and the train being delayed again, I thought I'd never get home.'

'The children missed you.'

'It's the weekend now, though. I'll make it up to you all.'

He squeezed her tight.

'Are you hungry?'
'Starving.'
'There's lasagne in the fridge.'
'You are the best wife, you know that?'
She slipped out of his arms and set about warming him some food. When she placed his dinner and a large glass of red wine on the oak dining table in front of him, he caught her hand and kissed it.
'Sit with me?'
'I would, Rick, but I'm exhausted. I need to go back to bed.'
'OK, well I'll eat this then follow you up.'
She nodded.
'See you in a bit.'
She left the kitchen, her heart heavy and her stomach churning, because something just wasn't adding up. Her husband had hugged her and seemed to be loving as ever, but she knew that years of competing in a high-pressured work environment had enabled him to perfect a cool, collected demeanour, even if inside his blood pressure was sky-high. Something about the way he'd felt when he held her close was off: he was too thin now, his body leaner than it used to be, as if the slight softening that had come with contentment and being a father had been eroded away. But by what? He had been working hard, putting in long hours, and when he was home, he was always doing something around the house or garden. So it was probably just that and her own insecurities rooted in her self-consciousness about her changing body, as it once again became rounder and softer.
She was probably finding problems where there were none.
But as she climbed the stairs, she heard a familiar sound; it was Rick's mobile letting him know that he'd received a text message.
And she couldn't help wondering who would be texting her husband so late at night.

Chapter Three

As Dawn strolled along in the Saturday morning sunshine, she breathed deeply of the October air. Laura and James were just ahead of her, and her husband was at her side, her hand clasped in his. Everything seemed perfect. And that was the problem, the fact that to an outsider, they would appear to be the perfect little family, but Dawn knew differently.
Rick had not come to bed until gone two. What he'd been doing until then, she had no idea. She'd lain in bed, hoping that he'd come and cuddle her, spoon her in the way she found so comforting and that helped her drop off to sleep when she was at her most insecure. When he hadn't come, she'd strained to listen, to see if he was perhaps watching TV or loading his plate and glass into the dishwasher. She'd heard nothing. Then she'd fallen asleep, only to wake when he climbed into bed next to her and rolled onto his side, facing away.
She had sensed his tension, known that even though the hour was late, he had stared at the window until she'd drifted off again, a deep sadness tugging at her heart and fear gnawing at her edges.

When she'd risen at six, she'd rushed to the family bathroom where she'd dry retched over the toilet, not wanting to use the ensuite in case she disturbed Rick. James had come to the door and she'd had to pull herself together then, to reassure him that she was fine and just had a tummy bug. They hadn't yet told the children about the baby; they'd been waiting for the twenty-week scan to ensure that everything was all right and to give themselves some time to prepare mentally and emotionally, but as she was getting so big, she didn't think they could wait that long.

Perhaps today was the day...

'Penny for them.' Rick squeezed her hand.

'I was just thinking about the baby and when we should... you know.' She nodded at the children.

'I guess we can't keep it a secret forever. We could do it over breakfast? Or lunch tomorrow at your Mum's?'

She tried to work out his tone. Was it light-hearted and positive or was it forced, hiding something that he was struggling with.

'Really?' She glanced at him and her heart fluttered. She still found him so handsome. Even though they'd been together since university and had two children, he was still, in her eyes, the most attractive man she'd ever seen.

'Why not?'

'Thank you for this... taking us to the café for breakfast. It was a good idea.'

'I like to spoil my family but I don't get the chance that often.' He laughed but it sounded hollow, even outside on such a beautiful morning.

They reached the front gate of The Cosy Cottage Café and Rick opened it then stood back to let them all in first. Dawn's spirits rose; she loved coming to the café. It was such a warm and welcoming place to be and she felt safe there. Allie was a dear friend and they'd enjoyed many mornings with coffee and cake as well as some uplifting Tuesday evenings, when Allie, Dawn, her sister, Camilla, and their friend Honey, would gather together and eat, drink and put the world to rights. On those occasions they often laughed until tears ran down their faces and it felt so good to have such close friends, so good to be alive.

The café garden was breathtakingly beautiful in the sunlight. In the borders, orange, red and yellow hardy chrysanthemums bloomed in the mild October climate. Purple-blue spikes of lavender still towered above silver-grey foliage, its sweet crisp scent permeating the morning air. Creamy white dahlias swayed in the gentle breeze, their centres of their multi-layered heads a soft baby pink.

Suddenly, tears pricked Dawn's eyes as she recalled something she'd once read about the flowers. Apparently, the Victorians had used the dahlia to signify a lasting bond between two people, a lifelong commitment. She had always thought that she would be with Rick forever, but recently, she was starting to wonder if he felt the same way.

She blinked hard and gazed instead at the café itself, a converted old stone cottage with ivy climbing its front, pretty purple shutters adorning the windows and a traditional thatched roof. On the side of the building, a sign in the shape of a teapot glinted in the sunshine and a specials board stood to the side of the front steps next to some colourful milk urn planters.

Laura and James stopped at the door and turned to their parents, so Dawn nodded at them to go inside. She was about to follow when Rick tugged at her hand.

'Are you OK, Dawn? You seem distant this morning.'

I seem distant?

She swallowed the words, not wanting to cause a row when Rick was clearly trying.

'I'm fine. It's just... something happened yesterday and because you were so late home, I haven't had the chance to talk to you about it yet.'

'What was it?' His hazel eyes roamed her face and she found herself leaning towards him as if hypnotised by the golden ring that flashed at their core, as if he had trapped the sunlight there and pierced it with the fathomless black of his pupils.

'Something happened to—'

'Mum! I need a poo!'

Dawn started. James stood in the doorway hopping from foot to foot.

'To what?' Rick frowned, clearly concerned by what she was about to divulge.

'Mum! Quickly...' The speed of James's hopping had increased and his little face was scrunched up as if he was in pain.

'Oh it doesn't matter. I can tell you later.'

Rick nodded but as he released her hand, he whispered, 'Surely he should be able to go to the toilet alone by now?'

Dawn bit her lip then walked inside. That was the problem with having an absent husband. He didn't understand what she dealt with on a daily basis, the type of things she didn't like to bother him with when he came home from work fit to drop. He didn't know that James had a phobia of public toilets – that had left the little boy nervous about getting locked in – following an incident in a toilet at school. Her own mother, Allie, and other mothers she knew had all tried to reassure her that children had their quirks and idiosyncrasies, and that, if not dramatized, such things would pass. But she still worried that James would be scarred by what had happened; he was such a sensitive boy.

How many things did she fail to share with Rick these days because he was tired or she was tired or because it just seemed like too much effort?

She waved at Allie, who was standing behind the counter, as she headed towards the café toilet where she would wait outside the door just in case James started to panic. It wasn't glamorous, it wasn't much fun, but it was motherhood, and Dawn wondered if Rick had any understanding at all of her world now, or if he just couldn't see past his own expectations and preconceptions of how things should be.

Rachel Griffiths

Half an hour later, Dawn was cutting up a cinnamon waffle for James. Laura was tucking into her lemon and blueberry muffin and Rick was working his way through a full cooked breakfast. Dawn had nibbled at a piece of toast but her appetite appeared to have stayed at home.
'Everything all right?' Allie asked as she filled the children's glasses with freshly squeezed orange juice.
'Delicious, thank you.' Rick raised his mug of tea. 'If I ate here every morning, I'd get fat.'
'If you just slowed down a bit...' The comment slipped from Dawn's mouth and she sucked in a breath. But no one seemed to notice.
'Can I get you something else, Dawnie?' Allie placed a cool hand on her shoulder. 'It doesn't look like that's tempting you. How about some yogurt and honey? Perhaps with a banana?'
'No, I'm OK, thanks. Just eating in the morning is difficult.' She bit her lip and eyed her children but they didn't seem to pick up on her slip.
'I know.' Allie nodded. 'I'll be back in a minute.'
She disappeared and Dawn was left with her family again.
'I like waffles, Mummy,' James said. 'Can we have them every day?'
'If we did, you'd soon get tired of them, darling.'
Dawn thought of the different cereals she'd tried to tempt him, of the variety of scones and pancakes she'd baked that had soon been rejected, and of the mornings when she'd been on the brink of tears because her children just didn't want what she had to offer them for breakfast. Sometimes, parenting was so difficult; especially when you were doing it alone.
She shook herself. Why was she dwelling on negatives when she had her beautiful family right here with her and they were all enjoying

their selections from Allie's gorgeous menu? She had so much to be grateful for.

Laura finished her muffin then drained her glass. 'That was delicious, thank you.' She got up and went round the table to Rick and hugged him.

'Hey what was that for?'

'I love you, Daddy. Are you staying home today?'

'Of course I am. It's Saturday.'

Laura smiled then kissed his cheek. 'You can help me play with Lulu and Wallace and take some new photos of them for Grandpa and Instagram. You should see how fat Wallace is.'

'Really? Have you been overfeeding him?'

Laura shook her head.

'He's just put on some weight.' Dawn winked when Rick met her eyes.

'Oh he has, has he? Well perhaps we better put him through guinea pig boot camp.'

'What's a boot camp?' James asked as he dipped a piece of waffle into his juice.

'It's somewhere that people can go to exercise.'

'Is that with soldiers?'

'How'd you know that, Laura?' Rick asked his daughter.

'Saw it on TV.'

Rick grinned at Dawn and she shook her head. 'Must have seen it at my Mum's.'

Allie returned with a small plate.

'What's this?' Dawn asked as she met her friend's eyes.

'Ginger cookies. I baked them yesterday with stem ginger. They might help with the nausea.'

'Thank you so much.'

'No problem. I'll pack some up for you to take home, too.'

Dawn picked up a cookie and sniffed it. The warming aroma of ginger made her mouth water and she took a bite. The cookie was

fresh and crumbly with the gentle heat of the fragrant spice warming her mouth and tongue.
'Mmmm. It's delicious.'
'I'm going to see Chris,' James announced as he slid off his chair.
'James, Chris is busy. Don't bother him.'
'It's OK,' Allie said. 'Chris won't mind. Come on, James.'
She took his hand and led him over to her boyfriend.
'I'm going too.' Laura jumped down and rushed over to the leather sofa by the window, where Chris was sitting with his laptop on his knees.
'Sorry you're still feeling queasy. It'll pass soon though, right?' Rick reached across the table to take Dawn's hand.
'I hope so. It's draining feeling like I'm going to throw up all the time and it had passed well before this point when I was carrying Laura and James. Sorry.' She pointed at his plate.
'Don't worry. You won't put me off.'
'Are we going to tell them about the baby tomorrow?'
'I think we should.'
Dawn peered behind Rick to see Laura and James sitting either side of Chris as he showed them something on the screen of his laptop.
'I need to tell you something, too.'
Rick nodded then placed his knife and fork on the empty plate.
'Go ahead.'
'Yesterday, I went to clean the hutch out as usual. And I found—'
'A rat! A big fat white rat!' Judith Burnley, an elderly lady from the village, had entered the café and her words cut Dawn off.
'You don't say.' Her companion, a woman of around seventy, shuddered as they approached the counter.
Dawn watched them, her mouth hanging open.
'Dawn, what is it?'
'Shhh.'
'Don't shhh me.'
She waved a hand at Rick then got up and went to the counter where she stood behind Mrs Burnley.

Autumn at The Cosy Cottage Café

'Did you hear that, Allie?' Mrs Burnley asked.
'I did.' Allie flashed a glance at Dawn. 'You *saw* a rat?'
'Not exactly.' The elderly woman drummed her nails on the counter. 'Your cat, the grey one, dropped it on my doorstep then ran away.'
'Oh. Do you mean Luna?'
'That's the one. Total nuisance that cat, always leaving dead rodents on my step. Have to scrub it with bleach on a daily basis.'
'I am sorry, Mrs Burnley. But usually that's a sign that a cat likes you.'
Mrs Burnley sniffed. 'Only since you moved in with Chris.'
Dawn processed the information. Mrs Burnley lived a few doors down from Chris Monroe and Allie, and it seemed that Allie's one cat, Luna, had been leaving gifts for Mrs Burnley.
But a fat white rat?
'It had no tail either. The cat must have eaten it first.'
Dawn gasped and Mrs Burnley turned to look at her.
'I know. Disgusting, isn't it?'
Dawn nodded. 'Uh... What did you do with the... rat?'
'Threw it in the bin, of course.'
'The bin in your front garden?'
'Yes, of course.' The older woman frowned at her.
'Right. OK. Uh... thanks.' Dawn turned and hurried back over to Rick.
'What was all that about?'
She took a shaky breath as a wave of nausea hit.
'Dawn?'
'I don't think it was a rat.'
'What was it then?'
'I think it was Wallace.'
'Wallace?' His eyebrows shot up his forehead. 'You need to tell me what's been going on,' he said.
And she did. Quickly, before the children returned to the table. She told him about finding Wallace and about him disappearing from her bag and about how she'd found the pink tissue paper outside and about Allie and Chris producing a replacement.

Rick listened carefully, then nodded. 'So I'll go and check her bin. Make sure.'
'Please. I don't know if I could face it.'
'If it's him... I'll pop him home then come back for you.'
He pecked her on the lips, then said something to the children, before leaving the café.
And Dawn sat there with her half-eaten ginger biscuit in her hand and her mug of tea going cold, wondering how she would cope if she ever lost him.

Chapter Four

The next day, Dawn was peeling potatoes in her mother's small kitchen. Rick and the children were in the garden playing catch.
'They all seem happy,' Jackie Dix said as she gazed out of the window at Rick and her grandchildren.
'They are. It's good for them to have some time together.'
'Rick still working late?'
Dawn nodded. 'He has a lot on, Mum.'
'I understand that, love.'
Her mother turned to her and Dawn met her green eyes, so much like her own and Camilla's, yet they carried something within them that told of hard times and disappointment.
'He's a good man, Mum.'
'I know. But even so, good men can change if their heads get turned.'
'Please don't.'
Her mother shook her head. 'I don't mean to, Dawn. It's just...'
'Not everyone is like Dad.'
'Nope. You're right. I just get scared for you and Camilla... and for my grandchildren. I don't want to see any of you hurt.'

Dawn bit her tongue. Her mother had a heart of gold but she'd never recovered after her husband's betrayal. He left when Dawn was eight and Camilla was ten, and now ran a bar in Benidorm with his third wife. Jackie had struggled to bring up her girls, working as a cleaner at several locations and taking in ironing just to make ends meet. Dawn admired her mother for what she'd done but also worried about her, as she'd never got over losing her husband. Although sometimes, it was almost as if she couldn't allow herself to move on.
'I won't be. Rick won't hurt me.'
'I thought the same about your father a long time ago but I was blinded by love and lust. Fool that I was back then. I suspected that he was having an affair but I tried to ignore it. I loved our family life so much and the idea that he would risk it all for a fling was more than I could bear to entertain.' She shook her head. 'Then the worst happened. I sometimes think it would have been better if he'd just died. At least he wouldn't have chosen to leave us all then.'
Dawn's mouth fell open.
'Oh, love, don't mind me. Forget I said that.' She rubbed Dawn's arm. 'Anyway, how're you feeling?'
'Not too bad this morning.' Dawn was glad of the change of topic. 'Allie gave me some ginger biscuits and some more of that peppermint cordial and the combination seems to be helping. Here,' she handed her mother the colander of potatoes, 'all done.'
'Right, you go outside and play with your husband and children and I'll finish up here.'
'Thanks, Mum.'
Dawn hugged Jackie then went out into the small back garden, her heart heavy with the knowledge of her mother's pain.

'Another cracking roast, Jackie.' Rick rubbed his belly. 'But I think I might have eaten too much.'

'Well that's a shame as I've made Queen of Puddings for dessert.'

'Oh... well I suppose there's a small space left.' Rick smiled. 'What do you say kids?'

'Yessss!' they replied in unison.

Jackie's desserts were legendary and when she had a chance, she took them to the café parties that Allie held. She wasn't always able to attend them because of her work, but when she did, people complimented her on her culinary skills. Before her husband had left, Jackie had always seemed to be smiling and baking. She'd been there to greet her daughters when they got home from school, usually with yummy freshly baked treats for them to enjoy and a hot meal that they sat around and ate together. That all changed after her husband had gone and she'd become withdrawn, depressed and irritable – and that was when she was home – because with the hours she had to work, Dawn and Camilla became latch-key kids. It had been hard returning from school to a cold, empty house, with no delicious aromas of cakes, biscuits or cottage pie greeting them. So Dawn knew how awful life could be if a couple split up, for them and for their children. And she had carried the fear of being betrayed and divorced throughout her life. Her mother's little reminders of how men could leave didn't help at all, although she understood why Jackie worried. It was natural for a mother to worry, after all.

Jackie got up to take the plates out but Rick held up a hand. 'I'll do this. You and my gorgeous wife have done enough.'

He stacked the dinner plates then carried them from the dining room.

'Laura and James, if you look in the cupboard there, you'll find the small bowls.' Jackie gestured at the Welsh dresser.

'I'll go and help Rick. He probably can't locate the spoons, knowing him.' Dawn got up and went through to the kitchen but Rick wasn't there. She paused and listened. Perhaps he'd gone to the toilet. Then she heard the low tones of his voice and looked through the window. He was out there, on his mobile phone, his cheeks flushed as he listened and nodded. She gripped the edge of the sink and watched him. Who was he talking to? He'd agreed not to take calls on a Sunday, as in the past, he'd been called into work on several occasions, and it always hurt Dawn to see him hurrying away when he should be spending time with his family.

He said something sharply, then ended the call and stuffed his mobile back into his pocket. A muscle in his jaw twitched as he stared blankly at the fence dividing Jackie's garden from her neighbour's. He looked so far away, so removed from the energetic, light-hearted man she'd met all those years ago at university. Back then, they'd had so much fun together. They'd both been young, hopeful, enthusiastic about life and what lay ahead of them, and had spent so many hours talking, planning, sharing their hopes and dreams, making love into the small hours of the morning and collapsing into bed as the dawn light flooded the sky. She'd been certain back then that this was the man for her, that he loved her as much as she loved him and that they'd always be together.

But that was then.

And this was now.

Rick was slipping through her fingers like sand in an egg timer, and she hadn't the foggiest idea how to stop him.

As Jackie served the Queen of Puddings, Rick clapped his hands together.

'Laura and James, we have a very special announcement!'

The children dragged their eyes from the dessert to look at their parents. Dawn shifted on her chair. Rick took her hand and kissed it.

'You are going to have a little baby sister or brother.'

A tiny line appeared between Laura's brows. 'A baby?'

'Yes. In about five months, give or take a week or two.'

Dawn suppressed a nervous giggle. Rick was always so careful with numbers, even with this news. And perhaps he was right to be. After all, Laura had arrived a week later than her due date and James had arrived two weeks before his. So expected dates of delivery were not necessarily precise, and with the children, they needed to ensure that they weren't expecting the baby to arrive right on time. Laura had a thing about times anyway, especially since Rick's working hours had increased again, and she would no doubt mark the baby's EDD on the rabbit calendar that hung on her bedroom wall and tick off the days as they passed.

'I want a brother.' James nodded as he accepted a bowl of dessert from his nanna.

'You can't decide what you're having, James.' Laura scowled at him. 'It just happens.'

'But I don't want a sister.' His bottom lip wobbled. 'I have you.'

Laura patted her brother's hand. 'I will always be your sister but you might have another one. Isn't that right, Daddy?'

'That's right, sweetheart. So are we pleased?'

Laura nodded and James shrugged, so that would have to do for now. It was a lot for them to take in, but they'd have time now to get used to the idea. Dawn hadn't wanted to tell them until the pregnancy was well established, because it would have been dreadful if they'd known, then she'd lost the baby. Of course, nothing was 100 per cent certain and things could still go wrong, but she was well past the three-month danger point, and had quite a bump already, so they had to tell them sooner or later. It was getting too hard to hide her belly all the time anyway.

'Here you are, Dawn.'

Her mother handed her a bowl and she took it then gazed at its contents. Growing up, Queen of Puddings had always been one of her favourites with its layers of light fluffy sponge, custard and jam, topped with soft, chewy meringue. But right now, she didn't fancy it at all.

All she did fancy was cuddling up with her husband and having him stroke her hair as he told her how much he loved her and the children and how he'd never leave them. But he was currently tucking into his dessert, seemingly oblivious to her vulnerability, and blissfully unaware that she'd seen him on his phone outside, lost in conversation with someone who brought a colour to his cheeks that Dawn didn't think she'd seen in quite some time.

Chapter Five

Dawn set up the ironing board in the quiet house. Rick had left at six-thirty, as he always did on Monday mornings, and the children were in school. She usually liked this time of day, when she could put the radio on in the sunny kitchen, make a cup of tea and read a magazine or a book, get some chores done or just sit and think.
She'd been out to check on Wallace the second and Lulu, and had found them quietly nibbling on hay, so she'd given them some carrots, changed the water in the bottle that clipped to the front of the hutch, then gone back inside to switch the kettle on. The new Wallace sure was hefty for a guinea pig. She wondered for a moment what had happened to the other little Wallace. She had asked Rick the previous afternoon, and he'd managed to tell her that he'd found Wallace and brought him home, but then they'd been interrupted by Laura and it had slipped her mind. She was suddenly overwhelmed with guilt and concern, and the only way she could ease it was to blame her pregnancy brain and reassure herself that Rick would have put Wallace somewhere safe. Somewhere the cats from the café couldn't find him, hopefully.

The thermostat on the iron clicked, so she picked a shirt from the ironing pile and slid it over the end of the board. She worked on autopilot: collar, sleeves, side, back, side. She'd done this so many times before that it was automatic, and before she knew it, she'd done four shirts and her tea was getting cold. She poured it down the sink then rinsed the mug.

Something was prickling at her subconscious and she'd been trying to keep it there, out of sight, not wanting to let it surface. But as she gazed at through the kitchen window at the generous garden – where even though it was still warm, the autumnal shades of red, orange and brown dominated – the question shot to the surface like a bubble and popped.

Was her mother right? Was Rick having an affair?

Her hand shot to her mouth. She knew that husbands and wives did cheat; she had her father's behaviour as a prime example. Plus the media loved to parade gritty stories of celebrity marital problems and affairs at the public all the time. She knew people whose marriages had failed because of it and those who'd stayed together, trying to work things out after one of them had cheated, and often they tried to make it work because of their children. But she had never really believed that it could happen in her own marriage. Not between her and Rick; they loved each other, didn't they? They had always sworn that they'd never disrespect each other in that way. But had Rick forgotten that as the years passed? Had someone in his busy, flashy, high-flying City job caught his eye and turned his head while his wife sat at home caring for their two children, getting fatter with her third pregnancy? Was Rick fed up with her or did he want to have some fun then come back to her? Could she allow that?

No she bloody well couldn't.

She took a deep breath. Her thoughts were racing away here and she might be imagining it all. This was Rick she was thinking about. He wouldn't cheat, surely? Not Rick.

She decided to leave the ironing for a bit and to check her Facebook page – that usually made her feel a bit better when worries rushed in. She could see if there was any news from her friends who'd moved away and from the friends she'd made at university. She retrieved the lightweight laptop that she shared with Rick from the study, then took it back to the kitchen, placed it on the kitchen island and switched it on.

It flickered into life and she was about to click on the Internet symbol when a folder caught her eye.

Rick's Stuff.

And her mother's final whispered words from yesterday – the ones she'd uttered into Dawn's ear, just before they left – came rushing back:

'You should check his emails, Dawnie. Just to be sure. It's not right that he's working so late, especially with you being pregnant. I read just last week in one of my magazines that a woman found out her husband was cheating with his secretary – oh the cliché – just from reading his emails. He'd forgotten to close down the account after using the family computer. Check them, then you'll know if there's something going on.'

She hovered the mouse over his folder, wondering if she could really do this. It was wrong and she knew that to the bottom of her heart but she also needed to put her mind at rest. And Rick was at work, probably wouldn't be home until late. If she did this, she could find the much-needed reassurance that she really was being silly.

She opened the folder and found several other blue folders, then clicked on the one labelled *Passwords*.

Bit daft having your passwords stored on here, Rick.

But then he had so many and was constantly having to change them as he'd forgotten them, so it seemed he'd decided to keep them all in one place. There were probably lots of people who did the same thing, in spite of the warnings about cyber security and hackers.

The folder opened and she found a six-page Word document with the names of accounts and the passwords next to them. She scanned down the pages, her heart beating hard and a sour taste filling her mouth. Because she knew this was wrong. Rick obviously didn't have anything to hide but then he wouldn't expect her to go snooping. He'd actually told her at one point that he'd made a list of all his accounts, just in case anything ever happened to him and she needed to access them. It would make things easier, he'd said. She'd tried to laugh it off, not wanting to think about the possibility of being without Rick, but he'd been true to his word and ensured that she'd know where everything was if she needed it.

Her eyes stopped on the heading *Rick's email account*.

She shouldn't really, but she could just take a peek then be done with all this worrying.

Before she could overthink it, she clicked on the Internet link and signed into the account with the password.

The first few emails were from the bank and PayPal. The next was from an online sports company that was headed FLASH SALE: 50% off selected lines today only. The next one looked more interesting. More worrying. It was from a Brianna Mandrell and the subject heading was FYEO.

FYEO?

Dawn's heart raced as she realised what that meant.

For your eyes only.

What the hell?

Her finger shook above the touchpad.

Her mind was screaming at her to stop; it was better not to know.

But...

She had to know.

She opened it.

And immediately wished she hadn't.

Dawn hurried up the path to The Cosy Cottage Café. She opened the door with such force that she nearly faceplanted onto the welcome mat. She steadied herself then glanced around. Five customers: two women, two male delivery drivers and Fred Bennett, an elderly man from the village who always came to the café on a Monday morning.

She couldn't see Allie, so she must be in the kitchen.

She went to the counter and stood there waiting, suddenly aware that she must look quite a state. After dropping the children at school, she'd changed into a pair of Rick's old lounge pants and a washed out black t-shirt. Comfortable clothes for wearing while ironing. After seeing that terrible email, she hadn't bothered to change. Her hair was in a messy ponytail and in her hurry to get to the café, the fringe she'd been growing out had slipped from its clip and now stuck to her clammy forehead. And as for makeup… she hadn't bothered with that. Who was going to see her at home? What did it matter anyway?

Allie didn't appear, so Dawn went behind the counter and into the kitchen. She found her friend scooping poached eggs from a pan then carefully arranging them on top of thick slices of toast covered with mashed avocado.

'Dawn! You gave me a fright then.' Allie paused, an egg suspended on the spatula in mid air, its golden yolk shiny and perfectly round, just waiting to be pierced by a fork. Dawn's stomach rolled.

'Sorry. I had to come to see you. I can't go to Mum's as she'll be doing her cleaning rounds and Camilla's in work and I didn't know who else to go to and…'

Allie's expression changed as she took in Dawn's appearance.

'Hold on.' She laid the egg on a slice toast then put the saucepan on the worktop. 'Now, do you want to take a deep breath then tell me what's going on? I love you, Dawnie, and you can always come to me when you need to but to be quite frank, you look like you've been dragged through a hedge backwards.'

Dawn took a breath and was dismayed to find her vision blurring. Her throat ached as a lump rose there and she tried to speak but it emerged as a squeak.

'OK, you stay here. I have to take these breakfasts out but I'll be right back.' Allie dusted her hands on her apron then pushed Dawn onto a stool that she'd pulled from under the kitchen island, before disappearing with two plates.

Dawn took the time to try to pull herself together. Allie was always so kind and caring that whenever Dawn was feeling emotional, her composure usually slipped. She'd always worn her heart on her sleeve and her mother had often remarked that she was very different to Camilla in that respect. After their father had left, Camilla had seemed to toughen up, taking care of Dawn and their mother like they were her responsibility, even though she'd only been ten. Jackie had fallen into a deep depression and ten-year-old Camilla had taken over the running of the house while Jackie was out at work, ensuring that she and Dawn had clean uniforms and got to school on time. Camilla had made excuses to her teachers when her mother hadn't shown up for parents' evenings and had used her saved pocket money to purchase tins of beans and loaves of bread from the local shop to feed them. Jackie had emerged from the worst of her darkness after about eight months, but it had been an awful time.

Camilla had been a rock. But it was as if the whole experience had left her scarred and scared. She'd never had a long-term relationship and very rarely ever let her guard down, not even to Dawn. Her decision to never have children had been one that had initially shocked Dawn, as she'd longed to be a mother after falling in love with Rick. However, as time went on and Camilla didn't falter in her decision, not even when she held her niece and nephew as tiny babies, Dawn realised that it was OK for her sister to lack maternal yearnings. As long Camilla was happy with her life, then Dawn didn't need to worry about her. Sometimes, she even envied

Camilla her freedom, her lack of responsibility, the fact that she could go into London and splurge on clothes and shoes then stay in a luxury hotel without worrying about the price or getting back for the school run. She wondered what it would be like to have a full night's sleep and to spend an hour lounging in a bubble bath without someone needing the toilet, or a drink, or having a fight over the TV remote.

But their lives were very different and their parents' divorce had affected them in different ways. Camilla swore she never wanted the whole marriage and children scenario while Dawn couldn't imagine not having that life that she treasured. If anything, seeing her mother's breakdown made Dawn crave domesticity. Her childhood had seemed perfect until her father left and in the weeks that followed his departure, she'd longed to come home from school to find her mother baking again, ready with a kiss and a smile at the door. But that idyllic stage of her life had passed and it never returned. Until Dawn married Rick and had her own home, and became determined to have the perfect family life, to be the wife and mother that Jackie had been before her husband had left. It was like she had a chance to recreate the early part of her childhood – the part that she'd enjoyed.

And now it seemed that it was falling apart, in spite of all her efforts.

'Right, Mrs,' Allie was back with a steaming mug and a ginger biscuit, 'I want you to take these then come and sit on my leather couch and tell me all about it.'

'Thank you, Allie.'

'No need to thank me, sweetheart. I'm your friend and that's what friends do. You need to tell me what's weighing you down and got you running around the village looking like you spent the night sleeping rough.'

Dawn tugged at the t-shirt, trying to stop it clinging to her belly.

'OK... but I have a feeling that you're not going to approve of what I've done.'

Allie placed a hand on Dawn's back then gently ushered her from the kitchen.

'I am quite sure that you can't possibly have done anything terrible, Dawn.'

Dawn swallowed a sob.

Because she was quite sure that as soon as she told Allie what she had done, her friend was going to change her mind.

Just as Dawn was about to tell Allie about the email, Camilla breezed into the café. As usual, she looked gorgeous with her dark elfin crop, her dazzling green eyes enhanced with shimmering emerald makeup and her designer charcoal-grey trouser suit and purple silk blouse. Her towering heels clicked across the floor as she made her way to the counter, then she caught sight of Allie and Dawn and did an about turn to join them at the sofa.

'Camilla, what're you doing here?' Dawn blurted.

'Well that's a nice welcome.'

'I didn't mean it like that. What I meant was, why aren't you in London?'

'Oh, I had a meeting with a local client then I thought I'd pop in for a coffee. Didn't expect to see you here either little sister.' Camilla peered at her. 'Have you been crying?'

Dawn shifted on the sofa.

'She's a bit hormonal.' Allie patted Dawn's hand.

'Yes it all gets a bit much sometimes.'

'Shall I pop you to the surgery? See if we can get your GP to take a look at you? Perhaps you need some iron tablets or something else...' Camilla's eyes were wary now, full of sisterly concern.

'No, no. I'm all right. No need for that.'

'Would you like a coffee, Camilla?' Allie asked.

'Yes, please, Allie, that would be lovely. Then I think we three need to have a chat.'

While Allie made the coffee, Camilla excused herself and popped to the toilet. Dawn took the chance to catch her breath. Part of her didn't want to tell her friend or her sister about Rick, because she didn't want to prejudice their feelings towards him, but part of her wanted, and needed, their support. How dare he do what it seemed like he'd been doing? If he had been doing anything at all. If only she could know for sure.

Soon, Camilla sat opposite her and Allie next to her.

'Um... please don't judge me, but I've done something and it's opened a can of worms.'

They both stared at her, their expressions unreadable as they waited for her to continue.

'I've had some suspicions about Rick for a while now and this morning, I just had to find out if they were true.'

'What suspicions?' Camilla asked as she shrugged out of her jacket then draped it over the back of the chair.

'That he might be cheating.' She pressed her lips together as Camilla's eyes widened.

'What?'

'Oh Dawn, but why?' Allie took her hand.

'He's been acting differently. Since before this pregnancy actually, although it has got worse. Or perhaps it's just me being paranoid and—'

'Dawn! Stop blaming yourself and tell us what's going on.' Camilla frowned.

OK...' She sighed. 'He works long hours, repeatedly claims his trains have been delayed and has more events in the City than ever.'

'But he works in investment banking. The demands are the same as they've always been but he's now competing with younger and probably more ambitious colleagues. It's a cut-throat career. You knew this when you married him and you said you could deal with it.'

'Don't judge me, Camilla.'

'No... I'm not judging you, darling. I'm just trying to understand what's going on here. If he is cheating then I'll kill him but you have to be sure. If you accuse him of this it could destroy your marriage and your life... your children's lives.'

'Don't you think I know that?' Dawn's voice cracked. 'Sorry, I don't mean to sound defensive. I just hate this. I mean... I love him so much but I can't deny that things have changed.'

'What evidence do you have that he's been cheating?' Allie asked.

'He's been getting calls and text messages at funny times. And I know it could be colleagues and clients but I just have a gut feeling that it isn't. At least not all of them.'

Camilla crossed her legs and drummed her fingers on her kneecap. 'But that's still not sufficient evidence to convict the man of adultery.'

'I went into his email account this morning.'

Camilla sucked in a sharp breath through her teeth. 'Oh dear.'

Dawn held up her hands. 'I shouldn't have and I feel dreadful for it. Snooping is the worst but I had to know.'

'What did you find?' Allie's tone was soft and inviting confidence.

'An email titled FYEO.'

'FYEO?' Allie shook her head.

'For your eyes only.' Camilla explained. 'Did you read it?'

'Yes, Camilla. Of course I did.'

'And?'

'It seems that my husband has been arranging a weekend away at a luxury spa with some woman called Brianna Mandrell.' Even saying the name out loud made her feel queasy.

'Oh.'

'Oh? Camilla, I thought you'd be furious.'

Her sister sighed. 'Look, Dawn, maybe it's not what it seems like. Maybe it's—'

'It does sound a bit suspicious, Camilla.' Allie chewed her lip. 'I'd certainly advise speaking to him about this as soon as possible, Dawn. Just to clear it up.'

'But if I do that, he'll know I've been snooping. He'll never trust me again. I mean... I've turned into a completely paranoid, emotional, swollen, pregnant snooper.' She huffed and covered her face with her hands.

'Insecurity can drive us to do things we wouldn't normally consider doing.' Allie rubbed Dawn's back. 'But this really would be best out in the open.'

'I know.' Dawn muttered into her palms.

'Or perhaps not.'

Dawn lowered her hands and met Camilla's eyes.

'You think I shouldn't say anything?'

'I just think you should give Rick a chance here. You know... he could have a perfectly good reason for this email and for all the other things that are worrying you. Why don't I have a word with him?'

'That's probably not a good idea. But thank you anyway.'

'I could do it from a sisterly perspective. If you do it, you'll get emotional, but if I do it, I can keep calm and find out the truth.'

'I don't know, Camilla.'

'Give me one chance. I'll be careful how I say it. I'll just... elicit the facts.'

Dawn looked from Allie to her sister then at her hands where they sat in her lap. Her nails hadn't received any attention in ages and the cuticles were ragged from where she'd chewed them. And as for her hands; they were red and chapped from where she'd washed them repeatedly then failed to moisturise them. She just didn't have time for such self-care anymore. Had Rick gone off her because she didn't make enough effort?

'I think I should try first, Camilla. I don't want to make things worse.'

'Up to you, sweetheart. But I'm willing to talk to him if you want me to.'

'Thanks. Right... I'm going to get my nails done.'

'What? Now?'

'Yes. I haven't had them done in a lifetime. I'm going to see if Jenny can fit me in at the salon.'

'I'll come with you.' Camilla started to rise.

'No, please don't. I need some time to think.' Dawn stood up.
'Thanks, Allie. Speak to you later, Camilla.'
She opened the door to the café then turned to wave at her friend and her sister, but Camilla had already taken Dawn's seat on the sofa and was deep in conversation with Allie. She glanced up and flushed when she spotted Dawn watching her.

Was something going on with Camilla too, or was she expressing her concerns at Dawn's behaviour?

Dawn shook her head then left the café, wondering how she was going to get through the next few months, but hoping that a manicure might be a good place to start.

Chapter Six

Sitting in the stylish salon, Dawn tried to focus on what Jenny was saying, but her mind was jumping around from one scenario to another.
'What was that?' Dawn asked. 'Sorry, Jenny, it's pregnancy brain.'
'Oh, so you are pregnant?'
'Yes. I take it you had your suspicions then?'
Jenny shrugged. 'Could've been that you'd put a few pounds on, so I'd never have said anything.'
'A few pounds?' Dawn lowered her eyes to her belly. 'We were going to tell people soon, make it all official, but we wanted to tell the children first.'
'Well congratulations! That's fabulous news.'
Jenny watched Dawn's face.
'Isn't it?'
'It is. Fabulous.' Dawn sighed. 'It was just a bit of a shock.'
'Not all babies are planned but they bring the love with them. Isn't that how the saying goes. At least, it's something like that. Anyway, good for you. I've always thought of you and Rick as the perfect couple. You seem so happy and so perfectly matched.'

Dawn bit the inside of her cheek. Was that how others saw her and Rick? As perfect? If only they knew the truth. She swallowed hard, trying to dislodge the painful lump that had lodged in her throat.
'Thank you. That's a very kind thing to say.'
Jenny smiled then looked down at Dawn's nails again. 'There you go. That looks much better doesn't it?'
Dawn admired the shimmering lilac polish that Jenny had applied to her nails. Her cuticles were now neat and her hands looked much better because Jenny had soaked them, exfoliated them, then smoothed in a rich rose scented lotion that made Dawn think of Turkish delight.
'Tell you what, shall I do you a pedicure too? On the house?'
'That would be lovely. But I'm happy to pay.'
'Won't hear of it. My way of saying congratulations.' Jenny shook her head and her long blue hair fell over her shoulders. Dawn found it hard to keep up with the stylist's changing hair colour, just last week it had been dyed different shades of grey and now it was a rich azure blue that reminded Dawn think of foreign summer skies.
'Well, thank you. But I do need to pop to the toilet first.'
'Of course.'
Dawn got up and made her way to the back of the salon then went through the black door and into the toilets.
Ten minutes later, she emerged.
'If you want to take a seat here, Dawn, I'll soak your feet in...' Jenny stopped mid sentence. 'Dawn?'
She hurried over and took hold of Dawn's arms. 'What is it? You've gone white as a sheet.'
Dawn opened her mouth to explain but the dull ache in her abdomen caused her to hunch over with fear.
'It's all right, lovely, just sit down. Everything will be OK.'
But as Jenny lowered her into a chair, everything went black.

The sound of whispering dragged Dawn from the warm, dark place where she'd been floating. The whispers sounded familiar and she knew, deep inside, that she had to surface.
But it was so nice in the darkness where she was weightless and didn't have to worry about anything.
Except for Laura and James!
She needed to pick her children up from school.
She opened her eyes and sat up quickly.
'Dawn?'
Rick leaned over her, his face pale and his eyes pools of concern. 'Dawn, lie back down.'
'What? Where are Laura and James? I need to get them from school.'
'No you don't. Your mother's going to pick them up today and give them dinner. Dawn you're in hospital. I came as quickly as I could. Camilla rang me. She said... she said that you'd collapsed at Jenny's salon and that Jenny called an ambulance then called her.'
As Dawn settled back on the pillow in its white starched hospital-issue pillowcase, it all came flooding back. She'd had her nails done then gone to the toilet. She'd discovered blood in her underwear. She'd gone back out to tell Jenny then felt all woozy and... that was all she remembered. Except for being in an ambulance with a very kind female paramedic then being wheeled into the hospital and into a room where she'd been told to rest while they organised tests and a scan.
'But I only fainted. I didn't need to come here.'
'They were concerned because you blacked out and because of the bleeding. Jenny was in a right old state apparently.'
'Poor Jenny.'
'Poor *you*!' He took her hand as he perched on the side of the bed. 'I don't know how I'd manage if anything ever happened to you, Dawn.'

'The baby?' She touched her stomach.

He shook his head.

'No!'

'They don't know what's wrong yet. That's why they want to scan you. They said... they said...' He sighed then rubbed his eyes. 'They said bleeding before twenty-four weeks is viewed as a threatened miscarriage but it could all be fine. The baby might be OK. Apparently, there are lots of reasons for bleeding in pregnancy.'

'But I fainted.'

He nodded. 'That could well be the shock of seeing the blood, and according to the paramedic, your blood pressure is quite low again.'

Dawn's heart melted as she took in how distressed he was. His tie was askew, his shirt crumpled and the fine lines around his eyes seemed deeper, as if the morning's events had aged him rapidly.

Whatever might be different between them, he did care, and that made her want to hug him.

'Come here.' She opened her arms.

Rick leaned forwards and gently embraced her. To be held by him, to breathe in the familiar spicy scent of his aftershave and to bury her face in his neck all made her want everything to be OK again. She couldn't imagine a world where she didn't get to hug him, where she didn't see him every day and know that he was hers.

But she might have to face up to all that if their relationship changed, if his feelings for her had altered as much as she feared.

He released her and she leaned back on the pillows, and he softly stroked her cheek.

'It's all going to be OK, Dawnie. I just know it.'

'I hope so, Rick.'

But she wasn't just thinking about the baby inside her, she was thinking about her whole life too.

Even though the Early Pregnancy Assessment Unit at the local hospital was extremely busy, they'd managed to fit Dawn in for a scan. Initially, she'd been told she might have to wait until the next day, but there had been a cancellation of a scheduled appointment, so they'd given Dawn the space.

And the baby had been fine. Heart beating strong and limbs moving around, safe in her womb. The relief had been overwhelming and Dawn had been struck by something; even though this baby's conception had not been planned, she did want it. With all of her heart. There was no doubt in her mind.

The medical team had run further tests but admitted that they weren't sure what had caused the bleeding. They'd also reassured her that although it might have seemed as though she'd lost a lot of blood, it was in fact not much at all. Sometimes, bleeding in pregnancy could be down to something as straightforward as changes to the cervix caused by pregnancy hormones, and the dull ache she'd experienced could have been down to those changes. They advised her to take it easy for the next few weeks, although how she was going to manage to do that with two children and a house to run, Dawn had no idea.

'Here's a cuppa, Dawnie,' Camilla entered the lounge where Dawn was resting on the sofa. Camilla and Rick had tried to persuade Dawn to stay in bed once they'd arrived home from the hospital, but Dawn had refused. She couldn't bear the thought of being upstairs alone, left to stew with her worries. So Camilla had insisted on bringing the quilt and pillows downstairs, then arranging them on the sofa.

Camilla put the mug on the coffee table then started plumping up the pillows.

'Will you stop?' Dawn swatted her sister's hand away.

'I'm just trying to make you comfy.'

'I know and I'm grateful but you don't need to keep fussing and if you keep making me all this tea I won't be able to rest anyway, as I'll be back and fore to the loo.'

Camilla nodded then slumped onto the end of the sofa.
'Ouch!' Dawn lurched forwards.
'Dawnie! What is it? More cramps?' Camilla's eyes were wide, her face contorted with worry.
'No, silly, you just sat on my foot.'
'Ooops!' Camilla moved to the arm of the sofa and perched there, her eyes restless, her fingers fluttering across her lap.
'Camilla, I'm fine.'
'But you're not. Or you weren't. What if you'd lost this baby? How awful would we all feel then? I'm going to have a word with Rick as soon as—'
'Please don't. He doesn't need to know what I did. Or that I know about the emails and whatever else. Today's scare has helped me re-evaluate. I'm not saying that I condone his... deceit, but I'm hoping there's a good reason for it.'
'And there is... I mean, I'm sure there is, but you really need to avoid stress. You can't be worrying that your husband's cheating or going off you or anything else for that matter. You need stability and taking care of.'
'I know. But I'll speak to Rick in my own time.' Dawn tilted her head. 'Where is he anyway?'
'Upstairs.'
'He's been gone for ages.'
'I think he's on the phone.' Camilla's eyes widened at her own words. 'It's probably just work.'
Dawn slumped onto the pillows. 'Probably.'
Rick had rushed back to be at Dawn's side then insisted that he'd stay home for the rest of the week, so he probably did have things he needed to sort out. She hoped it wouldn't get him into trouble; she knew his bosses didn't like their employees missing time. But surely this was a good reason to take some compassionate leave or even to work from home?

The next morning, Dawn sat in bed fighting the urge to get up and go downstairs to see what was going on. So far, in the forty-five minutes since Rick had got the children up, she'd heard Rick swearing, Laura reprimanding her father and James crying. She could smell burnt toast and the tea Rick had brought her, which was rapidly cooling on her bedside table, tasted faintly of washing-up liquid. It seemed like everything that could go wrong had gone wrong.

But Rick had told her to stay in bed and that under no circumstances was she to get up until the children had left for school. When she'd gone to the toilet first thing, she'd seen traces of blood, so she knew she had to listen, but there was less than yesterday.

She was also trying not to worry, because stressing wasn't going to help.

About the baby and about Rick. He'd been so loving and attentive since he'd brought her home, and she was even wondering if she'd imagined the email. Had she dreamt it, perhaps? Or read things into it that weren't really there? Was she being oversensitive?

She decided to push it from her mind and to focus on resting and enjoying the week with Rick. It wasn't often that they had time alone together, without the children around, and it would be nice to have that quality time. Perhaps this time alone would strengthen their relationship and prepare them for their new addition.

Footsteps on the stairs alerted her to an approaching child.

'Muu-uum!' It was James.

'Morning, angel.'

He ran at the bed and flung himself onto her just as Rick stormed into the room.

'James! Don't run at your mum like that. Remember what we spoke about?'

James gently moved off Dawn and nodded, his cheeks blushing scarlet.
'You said we have to be good and gentle with Mummy because she's not very well.'
'That's right.'
'Oh James, I'm not ill but I do need to rest because I'm growing a baby.'
She didn't want her son worrying about her being ill. A girl in his class at school had lost her mother to breast cancer the previous year and she'd seen the terror in James's eyes when he'd heard about it. He was a worrier and she couldn't bear to think about him wondering when he'd lose her.
'But you'll be OK now?' he asked, his eyes wide.
'Yes, James, I'll be OK.'
She opened her arms and he crawled up the bed to sit next to her, then carefully snuggled into her.
'Is he all right there?' Rick asked.
'Yes, he's fine. Everything OK downstairs?'
Rick winked at her. 'Running like clockwork.' Then he mock wiped his brow. 'I have to be honest, I don't know how you make it look so easy.'
'Do you need me to come down?'
'Absolutely not! You have a cuddle with James. I'll go and—'
'Daddy, are you going to get us a new toaster?'
'What?' Dawn raised her eyebrows.
'Nothing to worry about. I just burnt a piece of toast then it got jammed in the toaster so I shook it and now it won't work.'
Dawn suppressed laughter. 'We needed a new one anyway.'
'We certainly do... now. Right, see you in a bit. James, make sure you let Mummy rest.'
'Yes, Daddy.'
Dawn held her son in her arms and sighed with contentment. He might be six but he was still her baby. She buried her head in his hair and breathed in the scent of apple shampoo. His hair was soft and

fine. She wondered if the new baby would look like her, or if he or she would be another mini-Rick. It was exciting to think that soon there would be another person joining them, another child for her to love. After she'd given birth to Laura, she'd fallen so much in love with her that she hadn't thought she could ever have room in her heart to love another child as much. Then James had arrived and she'd loved him equally. Maternal love wasn't limited and she had plenty to share with three children.

'Mummy?' James leaned backwards to meet her eyes.

'Yes?'

'Can the baby hear me?'

'Yes, darling. At least I think so.'

He pressed his mouth against her belly. 'Baby, I'm your big brother, James. Now don't you come out until it's time or you'll be too small. When you do come I will look after you. I promise.'

Dawn's eyes filled with tears at his sweet words.

Then she felt a fluttering in her belly, like bubbles popping and she gasped.

'What's wrong, Mummy?'

'The baby just moved.'

'For me?'

'Yes, James, I think it's because you spoke to him or her.'

She'd felt some movement over the past few weeks but hadn't been sure if it was the baby or wind, and hadn't made a fuss because the children still hadn't known about the pregnancy.

He grinned.

'Mummy?'

'Yes, angel.'

'How did the baby get in there?'

Dawn choked as laughter burst from her chest. She looked around, as if she could find an appropriate answer for a six-year-old, then at a loss, she grabbed the mug of tea and winced as she swallowed a sour mouthful.

'Now that's an interesting question, James.'

He watched her, his big eyes wide and interested.
'Tell you what, why don't you ask your father?'
James nodded then snuggled back into her, and Dawn bit her lip as she imagined Rick's face when his son asked him that age-old question. She hoped he'd have a good answer ready and knew that she'd want to be there to listen when James asked.

Chapter Seven

Over the next few days, Dawn tried to rest. It was difficult when she saw Rick struggling with things and she had to stop herself taking over. He did try really hard but he wasn't used to the domestic side of things around the house as Dawn had always done them. It had worked for them because Dawn had wanted it to. Rick did the traditionally male things and Dawn did the housework and chores; it was the way it had been since she'd given up her teaching post after having James. And, of course, her desire for the more traditional family lay rooted in her past and her yearning for the stability and happiness she'd enjoyed as a young child. Besides which, by the time Rick got home in the evenings, he was usually so tired that she didn't have the heart to ask him to run the vacuum round or to do the ironing, and on weekends she wanted him to spend quality time with the children.

She realised now though, that something would need to change, because with a new baby on the way, she wouldn't be able to do everything that she had been doing.

But this week, as she'd lain on the sofa watching daytime TV, Rick had managed to wash a black sock with the whites, which had made them all grey. Then he'd shrunk one of her favourite cashmere (hand-wash only) cardigans by putting it on a boil wash. He'd put frozen chips in the oven to go with fried eggs, but forgotten to turn the oven on, so when the eggs were ready, the chips were still ice-cold. He'd been ironing his work shirts and answered a call on his mobile, leaving the iron face down on a shirt and burned a hole in it. And he'd gone food shopping and spent three times Dawn's usual budget by picking up the first version of everything on the list she'd written, and not searching around for the best value products like Dawn did. But he'd been trying so hard and she loved him for it, and, she could see that he was learning fast. His latest attempt at ironing had been very impressive, especially as he'd done it while Skyping a client. The camera on his laptop had been positioned so that only his head was visible though, so he didn't seem unprofessional. Then he'd boiled all the whites he'd dyed grey and returned them – almost – to their former condition.

As for Dawn herself, she was feeling much better, and thankfully the bleeding had stopped. She wasn't out of the woods yet but a few more days and she felt sure she'd be able to resume some of her normal tasks, just slowly.

Friday had arrived, the children were at school, and Rick had insisted that she have a lie in and breakfast in bed. He'd toasted her crumpets, in the new toaster, and served them with real butter and some of the homemade strawberry jam that Allie had given them recently, insisting that she had a surplus after the summer. He'd brought her a big mug of tea and a glass of freshly squeezed orange juice too. As she ate, he sat next to her on the bed and read the paper on his tablet.

'This is nice.' She dabbed her mouth with the paper napkin.

Rick turned to her. 'It is, isn't it?'

Their bedroom was warm with autumn sunshine and outside, the breeze toyed with the few remaining leaves of the silver birch in their front garden.

'I love the autumn.'

'I know you do.'

'It reminds me of our New York trip.'
'Back in our youth?' He grinned.
'Well, we were young, yes.'
'What and we're ancient now?'
'No, but... well things change don't they? And we were only in our twenties when we went out there. It was such a great week. I wish...' She bit her lip. She was about to say that she wished they could go again and be like they used to, but that wasn't going to happen for a while, not with a new baby and two young children.
'What do you wish?'
'Oh it doesn't matter.'
He placed his tablet on the bedside table and turned around to face her properly. 'Tell me.'
'I just miss how good things used to be between us. Back when it was fresh and new and exciting.'
'And when we weren't sleep-deprived and trying to do a million things while feeling guilty about the things we're not doing.'
'Yes. It's hard sometimes. I love Laura and James... they're my world. Our world. But I miss just being with you.'
Rick took her hand. 'I love you, you know.'
'I love you too.' She sighed. 'And I feel guilty now for wishing for things when I have so much to be grateful for.'
'You should never feel guilty. And I miss having more time with you too. But I do love our life and our children and even though sometimes it's so hard I could sleep standing up; I still wouldn't change a thing. Well... except for...' He shook his head.
'Except for what? Rick?'
'Nothing. Nothing at all, my beautiful wife. I'm just a bit tired. Right then... how about you take a nice long shower then smother yourself in that luxurious – and very expensive – moisturiser that the children bought you for Mother's Day?'
'OK.' Dawn wanted to ask him again what he was going to say but it was clear that he wanted to move the conversation on.
'I'll take your breakfast things down and make the sofa up for you.'

'Rick, I think I can manage without a quilt on the sofa today.'
He frowned.
'Perhaps. But you still have to take it easy.'
She nodded.
'I have a little surprise arriving later that I'm hoping you're going to enjoy.'
So he was planning surprises for her. That must mean that nothing was wrong and that he hadn't been about to tell her something to upset her. She was being too sensitive again.
So she would forget that Rick had said *except for...* and get on with her day. It would be their last full day alone together anyway, as the children would be home over the weekend, then Rick had to go back to work on Monday. Exactly how she'd manage then, she wasn't quite sure but she'd cross that bridge when she came to it.
She pushed back the quilt and slid her legs over the edge of the bed and wondered exactly what surprise it was that Rick had planned for her.

Dawn descended the stairs quietly. She was sure she'd heard voices when she'd got out of the shower. She had moisturised then dressed as quickly as she could without getting moisturiser all over her clothes. Her regular jeans were all too tight now, so she'd pulled on a pair of grey linen trousers with an elasticated waist and a loose black tunic top.
At the bottom of the stairs, she paused. She could definitely hear Rick speaking to someone. Her heart jolted. Was he on the phone again? She marched into the kitchen, about to give him a piece of her mind, but found Allie at the kitchen table unloading a large basket.
'Allie!'
Her friend turned and smiled.

'Hey, sweetheart. How're you feeling?'

'Better. Yes, much better, thanks. What are you doing here? Gosh… that sounded terribly rude and I didn't mean it like that. I was just surprised.'

Allie laughed. 'Well that's for Rick to explain.'

Allie turned to her husband.

'This is your surprise. I asked Allie if she'd have time to prepare us a nice lunch for today, seeing as how it'll be our last bit of peace and quiet for a while.'

'You weren't too busy?' Dawn asked Allie as she took in the number of foil containers and various bowls on the table.

'Of course not. I mean, we're always busy but Jordan is working today and he's enlisted Max to help him out. Which freed me up to do this for you.'

'That's so kind of you.' Dawn smiled.

'Rick is paying me for it, so…' Allie's cheeks coloured.

'I bloody well hope he is. You have a business to run, you can't keep giving stuff away, you know.'

Dawn crossed the room then gave her friend a hug.

'And Rick… This is so thoughtful of you. Thank you so much.'

The aromas coming from the table were making her mouth water, even though she hadn't long had breakfast.

'I must be getting better. My appetite seems to be returning with a vengeance.'

Rick came and stood next to her then slid his arm around her waist.

'I'm glad to hear it. I've been so worried about you.'

He kissed the top of her head and she leaned into him.

'I think everything you need is there, Rick. I've written down some warming instructions, although everything can be eaten cold if you prefer. Oh, and I'll just pop the ice cream in the freezer.'

'Thanks, Allie.'

'And you're all sorted for collecting the children from school today?'

'Yes, I'll get them. I'm quite enjoying being able to do the school run. It's amazing what you miss out on because of work.'

Allie nodded.

'I'll see you out then.'

Rick escorted Allie to the door and Dawn eyed the food on the table. It was still early, so they couldn't enjoy it yet, but it was certainly a lovely surprise.

'What time do you want to eat, my gorgeous wife?' Rick entered the kitchen. 'I don't know about you but I won't be able to wait too long.'

'I'm so glad you said that. Shall we give it an hour though?'

'An hour maximum.'

'What do you want to do now?' Dawn peered up at him, taking in his strong jaw, his broad shoulders and his slim hips. Something stirred inside her that she hadn't felt in quite some time.

Rick stepped closer and cupped her face. 'I know what I'd like to do but I don't think it's wise right now.'

Dawn leaned her head against his chest, breathing in his delicious scent.

'I know, you're right. We probably shouldn't.'

He lifted her chin and gazed into her eyes. 'It's not that I don't want to, because I really, really do. I love you, Dawnie, and desire you more than you could imagine. But I would be too worried because of what happened.'

'Me too.'

She closed her eyes as he gently kissed her lips.

'How about a head massage instead while we watch some daytime TV?'

'With a cuppa?'

'Now you're talking. You go and switch the TV on and I'll boil the kettle.'

Dawn nodded then left the kitchen, her body conflicted between desire for her husband and a maternal need to protect her unborn baby. But her heart felt lighter than it had done for weeks. Because Rick had told her that he loved and desired her and was trying to show her that in a variety of ways. So daytime TV and a cup of tea would have to be a substitute for passionate lovemaking – for the next few months, at least.

Dawn moaned with pleasure as Rick gently massaged her head. He was sitting behind her on the sofa with her head resting on his chest. He ran his fingers through her hair then rubbed her temples and worked his hands backwards to behind her ears.
When he stopped, she was weak and completely relaxed.
Then there was a knock at the door, so Rick slid out from behind her and went to answer it. Dawn strained to listen but Rick soon returned, holding a large box.
'What's that?'
'Get your shoes on and come out the back garden with me.'
'What? Why?'
'There's something we need to do.'
Dawn fetched her shoes then followed Rick outside. He carried the box down to the bottom of the garden then set it in front of the flowerbed.
There was a slightly raised mound of earth there and she let out a sigh. 'I'd forgotten to ask if you'd had a chance to bury him.'
'Yes I brought him out here because I thought you'd want him to stay at home. He's all wrapped up in a shoebox and I dug quite a deep hole, so there's no chance of anything... you know...'
'Digging him up?' Dawn's bottom lip wobbled. 'Poor Wallace.'
'Hey, don't get upset. He had a good life.'
'But he was so young.'
'He was but he could have had a medical condition we didn't know about.'
Dawn nodded. 'It's still sad though.'
'And part of life. But at least he's home again.'

'I know. If you hadn't found him, it would have been awful.'
'A giant white rat!' Rick shook his head.
'I bet it did give Mrs Burnley quite a fright. So what's in the box?'
'I thought we should have some way of marking this spot. And one day, when the children are a bit older, we can tell them the truth about Wallace.'
'If they don't already suspect. Laura's quite sharp, you know.'
He smiled. 'Don't I know it? You should've heard her bossing me around this week in the mornings.'
'I did, don't worry. She doesn't miss much.'
'She certainly doesn't.'
Rick opened the box and lifted out a bare root rose that sat in a small plastic container. 'It'll need to soak in water for at least two hours then I can plant it here.'
'Let me guess... the roses will be white?'
'Of course.'
'Thank you.' Dawn's vision blurred and she blinked rapidly.
'Don't thank me. This is what we do, Dawnie. We support each other and look after each other and our family.'
He wrapped his arms around her and held her tight, and she relaxed against him, knowing there was no place she'd rather be.

'Have you tried the couscous yet?' Rick gestured at Dawn's plate with his fork.
'No.' She lifted a forkful to her mouth. 'Mmmmm.'
'How good is that?'
'Delicious.'
They were sitting at the kitchen table, tucking into the food Allie had delivered. And what a feast it was: small cheese and sun-dried tomato tartlets, roast-vegetable couscous with a basil olive-oil drizzle, green-

lentil tabbouleh, asparagus, spinach and halloumi salad, chicken panzanella and for dessert, a large cherry pie and homemade coconut ice cream.

Allie had also provided a bottle of cloudy elderflower lemonade, that was sweet, refreshing and zesty and went perfectly with the food.

'This has been a wonderful day, Rick.' Dawn raised her glass. 'To family.'

'To our wonderful family and to you for growing our baby.'

They clinked glasses.

Ten minutes later, Dawn looked at the food that was left.

'I don't think we're going to be able to eat all this. I'm stuffed as it is.' She gently patted her belly that was straining against her waistband.

'Well the children can enjoy some of it for their tea, can't they?' Rick asked.

'Good idea. Save me... I mean, *you*... cooking.'

'Hey, I would've cooked for them anyway. I'm quite enjoying learning.'

'I have to try to get back to normal, Rick, I can't lie down forever.'

'I know, but not just yet. Besides, I want us to share more of the household chores now, as well as the cooking. I was quite a good cook back when we first got together, but when we bought the house, then had the children, I'm a bit ashamed to admit that we fell into stereotypical roles.'

'We did, I know, and that was partly my fault for pushing us into them.'

'I didn't put up much of a fight though, did I? I've just been so tired all the time.'

'But how is that going to change, Rick?'

He blinked then worried his bottom lip.

'It will. Somehow. Look... we still have the weekend and I have one more surprise for you.'

'You do?' Dawn laughed. 'But you've spoiled me so much already. What else could you possible have planned?'

He tapped the side of his nose. 'You'll know soon enough. Right, I'll

get the dishes done then it's time for another cup of tea and an afternoon snooze.'
'Ooh, sounds good.'
'You can make the tea if you like while I tidy up.'
Dawn switched the kettle on while Rick put lids back onto foil containers then placed them into the fridge. He had been so good to her this week and she found it wonderful yet strange, as if she should always be the one doing things. Of course, when her mother had visited earlier in the week, she'd muttered that it wouldn't last. And that had left Dawn biting her tongue as usual. What was it with her mum? Why couldn't she be happy when something nice happened, even if it was on the back of a difficult time? She knew her mother had been hurt and never got over it but still... surely it was time to move on? But then she thought of Camilla and her refusal to fall in love, and knew that for some people, time didn't move on. For some people, it very sadly remained the same.
'What was that sigh for?' Rick asked as he slipped his arms around her waist then leaned his chin on her shoulder.
'I didn't realise I had sighed.'
'You did. And it sounded like you're carrying the weight of the world on your shoulders.'
'I was just thinking about Mum and Camilla. About why they can't get over what Dad did. It was such a long time ago.'
She poured boiling water onto teabags.
'Camilla's OK isn't she?'
'Well, yes. But she's never had a proper relationship and I don't know if she ever will.'
'She seems to be enjoying herself.'
'Seems... And then there's Mum. Won't look at a man, which is fine, but she also carries so much bitterness around with her.'
'I guess she was badly hurt.'
'She was, but the way she hangs onto it and constantly bringing it up hurts me too. Sometimes I just want to live life without comparing everything to what my dad did, you know?'

Rick turned her in his arms.

'I do know, Dawnie. It must be hard for you and you are very patient with her.'

'I love her and she does so much for me... for us. I can't tell her because it would hurt her and I doubt anything would change.'

'Probably not. But perhaps you do need to have a gentle chat about it. Just not at the moment. Wait until you feel stronger.'

Dawn nodded. 'Perhaps. Anyway, right now I'm going to forget about it and enjoy being with you. We have about two hours until the school run, so let's take our tea upstairs and lounge in bed like we used to when we were students.'

'How decadent!' He winked at her. 'Going to bed in the afternoon... when it's still light.'

He released her then got the milk from the fridge and Dawn poured it into the mugs.

"I never want to feel the way my mother does, Rick.'

'You never will, I promise.' He picked up the tea. 'Come on, let's go lounge.'

Dawn followed him out of the kitchen and up the stairs, trying hard to banish all thoughts of the email she'd seen from her mind. Trying to hold her husband's promise there instead, because what was better than his word?

Chapter Eight

Dawn stretched and savoured the delicious tingling in her limbs. She'd had the loveliest nap followed by a refreshing cup of mint tea – that Rick had brought to her in bed before leaving to pick the children up from school. They'd be home soon. She should probably get dressed again. She'd slipped into soft pyjamas for her nap, not wanting to crease her clothes.
The sound of a car entering the street made her sit up. That couldn't be Rick; he'd walked to pick up Laura and James as it would be lazy to drive the five minutes to the school.
She was about to lie back down again when she heard footsteps on the path. Was that Rick? An urge to throw herself into his arms and tell him how much she loved him consumed her. Recently, she'd been beset by so many doubts but the way he'd treated her this week had to show that he loved her, surely?
Dawn reached for her dressing gown and slipped it on then descended the stairs, her heart full of love and happiness. She unlocked the front door then swung it open, about to greet her husband, and she stopped dead. Because the person on her doorstep was not the one she'd been expecting at all.

'Hello, Dawn.'

She opened her mouth but nothing came out.

'What's the matter, dear? Didn't Rick tell you I was coming?'

Her mother-in-law gave her a quick once over with her hard olive-green eyes then patted her dyed chestnut hair.

'Are you still in your dressing gown?'

'Yes actually, Fenella. I was having a nap. I've been told to rest.'

'Yes, I know that.' Fenella Beaumont sniffed. 'So let's get you back to bed then.'

She pushed her way into the house.

'My suitcase is in the car but Rick can get it when he comes home.'

'Suitcase?'

'Yes, dear. I've come to stay.'

Dawn's heart sank.

'Sorry?'

'It was going to be a surprise. Rick said not to let on.'

I bet he did.

Dawn closed the door.

'Right, dear. It was a long drive so I'd love a cup of tea. I'll make it of course as you need to go back to bed.'

'Of course. No. I mean... I'll make it now.'

'I'll just go and powder my nose.'

In the kitchen, Dawn filled the kettle and noticed that her hands were shaking. She couldn't believe that Fenella Beaumont was actually here. It wasn't that she didn't get on with her mother-in-law, more that she enjoyed the fact that they lived a good two hours' drive apart. It meant that family get-togethers were limited to once or twice a year. Fenella was a very proud and opinionated woman and Dawn always found being in her presence somewhat tiring. So the idea of dealing with Fenella in her current fragile condition was something that made her anxious.

It wasn't Rick's fault, of course. Dawn had never told him about the things his mother said that made her uneasy, or that led her to doubt her own abilities as a wife and mother. She'd never wanted him to be

in a position where he felt awkward having the two women under the same roof. But then that had never happened on more than a handful of occasions and then it had only been for a night or two.
But now...
It seemed that Fenella Beaumont had come to stay and Dawn had no idea how long for. Or how she would manage. Or how this would help her to relax.
When she heard Rick's key turn in the lock, she took a deep breath. She had a feeling it was going to take all her strength to stay positive.

'I'm the winner!' James shouted as he ran into the hallway.
'Really James, I wasn't even racing you.' Laura shook her head as she removed her coat, eight going on eighteen.
'Hello guys.' Dawn opened her arms and hugged them both. 'How was your day?'
'It was OK.' Laura shrugged.
'Great, Mummy, we played football in afternoon playtime and I was the winner!'
'James!' Laura scowled at her brother.
'I was under the impression that footballers played in teams.' Rick closed the door behind him.
'I told him that, Daddy, but he won't listen. He's just *obsessed* with winning.'
'Good word, Laura.' Dawn smiled.
'We had theassawsuses today for creative writing.'
'Theassawsuses?' Dawn frowned.
'Yes, you know with all the different words in. Not to be confused with dictionaries!' She wagged a finger at her mother.
'Ah... you used a thesaurus.'
'That's what I said, Mummy.'

Dawn met Rick's laughing eyes and pulled a face. 'Silly me. Uh, Rick... I think my other surprise has arrived.'

'Oh?' He raised his eyebrows.

'Yes.'

'Ohhhh... I thought I saw an unfamiliar car on the road. Dad no doubt changed it again.' He shook his head. 'Are you OK with the... uh... surprise?'

'What surprise, Daddy? I want to see!' James tugged at Rick's hand.

'Well if it isn't my beautiful grandchildren!'

'Nanna!'

'Nanna!'

Fenella enveloped the children in floral-scented bear hugs and Dawn suppressed a smile as she noticed James trying to wriggle free. He still liked hugs but didn't enjoy being squashed.

Then Fenella went to her son and took his face in her hands.

'Darling Rick, you look tired. Are you all right? I bet you're working too hard and trying to run the house now that Dawn's incapable. I mean incapacitated.'

Rick glanced at Dawn, evidently uncomfortable with his mother's effusiveness and with her wording.

'Yes, I'm fine, thanks. It's Dawn that we've got to look out for.'

'And that's why I'm here. To help you all out while darling Dawn rests.'

Dawn swallowed her disappointment.

'Rick, be an angel and get my suitcase from the car. It's that flashy new Jag out on the road. Your father's choice, not mine. Laura and James, come with me and I'll fix you a healthy snack.'

'There's food in the fridge actually,' Dawn said. 'Left over from lunchtime.'

'Left over?' Fenella's drawn on eyebrows shot to her hairline.

'Yes. Allie brought lunch over for us... Rick asked her to. It was delicious. All freshly cooked and plenty of variety...'

Fenella shook her head. 'Well, there'll be no need of that now I'm here. Nanna Beaumont will take care of everything, don't you worry.'

But as her mother-in-law took Laura and James into the kitchen, Dawn was unable to comply. Of course she was worried. Fenella was overpowering, bossy and hard work at the best of times. Dawn needed to be at full-strength to deal with Fenella and right now she wasn't.
So she had a feeling that the duration of Fenella's stay would be challenging indeed.

The bedroom was grey with early morning light when Dawn woke. She blinked hard. It was too early to be awake yet something had disturbed her.
She held her breath and listened carefully, wondering if it was one of the children. But neither of them was calling her.
Rick was on his side next to her, his breathing deep and regular.
So what was that banging?
She slid out of bed and shrugged into her dressing gown then crept across the landing and checked on Laura and James. They were both sleeping, Laura on her back with her hands on her chest like a fairy-tale princess, and James across his bed with his head hanging off the edge. She gently repositioned him so his head was on the pillow then tucked the duvet back around him.
As she pulled James's door closed behind her, she noticed that the door to the guest bedroom was open. She stuck her head around it and the bed was made, the curtains open and Fenella was nowhere to be seen. For a moment, she wondered if she'd imagined her mother-in-law's arrival, or if the older woman had decided to leave under cover of darkness like some blood-sucking vampire – only in Fenella's case it was soul-destroying she practised rather than drinking blood – but no, the dressing table was groaning under Fenella's paraphernalia. Bottles, jars, tubes, curlers, brushes, lipsticks

and a small jewellery box had been arranged in order of size and colour.

Dawn shivered. From the look of that lot, Fenella was in for the long haul.

There was a book on the bedside table and Dawn peered at it, wondering what Fenella liked to read.

Walk With Poldark

She recalled Rick saying something about his mother's obsession with the TV show but apparently his father didn't feel the same. Married couples didn't have to like everything their partner liked, although she believed that they needed to have some common interests. Dawn and Rick did; they still laughed at the same things, still enjoyed spending time together. She just wished she could shake the final nagging worries about their relationship from her mind.

Downstairs, she steeled herself before entering the kitchen. The sounds coming from in there made her wonder what on earth was going on. There was the clattering of baking trays, the rustling of plastic and the grunting of a woman labouring. And not in childbirth. As she crept in, she almost screamed.

'Fenella… What have you done?'

'Sweet peas and piglets, Dawn! You frightened me half to death.'

'I… I'm sorry but what…' Dawn stared at the kitchen she had loved the moment she'd seen it, with its clean cream-shaker cupboard doors and its black-granite worktops. She'd had everything where she wanted it; from the freestanding range cooker to the coffee machine and the digital radio Rick had bought her last Christmas that resembled an old jukebox.

But now…

Everything had been moved and the surfaces that she made an effort to keep scratch-free, were covered in things that Fenella had pulled from her cupboards, the things Dawn kept even though she knew she'd never use them. She fought the urge to check under the cast-iron bake stone that had been moved from the top of the range – where she kept it for making pancakes and Welsh cakes – and

dumped onto the worktop next to the sink. It was very heavy and could easily scratch the granite if not handled carefully. She wondered if her mother-in-law had considered this.
'I've been giving everything a good clean and sort for you.'
'But I didn't ask you to.'
Fenella held up a hand. 'I know you didn't, dear, but let's be honest, it needed it. And had done for quite some time. Once I've finished cleaning out the cupboards, you can help me to decide what's going out.'
'Going out?'
'Yes of course. There's a lot of junk here.'
'But...' Dawn bit her lip. There was no point keeping on with the *buts*. Fenella was obviously trying to help and she didn't mean any harm. 'OK.'
'Why don't you have a cup of tea first though?'
'Yes. I think I will. Do you want one?'
'Not for me. I'd rather keep going.'
Dawn made tea for her and Rick, trying not to stare at Fenella as she continued her mission. Because that's clearly what it was. She intended to sort out the kitchen and would not be stopped.
'I'm going to take this up to Rick.' Dawn held up two mugs.
'You do that. I'll call you in about an hour, shall I?'
Dawn glanced at the clock on the wall.
'It's only five-thirty.'
'Early bird catches the germ.'
'Worm.'
Fenella threw back her head and laughed. 'In this case, it's the germ, dear. The germs in this kitchen must have been having the party of a lifetime.'
'Right,' Dawn forced out the word through gritted teeth. 'No need to call me. I'll be up soon enough.'
She left the kitchen quickly before Fenella could deliver any further insults, then climbed the stairs, taking care not to spill the tea. After

all, she didn't want to give the older woman something else to comment on.

'I'm sure she didn't mean it like that. She was just joking, Dawnie.' Rick smiled at her. As she took in his sleep-rumpled hair and his broad shoulders, currently bare due to the fact that he only ever wore a t-shirt in bed when it was freezing out, she tried not to be distracted. She knew how yummy his warm skin would smell if she snuggled into him and how good it would be to have his strong arms wrapped around her.
'I don't think she was, Rick. She basically told me that I'm a slob.'
'You're not a slob.'
'Your mother thinks I am.'
He shook his head.
'Anyway, how long's she staying?'
'I told you last night, as long as you need her.'
But I don't need her.
Dawn took a swig of tea to prevent the response escaping. The last thing she wanted to do was appear ungrateful and upset her husband. He was just trying to help and she knew he'd feel terrible going back to work if he thought she'd be struggling and risking her health and the baby.
'Rick, I need some sort of idea how long because I like some space. You know... when I'm at home.'
'Dawnie,' he took her hand and kissed it, 'I need to know you'll be OK when I'm not here. I'll worry anyway but at least if Mum is with you, you'll have to take it easy.'
'But she'll change the whole house around.'
Rick kissed the tip of each of her fingers and Dawn's mind grew fuzzy.

'No she won't. I'll have a gentle word with her.'
He ran soft kisses along her wrist and Dawn struggled to focus on her point.
'And... ask her not to throw anything out without checking first?'
Rick let go of her hand then kissed her cheek before picking up his tea.
'Of course.'
Dawn sank back onto the pillows.
'Now how about we grab another hour of snuggling before the children wake up? You know I love any excuse to feel your curvy body against mine.' He wiggled his eyebrows.
'I thought you said we shouldn't—'
'Well yes... but I can still show you how much I love you, can't I?'
He opened his arms and Dawn moved into them, the warmth of his body and his delicious male scent making her love him even more. Then Rick's mouth met hers and she floated away, caught on a cloud of love and desire, until their bedroom door swung open and heavy footsteps entered the room.
'Rick, dear?'
He poked his head above the covers.
'Mum?'
'I need your help moving something downstairs.'
He rubbed his eyes as Dawn peered out from beneath the quilt too.
'Can't it wait, Fenella?'
'I'm afraid not, Dawn.'
'All right, Mum, I'll be down in a minute.'
'Don't be long!'
Fenella left with a humph and Rick slumped against the pillows.
'She can't go bursting in like that, Rick.'
He met her eyes and she saw uncertainty wavering in his. 'No, I know. I guess she's just finding her feet around here.'
'Finding her feet?'
'I'll have a word.'

'Please do. And quickly. Because I can't deal with this if we're not going to have any privacy, Rick.'
He nodded.
'I'll get dressed and go and see what she wants.'
Dawn turned onto her side and closed her eyes. She kept them closed until she heard him leave the bedroom, because she didn't want him to see her tears. The last thing she wanted was for Rick to feel torn between his wife and mother; that wouldn't be fair at all. But she hoped he really would ask Fenella to tone it down a bit, or having her around would cause more damage than it would if Dawn was left alone to manage. And with her marriage already being a bit unsteady – at least in her own head – Dawn didn't think she had the energy to deal with an interfering mother-in-law too.

Chapter Nine

'This chocolate cake is delicious, Allie,' Camilla said before she took another bite.
'It really is.' Honey smacked her lips. 'You're going to make us fat.'
'Some of us already are.' Dawn rubbed her belly.
'That's not fat, you're just keeping my niece or nephew warm.' Camilla smiled at Dawn across the table.
'Thanks, Camilla.'
'What are big sisters for?'
'How are things going with the mother-in-law, Dawn?' Allie asked.
'Monster-in-law more like,' Camilla blurted.
'Camilla!' Dawn frowned at her sister.
The women had gathered for a Tuesday evening get-together at The Cosy Cottage Café. It had become their routine and only didn't happen if someone was ill, away, or if there was, in Dawn's case, a childcare issue. Dawn hadn't been able to make the previous Tuesday because of her condition but this week, as she was feeling stronger, she'd wanted to come. To get out of the house for a bit while she could.
'I'll be honest with you... my house has never been so clean.'

'Well that's fabulous. Wish someone would come and clean mine,' Allie joked. 'But that's not a good thing for you because…'
'I don't want to seem ungrateful.'
'You can tell us anything,' Camilla said.
'I'm not so sure about that. I mean, you just called her my monster-in-law and I only ever said that once when I was drunk. And I didn't mean it. Fenella tries hard, it's just that she's also—'
'Very trying?' Honey finished her sentence, her brown eyes warm and understanding.
'Yes.' Dawn put her fork down. 'She's cleaned everything from cupboards to shoes to behind the downstairs toilet, but it's strange having another woman doing that. It's like my space has been invaded.'
'A space-invader monster-in-law!' Camilla snorted. 'Well Rick should have been doing his fair share too, Dawnie.' She took a swig of her wine.
'I've told you before that he does what he can but with his job and the hours he works, it's very difficult. That's why we have had more traditional roles, I guess.'
'It was like that with Roger and me,' Allie said.
'Was it?'
'He was…'
'Difficult. A chauvinist.' Camilla took Allie's hand. 'You don't have to be kind about him in front of us, you know.'
'I know. I just don't like calling him over. It seems like I'm betraying the kids.'
Dawn and the other women knew how tough life had been for Allie in the past. She'd revealed some of the details of her marriage to them that summer, after Chris Monroe had arrived in town, and they'd been shocked that she'd kept them to herself for so long. But Dawn knew that people did keep secrets, even from their friends and relatives. She'd been glad that Allie had unburdened herself and it was wonderful to see her so happy with Chris now.
'Rick isn't a chauvinist though, Camilla.'

'I know that. He just needs a bit of a kick up the bum sometimes to get him into gear.'
'He'd do more if he had more time.'
Camilla nodded. 'All right, all right. I know how much you love him.'
'And as for Fenella, as much as she might be… treading on my toes, she's the one looking after Laura and James this evening.'
'It'll be good for her to spend some time with them.' Allie smiled. 'It's nice for children to have extended family.'
'James isn't so sure. He was delighted at first but now he knows that she's going to make him eat his greens and tidy up the toy room when he's finished playing, he's not so sure. And she's making Laura practise her times tables every night, which my daughter does not find amusing.'
Dawn thought of the rhythmic chanting that took place after the children had eaten dinner. Still, it was how she'd learned her tables and every child should know them.
'I can understand how it must be challenging but try to take whatever time you can to rest, Dawn. You need it. I doubt she'll stay permanently?' Allie ended on a question.
'God I hope not. Can you imagine?'
'She'd be getting you to express so she could test the quality of your milk.' Camilla giggled. 'Sorry! I think I've had too much wine. Just let her know if she's bugging you.'
Dawn nodded but inside she was wilting. Fenella had been with them for just five days and her domineering presence had left Dawn drained. Keeping her mouth shut when her mother-in-law made sniping remarks was taking all the strength she had. But she didn't want to snap and hurt the older woman and she also didn't want to seem ungrateful.
'I'm sure she'll leave in a week or so.'
'Doesn't her husband want her at home then?' Honey asked, twirling a strand of her rainbow-dyed hair around her fingers. 'You'd think he'd have come too.'

'He's probably enjoying all the extra time he can spend on his boat, playing chess, golfing and whatever else it is that he does now.' Dawn thought of her father-in-law and how he liked his time outdoors, often spending weekends at the docks or out on the water. When he wasn't sailing the boat, he was polishing it or conducting repairs. At least that's what he told Fenella and she seemed to have bought into it. Was that what happened to marriages long-term then, if they went the distance? Did people accept their partner's excuses because it was easier to nod along, or because they just liked having time apart?

Something struck her then.

What if Fenella was actually lonely?

After all, Rick's younger brother, Kyle, had moved away straight after university, just like Rick had. Kyle had a family of his own now and he lived on the Isle of Wight with his wife and three-year-old twin girls. So it was possible that Fenella didn't see much of him, although she never let on.

Dawn was overwhelmed by a wave of compassion for Rick's mother. It couldn't be easy when your children left, especially if they moved far away.

She resolved to try to be extra kind to Fenella when she went home later, and to try to make her mother-in-law feel appreciated. Because everyone deserved that, didn't they?

'Hello?'

Dawn locked the front door behind her.

'Fenella?'

'SHHH!' Came from the top of the stairs followed by the appearance of her mother-in-law in a long white nightgown with a frilly collar, that made Dawn think of those she'd seen in faded Victorian photographs.

'Hi Fenella. Where are the children?'

'In bed, of course.' Fenella replied as she descended the stairs, shrugging into a purple cord dressing gown. 'I've read them both a story and they're fast asleep.'

Dawn checked the clock on the wall. 'But it's only eight. Are you sure they're sleeping?'

'I did have children of my own you know.' Fenella scowled at her.

'Oh, I know that. It's just that even when James drops off, Laura often takes a while. She tends to spend time thinking and processing her day before she goes to sleep. A few times I've even found her still awake when I've popped up to check on her and it's after nine.'

'After nine?' Fenella tutted. 'No wonder that little girl has trouble concentrating.'

'What do you mean?'

Dawn removed her coat and hung it over the bannister. Fenella eyed it then gave a small shake of her head.

'She told me she's having trouble with maths.'

'When?'

'Yesterday. I didn't want to worry you.'

'Well you should have told me. When I saw her teacher recently, she didn't say there was a problem.'

'Hmmmm. Well if she got more sleep there wouldn't be.'

'Fenella...' Dawn took a deep breath.

'Yes.'

'Oh... nothing. I'll just pop up to give them a kiss then make us a cup of tea. Rick's not back yet then?'

'No. He's rather late too, isn't he?'

'He's been later. It depends what time he gets out of work. I'll text him to find out when he'll be back.'

Fenella nodded then went into the kitchen and Dawn climbed the stairs. She'd had a lovely evening at the café and coming home to

Fenella's disapproval was difficult, especially as she just wanted to put her pyjamas on and lie on the sofa watching some mindless TV. And she'd been intending on being kind to her mother-in-law. Upstairs, she pushed James's door open and found him sleeping across the bed, so she gently wriggled him around, then kissed his forehead. He smelt of honey and lemon and a scent that was all his own, one that she'd know in a room full of children even if she was blindfolded. He was her little boy and her heart brimmed over with love for him.

When she went into Laura's room, she crossed the pink rug to the bed and leaned over. Laura turned suddenly and sat up.

'I thought you'd still be awake.'

'Oh Mummy, you know I need to read before I go to sleep. But Nanny said I couldn't. I told her she was being a big fat bossy boots.'

Dawn swallowed a giggle. 'You didn't?'

Dawn saw a look of scorn passed over Laura's face in the light from the hallway.

'Well I almost did. I said she was a bossy boots but I didn't say the fat bit. Mummy... when's she going home? I like her and everything but she's not like you. She has different rules and ways of doing things and I don't like them. I want it to be just the four of us again.'

Dawn brushed Laura's hair from her cheek then sighed. 'I know, angel, that's how I like it too. Nanna's just here to help for a few weeks until I feel better.'

'But you are all better aren't you? And the baby is OK now.'

'Yes, I do feel much better. But it would be mean if we just told Nanna that and sent her packing.'

'Sent her packing?'

'Yes... on her way, back home.'

'Oh. Yes. Well let her stay a bit longer, but then send her packing.'

Dawn smiled. 'Deal. But try to be nice and polite for now.'

'Mummy, can I read now, please?'

Dawn chewed her lip. If she said yes, she'd be going against what

Fenella had told Laura to do but if she said no, Laura could well be awake when she came up to bed.
'For fifteen minutes. But no longer. Promise?'
'Pinky promise.' Laura nodded then switched on the lamp that was on her bedside table.
'And it's our secret.'
'Of course, Mummy. Between you and me.' Laura tapped the side of her nose.
Dawn was still smiling when she reached the kitchen. Laura was so much like Rick with his mannerisms and vocabulary, yet also so much like her. Dawn remembered struggling to sleep in her youth and lying in bed with her mind racing about everything from politics to whether or not Take That would ever get back together.
'Something funny, Dawn? Do share, I could do with a laugh.' Fenella was sat at the breakfast bar with a steaming mug of tea.
'Oh, I was just thinking about how much I love the children.'
'They are lovely. And even if I do think they stay up too late, you and Rick have done a good job, I must admit.'
'Uh... thank you.' Here she went again, being such a contradictory and confusing character. One minute, Fenella was undermining her, the next she was building her up. Albeit as a veiled compliment.
'Did you text Rick?'
'I forgot. I'll do it now.'
Dawn dug her mobile out of her trouser pocket and swiped the screen. It buzzed as a message popped up.

Staying in London tonight, Dawn. Late one working through, so no point coming home. Ring you in the morning. X

What?
Blood whooshed through her ears and her head spun. He was staying out all night. Granted, he'd done it before when he had an important

meeting or a very early start but never at this short notice. Now she'd be left on her own with Fenella and she didn't know where he was sleeping. Or who he was with.

'I've uh... I've got to do something a moment. I'll be back shortly,' she said to her mother-in-law.

'But Dawn...'

She opened the back door and went into the garden before Fenella could argue. This just wasn't on. What did Rick think he was playing at? She brought up her contacts list and scrolled down to *Rick* then pressed the call button.

When he answers, he's going to get a mouthful.

As she listened to the phone ringing, her breaths came shaky and fast.

No, not a mouthful but a few strong words.

It kept on ringing.

OK then, some questions.

Perhaps but...

His voice came on at the other end and she was about to say his name then realised she'd got his voicemail.

She waited until the recorded message finished then was besieged by doubts so she ended the call.

Should she leave him a message?

Yes, of course.

She dialled him again and waited for voicemail to kick in.

'Hi Rick, it's me... Dawn... you know, your wife. Hope you're OK. Could you ring me. Even if it's late when you get this. I just want to hear your voice. Love you.'

She stared at the black screen, seeing her face reflected there: pale, large eyes wide, fear in her gaze.

'What did he say?' Fenella was peering out of the door.

'He's not answering. But I left a message.'

'Cup of tea in here for you.'

'Thanks.'

As she followed Fenella inside, the last thing Dawn wanted to do was to sit and drink tea, but if she didn't, she knew she'd go upstairs and cry. Although what comfort she'd get from the older woman, she didn't know. But at least it would be distracting and hopefully stop her imagining that Rick might be out drinking with women, smart attractive women in tight dresses and high heels, the type who worked hard and partied hard, who lived without commitments. Women who were a bit like Camilla.

Women who might not mind if a man had a wife in a little country village because they didn't want any commitment anyway.

She shook her head as if to shake the disturbing thoughts away, still holding her mobile tightly as she willed Rick to call. Just to put her mind at rest. If that were at all possible.

'So who is he staying with?' Fenella asked as she poured fresh tea from a teapot that Dawn didn't recognise.

'I'm not sure.'

'You don't know?' Fenella frowned. 'Well I wouldn't have that.'

'Look, I can hardly order him around can I? Besides, he didn't answer so I'm helpless right now.'

The reality of the situation swept over her. 'I can't even have a stiff drink to try to calm my churning belly or to at least numb my nerves. I want to know where he is tonight. But I don't have any idea...'

She glanced at Fenella and found that the older woman's eyes were wide as she stared at her. Great. So now she seemed like a suspicious neurotic wife.

'Of course you do. I'm sorry, Dawn, that was unfair of me. You must be worried.'

Again, Dawn had to try to keep the surprise off her face.

'I am.'

Fenella pushed a mug of tea across the breakfast bar. 'Drink this. It might help with your upset stomach.'
'Thank you.'
'You know... I'm quite annoyed at Rick.'
'You are?'
'He shouldn't do this to you. I mean, you've just had a pregnancy scare. That's why I'm here after all, and he's decided to stay in London without warning you before hand.'
Dawn sipped her tea. She was a boiling pot of contradiction right now, torn between being angry at Rick herself and wanting to defend him from his own mother. And that was ridiculous as Fenella was actually being supportive.
'Why don't you try to get some sleep and I'll stay up for a bit. Just in case he rings.'
'But he'll probably ring my mobile if he does call.'
'Well you can leave that with me if you like so it doesn't disturb you... or take it upstairs...' Fenella smiled. 'Because you probably won't rest at all if it's not right beside you.'
Dawn nodded.
'I guess I should try to get some rest.'
'You certainly should. Now take your tea up and get into bed. Perhaps have a read.'
'Thanks, I will.'
'Dawn?'
'Yes?'
'I am only here to help, you know. I'm sorry if I sometimes seem overbearing.'
'You're not overbearing, Fenella.'
'Really?'
'Well... uh...'
Fenella nodded. 'I know I can be. I just... when Rick called me, I was extremely worried about you and the baby but I was also grateful.'
'Grateful?'
'To feel needed. That's why I wanted to help as much as I could and

cleaning was one way I hoped to make myself useful. But afterwards, I realised that perhaps it was a bit out of order. After all, this is your home and there I was sticking my nose in. Paul did warn me before I left. He told me not to try to take over, as I can be quite overpowering when I do. He said I'd soon get my marching orders if I stuck my nose in too far and look at me... I've been doing exactly that.'

'No, Fenella, I'm really grateful. Honestly.'

'Thank you, Dawn. You're too kind.' She sighed. 'You know... oh it doesn't matter.'

'No it does. Please go on.'

'Are you sure? I don't really have anyone to talk to about these things and sometimes, it all builds up.'

'You can tell me, Fenella.'

'Thank you, dear. When Paul retired, I thought we were going to do all the things we'd planned years ago. We have National Trust membership and I was looking forward to visiting the places we'd admired for so long. He used to show me all these beautiful stately homes and castles on Instagram and we'd talk about how we'd visit them.'

'And it hasn't happened?'

She shook her head. 'He's always still so busy and I don't like to ask.'

'But you should, Fenella. You have a right to spend time with him too.'

'It's like retiring gave him a new lease of life and it doesn't involve me. I can't play golf, I'm terrified of going out on that damned boat because I can't swim very well and I'm not that good on social media, so I can't even get involved with Wallace and Lulu's Instagram page.'

'You could learn how to do that. If you like, I'll show you.'

'I'd be very grateful for some lessons in that respect, Dawn.'

'No problem at all. But what will you do about Paul? You should be honest with him because perhaps he doesn't even realise that he's neglecting you.'

Fenella shrugged. 'Perhaps I will. Or I'll just get on with it, I guess. I'm good at that. My sons and their families don't live close enough to visit every week, and Dawn, please don't think that's a criticism. My husband prefers sailing and golf to taking me around stately homes and castles. All I do have to enjoy is a slightly wicked crush on a TV character.'

Dawn smiled.

'You know, Fenella... It would really help us out if you could come to stay more regularly. Perhaps you could pick the children up from school once a week – I could speak to the head teacher and get your name on the trusted contacts list – and you could help me out with the baby. Even once a fortnight if it's too far to drive on a weekly basis.'

Fenella nodded. 'That's very kind, Dawn. I promise that I won't do any cleaning unless you ask me to do it.'

'That's settled then.'

'Every other Thursday?'

'Whatever suits you.'

'Now go and get some rest, dear.'

'Thank you. Good night, Fenella.'

'Call if you need me.'

Upstairs, Dawn changed into her fluffy pyjamas then slipped under the quilt. A noise outside made her jump but she realised it was the wind. It had been breezy all day and the wind was now picking up. Perhaps the weather was changing and the Indian summer they'd talked about was on its way out.

She wondered what Rick was doing. Was he sleeping or engaged in conversation in some swanky London club? Was he poring over figures and offering advice, or was he laughing with some attractive woman who was pawing at his arm and fingering his tie as she hung on his every word...

Stop it!

This wouldn't do anyone any good.

She picked up the top book off the pile on her bedside table – a psychological thriller that had been raved about recently – and opened it. But the words swam before her eyes and she tried to read the page four times before realising that this wasn't going to work. Instead, she tried to think about her conversation with Fenella. It had been one of revelations and she hoped that their relationship would be stronger because of it. And that Fenella would feel needed, because she hated to think of anyone feeling lonely or left out. There was no need for that at all.

Chapter Ten

Dawn woke to a buzzing sound. She reached for her mobile then peered at the screen. It was six o'clock and she'd received an alert from the mobile network about cinema tickets. As if that would be her first concern on waking. She realised that she must have fallen asleep trying to meditate, as the lamp on her bedside table was still on. Exhaustion had obviously claimed her in spite of her reservations about being able to rest.
She sat up and propped the pillows up behind her then took a few deep breaths before looking at her mobile again. There were no missed calls and no text messages. Rick hadn't tried to make contact at all.
Well she was not going to spend the day moping around. There was probably a perfectly good reason why her husband had not called her and she would have to give him the benefit of the doubt or go mad. Besides, all this stress wouldn't be good for the baby.
She got up, showered, dressed then went downstairs. Fenella was in the kitchen making pancakes. Laura and James were sitting at the breakfast bar, fully dressed, tucking into pancakes covered in chopped banana.

'Good morning,' Dawn said as she kissed their heads.
'Morning, Mummy.'
'Hi, Mummy.'
'Morning, Dawn. Pancakes?'
'Uh... yes, please. I actually feel quite peckish.'
Fenella handed her a plate then loaded it with two pancakes and gestured at the bottle of maple syrup. 'You want that, bananas or both?'
'Banana will be fine, thanks.'
Fenella nodded then chopped up a banana into a bowl and passed it to Dawn.
'Thank you.' Dawn smiled at her mother-in-law and saw warmth in the older woman's eyes. It lifted her own spirits and she wondered if it was usually there, and if she failed to see it because she had a version of Fenella in her head and that version hadn't been warm and kind. Until now.
'I was thinking that I can drop the children off at school this morning then go shopping for you. Do you want to write a list?'
Dawn swallowed the banana she'd been chewing.
'That's really kind of you, thank you.'
'I'll do that then when I come back, I'll pack my things.'
'What?'
'Well it's probably time for me to be going, Dawn. Give you some space to sort things out here.'
'You don't have to do that.'
Fenella nodded. 'I do. You're better now and if you need me again, you just ring and I'll come straight back. But you and your family need some time alone to prepare for the little one.'
'But who will make me pancakes, Nanna?' James asked.
'I'll make extra then freeze them, so all your mum needs to do is heat them up in the mornings. How does that sound?'
'Like a good plan.'
Dawn smiled at her son. He was so easily bought with food.

'Nanna is going to visit more often now, so she'll be able to make you pancakes when she comes.'
'Are you, Nanna?'
Fenella nodded. 'Whenever your mummy needs me.'
Laura was chewing absently, silently, her eyes focused on something in the garden.
'Laura, what's up?'
'Nothing.'
'Are you sure?'
'I just need to check on Lulu and Wallace before school, so I'm trying to eat my breakfast quickly.'
'Good idea.'
When they'd finished eating, the children went outside and Dawn helped Fenella to tidy the kitchen.
'Thank you.'
'What for?'
'Well, for being understanding.'
'I might seem like a pompous old bag at times but I do mean well, you know.' Fenella shook the cloth she'd used to wipe the cooker top over the sink then rinsed it.
'You're not a pompous old bag.'
Fenella chuckled.
'We all go through trials in life, Dawn, and marriage certainly isn't easy. I do hope that you and Rick manage to sort this out but even if you don't, I hope you'll be happy. Life is so short.'
She placed a hand on Dawn's shoulder. 'You're a good mum and a loving wife. You deserve to be treated well. Make sure you're honest with Rick. Do not let him off the hook.'
Dawn inclined her head.
'Same goes for you with Paul.'
'Unfortunately, I'm not very good at practising what I preach.'
Fenella pressed her lips together.
'Mummy!
James ran into the kitchen.

'No, I want to say!' Laura pushed past him and stood in front of Dawn panting.
'What is it?' Dawn scanned her children's red faces, met their shining eyes.
'It's Wallace.'
Oh no... not again... The new one couldn't possibly have died too.
'What's wrong with Wallace?' Dawn steeled herself.
'Come and see!' James grabbed her hand and pulled her outside.
In the garden, Laura knelt in front of the hutch then slowly opened the door to the sleeping compartment. Dawn noticed that her daughter had put Lulu into the garden run. She steeled herself, preparing to see a stiff little body, but instead, Wallace was there, eyes wide and nose twitching as he spotted his owners.
'Wallace is a mummy!' James shouted.
Dawn stared in shock at the straw.
From behind her, Fenella laughed. 'How on earth did that happen? Wallace is a boy isn't he? And even if he wasn't... You only have one guinea pig don't you?'
'Yes.' Dawn turned to meet her mother-in-law's eyes then she winked at her. 'I'll explain later.'
'Yay! Can we keep them all?'
Dawn looked at the four tiny white guinea pigs, then at her children's delighted expressions and knew that she couldn't refuse. They'd already lost one guinea pig, even if they knew nothing about it, so she could hardly deny them this.
'I guess so. But I think we'd better give them some darkness now and close the door so they don't get cold. Wallace has a big job ahead of him... I mean her.'
'Wallace is a girl!' Laura shrieked then she held her belly as she giggled.
'Indeed she is.'
'Can we have a boy baby then Mummy, because there are too many girls now.' James frowned, his light brown brows meeting in the middle of his smooth forehead.

'I'll see what I can do.' Dawn ruffled his hair then ushered the children towards the house. 'Come on, time to get ready for school.' Fenella led them inside and Dawn turned and gazed at the garden. Lulu was hopping about in the run, stopping to nibble at the grass. Dawn realised that it was lucky that the rabbit hadn't attacked the baby guinea pigs – she thought she recalled reading that they were called pups – or even eaten them. That thought turned her stomach but she knew she'd read about rabbits turning on their own young. They would need to get another hutch now to give Wallace some space to raise her family. Especially as it had turned colder and Lulu couldn't stay out in the run all day.
More than ever, she wished her husband was here, so she could speak to him about what had happened and so that he could help her to decide on what needed to be done.
She stepped inside the kitchen and closed the door.
Then her heart leapt as she spotted Rick standing in the hallway, his face dark with stubble, his eyes red and his suit crumpled as if he'd slept in it. Laura and James were clinging to his hands, asking him why he'd come home from work at this time and Fenella was trying to get them to go upstairs to brush their teeth.
'Laura, James, go on upstairs. I'll be up in a bit.' Dawn used her strictest voice and the children listened, as if aware that their parents needed some time alone.
'I'll be upstairs if you need me.' Fenella gave a quick wave.
Then it was just Dawn and her husband and the air was filled with tension so thick she could barely breathe.
'I am so sorry,' he whispered. 'I've done something terrible.'

Dawn wobbled and Rick was suddenly beside her, taking her arm.

He helped her to a chair and she sat down then placed her palms flat on the kitchen table as if to anchor herself.

Rick took the chair next to hers and sat facing her. She noticed that he couldn't keep his hands still, he was wringing them together, his knuckles were white and his cuticles were ragged as if he'd been chewing them through the night.

'So you've done something terrible?'

'Yes. Well I think so. Although it might not be terrible... it depends how you see it, really.'

'Something unforgivable?'

'I'm not sure.'

The ground shifted beneath her and she gasped.

'Dawn?'

'I'm all right. Just a bit dizzy.'

'I am so sorry for putting you through all of this.'

'Rick, if you'd just let me know where you were last night. I was so worried.'

'God, I know.' He rubbed his eyes with the heels of his hands. 'I'm sorry, I was in such a state. Jake took me to a bar and we got drunk and... I'm just sorry. I was in no fit state to come home.'

'You didn't come home because you got drunk? What if something had been wrong with one of the children or with the baby... I wouldn't have been able to reach you.'

Dawn expected to feel anger rising again but instead a strange numbness was taking over, spreading like ice through her limbs and dulling her thoughts. Making them sluggish.

'Dawn, I'd better just get straight to the point here. I got drunk because of what I did.'

'Did you... did you cheat, Rick?'

She clamped her jaw shut to stop herself crying, although a lump had risen in her throat and her eyes were burning.

'Did I cheat?' His bloodshot eyes widened. 'Me?'

'You've been acting strangely. You've been distant. You didn't come home last night and now you're telling me you did something terrible. What's worse than cheating?'

'Dawnie, I love you, I would never cheat on you. Is that what you thought?'

'Well look at me!' She gestured at her jogging bottoms and baggy t-shirt then at her face, where she knew she had a line from a crease in the pillowcase. Her hair was pulled into a messy ponytail and she certainly didn't feel at her most attractive.

'Look at you? Dawn you're the most beautiful woman I've ever seen.'

'But right now I'm all fat and swollen and...' Her lip wobbled so she stopped talking.

'You're absolutely gorgeous. I love you so much and even if you put on twenty stone, I'd still love you because you would be you. Don't you get that? And right now, your body is changing again because you're carrying our baby. That, to me, makes you even more beautiful.'

'Really?'

He took her hands. 'Really. I'll never ever want anyone else. That's why I married you. I have never ever cheated and I never ever will.'

'So what's wrong then? Why all the secretive phone calls and longer hours and the distance between us? When you were home last week, things seemed so much better but then you stay out all night...'

'If you think I've been distant then I'm sorry. I didn't mean to be at all. I've just had a lot on my mind. I did before you found out you were pregnant again but it kind of added to the pressure.'

'It wasn't the best time, was it?'

He shook his head. 'No, but I don't care about the timing now. I'm delighted that we'll have another child, but for me, I need to be able to provide for you all. I want you to be happy and secure and if you've been feeling the opposite of that then it's an ironic mess.'

'Oh Rick.' She squeezed his hands.

'Dawn... yesterday I quit my job.'

'What?'

'I quit. Well, I didn't exactly walk out empty-handed but the

company has suffered some losses recently and they asked for volunteers to come forward to accept redundancies.'
Dawn's mouth had fallen open so she forced it shut.
'You don't need to worry, Dawnie, it's a good package. I wouldn't have considered it otherwise. I promise you that.'
'You gave up your job?'
His cheeks blanched. 'You're not happy. See, this is why I was concerned you'd think it was terrible. The last thing I want to do is to put you under more pressure. But honestly, angel, we have more than enough money to pay the mortgage and bills for two years... more if we're careful. I know it's not the best time to be careful with money with a new baby on the way but I won't just sit around doing nothing. I have some ideas... and contacts. I know people who'd give me a job tomorrow. I'll need to go into the City for a few days next week just to tie up loose ends but then I'll be free.'
Dawn started to laugh.
'Dawnie?'
'Rick, I'm not worried. We still have money that we saved when I was working. We won't be broke; I know that. And if it came to it we could sell this house and downsize.'
'I don't want to do that to you and the children.'
'No, I know. But it's always an option. And after the baby's born, I could look for work. Do some supply teaching just to keep some money coming in. I was hoping to go back to work anyway, wasn't I... before we found out we were expecting again?'
'So you're not mad?'
'Not at all. In fact, I'm delighted. Just think of the time we can spend together. It was so lovely having you home last week.'
'Well, that was one of my ideas. I could set up as an independent financial adviser. Work mainly from home and go out when necessary. It would mean I'd be around more for when baby number three comes.'
'Oh Rick I love that idea.'

Chapter Eleven

'Oooh, look Mummy!' James pointed at The Cosy Cottage Café as they walked through the gate. The path and steps were lined with pumpkins of varying sizes. Each one had a different expression and glowed in the twilight. Dawn knew they had LED tea lights inside them instead of naked flames. Allie always considered the safest option with children around, which Dawn was glad of as James's curiosity meant he'd probably try to examine their light source.
The trees in the café garden and the pergola were draped with strings of tiny pumpkin-shaped lights and a few black bats dangled from them, swaying in the gentle evening breeze.
The front of the café itself was dressed with fake cobwebs that hung from the shutters, and to the side of the front door, was a four-foot skeleton. As the café door opened and Allie emerged carrying a tray, the skeleton cackled and shook.
'Mummy, it's alive!' James grabbed her hand.
'Don't be silly, James,' Laura said. 'It's obviously activated when someone goes near it, which means it has a movement sensor.'
Dawn looked at Rick and he shrugged. 'I guess she's learned about it in school.'

'I take it that you two worked things out then?' Fenella eyed them both. 'Not my business, I know... well it is because I love you both and want you and my grandchildren to be happy... and you look... happier.'
'Everything's sorted, Fenella. Life is going to be much better now for all of us.'
'I'll fill you in later, Mum,' Rick said. 'But right now I think we'd better go and check that James isn't handling the new additions to the family. He'll scare them half to death.'
'And we don't want another dead guinea pig round here.' Dawn gasped as she realised what she'd just said.
Fenella frowned. 'Another dead guinea pig?'
'Something else I'll explain,' Rick said.
They followed Fenella out into the garden and Dawn's heart was so full of love that she thought she might just float off into the sky, if Rick wasn't holding her hand so tight.

'Of course.'
Relief washed over her.
'Rick, I'm so relieved. I spoke to Camilla and she insisted it was nothing to worry about and said she'd speak to you. It all makes sense now. She was probably going to tell you to talk to me about it, so I'd stop worrying.'
He opened his arms and she moved into them, sitting on his lap as he kissed her gently.
'I thought I was losing you.'
'You'll never lose me.'
'I love you.'
'And I love you.'
'Daddy!' James shot into the kitchen closely pursued by a red-faced Fenella.
'James! Come here right now. I'm so sorry. I told him you needed time to talk but he was desperate to tell you.' Fenella straightened her blouse.
'Daddy!'
'No let me tell him.' Laura ran up to her father and took hold of his face. 'Stop looking at Mummy for a minute and concentrate.'
Rick winked at Dawn then nodded at his daughter.
'Laura, you have my undivided attention.'
'Good.'
'It's Wallace,' James blurted. 'He's a girl.'
'James!' Laura turned to her brother. 'Shut up.'
'Wallace is a girl?' Rick's eyebrows shot up and colour flooded his cheeks then he started laughing. 'Well that's a shocker. But how do you know for sure?'
Laura folded her arms and rolled her eyes. 'She had babies Daddy.'
'Babies?'
'Yes. Lots of tiny white babies and Mummy said we're going to keep them all.' James jumped up and down. 'Yay for baby guinea pigs!'
'Let's go and see them again, James.'
The children hurried out into the garden.

'And if you want to return to work next year, then that's up to you, but you know you don't need to.'

'I know that, but I think I'd like to. Even if it's just for a day or two a week.'

Her heart soared as she let everything sink in. Rick wouldn't be working such long hours anymore. He wouldn't have to leave for the train at the crack of dawn or return after Laura and James had gone to bed. It would be so good for the children. So good for them.

Then a thought struck her like a bucket of ice-cold water.

The email.

There was still the issue of the email.

'Rick.'

'Yes.'

'There's one more thing.'

He nodded.

'I was upset... because I'd got it into my head that you were cheating. And I'm so glad that isn't the case but I did something I shouldn't have.'

'You did?' He watched her, his hazel eyes wary.

'I went into your email account.'

He shrugged. 'I wouldn't have thought you'd do that but there's nothing in there to worry about.'

'I found an email. Titled FYEO. About a weekend away. From another woman. Brianna Mandrell.'

Understanding filled his eyes.

'Ahhhhh...'

'But you're not cheating?'

He smiled. 'No, but I'm gutted you found that. It was meant to be a surprise. I was trying to organise a weekend away for us without the children. I'd enlisted Camilla and your mother to take care of Laura and James. I wanted to take you away for a weekend of pampering, to ensure that you got some rest and so that we could have some quality time together.'

'It was about a booking for us?'

'Or watching the Discovery Channel.'
'Hello!' Allie called as she approached them, depositing the tray she was carrying on a nearby table.

In keeping with the café theme, Allie was dressed as a giant pumpkin. She was wearing black tights and boots with a velvet pumpkin dress that hung to her knees. On her head was a green headband with a thick green stalk sticking out of it. She'd tied her hair back and painted her face orange.

'You look amazing, Allie. You always make such an effort.'

Allie smiled warmly.

'Have you seen Jordan and Max yet?'

Dawn looked around and spotted the young men at the drinks table. She took in their matching grey werewolf costumes. They'd outlined their eyes with coal pencil and drawn whiskers around their stick on snouts.

'I told them they'd terrify the children looking like that but Jordan insisted that kids these days aren't scared by werewolves. Popular culture means that if they saw a zombie walking along the street they wouldn't bat an eyelid.' Allie shook her head.

'How things change, eh?'

'And you guys look great! Laura, I think you are the scariest vampire I've ever seen.'

'I'm not a vampire, I'm a witch.'

'Oh!' Allie grimaced at Dawn. 'Of course you are. And James… you are a terrifying ghost.'

'You can see me?'

'Who said that?' Allie frowned and batted the air around her, causing James to giggle.

'You can see me when I say you can,' James said, throwing back the hood of the white robe that Dawn had fashioned out of an old sheet. It was a simple costume but James had insisted that he wanted to be a ghost like the ones in the old movies, because then he could be invisible. 'See me now!' He clapped his hands and Allie gasped.

'Well that's just amazing.'

James giggled. Dawn wasn't convinced that he believed he was invisible but he was enjoying himself, so it didn't really matter.

'Allie, did you hear about Wallace?' Laura asked.

'No...' Allie glanced at Dawn and Dawn shook her head.

'He's a she and she had babies.'

'Really?' Allie raised her eyebrows. 'That's amazing.'

Dawn bit her lip to hold her laughter in. She had told her friend about the replacement guinea pig's surprise delivery the previous Tuesday, when she'd met up with her friends at the café, but she'd told Allie that the children would probably want to tell her all about it themselves.

'I had my suspicions that something was wrong because Wallace was so fat.' Laura nodded.

'You did?'

'Yes. And... the strangest thing was that his... *her*... eyes changed colour.'

'Did they?' Dawn blurted the question before she could stop herself.

'Oh yes. I noticed that there was something different about Wallace at the same time I noticed that she was fatter.'

'I see.' Rick's smile was getting bigger by the minute.

'Wallace's eyes were pinky-red but they changed to blue. It must have been because she was going to have babies.' Laura folded her arms and turned to Dawn. 'When will your eyes change colour, Mummy?'

Dawn gulped under her daughter's scrutiny and Allie snorted loudly.

'What? What's wrong?' Laura asked. 'Why is that funny?'

Rick squeezed his daughter's shoulder. 'We'll talk about it later, angel. I think Mummy and I need to explain a few things to you.'

'Yes, I think we do,' Dawn said.

'Oh, OK. Can we go and get a drink, Mummy?' Laura asked.

'Of course.'

Laura and James went over to the drinks table and James tugged on Jordan's furry tail. Jordan kept turning around, pretending not to know who was there.

'Well that's something we can't allow her to believe, Rick.' Dawn shook her head. 'I think we'll have to tell her the truth about Wallace.'
'She's pretty sensible, Dawn, so I think she'll understand why you did it.' Allie smiled.
'I think she will, too. At least if she is sad about Wallace the first, the new guinea pigs will help to cheer her up. Although I do miss the original Wallace, I have to be honest.'
'Well you'll have our new baby to cheer you up soon.' Rick slid his arm around Dawn's shoulders. 'And this is yet another amazing party, Allie.'
'Most of this was down to Jordan and Max. They're a very efficient couple. Although, I have to admit that Chris did prepare a lot of the food.'
'Again? Wow, he's definitely a keeper.' Dawn didn't try to hide her delight from Allie. She was so happy that her friend had found such a good man.
'Come and have a look at the food. It's incredible.'
'I'll keep an eye on the children.' Rick kissed Dawn's cheek.
She went over to the long trestle table that was covered in an orange cloth, and eyed the Halloween delights that Chris had made that afternoon. Savoury foods included witch fingers, ham and cheese bread bones, mummy dogs, pumpkin risotto and cheese and pretzel broomsticks. Then there were toffee apples, chocolate apples, chocolate bat-shaped cookies, meringue ghost tartlets and mini mice cakes. Chris was standing behind the trestle table wearing a black suit and cape, complete with drawn-on widow's peak and plastic fangs.
'Hello, Dawn! Can I offer you a mummy dog?'
She laughed. 'Not just yet thank you, Nosferatu, but they do look delicious.'
'Nothing but the best for the village.' He winked. 'You might also want to try the blood beetroot mocktail that Jordan is serving. The cocktail version is pretty tasty but I know that at the moment...' He nodded at her bump.
'No alcohol for me.' Dawn placed a hand on her belly. 'Only another

twenty or so weeks to go, depending on whether baby comes early, on time or late. And even after she arrives, I'll be unable to drink for a while if I'm breastfeeding.'

She realised Allie and Chris were staring at her.

'What? Is it because I said breastfeeding?'

Allie's eyes had filled with tears.

'No. You said... *she*.'

Dawn gasped. 'So I did! We weren't going to tell people but we found out at the twenty-week scan. Rick said not to ask but it was quite clear that there was no little penis there.'

'Oh that's so wonderful! Congratulations!' Allie hugged her.

'Don't say anything, though. We need to tell Laura and James first and I don't think our son will be too pleased.'

'He wants a brother?' Chris asked.

'Really badly. And after finding out that Wallace number two was a girl, well... he feels outnumbered.'

'You can always try for a boy next time.' Allie winked.

'We'll see. I know we're making some big changes to our lives but this baby was a surprise, so I don't know about a fourth one.'

'And sorry about the hiccup with Wallace.' Chris shook his head. 'It was just such a rush to find a replacement that I didn't think to check. And then for her to be pregnant on top of it.'

'Don't worry about it. The children are delighted to have all the pups too.'

'Shall we get a drink?' Allie asked.

'Lovely.'

At the drinks table, Allie ladled a ruby coloured liquid into two plastic cups.

'Do you want to sit down?'

Dawn nodded so they took seats under the pergola.

'How're you feeling now?' Allie asked.

'Much better. Clearing the air was the best thing we could have done. And now that Rick is going to be home all the time... well...' Dawn leaned back in her seat and stared up at the tiny pumpkin lights. 'I just feel so lucky.'

'I'm so glad it worked out for you both.'

'Thank you for being there for me. You're such a good friend.'

'Stop it or you'll have me tearing up again.'

'Anyway, cheers!' Dawn held out her plastic cup. 'Here's to the future.'

'A future that looks very bright indeed.'

They tapped their cups together.

'And how is Fenella?'

Dawn had outlined the basics about her chat with her mother-in-law when they'd met up last week, and about their plans for Fenella to visit more regularly, but she'd held back the more personal details, of course.

'Well… I told Rick about how his mother was feeling; I couldn't keep it from him really, and he insisted on speaking to his father. Paul admitted that he'd probably got a bit carried away with his hobbies since he retired, then he promised to make more of an effort with his wife. I rang Fenella yesterday to ask if she's coming to stay this Thursday, and she said she'd have loved to but she can't as Paul is taking her to Cornwall… Poldark spotting!'

'No!' Allie laughed.

'Yes! She's delighted. She even asked me if I thought she might see Aidan with his shirt off.'

Allie clutched her stomach as she laughed and Dawn covered her bump with her hands; the baby was fluttering there, as if she was enjoying the joke too.

'I hope you told her to take lots of photos if she does see him.'

'Of course.'

'Hello darlings!' Camilla sashayed towards them. 'What's so funny?'

Dawn's jaw hit the ground as she looked at her sister's outfit.

'Camilla, that's what I call a costume.' Allie wolf-whistled. 'It's like that scene out of Grease when Sandy turns up all sexy.'

'Are you all right, Dawn?' Camilla asked.

'Yes... fine... I just saw your... costume and... wow!'
'It's a little something I had in the cupboard.'
'You fibber.'
'OK, well it's a little something I ordered especially for this evening.'
'From the cat-alogue?' Allie giggled.
'I don't care where you got it from, Camilla, but I don't think it's appropriate for a children's party.' Dawn eyed her sister. 'It's barely there.'
Camilla was wearing a metallic-black wet-look jumpsuit with a zip-up front, slashed leg detailing and cut out shoulders. It clung to her svelte frame like a second skin. To top it off, she had on a black cat mask that covered her eyes and forehead and sparkled with silver glitter. Her short dark hair had been gelled into spikes.
'I've just popped by to say hello. I'm off to another party later on.'
'Oh?' Dawn raised her eyebrows.
'Yes, *oh*.' Camilla grinned.
'In the village?'
Camilla nodded.
'Is it at the new vet's house?' Allie asked.
'That's the one.'
'We had invites too but I didn't really fancy going. I'm quite partial to my evenings on the sofa followed by an early night.' Dawn thought about the past couple of nights, where after the children had gone to bed, she and Rick would cuddle up on the sofa and watch TV together. It was so nice, so much better than sitting alone wondering what time he'd come home. She had asked Rick if he wanted to go to the fancy-dress party, suggested asking her mother to babysit, but he'd told her he just wanted to know his children were safely tucked up in bed and that his wife was in his arms. It was almost like they were rediscovering each other all over again and Dawn knew that she didn't want to be anywhere else of an evening either. There would be plenty of time for parties and the like after baby number three joined them.
'Chris and I would have gone too but it'll be late by the time we've

cleaned up here and he's got edits to work on tomorrow, so a late night isn't the best thing for him.'

'Well you party poopers, I intend to enjoy myself.'

'Hold on…' Allie placed a finger on her lips. 'Isn't the new vet… what's his name—'

'Tom.' Camilla blurted.

'That's it! Tom Stone. Isn't he pretty good-looking?'

Dawn watched her sister's cheeks darken.

'He's all right. For a vet.'

'Is that why you're looking so sexy?' Dawn giggled. 'You fancy the vet.'

'I do not.' Camilla pouted. 'And keep your voices down, won't you? I don't want this getting back to him.'

'What because that outfit won't give him ideas?'

'You know I don't date anyone from the village,' Camilla said. 'It's far too risky to get involved with someone local.'

'Perhaps he'll offer you a free examination though.' Allie snorted. 'You know, with you being a cat and all. He might even take your temperature…'

'Oh stop it.' Camilla flicked the stick on tail that she'd been toying with. 'I'm just going to a party, I'll have a few drinks then I'll head home. *Alone.*'

'Just be careful.' Dawn pointed a finger at her sister. 'But have fun.'

'What's all this then?' Rick asked as he joined them.

'Camilla's having a night on the tiles.' Allie blurted.

'She's like a cat on a hot tin roof.' Dawn added.

'Watch you don't get stuck in the cat flap if you get home late.' Rick joined in.

'Right, that's it, I'm off. I'm not staying here for you to poke fun at me.'

'Ring me in the morning.' Dawn met her sister's green eyes. 'Let me know how it goes.'

'OK, Dawnie.' Camilla kissed her cheeks then Allie's before sauntering along the path and out onto the street.

'I hope she knows what she's doing,' Allie said.
'She probably does. My sister never does anything without thinking it through. Although he must be pretty special if she's breaking her no dating anyone from the village rule.'
'Let's hope so. Anyway, I'd better go and give Chris a hand.' Allie got up and took Dawn's empty cup. 'You want a refill?'
'Not just yet, thanks.'
'Why's Camilla so dressed up?' Rick sat next to Dawn.
'Fancies the vet.'
'Does she now? But Camilla never dates anyone local.'
'Perhaps this time is different.'
'I take it he's hot then?' Laughter danced in his eyes.
'I have no idea.'
'You can tell me.'
'I haven't seen him yet.'
'Shall we fabricate an animal emergency so we can check him out?'
'Rick...' Dawn nudged him. 'We can't do that.'
'Sure we can. Actually we've had an animal emergency, haven't we? We could ask him to come round to check on the baby guinea pigs.'
'Oh, I don't know.'
'Don't you want to make sure he's good enough for Camilla?'
'I'm sure she can take care of herself. She's been doing it for long enough.'
Camilla had protected her heart for all of her adult life, but Dawn always worried that her sister would get hurt at some point. If she hadn't already been hurt that was. After all, it wouldn't be like Camilla to let on if she had been.
Squeals of excitement broke into her thoughts and she looked over to where Jordan was guiding tiny ghosts, pumpkins, fairies, witches and skeletons around the garden. It seemed that some of the children were looking for clues in some sort of monster treasure hunt. Max, meanwhile, was supervising the games of Frankenstein bowling, which involved knocking down tins painted with monster faces, and every time someone hit them over, there was a loud cheer.

'We're so lucky to live in Heatherlea,' Dawn said, as Rick wrapped an arm around her shoulders.
'Wouldn't want to be anywhere else.'
'Are you sure?' Dawn asked her husband as she gazed into his eyes.
'Never been more certain about anything. I love you Dawn Dix-Beaumont and I always will do.'
He cupped her chin then kissed her gently.
'Oh!' she gasped.
'What is it?'
'Feel.' She guided his hand to her belly and he smiled.
'Little one is busy tonight.'
'She certainly is.'
'Just like her mum always is.'
'Not as much now that you're home.'
'And I bet she'll be beautiful… just like her mum.'
'Thank you.'
'No, Dawnie, thank you.'
'What for?'
'For making me happier than I could have wished for.'
Dawn sighed with contentment as she snuggled into him.
'I'm happier than I ever could have imagined too.'
And they stayed that way for some time, on a perfectly cool and crisp autumn evening, watching their two children as they played on the lawn of The Cosy Cottage Café.
Life wasn't always perfect; there were bumps and grooves in the road, and there would no doubt be more ups and downs along the way. But Dawn and Rick had each other and their wonderful family, so they knew that they would be OK.

The End

Winter at the Cosy Cottage Café

Winter at The Cosy Cottage Café

Camilla Dix has kept her heart firmly closed to love. Tom Stone moved to Heatherlea for a fresh start. When Camilla and Tom meet, they can't deny their mutual attraction, but can they trust each other enough to let love in this Christmas in Heatherlea?

Chapter One

'Would you like it wrapped?'
'I'm sorry?'
'The scarf. Is it a gift for someone?' The shop assistant blinked, drawing Camilla's attention to the larger-than-life false black lashes that surrounded her big blue eyes.
'Oh! Yes... yes, please.'
Camilla nodded and watched as the younger woman, who could well have been a university student with a Christmas job, produced a perfect square of gold foil paper then wrapped the gift effortlessly, before adorning it with a shiny red bow.
'There! How's that?'
'Fabulous, thank you so much.'
'Would you like a bag?'
'No, thanks. I'll tuck in here.' Camilla held up her Marc Jacobs leopard-print cotton-canvas tote – that had cost her over three hundred pounds in July, then she'd spotted in the sales a week later with fifty percent off – and the shop assistant nodded her approval.
Camilla slipped her credit card from her purse and slid it into the payment machine on the counter. As she went through the familiar

process of typing in her pin then waiting for the transaction to be processed, she gazed around the department store. Bright strip lights in the ceiling gave everything a surreal glow and bounced off shiny surfaces, mirrors and metallic clothes stands. (She was surprised the shop workers didn't have permanent migraines.) People shuffled around like penguins, weighed down by their shopping bags, picking up items then discarding them as their eyes were drawn to other, better gifts. Strategically placed Christmas trees dressed with this year's must-have festive decorations reminded shoppers that Christmas was on its way and that they didn't have long to find the perfect presents for colleagues, friends and loved ones. And from the speakers around the store, carols blared, adding to the sense of urgency while disguising it as a time of fun, relaxation and togetherness.

Scarf paid for, Camilla tucked her card back into her purse then took the gold package from the counter and carefully put it into her bag. She wished the shop assistant a merry Christmas, but the woman was already peering at the next customer. Camilla sighed; a handsome young man carrying a box of luxury crackers and a pair of corduroy slippers had quickly replaced her.

She pushed her way through the crowds, which wasn't easy as she was going against the flow, then emerged onto the cold street where she gratefully filled her lungs with the icy December air.

Despite her best intentions, she had failed to complete all of her Christmas shopping by mid-November, and instead, it was the first weekend of December and Oxford Street was heaving. Still, there was no time to regret being disorganised; she had gifts to buy, so she'd better get on with it.

She hoisted her tote onto her shoulder then set off towards Selfridges. The regal exterior of the department store always lifted her spirits with its towering stone columns and the ornate clock at the building's main entrance. The window displays were as famous as the store itself, and the Christmas ones always attracted a lot of excitement and attention.

Camilla stopped in front of the nearest window and smiled. It featured a ski lift with Santa Claus in his traditional red suit the middle, with skis strapped to his feet, and on either side of him sat two mannequins. They wore festive outfits and ice-skates as if they were ready to slip off the lift and onto the ice at any moment. Beneath the lift was a pile of soft white snow that looked good enough to dive into headfirst, and tiny white reindeer frolicked at the front of the window.

Camilla moved along and found a space at the next window. This time, Santa Claus was decked out in a red sequin outfit with his fur trimmed hat perched at a jaunty angle on his head. He was emerging from a white personal jet and in each hand he held a lead, at the end of which were two grey toy poodles. In this scene, one of the mannequins wore checked pyjamas while the other wore a knee-length fur gilet and high waisted blue trousers. Suitcases lay scattered around them and some of them were open, spilling their contents – including hot water bottles, fluffy socks and hats – onto the snow. The scene was framed by towering evergreens decked with sparkling white fairy lights. As she gazed at the plane, Camilla wished, not for the first time, that she'd arranged to go away for Christmas. After all, it wasn't as if she hadn't had offers…

Harlan Wright, a long time friend of Camilla's, had invited her to New York for a ten-day trip. A native New Yorker, he jetted around the world with his freelance photography business. The first time Camilla had met him, at a bar in Soho, he'd raved about her looks and told her she could be the modern day Elizabeth Taylor with her delicate features and cropped dark hair. Camilla had been three Manhattans in by then and suspected he was hitting on her until he'd introduced her to his boyfriend, Lance Havisham, a movie extra who'd appeared in lots of films Camilla had never heard of and didn't think she ever wanted to watch.

She'd also been invited to spend Christmas with Malcolm Ferguson, a Scottish Venison farmer. They'd been introduced by a mutual acquaintance at an international rugby match. Malcolm was a giant of a man with a fashionably bald head and thick sandy beard, and had once played rugby himself, but been forced to quit because of a shoulder injury sustained when he was kicked by a pregnant doe. Camilla quite fancied Malcolm, but apart from a physical attraction to him, there wasn't much else she was drawn to and she'd worried that accepting his invitation to snuggle in front of a smouldering yule log while sipping Scotch might send the wrong message.

Then there had been William Roscoe, the wealthy Englishman ten years her senior, who reminded her of Hugh Grant. She had a very soft spot for William. In fact, she had, up until October, wondered what it might be like to allow her friendship with him to develop into something more permanent. Though she hadn't admitted this to anyone else, of course. He had money, a large house in Kent, and a villa in Malcesine on Lake Garda, and he'd asked her to fly to Italy with him and some friends to enjoy Christmas at the lake. But she'd hesitated when he'd invited her, not really sure why at the time, although she'd told him it was because her mother would need her at home to help with the festivities.

In reality, there was another reason why she couldn't bring herself to accept, and Camilla knew it was a very silly reason indeed. It had something to do with a particular vet...

'Penny for them!'

Camilla turned to find her close friend, Allie Jones, smiling at her from beneath a woolly russet beret.

'Allie...' Camilla flung her arms around the other woman's neck, delighted to have been rescued from her thoughts.

'You OK, lovely?' Allie asked as Camilla released her.

'Yes... well, kind of. It's just great to see you. Is Chris with you?' Camilla peered over Allie's shoulder and scanned the crowds for the George Clooney lookalike.

'No, I came into London alone today so I could shop in peace. Jordan and Chris are looking after the café.'

'Well if I'd known, I'd have caught the train with you.'

Allie smiled. 'It was a bit last minute to be honest but now we're here, why don't we go shopping together?'

'That's a great plan.' Camilla hooked her arm through Allie's. 'And how about if we start with a glass of bubbly in the Selfridges Champagne Bar?'

Allie's blue eyes lit up. 'You had me at bubbly!'

'Come on then.'

They made their way through the crowds admiring the window displays, and into the department store, with Camilla nursing a secret delight that she'd bumped into her friend, because Allie would take her mind off her own musings as well as helping her to make the most of the festive atmosphere.

'I don't think I should have had two glasses of champagne, Camilla. You're a bad influence.' Allie giggled as they wandered around brightly-lit Wonder Room in Selfridges. 'What if I accidentally buy something really expensive?'

Camilla smiled. 'You deserve it.'

'Not if I bankrupt myself and Chris in the process.'

Camilla shook her head. 'I'm sure he'd live in a cardboard box as long as it was with you.'

Allie blushed and her eyes took on that far away look she got whenever Chris was mentioned. 'I'm so happy, Camilla. I still have to pinch myself every morning when I wake up and see his handsome face on the pillow next to me, just to make sure I'm not dreaming.'

'You deserve to be happy, Allie. You weren't for a long time.'

Allie had spent years single after the death of her husband Roger. She had focused on being a mother to her children and on building her business The Cosy Cottage Café. Her daughter, Mandy, lived in London where she worked in publishing, and her son, Jordan, helped run the café along with his boyfriend, Max. That summer, author Chris Monroe had returned to the village of Heatherlea for his mother's funeral and realised that the feelings he once had for Allie – before her marriage to Roger – were still there. Luckily, the feeling was mutual. They were so in tune that Camilla often thought they could have been together for years not months, as if time had fallen away and they'd never been apart.

'And what about you, Camilla?' Allie squeezed her arm as they stopped in front of a glass display case full of sparkling diamond engagement rings. 'Still no one special?'

Camilla suppressed a groan. She loved her friends and her sister, Dawn, but they often asked her about her own love life and it wasn't something she'd ever liked to discuss. Mainly because she felt that if she kept it to herself, then it would remain uneventful and within her control, just the way she liked it.

'Nope. You know me, Allie. I'm independent and that's the way I want to stay.'

'Just because you have a relationship with someone, it doesn't mean you have to lose your independence.'

'I know. But I do worry that I would. If I ever fell in love.' She sighed. 'Which is never going to happen.'

'Never say never.' Allie leaned forwards to look at some of the rings. 'Ooh! I almost forgot about the vet. Still nothing going on there?'

Camilla cringed. For the past month, since Halloween in fact, she'd done her best to avoid these questions from Dawn and her friends and had become adept at changing the subject quickly to divert their attention.

'Let's go and look at the Cartier watches. You know they make some of the finest—'

'Oh no you don't!' Allie shook her head. 'Not today, Camilla Dix. I know you've avoided this question since the Halloween party at the vet's house... What's his name again? Tom Stone isn't it? Anyway, I want to know what happened and I'm not moving until you tell me.'

Allie crossed her arms and stood facing Camilla, her blonde eyebrows meeting above her nose and her mouth screwed into a pout. Camilla couldn't help herself; she burst into laughter.

'What? What's funny?'

'You, you daft woman. Scowling doesn't suit you, Allie. You're far too sweet for that.'

'See... distraction techniques again. Just tell me what happened.'

'OK. OK. I will. But it's not a pretty story.'

Camilla took a deep breath and glanced around to check that no one was in danger of accidentally eavesdropping, then she met Allie's curious gaze before exhaling.

'So you really want to know?'

'I do.'

'OK then. On Halloween, I went to the party...'

Chapter Two

'And?'

'Promise you won't tell anyone?' Camilla scanned the jewellery department of Selfridges and realised that there was no escape. She'd have to tell Allie about Halloween.

Allie raised her eyebrows.

'OK, well promise you won't tell anyone other than Chris? I don't expect you to keep secrets from him.'

'It depends on whether this is something you need help with... from Dawn and Honey. You know they think the world of you.'

'I think the world of them too. I mean... Dawn is my baby sister, so of course I adore her and I don't want to keep secrets from her. It's just that Halloween was quite... embarrassing.'

'But why?' Allie reached out and rubbed Camilla's upper arm. 'What could have happened that was so bad you haven't told us about it?'

Camilla chewed her bottom lip.

'Well you know I was dressed as a cat?'

'Yes.' Allie smiled. 'If I recall correctly, you were wearing a rather sexy cat costume.'

Heat crawled up Camilla's throat and into her cheeks.

'Well I went to that party feeling quite smug and satisfied, in spite of the cat jokes that you all subjected me to before I left the café.'

'Sorry, lovely, we were only teasing.'

'I know that.' Camilla ran a hand through her short hair as she wondered if Allie would judge her. But of course she wouldn't; Allie had a heart of gold. 'Anyway… when I arrived at Tom's house, the party was in full swing. There were some people there from the village but there were also some I didn't know, including the man who let me in then handed me a glass of wine. I downed the drink pretty quickly because I was so nervous.'

'You were nervous?'

Camilla nodded.

'I don't think I've ever seen you nervous, except for when you're worried about Dawn.'

'Well I was. I don't know if it's because I was at a stranger's house or because I wanted to make a good impression or because I was wearing that ridiculous costume, which compared to everyone else's seemed rather risqué.'

'Oh no!' Allie shook her head.

'Oh yes. They were dressed up but as zombies and movie characters, there was even one bloke dressed as a pumpkin and his costume was so big he was having trouble fitting through the doors. I felt a bit… exposed, to be honest. So I had another wine, thinking it would give me some courage to go and speak to Tom, but it was quite strong and my head started to spin. I didn't want to approach him and slur, so I let myself out into the back garden for some fresh air.' She swallowed hard. 'And while I was out there…'

'Yes?' Allie nodded, her eyes wide as she waited in anticipation for the rest of the story.

'While I was out there, I met Tom's dog.'

'He has a dog?'

'A rescue dog.'

'What breed?'

'A British bulldog. He's huge. His shoulders are like that.' Camilla held out her hands to show Allie just how big.
'I love bulldogs. They have such squishy faces.'
Camilla shuddered. 'This one had a squishy face all right but it wasn't cute when he started growling at me.'
'Yikes!'
'Exactly. Anyway, it was dark outside and I didn't see him lying on the decking, so I tripped over him. Tom later told me that the dog likes to go out to cool down and with all the people there, it was really warm in the house.'
'He isn't friendly then? If he was growling at you?'
Camilla shivered at the memory. 'It was because I startled him and as a rescue dog, he's a bit jumpy, but once he realised I was vulnerable… you know, because I was face down on the decking after tripping over him, he decided to make friends with me.'
Allie snorted.
'It's not funny. He's so heavy and when he came and stood over me, I just couldn't get up. Then he…' She shook her head. 'Remember that I was lying there dressed as a cat. A sexy bloody cat!'
Allie was visibly trying to control her mirth.
'How did you get him off?'
'I couldn't. He had me trapped and he wrapped those muscular front legs around my thigh and went for gold.' She rubbed her eyes as if she could erase the memory. 'He took advantage of me.'
Allie turned away for a moment but her shoulders were shaking.
'I know you're laughing and this was why I didn't tell you. It was traumatic and I kept trying to move out from under him but it just made him more excited.'
'I'm sorry, Camilla. It must have been terrifying.'
'Kind of. But I was in shock more than anything. Then, just when I thought I was done for, the back door opened and the security light came on.'
'Like a spotlight?'
'Yes. It's positioned so it highlights the decking. Shame I didn't see

the switch next to the back door as I might not have tripped over the dog. Anyway... Tom came out.'
'And caught you?'
'Yes. He peered at us first of all then his face dropped and he shouted at the dog to stop. But it wasn't just that... it was the dog's name.'
'What's he called?'
'Hairy Pawter.'
Allie guffawed and her eyes shone. 'Really? Hairy Pawter took advantage of you?'
'Yes. So Tom's there shouting 'Stop it, Hairy Pawter!' And I'm there whimpering and wriggling then...'
'What?' Allie's eyes were wide as saucers.
'Everyone else came out to see what was going on.' Camilla covered her face as her cheeks burned.
'So everyone at the party saw you being humped by Hairy Pawter while you were dressed as a sexy cat?'
'Yes.'
A tear slipped from Allie's eye and rolled down her cheek. 'I'm sorry but this is the funniest thing I've heard in ages.'
'I know. And if I hadn't been so humiliated, I'd have found it funny too.' Camilla started to giggle, her embarrassment fading slightly as she shared the story with her friend. 'And with champagne inside me, it actually does seem quite amusing.'
'What happened then?'
'Tom managed to get the dog off then he helped me up. He asked me if I was hurt but I wasn't, just a bit shaken. He was very nice and polite and apologetic and he actually told me that it means Hairy Pawter likes me.'
'Kind of a doggy sign of approval?'
'Exactly.'
'Did you stay for the rest of the party?'
'Did I hell! I made my excuses then scarpered.'
'Have you seen him since?'

'Twice. Once as he was going into the post office and once when I drove past as he was out running. But I pretended not to see him.'
'You know, Camilla, I bet he was embarrassed that his dog did that to you. He's new to the village and he had that party to try to get to know people then you were assaulted by his dog.'
'Who knows, eh?'
'It's a shame really as we... Dawn and I... thought you seemed to fancy him.'
'He's an attractive man but I had no intention of going after him. We live in the same village and imagine if we did have a fling and it ended badly. It's simply not part of my love them and leave them policy.'
'You don't really do that though, do you, Camilla?' Allie's pupils dilated and Camilla felt as though her friend could see into her heart.
'Course I do, Allie. No commitment for me.' Allie nodded but Camilla wasn't sure if her friend believed her. 'Let's get shopping, shall we?'
'Of course. Shall we start with something for Honey?'
Camilla nodded and they set off around Selfridges to try to find the perfect gift for their very sweet friend.

Chapter Three

'How did your shopping trip go?' Dawn asked Camilla as they sat down to Sunday lunch at their mother's the next day.
'It was fairly successful.' Camilla dropped a scoop of mashed potatoes onto her plate then handed the bowl to Dawn's husband, Rick. 'I still need to get a few things before the big day...' She glanced at her sister's children, Laura and James, and found them both staring at her, eyes wide.
'You went Christmas shopping, Auntie Camilla?' Laura asked.
'I did. In London where all the best shops are.'
'What did you buy?'
'I can't tell you because some of it's for you and James.'
'Awwwww!' James pouted. 'Whisper it!'
'Uh uh.' Camilla shook her head.
'Kids leave your Auntie Camilla alone.' Rick dropped a scoop of mash onto Laura's plate then one on James's before passing the bowl to his wife.
'Anyone fancy a glass of wine with dinner?' Jackie waltzed into the dining room with a bottle of Chablis in her hand.

'That would be lovely, Mum.' Camilla got up and fetched the wine glasses from the dresser.

'Not for me.' Dawn grimaced as she pointed at her bump. 'Not for about another thirteen weeks.'

'You could have a drop, Dawnie,' Camilla said as she took the bottle from her mother and filled three glasses.

'The heartburn is already so bad that I wouldn't want to risk it.' Dawn replied as she raised her glass of water. 'But cheers anyway. You three enjoy.'

They tucked into Jackie's roast chicken dinner as The Carpenters' Greatest Hits flowed into the room from the speakers on top of the dresser. Camilla looked around the table at her family. Jackie looked good for sixty-five with her short black hair and bright green eyes, but there was always something in her mother's gaze that made Camilla sad. It was, she knew, because Jackie had never got over her husband leaving her when the girls were young and she'd never been able to move on. In fact, she was rather vocal about it a lot of the time and it had affected Camilla growing up, as had the fact that her father had walked out on them, of course. She'd veered on the side of caution, never wanting to commit to a man, while Dawn had been almost desperate to create a stable family of her own where she could be the perfect wife and mother.

Over the past year, Dawn and Rick had been through some ups and downs, and Camilla had been quite worried for a while there, especially when Dawn had admitted that she was pregnant with her third child and that the baby hadn't been planned. But during the autumn, her sister and brother-in-law had managed to work through their problems and were now happier than ever. Which pleased Camilla immensely, as she wanted nothing more than to see her sister, her niece and nephew happy and settled. And Rick too for that matter. He was a good man and he clearly loved Dawn. He'd left his high-flying job in the City recently and the flexibility of working from home suited him. He looked healthier and more contented than ever. As for Laura and James, they physically – in Camilla's eyes, at least –

were a mixture of their parents, but their mannerisms and idiosyncrasies often reminded her of Dawn as a child. The children were happy and funny and a joy to be around. Camilla enjoyed spending time with them, especially on Sunday afternoons after lunch, when she could curl up on the sofa with them and listen to them talk about their week. Laura often entertained her with stories about their guinea pig, Wallace, and her babies, as well as tales of Lulu the rabbit and how she was adapting to being an auntie to the small guinea pigs. Camilla knew that Dawn had tried to gently persuade the children to consider giving the baby guinea pigs away, but Laura and James had been stubborn, and Rick had suggested keeping them because – as he'd said – he was home now so could help to care for them. This had led to them buying extra hutches for their garden and to Rick and his father, Paul Beaumont, erecting a larger shed in the back garden where the animals could live during the winter months. The shed resembled a Canadian log cabin and Camilla quite fancied staying in it herself.

As for Camilla's life, she lived alone in a small cottage on the outskirts of Heatherlea, that was a five-minute walk from Jackie's and, in the other direction, from Dawn's. Her family members were close enough that she could get to them with ease but far enough away to allow her some space. Although recently, even though she still kept busy running her accountancy business, with regular meetings with clients and trips into London, she'd begun to feel that something might be missing. Coming home to an empty cottage, however pretty and cosy it might be, wasn't as much fun as it had once been. She suspected it just had something to do with the dark nights and mornings that came with winter and that as soon as spring made an appearance; she'd feel more positive again.

'More wine, Camilla?' Jackie held up the bottle.

'No thanks, Mum. I haven't drunk this glass yet.'

Camilla took a sip of the Chablis and enjoyed its honeyed-stone fruit flavour balanced with a pleasant minerality.

'Rick?' Jackie held up the bottle.

'Just half a glass, thank you. I've promised Laura and James a kick around later, once dinner goes down.'

Jackie poured wine into his glass then filled her own. Camilla swallowed her surprise as her mother knocked back her drink then refilled her glass again. She was about to make a joke of it when Jackie raised shiny eyes to meet Camilla's. Now might not be the best time to raise the topic, even in jest. Her mother had never had an alcohol problem, but perhaps she had had a tough week and was just letting her hair down. After all, she rarely went out and still worked hard on her cleaning rounds, so she deserved to relax over Sunday lunch with her family.

'We made a trip to the vet yesterday.' Dawn speared a piece of broccoli with her fork then raised it to her mouth but kept her eyes on her plate.

'You did?' Camilla ran a hand through her hair. 'What for?'

'Poor Lulu was limping. At least Mummy said she was but I thought she looked fine,' James said. 'Mummy was worried she'd broken her leg.'

'How would she have managed to do that?' Jackie asked.

Dawn shrugged. 'Hopping around.'

Camilla turned her gaze to Rick and noticed that his cheeks were slightly flushed.

'Hopping around? What she suddenly hopped a bit too hard?' Camilla stared at her sister.

'She wasn't herself and I thought she was reluctant to put weight on her back right leg, so we decided a trip to see the vet might be best. Just to be sure.'

'Of course. And what did Tom... I mean, *the vet*, say?'

'Nothing wrong with her that he could see. He suggested keeping a close eye on her over the weekend and that if I see her limping again, to take her back on Monday and he'll consider doing an x-ray.'

'So you basically bothered the poor man on a Saturday for nothing.'

'It wasn't nothing,' Dawn replied. 'It could have been something and after what happened to Wallace—' She bit her lip and glanced at her children. 'I mean... you know...' Dawn's cheeks glowed and Camilla had to take a gulp of wine to stop herself smiling.

'What Dawn means, is after we found out that Wallace was a girl, when all that time we'd believed she was a boy...' Rick leapt in to rescue his wife then stared meaningfully at Camilla. 'We don't want to take any chances with their health.'

Camilla nodded. She knew that Dawn had almost slipped up about how they'd lost their first guinea pig suddenly then Allie and Chris had rushed to find a replacement, but the replacement had turned out to be a pregnant female.

'Anyway...' Dawn sipped her water. 'Doctor Stone... or is it Mr Stone... I'm never sure with vets... seems very nice. Wasn't he nice, Rick?'

'He was indeed. Seems like a decent enough sort.'

Rick and Dawn smiled at Camilla and she wriggled in her chair.

'Well that's great. I'm really happy for you both. And I hope that poor Lulu will be OK.'

'I'm sure she will.'

'Can we have dessert now, please?' James asked.

'Of course, darling.' Jackie drained her glass then pushed her chair back. She reached for the gravy jug but it slipped from her grasp and clattered onto her plate, sending gravy and bits of roast potato everywhere.

Laura gasped. 'Uh oh... Look what you did.'

Jackie pursed her lips. 'Ooops! Butterfingers. Nothing that won't clean up.'

She picked up her plate and kept one hand on top of the gravy jug to stop it sliding off then lifted her chin and left the dining room.

Camilla met Dawn's eyes and mouthed *What's going on?*

Dawn shook her head.

'I'll go and give Mum a hand.' Camilla stood up and took some of the plates through to the kitchen. She found Jackie standing in front of the sink, gazing out at the garden.

'Everything OK, Mum?' She put the dirty plates on the worktop then rubbed her mother's shoulders.
'What?' Jackie turned to her. 'Oh... yes, Camilla, everything's fine.'
'Are you sure? You've been a bit distracted today.'
'I'm fine, darling.' Jackie went to the fridge. 'I made a simple trifle for dessert. I hope that's OK.'
'Trifle is lovely.'
Jackie nodded then placed the familiar cut glass bowl that she always used for trifles on the worktop and opened a drawer to find a serving spoon.
'It's just... I had an email you see.'
Camilla frowned. Hadn't they just been talking about trifle?
'An email?'
'Yes, darling. This morning. I opened my emails to check when my Amazon order was coming and... ooh, do you know, I forgot to check if the full order had been despatched. I ordered the loveliest pyjamas for the children and for Dawn I ordered a pair of those stretchy jeans with the panel for her tummy. She is getting quite big now isn't she?'
Jackie smiled. 'Ah... a new grandchild on the way. Just delightful.'
'Mum? You're worrying me now. Can you tell me what the email said?'
'Email?' Jackie's green eyes flickered. 'Oh, yes! It said—'
The doorbell rang, its tinny rendition of The White Stripes *My Doorbell* echoing through the house. Rick had bought it for Jackie for her birthday, telling her it made her a trendy grandmother.
'Saved by the bell!' Jackie grinned then strode out of the kitchen and through the hallway.
Camilla held her breath to listen. It was rare that people called round on Sundays, especially to her mother's house. It was probably someone collecting for a charity or a client of her mother's come to pay for a recent cleaning job.
She went to the sink and squirted lemon washing up liquid into the bowl then turned the hot tap on. She wrinkled her nose as the steam sent the fake citrus smell into the air. She heard the front door close

again. Presumably, her mother had dealt with their visitor quickly and efficiently, as was Jackie's way. Sometimes she could be eye wateringly abrupt, and had made Camilla and Dawn cringe on more than one occasion.

'Who was it, Mum?' Camilla asked as footsteps entered the kitchen behind her.

'Someone you may or may not be pleased to see.' Jackie said.

Camilla turned around slowly, wondering why her mother had invited someone inside when they were about to have dessert.

Her mouth fell open.

Her heart flipped.

And she blurted, 'What the hell are you doing here?'

Chapter Four

'You'd better turn that tap off love, or the whole kitchen will be flooded.' His voice was familiar, though she'd not heard it in years, but it was also gravelly now, the voice of a heavy smoker.
'What?'
'The tap. The sink will over flow.'
Camilla turned the tap off then took a few deep breaths to steady herself. She looked down and her knuckles were white where she gripped the edges of the apron fronted sink.
'Camilla? That's no way to greet someone is it?' Jackie's voice had a strange edge to it, as if she was trying to sound calm and controlled when inside she was on the verge of screaming.
Camilla spun round. 'I asked you a question.' She swallowed hard. '*Dad!* I said… What the hell are you doing here?'
Her father opened his arms and smiled.
'How's my little girl, then? Such a beauty, isn't she, Jackie? Just like you.'
Camilla watched as he turned his blue eyes on his ex-wife and she gazed up at him.
'Dad!' she snapped, keen to break whatever spell it was that he

seemed to be casting over her mother. 'What are you doing here? More to the point, when did you get to England?'

He waved a hand. 'So many questions… and I'm absolutely parched. Put the kettle on and make your old man a cuppa, love. There's a good girl.'

Camilla bristled. *Good girl!* What was she… a dog?

She was about to give him a tongue lashing when something occurred to her. She was shocked, yes. But Jackie didn't seem shocked, so presumably the strange mood she'd been in was because her father had emailed to say he'd be visiting. But Dawn didn't know he was here yet. And Dawn was pregnant and had been unwell over the autumn, so she needed to be spared any sudden surprises. Camilla had to protect Dawn.

She rushed across the kitchen and into the dining room.

'Camilla? Where's the fire?' Rick laughed as she reached the table and gripped the back of her chair.

'No fire. Not yet anyway. No fire. Uh… but… Dawn. Mum has a visitor.'

'Yes, we heard the doorbell. Charity collection is it? Don't tell me she's invited them in for dessert.' Dawn picked up the almost empty wine bottle. 'Exactly how much of this did Mum drink?'

'NO!' Camilla's shout made Dawn, Laura and James jump and they all stared at her. 'Just listen. There's not much time.'

Rick pushed back his chair and straightened his shirt.

'Camilla?' He raised his eyebrows. 'What's wrong?'

She sighed. *Here goes.*

'The visitor. It's—'

'Me! Your dad!'

Camilla turned quickly to find Laurence Dix filling the doorway. Dawn gasped. Rick groaned. Laura and James squealed.

'I'm home, darling. I've come home for Christmas.'

'I'm so sorry, Dawn. I was trying to warn you.' Camilla shook her head.

Dawn gently pushed back her chair and stood up. She placed her hands on the table to steady herself, and Camilla, overwhelmed by a need to protect her younger sister, went to her side and slid an arm around her waist.

'Girls? Aren't you pleased to see me? I know it's been a... a while. But I'm home now so we can make up for lost time.'

'Lost time? A lost lifetime more like.' Camilla muttered through gritted teeth.

And as they stared at the man they hadn't seen in years, the man that Laura and James hadn't even met, the Carpenters *Close to You* filled the room, and Dawn burst into tears.

Camilla curled up on her sofa, pulled the soft fawn blanket over her legs then wrapped her hands around her mug of tea. Her head ached, her eyes burned and her bottom lip was sore from biting it as she'd held back her anger earlier that afternoon. It was only just gone six in the evening, but she felt as if it could easily be gone eleven.

She gazed around her small, cosy lounge and sighed. In the silence, her sigh seemed as loud as a shout. She'd lit the log burner when she got back just after four, and its warmth permeated the room, but she was chilled to the bone. And she knew why.

Her father had turned up after twenty-five years and acted as if he'd just popped out for milk. He'd missed seeing her and Dawn grow up and missed the first years of his grandchildren's lives. Who the hell did he think he was? It had taken all of Camilla's strength not to run at him and pound him with her fists. For hurting her mother. For hurting Dawn. And for hurting her.

Because Camilla had been badly hurt by him, by the man who should have adored her, loved her and supported her. He'd left her and Dawn as little girls with a broken mother and a lifetime of doubt ahead of them. For Dawn, finding love and security had been paramount, but for Camilla, she'd barely been able to face a second or third date with a man just in case she fell for him. She'd refused to make herself at all vulnerable. Of course, she knew she couldn't place all the blame on Laurence now, because she could have fixed herself and moved on. People did move on and it was wrong to languish in self-pity when there was a life to be lived, and for the most part, Camilla did enjoy her life. But as far as relationships were concerned, she steered well clear. So she didn't hurt anyone and they couldn't hurt her. It was safer that way.

Yet at times like this, it would be nice to have someone to talk to. Someone to cuddle her and stroke her hair and tell her that it would all be OK, that she would survive whether Laurence chose to stay in Heatherlea or went back to Benidorm.

Her father had been evasive when Camilla had asked him outright what his plans were and she didn't like that at all. Not long after he'd arrived at their mum's, Rick had taken Dawn and the children home – with trifle, at the children's insistence – as he'd been worried about the effect the shock could have on his pregnant wife. Camilla loved him for it; Rick was Dawn's rock now, whereas once it had been Camilla. That had left Camilla alone with her parents, something that hadn't happened in decades, and it had not been comfortable at all.

Jackie had pottered around, still slightly inebriated, chattering on about nothing in particular, as if her ex-husband turning up was an everyday occurrence. Laurence had been smiley, made silly jokes and appeared to be carefree, but whenever Camilla had met his eyes, he'd looked away, as if afraid that she would see something there that would betray his intentions. *Shifty* was the word that had sprung into her head and she'd wanted to drag him into the garden and ask him exactly what he was playing at.

But she hadn't. Because Camilla was good at suppressing her feelings; she'd had years of practice storing them away in a locked box at the back of her mind. She wasn't one for emotional displays or outbursts, even when a thirty-kilo bulldog was humping her. Camilla had perfected the art of picking herself up, dusting herself off and walking away with her head held high.

She eyed her small Christmas tree that was tucked neatly in the corner of the room. The lights were dark and the tinsel reflected only the flames from the log burner. She hadn't had the heart to switch the silver fairy lights on; it hadn't seemed right to think of Christmas while in her current mood.

After the dinner things had been cleared away and Camilla had realised that Jackie was trying to encourage Camilla to give her and Laurence some space, she'd pulled on her boots and coat then hugged her mother and told her to be careful. Jackie had nodded against Camilla's shoulder and murmured, 'I know.' Then Camilla had swapped mobile numbers with her father and asked him to meet her for a drink the next day. He'd agreed, and told her that he'd text her a time later that evening.

Her mobile sat on the arm of the sofa. It was quiet, just as it had been all evening. Its black screen hadn't lit up once. And what did she expect? For him to contact her immediately? She evidently wasn't – and never had been – his priority. Of course, one reason why Camilla wanted to meet Laurence alone, was to speak to him before he went near Dawn again. Although Rick was there to protect her, Camilla still didn't want him charming Dawn if he had no intention of sticking around. And what if he did? Where would that leave them all?

Just then, her mobile buzzed making her jump. She picked it up and swiped the screen. It was a message from Jackie:

Camilla,
Don't be mad with me but Dad is staying here for a few days. He was going to see if they had a room at the pub but I told him not to fritter away his money. We're going to have a big talk now.
Love, Mum X

Just as she put her mobile back down, it buzzed again. This time the message was from her father:

Camilla,
Shall we meet tomorrow at The Red Fox pub at 4? Be great to catch up.
Love you,
Dad

Camilla shook her head. So he'd wheedled his way back into Jackie's home already and was acting as if he'd done nothing wrong. Well tomorrow, Camilla would have a chance to find out exactly what he was doing back in Heatherlea and to let him know how much he'd hurt them all those years ago. In her usual cool, calm and collected way of course. There was no way she'd show him a glimmer of emotion; he didn't deserve to know that he mattered to her. Still. In spite of everything. Especially seeing as how she knew that she meant absolutely nothing to him at all.

Chapter Five

Monday morning, Camilla was up bright and early following a rather restless night. When she had opened her eyes, she had a few seconds of blissful ignorance about the previous day's events, then suddenly, it came rushing back and gate-crashed her peace of mind. There was no way she was going to be able to get any more sleep after that, so she decided to go for a walk before breakfast. She'd kept today meeting free, as she had some work to catch up with for her existing accountancy clients, so the day was hers to plot out as she wished, which was certainly an advantage of being self-employed.

She wrapped up in her North Face bomber jacket, scarf, hat and boots then pulled on her gloves and opened the door. The December morning was crisp and fresh and she savoured the air as she stepped into it. She never usually left the house before nine in the morning – as she tended to meet her clients late morning or for lunch – so going out at eight seemed quite adventurous, especially seeing as how it wasn't yet fully light.

However, a brisk walk around the pretty village would be good for her. Just the thing to clear her head and help her to prepare her for speaking to her father later on. If he was even still in the village, that was.

She set off along her road, passing the pretty cottages with their smoking chimneys and frosty window panes, then took a right and headed past the village green and the small medieval church with its mossy dry stone wall. Light was creeping into the sky now and everything seemed grey in the silvery-amethyst light, reminding her of an old photo of the village that hung on the wall of The Red Fox. She walked briskly, her breath emerging like puffs of smoke and as she inhaled, her throat and lungs felt as if they were being cleansed.

She passed the village shop and post office then froze. There was someone heading towards her with what appeared to be a short lion on a lead.

A lion?

A bulldog more like.

She turned quickly, keen to get out of sight, but there was nowhere to hide, so she scanned the road in both directions. The only thing she could see was the small graveyard in front of the church, so she hopped over the wall and landed on the grass on the other side. She lay there for a minute, holding her breath, then realised that her bottom and thighs were cold and wet where the frost was melting underneath her. So she slowly raised herself onto her haunches then peered over the wall to check if the coast was clear. And let out a screech.

'Hello... Camilla? Are you all right?'

It was Tom Stone and he was standing on the other side of the wall frowning at her.

'Oh... yes... I'm... absolutely fine, thank you.' She stood up slowly then dusted her behind off.

'What were you doing? One minute you were walking towards us then suddenly, you turned and ran in the opposite direction and leapt over the wall into the graveyard. I didn't know it was you, to be honest, what with the hat, scarf and padded jacket and wondered if it might be a criminal fleeing after committing a crime.'

'I was uh...' She lowered her eyes to find the bulldog, Hairy Pawter, gazing up at her, his big tongue lolling out of his mouth, casting steam out around his squishy face. 'I was doing my new exercise routine. It's a bit like circuits... you know, where you have to run backwards and forwards then jump over things.'

'I see.' His dark eyebrows disappeared beneath the rim of his grey wool hat and she noticed for the first time that he had a faint dimple in his chin. She had an urge to reach out and touch it. 'Well just be careful because the ground can be quite slippery and you could hurt yourself jumping over walls like that. Even low ones.'

'Of course.' She pulled her scarf higher to cover her cheeks as heat rushed into them. What an idiot she was. Tom didn't believe her and she knew he didn't. He probably knew that she knew and...

'I've been hoping we'd bump into you anyway. Not like this, first thing in the morning when I haven't even shaved or brushed my teeth.' He offered a small smile. 'I always get HP out for a walk before breakfast, you see. He's a bit of a lazy boy, so I promise him food if he walks first.'

Camilla nodded, finding herself unable to tear her eyes away from his. This morning, in the grey light, their brown seemed darker than it had when she'd last seen him and the shadow of stubble over his jaw was quite sexy. An image of it rasping against her cheek as he nibbled her earlobe sprang into her mind and she had to swallow a gasp.

'Anyway... as I said, I was hoping to bump into you but I've been so busy since I arrived in Heatherlea, that I haven't really been out much. And you're probably really busy with work too, aren't you? What is it you do again?'

'I'm an accountant. I have my own business.'

'That's right. Someone in the village told me something along those lines.'

Someone in the village had been talking about her with Tom?

'Look, uh... I wasn't snooping. I remember now... I went into the café last week and the man who works there... Jordan, is it?' Camilla nodded. 'He said something about you doing his mother's books so I put two and two together.'

'Right.'

'But I haven't seen you around at all. I suppose I could have come and knocked on your door but to be honest, I was embarrassed.'

'You were embarrassed?'

'After the Halloween Party. I am so sorry for HP's behaviour.'

'Oh. Uh—'

'It was out of order but he was overexcited anyway, what with the move then all the guests and you just took the brunt of it.'

'You can say that again.'

'I really am so sorry. I'd like to make it up to you, if I could.'

'Make it up to me?'

'Yes. Would you let me?'

Camilla could hardly believe her ears. She'd been mortified after the dog had assaulted her and never thought for a moment that Tom would have been embarrassed by what had happened. In fact, she'd rather suspected that it would be one of those tales to regale his colleagues with at those fancy veterinary dinners that he probably attended. *This one time I had a party and a guest dressed as a cat then got humped by my dog. Ha! Ha! Ha!*

'Camilla?'

'Yes?'

'You just went all glassy eyed. Is it low blood sugar? Have you had breakfast yet?'

'I'm fine. I just drifted off. Had a bit of a difficult day yesterday.'

'Would you like to talk about it? I'm quite a good listener. To be honest, I have to be in my profession.'

'It's nothing. Well, it's not nothing but it's kind of personal.'

'OK. No problem. I didn't mean to pry.' He chewed his bottom lip before meeting her eyes again. 'But about making it up to you…'

'Yes?'

'Can I buy you a drink?'

'There's no need. Honestly, it's all in the past. I'd quite forgotten about it.'
'Well I'm glad to hear that but you'd be doing me a favour if you agreed. See, although I had that party, and some of the villagers came, I'd still like to meet more of the locals. Sitting in the pub alone is a bit... awkward.'
Camilla sighed. What would be the harm in it? He was nice enough and he was living in Heatherlea now, so she'd bump into him from time to time. Therefore, getting to know him a bit better wouldn't be a bad thing.
'All right then. That would be lovely.'
'Say five-thirty pm? After I've closed up the surgery?'
She was meeting her father at four and that could be over quickly or take a while. Then what would she do? Go home alone and stare into a glass of wine? At least if she stayed in the pub to meet Tom, she'd have a distraction after she'd spoke to Laurence.
'See you later.'
She lifted her leg and cocked it over the wall then found herself standing next to Tom. Hairy Pawter immediately pulled on his lead to get closer to her, sniffing hard at her leg. She took a step backwards.
'He means well. He won't hurt you.'
'After our last encounter, he makes me a bit nervous.'
'He won't do it again, I promise.'
'I believe you.' She gritted her teeth. 'Hello HP.'
The dog's small stumpy tail wiggled and he huffed at her, seeming to smile.
'He really likes you.'
Camilla smiled. She smoothed the dog's head and he craned his neck to sniff her gloved hand. He was kind of cute.
'See you later then.' Camilla turned and started to walk away.
'Camilla?'
'Yes?' She turned on her heel.
'Not that I was looking... more that I couldn't help noticing... you've got a big slug on your bottom.'

'Oh!' She looked over her shoulder and sure enough, there was a large sticky slug clinging to her jeans. She pulled it off then threw it back into the graveyard where it landed on the grass. 'Bye.'
'Bye.'
She made her way home, conscious of how her wet jeans were clinging to her bum and thighs and that there might well be a slug slime over them too. But she didn't really mind, because she was meeting Tom later for a drink. And he'd seemed really nice in a shy, intelligent kind of way. He wasn't like the men she usually dallied with – they were loud, confident and even brash – but Tom was quiet and even sweet. It was refreshing.
When she reached her front door and let herself in, she realised that she was glad she'd bumped into him, because now she had something to look forward to. Something to take her mind off what she had to do first. Because she knew that speaking frankly to her father after twenty-five years of estrangement was not going to be easy at all. In fact, it was going to be very difficult indeed.

Chapter Six

Camilla immersed herself in numbers and spreadsheets all day, so when she looked at the clock and saw that it was gone three, she was surprised. The time had passed without her worrying and she patted herself on the back again for her chosen profession. There was nothing like a spreadsheet, or ten, to keep your mind busy. She supposed that her love of numbers might have begun when her father left and she had to try to make her savings stretch to feed her and Dawn, when she didn't want to worry her mother by asking for money to buy groceries, so she'd eek out her coppers to buy bread and tins of beans. She'd known the price of everything in the local shop as well as how far three tins of beans and a loaf of bread would stretch. She shook her head. It had been a difficult time but Jackie had emerged from her depression and life had continued, if in a different direction than the one they'd thought it would: without Laurence. And now he was back.

She swiped the screen on her mobile then typed a brief text to her mother and one to Dawn, letting them know that she was meeting with Laurence – leaving out the details about meeting Tom afterwards – and would text them later to let them know how it went. She was curious to know how things were going at Jackie's anyway; how did someone react when their ex returned after a quarter of a century and asked to stay? Dawn replied instantly telling her to take care and that she loved her.

Camilla hurried upstairs to change and brush her hair. She didn't want to look like she'd made a lot of effort for her father but she also wanted to look presentable and the leopard print onesie with the hood with ears, that she'd donned to work on the accounts, wasn't quite what she had in mind. Especially as she was meeting Tom afterwards. She didn't want him to start thinking she had a thing for dressing up as cats.

Outside The Red Fox, Camilla paused. The sky had turned gunmetal grey and an icy wind whipped around her ankles and buffeted her as she stared at the pretty pub with its stone façade and small paned glass windows. Inside, she could make out the glow of the fire and see a few people enjoying a quiet Monday afternoon drink.

She'd been in the pub so many times over the years with friends, family and clients, but never with her father. At least not since she was a child. She'd only been ten when he left and vaguely remembered having Sunday lunch in there a few times as a child and she thought she recalled him buying her a glass of Coke once, but sometimes she couldn't be sure if they were actual memories or things she'd wished for. They could even be things she'd seen on TV for all she knew.

'Come on, Camilla. No point dawdling. Let's see what he has to say.' She spoke firmly, gathered her courage then opened the door and went inside.

At the bar, she ordered a coffee then, seeing no sign of her father, she went over to a corner table and sat down. She had a clear view of the bar and the front door from her seat, so she wouldn't be taken by surprise when Laurence arrived.

The hands on the clock above the bar moved round and Camilla drank her coffee. She tried to take her time, but she needed something to do with her hands. When she drained her mug, she thought about ordering another one, but knew that the caffeine would make her more jittery than she was, so she went to the bar and ordered a sparkling water instead.

Back in her seat, she gazed around at the festive décor. The pub was always cosy with its exposed beams on the low ceiling and the open fireplace with its thick oak mantelpiece. The fire burned in the grate sending out a warm orange glow into the pub as the afternoon light faded. The mantelpiece was adorned with holly and ivy that draped over the sides and almost reached the floor. In amongst the greenery, tiny fairylights twinkled. To the left of the fireplace a tall Christmas tree stood in a deep red bucket. The tree was decorated with silver and gold bows and a fairy in a silver sequin dress sat at the top, smiling down at the pub's patrons. The bar itself was trimmed with silver and gold tinsel and at intervals, sprigs of mistletoe dangled from the ceiling beams. It was a perfect festive setting and Camilla knew that on any other day, she would have appreciated it, but today, she couldn't reach past the icy blockage in her chest to locate her heart. It was just fear and anxiety, she knew that, but its physical manifestation was horrid.

The clock struck four-thirty. Where was he? Why was he so late? She sipped her water and took a few slow deep breaths then checked her mobile.

Nothing.

Then she saw him, entering the pub in a dark wool coat with a flat cap on his head, his cheeks ruddy and his face lit up with a smile. The blockage in her chest swelled, threatening to choke her. Here she was, building herself up into an anxious tizzy, and he walked in late and beaming. *Bloody hell!*

He removed his cap and coat and hung them on the coat stand near the door then looked around. When he spotted Camilla, he waved then gestured at the bar. She shook her head, trying not to scowl. She had to give him a chance, however difficult this might be. It wasn't just about her but about Jackie and Dawn, as well as Laura and James.

'Hello, Camilla. Great to see you again so soon.'

Laurence put his pint of beer down on the table then pulled out a chair.

'You're late.'

He frowned. 'Am I?'

'Yes.'

He glanced at the clock. 'So I am. Apologies, sweetheart. I took a walk around the village and got caught up in nostalgia. You know, I walked past the old park and it was like I'd gone back in time. I remember one day when I took you and Dawn there... gosh you must have been about six and she would've been... about three—'

'Four!'

'What?'

'If I was six, Dawn would have been four. She's two years younger then me, Dad.'

He nodded. 'Yes, of course.' He sipped his beer and when he put his glass down, froth clung to his moustache. Camilla pointed at it and he wiped it away with the back of his hand. 'So you were six and Dawn was four. We went there for a picnic and spent all day playing and eating strawberries straight from the punnet along with whippy ice creams from the van that parked there in the afternoons every summer holiday. It was a fabulous day. We had so much fun but then... you both got sunburn.'

'Sunburn?'

'Yes and the ice cream... or the unwashed strawberries... upset your tummies. Your mother went mad.'

'And so she should have. Don't you know how dangerous sunburn is? It leads to skin cancer and all sorts of nasties.'

He shook his head. 'Back then, Camilla, we didn't know so much about all that. But it was a bit irresponsible of me, I know that. I just... I tried to be a good daddy, although I guess I wasn't always that good at it. You know... I was good at the fun stuff but not so good at the other things. How was I to know the ice cream or the strawberries would give you both the runs?'

Camilla watched him carefully as he spoke. His eyes had glazed over and he seemed to have travelled to another time and place. He'd changed so much. The memories she had of him were of a tall, broad-shouldered man with a thick ginger beard and hair swept back with wax. He'd had smiling blue eyes with sandy lashes and eyebrows and a strong lean physique. As a little girl, she'd admired him and yes... a lump rose in her throat... she could even remember now telling one of her friends that she wanted to marry a man just like her daddy when she grew up.

But now... the strong young man was gone and in his place sat a shadow. He still had that same big smile that spread from ear to ear but his hair had thinned and turned grey, its red long gone. His beard was mainly white but still had some flecks of rust, a reminder of his youth. He was tanned but the sun and smoking had aged his skin and thick grooves ran from his eyes, over his forehead and from the corners of his mouth, the latter ones disappearing into his beard. His neck was haggard below the beard, the skin loose and his Adam's apple was exposed. As she stared at him, it bobbed in his throat and she realised that for all his bravado, he was actually nervous too.

'I guess I failed you then... before I even left.'

Camilla met his eyes and was surprised to see that they shone.

'I don't really remember much about the time before you left, Dad. After you'd gone... it was tough. That time is etched on my memory but the life we had before... I don't know. There are fragments of memories but nothing solid.'

'I understand. Camilla... I want to say sorry.'

She gasped as the blockage in her chest shifted. 'It's a bit late for that don't you think?'

'Is it? Is it ever too late to say sorry? I don't know. I hope not. I've come home, Camilla, and I want to make it up to you all.'

'All?'

'Yes, of course. You, your mum and Dawn. My grandchildren.'

Camilla swallowed hard. She had so many retorts on the tip of her tongue but she didn't want to free them. If she started berating him, she might never stop and there was so much pain in her heart that she knew her words would be harsh. And she didn't want to be harsh. As much as this man had hurt her and her mother and sister, she didn't want to hate him. She just wanted... for him to love her.

To her horror, tears rolled down her cheeks and a sob burst from her.

'Oh my girl.'

Laurence jumped up and rushed around the table. He knelt next to Camilla and took her hands. She screwed her eyes shut, afraid to look at him, afraid to show him how much she was hurting. This wasn't like her; she was strong, firm, and unemotional. Camilla wasn't weak, tearful and vulnerable. She just didn't do all that.

But now she did. Apparently. And all because a sixty-five-year-old man had turned up on her mother's doorstep and told her he was sorry.

'Do you have any idea how many times I wished you'd turn up when I was a child?' she asked as she peered at him from behind her wet lashes.

'I thought about it so many times, too, Camilla. I swear it to you.'

'Why didn't you phone more than once or twice a year?'

He frowned. 'I did.'

'No you didn't.'

'I did. At first. I rang every day then every week and every month and I sent you cards and letters but your mother...' He bit his bottom lip.

'My mother what?'

'It doesn't matter.'

'Yes it does. What...' A horrible thought crashed through Camilla's mind. 'Are you saying that you did ring and send us letters but Mum didn't tell us?'

His cheeks coloured. 'It's all in the past now.'

'Evidently it isn't or I wouldn't be so upset.'

'Look... I was in the wrong. I left your mum and you two girls. I should have stayed around. It was my fault and I am so, so sorry.' He grimaced. 'I'd better get up or my knees will stick like this.' He pushed himself up slowly then hobbled back to his seat.

'So why now? Why come back now?'

He sipped his pint then wiped his moustache. 'It was time. High time, I mean. There are lots of reasons and I'd been thinking about it for a while but then I caught my wife... my third wife, with someone else.'

'You did?'

Camilla recalled Dawn forwarding her an email from Laurence about his third wedding. He'd written to Dawn presumably because she'd be less likely to reply negatively than Camilla would. There was a photo attached, taken on a mobile phone, of Laurence in shorts and t-shirt with his arm around a much younger woman. The woman had been extremely thin and tanned with sleek blonde extensions and large cobweb tattoos that covered her chest and disappeared below the neckline of her very low-cut white top.

'You mean the one with the cobweb tattoos on her—'

'Boobs?'

'Yes.'

'That's right. Beautiful girl she was... *is*... but she was way too young for me. I should've known she only wanted me for the bar.'

'She took your bar?'

He sighed. 'I signed half of it over to her as a wedding gift. Then a month ago, I caught her shagging a tourist behind the barrels out back.'

Camilla shook her head.

'So now she's running the bar for you?'

'Uh... no. I sold her my share.'

'You've sold your livelihood? I hope she gave you a good price for it?'

'Wrong again.' He blinked. 'And I had some... urrrr... debts.'

'You mean to tell me you have nothing left, Dad?'

'Nothing at all. Kind of like retribution, right? No less than I deserve.'

'Oh Dad...'

Camilla was overwhelmed with tiredness. There was so much to take in and she'd been through so many emotions. But as she sat there, listening to him, she realised that the blockage in her chest had shrunk a bit. This man did have feelings and he had been through some tough times too. He was in a bad place and as much as he'd hurt her and her family, he had nowhere else to turn.

'I'm sorry for what you've been through. Are you... OK?'

He nodded. 'I wasn't that surprised she cheated to be honest. I had my suspicions that monogamy wasn't her thing when we married.'

'Why did you marry her then?'

He shrugged. 'I'm an old fool. I wanted one last shot at youth. I don't know really, Camilla. I've made so many mistakes along the way. I wish I could have my time over but no one can turn that bloody clock back.'

'No they can't.'

'I'm not here to hurt anyone, Camilla. Please know that. I came back because I felt this was where I should be. If you want me to leave... if you think that's best, then I'll go.' He looked down at his shoes and Camilla followed his gaze. He was wearing shoddy brown brogues that she suspected he'd bought before he moved to Benidorm. Her heart squeezed and something rushed through her. Was it pity? Love? Misplaced loyalty? She didn't know. She needed time to think about everything he'd told her, time to digest what he'd said.

'What do you want then, Dad?'

'To spend some time with you all over Christmas. If that's OK? Then, if you can't stand me...' He gave a small laugh but his eyes were cloudy. 'I'll go again.'

'Where would you go?'

'Wherever. It won't matter if I leave here. There's nothing left...' He shook his head. 'Sorry. I'm not about to indulge in self-pity now. You take your time and make your decision and I'll do my best to make it up to you. Or, if I can't make it up to you because it's been so long and because I'm such an idiot, then I'll leave you in peace.'

Camilla sighed. 'Are you going to speak to Dawn too?'

'Do you think I should?'

'She's sweet and soft. She's not like me.'
'You're softer than you think.'
'No I'm not. This has just...' She threw her hands up. 'This has rocked me.'
'I'll go and see her this week and speak to her. Try to explain.'
'Well make sure Rick's there when you do. She's not had an easy pregnancy so far.'
'A third baby on the way.' His lips curved slightly and he nodded. 'Yes. So be gentle with her.'
'I will.'
'I take it you've told Mum all this?'
'Your mum and I had a good long talk last night.'
'And how does she feel about it?'
'Who knows? She's a strong woman your mother. She's sensible too.'
'You broke her heart.'
He hung his head.
'I don't meant to be hard but you did. I thought she'd never recover and she's never found anyone else.'
'I promise I'm not here to hurt her.'
'You better not be.'
Movement at the bar caught Camilla's eye and she looked over to see Tom smiling over at her. Heat rushed into her cheeks. How long had he been there? Watching? Trying to catch her attention.
'Look Dad, it's five-forty and I'm meeting someone else.'
Laurence followed her gaze. 'The handsome guy at the bar?'
'Yes. Tom Stone. He's the new vet.'
'Vet eh? Good for you.'
'He's just a friend.'
'I'd say the way he's looking at you that he wants more than friendship. That's the look of a man who's smitten.'
'Don't be silly.' She waved Tom over. 'Let me introduce you. And we'll speak again soon?'
'I'd like that.'
'Hi Tom.' Camilla stood up. 'This is my father, Laurence.'

'Pleased to meet you.'
Tom and Laurence shook hands.
'Can I get you a drink?'
'No thanks, I was just leaving.' Laurence walked around to Camilla and gave her a peck on the cheek. 'Have a lovely evening, sweetheart.'
'Thank you.'
Camilla watched as he put on his hat and coat then left the pub. Through the window, she saw him pause then smoke billowed around him as he lit a cigarette. She was suddenly so tired she could have curled up under the table and gone straight to sleep.
'Everything all right?' Tom asked.
'Oh... yes. Yes, thank you.'
'Can I get you another drink?'
'What're you having?'
'Well I wasn't sure what to order so I told the barman I'd see what you wanted. Do you fancy sharing a bottle of wine?'
'I could use a glass of red right now.'
'Red it is then.'
Tom draped his wax jacket over the back of the chair that her father had recently vacated then went back to the bar. Camilla took the time to gather her thoughts. She wasn't entirely sure what she'd been expecting her father to say but she didn't think she'd end up getting emotional. His third wife had basically cheated then taken his bar, he'd lost all his money and he'd come back because it was time. Or was it just because he had nowhere else to go? Did he think they were needy fools who'd believe everything he told them? Or did he genuinely want to make amends? They could turn him away or they could give him a chance. The question was, did Camilla want to give him a chance, or would it be easier to send him packing?
When Tom returned with a bottle of Shiraz and two glasses that he filled, she accepted hers gratefully.
'I'm a good listener.'
'Pardon?'
'If you want to talk about it.'

'I wouldn't know where to start.'
'Try the beginning. I'm in no rush. I've got a casserole in the slow cooker and I popped home to feed HP after work, so he's snoring his head off in front of the log burner. I have all the time in the world.'
Camilla eyed him over her glass. Could she really discuss her innermost feelings, doubts and fears with this man?
'Look... in my profession, I hear everything and I never repeat a word. People just like to talk to me, kind of like their GP or their beautician. Cross my heart, I won't tell a soul what you say and if you need some advice, I might be able to help.'
His eyes were so warm and friendly, that she felt her resolve not to share her feelings with anyone waning. She could talk to him, couldn't she? Get an impartial opinion. If she spoke to Allie or Honey, they'd be too involved to be objective. And she couldn't expect her mother or Dawn to weigh it all up rationally either. So speaking to Tom seemed like her best option. She could get a male perspective on it.
'OK then. Thank you.' She sipped her wine. 'I hope you like sad stories.'
He smiled at her, leaned forwards and clinked his glass against hers.
'I have a few of my own, believe me.'
'I'll tell you mine if you tell me yours.'
'Sounds like a plan!'

Chapter Seven

Over a bottle of very nice wine, Camilla gave Tom the potted version of her father's explanation, as well as filling him in about when Laurence had left and how they'd rarely heard from him over the years. Tom listened carefully, his brown eyes fixed on hers as Camilla relayed the details as calmly and clearly as she could. Twice, she became a bit emotional, and had to pause, but Tom waited quietly and she found his presence soothing and reassuring. It was strange, to feel so comfortable with a man, and when she hardly knew him, but she also didn't feel under any pressure to impress him. Camilla had never felt like that with a man before, except for Rick and Chris, and one was her brother-in-law, the other her best friend's partner.
'And that's my life story.'
Tom nodded. 'Quite a story too.'
'What do you think?'
He sighed. 'I think that you lost your father when you were very young and that's got to be hard for any child. The fact that he left, rather than passed away, must have been difficult because he was still out there somewhere. You, Dawn and your mum have had it rough but you've done amazingly.'

'Amazingly?'
'You have a great job, you're independent, you clearly love your family and now... you have some difficult decisions to make.'
'What would you do?'
'I have no idea, Camilla. I've been very lucky in that my parents are still together. They get on well, they're both retired and still live in Brighton where I grew up. They were strict when I was younger but not ridiculously so and they always made me feel secure. They were there when I needed them. I hope I never took that for granted but I don't think I did because I had friends whose parents divorced and I saw how difficult it could be for them, although having said that, for some it was a blessing.'
'How so?'
'Well if two people are together and they're making each other unhappy, then surely it's better to separate? Not all marriages work out.' He winced and reached for his glass.
'Do you have first hand experience of that or are you talking about a friend?'
He shook his head. 'We're still talking about you.'
She glanced at his left hand but he wasn't wearing a ring.
'Are you hungry?'
'Starving.' She placed a hand over her belly and it grumbled. 'I think it's all the emotion.'
'That casserole will be ready soon and it goes very well with fluffy mashed potato. How'd you fancy that?'
'It sounds so good.'
'And I popped into The Cosy Cottage Café at lunch time and picked up some mince pies.'
'Now you're torturing me.'
'Would you like to come to mine for dinner?'
Camilla finished her wine. 'That would be very nice indeed. Oh...'
'Are you thinking about HP?'
She nodded.

'He'll be on his best behaviour, I promise. I'll warn him when we get there that if there's any nonsense, he'll be sent straight to his room.'
'He has his own room?'
'Not really, the daft dog has the run of the downstairs but I can close the kitchen door if he's bothering you. He has a bed in there and one in the lounge and one in the office.'
'Doesn't he go upstairs then?'
'No. I don't let him because he'd struggled to come down without help and I worry that he'd hurt himself in the day when I'm at work. With his huge shoulders, he's a bit top heavy, and he'd come down too quickly.'
'Of course.'
Tom stood up. 'You coming then?'
'I am.'
Camilla and Tom made their way to his cottage. It was one of the largest in the village and had been renovated recently by the previous owner's son before it was put up for sale. Tom had paid a hefty price for it, Camilla knew because news travelled fast in the village, but it was a fantastic property and she hoped he'd be happy in Heatherlea. As they walked, he asked about life in the village and about the locals he'd met already and Camilla was grateful to have her attention diverted from her own worries. At one point, Tom took her arm to guide her over a patch of black ice that she hadn't even noticed, and she found herself comforted by his consideration. Not only was he incredibly handsome but he was kind, considerate and funny. And he was, as he had told her, a very good listener.
They soon reached his cottage and as they walked up the path to the front door, she heard a loud bark from inside.
'The sleeping prince awakens.' Tom grinned as he unlocked the door. 'Just let me go in and speak to him for a moment so I can calm him down.'
Camilla nodded and stood on the step, gazing at the small front garden. In the warm glow from the streetlight, she could see that it had been cut back for the winter months and the flowerbeds were

dark and bare. Ivy climbed the front of the cottage, its dark green foliage neatly trimmed, and the rose that wound its way around the front door was bereft of flowers. Camilla knew that in the summer months, the plants would flourish with gorgeous scents and colours, and she wondered if she'd come here to see Tom then. But that was a foolish thought. Unless they stayed friends, of course. Although by then, Tom might well be involved with someone and who knew what situation Camilla would be in? If Laurence proved to be a rogue, she might well have packed her bags and set off around the world herself. The door opened and Tom peered out. 'You can come in now. HP promises he'll behave. He'll just want to sniff you a bit.'
'OK.'
Camilla entered the dark hallway and the mouth-watering aroma of chicken casserole met her nostrils. It was a comforting, homely smell and one that made her empty stomach rumble.
'HP, say hello to Camilla.'
The dog waggled his bottom as he approached Camilla and she tensed.
'Hello HP. How are you?'
'It's OK, he won't jump up.'
Camilla nodded and leaned over to stroke the dog but he moved sideways and sniffed her hand then her wrist before giving her hand a gentle lick.
'There... see. He knows you now. Shall I take your coat?'
Camilla shrugged out of her jacket and Tom hung it under the stairs.
'Come on through to the kitchen.'
'Shall I take my boots off?'
'No, don't worry the floors are all wood or tiled so you'll have cold feet if you do.'
Camilla followed him and HP trotted at her side like an escort, or as if he was keeping an eye on her, she wasn't sure which. Everything looked different than it had on Halloween, but that could be because then it had been full of people and decorated with pumpkins, skele-

tons and cobwebs, whereas now, it was just the two of them and the big British bulldog.

The spotlights were on in the kitchen and Camilla was struck by how warm and cosy it was with the Aga set against the chimney wall and the limed oak units.

'Can I get you a drink?'

'Yes please.'

'More wine?'

'Lovely.'

'Take a seat.'

He gestured at the table near the French doors that overlooked the garden. Camilla sat down, conscious of the fact that her reflection in the glass doors was pale and dark eyed. She hoped she didn't look that bad but then she had been through an emotional afternoon.

Tom handed her a glass of wine and HP sniffed her boots then plonked himself on her feet.

'You have the official HP seal of approval there.'

'What his bum on my toes?'

Tom nodded. 'He trusts you enough to sit on you.'

'Or he doesn't trust me so he's keeping me pinned in one place.'

Tom laughed.

'I'll peel some potatoes then we can go and sit in the lounge while they cook.'

'I'll do them if you want?'

'Absolutely not. You're my guest. In fact, why don't you go into the lounge and sit on the sofa and I'll come on through in a bit?'

'No, it's OK. I'll sit here and wait. Your kitchen is lovely.'

'You're the guest.'

Tom went to the dresser at the side of the table and music filled the kitchen. Camilla realised that what she had thought was a small radio was actually an iPhone dock. As Michael Bublé's Christmas album played, Tom pottered about the kitchen and HP warmed her feet, and she felt herself begin to relax.

And she was glad that she'd agreed to meet Tom that afternoon, because if she'd gone home alone after meeting her father, she'd have been lost in introspection and loneliness. Instead, she had someone to talk to and he was even making her dinner.

They didn't make it to the lounge because once the water in the saucepan of potatoes was bubbling, Tom sat at the table and they started talking.
'Camilla... I know you've had a difficult day with the arrival of your father in the village, but apart from that, what can you tell me about you?' His hands were resting on the table next to his wine glass and Camilla looked at his short clean nails and long slim fingers.
'What do you want to know?'
'Well... more about you. Likes and dislikes, that kind of stuff.'
'Kind of like speed dating?'
'Sorry?' He tilted his head.
'Well, we only have until the potatoes are cooked, so whatever I tell you won't be particularly detailed. When you go speed dating, you have a limited amount of time to tell someone about you.'
'I've never done any of that stuff.'
'Speed dating?'
'And the rest. I have friends who've done it but I just couldn't bring myself to try it.'
'What, no Tinder or Match or any of those?'
'Never.'
She nodded. 'I can understand that. I've only tried speed dating once, but it was all so fast that I kept giggling and that didn't go down well, and I tried Tinder.'
'Did you actually date anyone you met because of it?'
Camilla paused, not sure how much she should tell him because if this was kind of like a date, then the wrong thing to do would be to

tell him about her exes. But then, if it wasn't a date and they were just friends, it would be fine. But which was it? After all, Tom was from the village and Camilla had a rule about that. Yet, with him it seemed like a rule she could break. He'd been so kind to her today and she was so comfortable with him that she wanted to get to know him better.

'Camilla?'

'Yes?'

'You drifted off.'

'Sorry... I was just wondering if I should tell you about past dates, really.'

'Why not?'

'Well, because...'

'Because?'

'Nothing.' She worried her bottom lip.

'No, you have to tell me now.'

She sighed. 'Tom, I really like you. But I'm not used to this.' She waved at the air between them. 'At being friends with guys that I... I'm attracted to. Usually, not that I date a lot, you understand, but I do have friends who are guys and guys who are, well, dates, I guess, but the lines don't get blurred. No, that's not right because the guys I date... well sometimes they're friends. I'm making a right mess of trying to explain myself here aren't I?'

'I think I understand your point. Are you talking about friends with benefits?' He raised his eyebrows.

'That sounds terrible, doesn't it?'

He held up his hands. 'Hey, I'm not judging anyone here. If you have male friends you can call on to take you out and make you feel special then good for you. Although, I have to admit that I'm a teensy bit jealous of them.'

She smiled. 'You're jealous?'

He nodded and spots of colour appeared on his cheeks. 'I am. I really like you, Camilla. You're smart, funny, pretty and you smell good.'

'I am? And I do?'

'I fancied you the moment I saw you walking through the village.'
'You did? I had no idea.'
'I'm also kind of... shy.' He lowered his gaze to his wine and swirled it around in the glass. 'I don't find talking to attractive women easy at all, yet with you, I'm fairly relaxed. And, of course, the wine is helping to loosen my tongue.'
'Mine too, I think.'
'I'm also excited. If that makes sense. By being around you. I want to make you smile and to impress you but I also feel that I don't have to.' He rubbed his eyes. 'Look at me spouting nonsense now. I bet I don't make sense either.'
He smiled.
'It's not nonsense and I know exactly what you mean. I feel at ease around you. I've told you more today than I've ever told any of my dates.' She used her fingers to air quote *dates*. 'But because I like you, I'd prefer not to analyse my past... encounters, except to say that there's never been anyone serious.'
'What? Never?'
'Nope. I never met anyone I wanted to settle down with.' She held back the fact that she'd never *let* herself get involved in case he thought that was strange. She didn't want to ruin the moment with brutal honesty or to seem totally screwed up. 'And I'm thirty-five, so that's quite a long time to be single.'
He shook his head. 'No point rushing into anything if it's not right.'
'And what about you? I'm not asking for an analysis.' She ran her finger around the bottom of her wine glass. 'I just meant, has there been anyone significant?'
He took a sip of his wine and swallowed then placed his glass back on the table. 'There was someone, yes. She was a vet too, from Peckham originally, and we met at university then got jobs in Brighton. We've been separated for two years.'
'I'm sorry to hear that.'
'It's OK. It happens. We were young when we met and we grew apart. It hurt but that's life.'

Camilla finished her wine then returned her glass to the table.
'And are you all right about it all?'
'I'm fine.'
'Is that why you moved?'
He met her eyes and she saw sadness in his, even though he'd claimed that he was fine.
'Yes. I needed a fresh start. It was too difficult bumping into her around our old haunts in Brighton and supermarket trips just became a nightmare.'
'She couldn't have shopped elsewhere?'
'She should have, really. It was my supermarket first.' He laughed. 'It wasn't an easy time but it's all over now.'
'Life and relationships can be difficult.'
'Sad but true. That's life though, eh?'
He got up and went to check the bubbling pan.
Camilla cringed inwardly. Had she just said completely the wrong thing? Had she pried too much? Tom might well have more secrets in his past and that was fine; it was his prerogative to tell her or not, as he wished. The last thing she wanted to do was to upset him and ruin what had been a lovely evening so far. She'd do her best to make him smile again, because he had the loveliest smile she'd seen in what felt like a lifetime.

Chapter Eight

After they'd eaten, Camilla helped Tom to tidy the dinner things away. The casserole had been as delicious as it had smelt, Tom's mashed potatoes had been fluffy and creamy and she was now fit to burst.

'My belly is straining against my jeans, Tom.' She patted it gently.

'Mine too. But I can't resist mashed potato.'

'Me either. Thank you for dinner. It was wonderful.'

'My pleasure.'

'I suppose I should get going.' She glanced at the clock on the dresser.

'You don't have to go yet.' Tom leaned against the worktop. 'We could finish the wine.'

'OK then.'

'Let's go into the lounge now, shall we?'

'What about HP?'

'He'll come on through if he wants to.'

HP was snoring loudly in his bed next to the dresser and every so often, his eyebrows wiggled up and down. He didn't look as if he'd be moving for the rest of the evening.

'Is he dreaming?'

'Probably. Sometimes we have full on whimpering and leg movements that suggest he could be running in his dream. For a dog that doesn't like walks, he gets a lot of exercise when he's asleep.'

Tom handed her a fresh glass of wine then held out his arm to indicate that Camilla should go in front of him, and they made their way through the hallway that was now rather chilly compared to the cosy kitchen, and into the lounge.

Two lamps at either end of the room gave it a warm glow. There was a large squishy red sofa and a matching chair that was positioned next to the hearth where a fire burned in the grate. The room smelt of cinnamon and pine and the real Christmas tree – in front of the French doors that led into the garden – was lit with red orb fairy lights that matched the room's décor.

'It's a non-drop Norwegian Spruce.' He nodded at the tree. 'I always get the tree up early or December just flies past and it's time to take it down again.'

'I have my tree up too. It seems sad not to make an effort, even though it's just me.'

'I know what you mean. Take a seat.'

Camilla sat on one end of the sofa and expected him to take the chair but he sat on the sofa too. They sat there in silence for a few moments, gazing into the fire. Camilla wondered if he could see the same things she could in the flames that licked at the logs.

'I'm sorry if I said the wrong thing in the kitchen.'

'In what way?'

'About life and relationships.'

'We were talking openly. You didn't say the wrong thing at all.' He turned on the sofa so he was facing her and rested his left arm along the back. His fingers were just a few centimetres from her shoulder. 'Tell me more about you, Camilla. Why did you become an accountant?'

'I've always loved numbers. I like how they make sense, how they work together and there's always a right answer.'

'Unlike life?'

'Exactly. You can't always predict how people will act or how circumstances will pan out but numbers won't let you down. Well, having said that, they do let some of my clients down but that's more to do with the success or failure of their ventures, savings and so on. But numbers are numbers and there's always a clear solution.'

He nodded. 'I get that. You never wanted to be anything else?'

'I went through some of the usual dream careers when I was younger. At one point, I think I wanted to act and at another I wanted to be a dancer but after Dad left, all that faded away and I became more practical and focused. I wanted a career that I could control, hence working for myself, and that would always earn for me. I've worked hard to build my own business and I'm proud of what I've achieved.'

'Good for you.'

'Thank you. Did you always want to be a vet?'

'Yes. Bit of a cliché I guess, but from about six, I knew how much I loved animals and wanted to work with them. I was a bit of a geek growing up. I studied hard, wasn't big on partying or drinking. I like beer, wine and a good whisky but while the lads in uni were big on going out and drinking until they could barely stand, I preferred to go for a meal or to the cinema. Don't get me wrong, I did go out and drink but not as much as them and if I could avoid it or persuade them to try something else, I did. We were in London, after all. We had so many things on our doorstep to see and do, and drinking wasn't the most exciting one I could think of. Then I met Danni – she was a year behind me – and life changed anyway. I don't regret being with her because there's no point, is there? It's just a waste of emotion and I don't want to waste any time on it. I try to live in the present and to plan for the future.'

'What plans do you have?'

'I have places I'd like to visit. I want to go to New York, China, Italy...'

'New York is incredible.'

'You've been?'

'Twice.'

'Recently?'

'Two years ago. I went with a friend who was out there for a business trip and wanted some company and I went on a hen weekend with a girl, or woman now, from school. I didn't know her really well but she wanted to make up the numbers. To be honest, while they were getting drunk, I sneaked off for cheesecake at Times Square and went to Central Park to see all the landmarks.'

'Lucky you.'

'Why haven't you been?'

'Never the right time.'

'Well we must go!' Camilla's eyes widened as she realised what she'd said.

'We?'

'Oh... I wasn't presuming anything there, Tom. It's the wine.' She put her glass on the table. 'It's making me say way too much.'

'I'd love to go to New York with you. When were you thinking?'

'Uh...'

'I'll just get my diary.' He made to get up then slouched back down again. 'You should see your face.'

Camilla covered her cheeks with her hands. They were scorching.

'I'm not backtracking. I'd love to go again and if you haven't been then I know my way around. I could show you the sights... sometime.' She added the extra word just to offer him a get out clause, in case he was feeling a bit trapped.

'Sometime... that would be lovely.'

A snuffling from the doorway diverted their attention and Camilla looked up to see HP shuffling in, his ears slouching and his eyes half-closed.

'Hello, boy. Did you have a good nap?' Tom asked.

HP responded by stretching and yawning, then he approached the sofa and stared at the space between Camilla and Tom.

'He wants to come up.'

'He comes on the sofa?'

'It's why I bought a low one. So he can get on and off without hurting himself. I always put a blanket down for him though, to save the material from his fur. He moults a lot.'

Tom reached down next to the sofa and produce a grey faux fur throw that he draped over the cushion then HP jumped up next to him and sat between them, alternately staring at Tom then at Camilla.

'He's funny isn't he? It's like he knows what we've been talking about.'

'He's an intelligent dog. He's been great company and I'm really glad I adopted him.'

'How did you end up homing him?'

'An elderly client passed away. His son bought HP for him but never helped train him. When the old fella died, HP was a bit overweight and under-exercised. The son brought HP into the surgery and asked if I knew anyone who'd want him. I just couldn't see him go anywhere else. Bulldogs take quite a lot of daily maintenance with their nose rolls and skin conditions and although HP has been lucky in that respect, he still has to be properly cleaned and I keep an eye on his diet too. He's a greedy sod and would keep eating until he burst.'

Camilla rubbed HP's ears and his thick neck and his tongue slipped out the side of his mouth as he gazed at her with his big brown eyes. 'He's lovely.'

'I think so. And it seems he likes you too. Let me get some more wine.'

They spent the next hour laughing and chatting and Camilla slipped into an even more relaxed state than she'd thought possible when HP snuggled down with his large head on her lap. He was soft and warm, his gentle snoring almost hypnotic, and all her previous wariness of him drifted away. HP was a big and powerful dog, but he was also a total softy and his approval made her feel kind of special, as if the fact that he trusted her enough to sleep on her showed that she was a good person.

When Tom leaned forwards to put his empty glass on the table then took Camilla's from her hand, she had to swallow her disappointment.

'It's getting late,' she said, wanting to say it first so he didn't have to, although the thought of returning home alone now didn't seem at all pleasant.

'I've had a lovely time.'

'Me too.' She looked down at HP. 'I hate to move him.'

'He'd sleep there all night if you let him.'

'I think I might lose all feeling in my leg though.'

'You would.'

Tom gently shifted HP so Camilla could move but as she did so, the dog opened his eyes.

'Sorry, boy, but I have to go home. See you soon.' She pressed a kiss on his head and he closed his eyes again.

'Thanks for a lovely evening, Tom.'

'And thank you. It was great to have some human company.'

They walked through the cool hallway to the front door and Tom helped her into her coat then he leaned forwards and he seemed to be about to kiss her. Camilla instinctively closed her eyes and pursed her lips but the kiss didn't come. Instead, she realised as she opened her eyes, that he had, in fact, just been reaching around her to open the door.

She coughed and stretched to hide her embarrassment. Perhaps he hadn't noticed though? Perhaps...

'Good night then.' She turned to step outside but felt his hand on her shoulder.

'Camilla.'

'Yes?'

'Turn around.'

She did so slowly, willing herself to stay calm.

Tom's eyes were dark as they roamed her face, his lips slightly parted. He reached out and stroked her cheek gently. The moment was filled with tension and electricity and every fibre of Camilla's body was alert, her heart was pounding and she longed for him to pull her close and kiss her.

But he didn't.

His touch on her cheek was soft as a butterfly's wings and he was close enough that she could feel his heat, yet he wasn't quite pressed against her. His scent was of ginger and sandalwood, mellow yet spicy, and she breathed it in, wanting to carry it home with her.

'I should walk back with you.'

'No need.' Her voice came out as a squeak.

'I should. I'll grab my coat.'

'It's only five minutes and I've lived here all my life. Besides, I'm trained in self defence.'

'You are?'

'Yes, didn't I tell you?'

'No. And you didn't look like you were when HP... you know... at the Halloween party.'

'I wouldn't use it on a dog. But if anyone attacked me, I'd take them down.'

He shook his head. 'You're quite a woman, you know?'

'Thank you.'

'But I do need to walk you home. I'll worry all night if I don't come with you.'

Camilla shrugged. She didn't need to be walked home but it also meant that she could spend a few extra minutes with him, so she'd go along with it.

Tom pulled on his coat and hat then stepped into his boots. He'd been wearing thick socks around the house even though he'd insisted that Camilla could keep her boots on.

'What about HP?'

'I won't even try to get him out for a walk now. He'd be appalled.'

Tom held out his arm and Camilla slid hers through it then they walked the short distance to her cottage. The air was crisp and the ground was frosty and she was glad of Tom's arm to steady herself. When they reached her cottage, she paused by the gate.

'Would you like to come in?'

'I would, but…'

'Not tonight.'

'Not tonight. But I would really like to see you again.'

'You have my number.'

'And I know where you live.'

'You do.'

She smiled at him. 'Night then.'

'Night.'

Then before she could overthink it, she raised onto her tiptoes and planted a kiss on his lips before turning and hurrying to her front door. She unlocked it, pushed it open and rushed inside, closing it behind her before she could see his expression.

And she burst into laughter, because careful, controlled Camilla had just done something she would never normally do. She'd let her guard down and enjoyed a man's company. She'd felt things she'd never felt before that had been roused by his gentle touch, his warm brown eyes and his compassion. She liked the way he made her feel. It was, she realised, as she removed her coat and boots then plodded up the stairs, a very nice feeling indeed.

Chapter Nine

The next day, after returning from a meeting in London, Camilla went straight to her mother's house. There were things she needed to ask Jackie and they couldn't wait. Even over lunch with one of her most important clients, she'd found herself drifting back to her discussion with her father when he'd told her that he had tried to stay in contact with his daughters. Had he been telling the truth?
She let herself into Jackie's and called out, as she always did, to let her mother know she was there. It was five-thirty and the house was dark, which wasn't that unusual as Jackie often worked on if she was needed, or if she got chatting to one of the people she cleaned for, but she usually left the lamp in the lounge on a timer.
She walked through the downstairs and there was no sign of life, so she went to the bottom of the stairs.
'Mum? Are you home?'
She heard a bang and someone swearing then a door upstairs creaked open.
'Camilla? Is that you?'
'Yes, Mum. Were you in bed? Aren't you well?'
Jackie appeared at the top of the stairs, tying her dressing gown belt.

Camilla flicked the switch on the landing light and stared up at her mother who was shielding her eyes in the brightness.
'God, Mum, what's wrong? Is it the flu? You look terrible.'
She slipped off her coat then hurried up the stairs.
'Come here.'
She wrapped her arm around her mother's shoulders then led her towards her bedroom.
'You get right back into bed and I'll go and find some paracetamol and make you a cup of tea. Actually, I'll go to the shop and get you some juice if there's none here. You look like you need some PENIS!'
In the doorway to Jackie's bedroom stood Laurence.
Wearing nothing except for an expression of horror on his face.
'Flipping heck, Dad, put it away!'
Camilla closed her eyes to prevent herself seeing the part of her father that she had never, ever wanted to see.
'Camilla!' her mother squeaked. 'I'm so sorry, love. You weren't meant to find out like this.'
'Is it safe to open my eyes?'
'Yes, love.'
Laurence stumbled out of the doorway, now clutching a towel around his middle.
'Camilla. Hello, sweetheart.'
Camilla gasped as she realised what was going on.
'I'm so slow!' She smacked her forehead. 'You two are... oh... oh no!'
She released her mother and rushed back across the landing then down the stairs. In the hallway, she froze, not quite sure what to do next. She wanted to run out of the door and never come back, but that wouldn't be very mature. Even as a teenager, she wouldn't have done that. So, instead, she did the grown-up thing and went into the kitchen to make a cup of tea.
When the kettle had boiled, she poured water onto the tea bags she'd put in the pot, then gently swirled it to allow it to brew. There was always comfort to be found in familiar actions and right now she needed comfort. After she'd splashed milk into the mugs, she poured

the tea in then dropped three sugar cubes into her own mug. She didn't usually take sugar in her tea, but she was in shock and wasn't that what they recommended on TV when someone had experienced a trauma?

She carried the mugs to the table in the dining room and sat down. The garden beyond the window was inky black so all she could see was her own white face. She got up and pulled the curtains then sat back down and sipped her tea, wincing as it scalded the tip of her tongue.

'Camilla.' Jackie entered the room, now dressed in jeans and a jumper, closely followed by Laurence who wore jeans and a t-shirt with a picture of a waterslide on it and The Biggest in Benidorm beneath it in neon writing. How inappropriate in light of what she'd just seen, crossed Camilla's mind.

They pulled out chairs and sat down stiffly, as if it was a formal meeting.

'Are you all right?' Jackie eyed her daughter

Camilla stared at her parents with their flushed cheeks and shiny eyes.

'Yes, I'm fine. A bit... surprised, I suppose, but you're both adults so I guess what you get up to is your own affair. Only... it's bit... strange isn't it?'

Jackie and Laurence looked at each other then back at Camilla.

'Why strange, love?' Jackie asked as she cradled her mug. Camilla noticed that she'd had her nails painted. Her mother rarely bothered with getting a manicure or pedicure, rarely ever had her hair cut at the salon, claiming that there was no need as who was going to look at her anyway.

'Well you two... Dad's been gone twenty-five years and as soon as he returns, you jump into bed with him?'

'We didn't mean for it to happen. It just did.' Jackie reached over and took hold of Laurence's hand where it rested on the table.

'Sex doesn't just happen, Mum. It takes effort.'

Jackie's cheeks flushed a darker shade of red and Laurence lifted her hand and kissed it.

'Camilla,' he took a deep breath, 'I have feelings for your mother. And I think she does for me.'

'How can you know that? You've been back for five minutes, Dad. If there's anything between you, it's nostalgia, surely?'

Camilla crossed her arms. Didn't these two realise that they were behaving like irresponsible teenagers?

'Look love, we know we're hardly Romeo and Juliet here, but even at our age, we still have sex... *romantic* feelings.'

Camilla wrinkled her nose.

'Don't pull that face, Camilla.' Jackie frowned. 'It's like you think sex after forty is gross or something.'

'It's not that!' Camilla slammed her hand on the table. 'I know people can have sex all their lives and I don't think there's anything wrong with it. What's wrong here is that Dad left us a long time ago. You were broken. You told me and Dawn, time after time after time that he was a bad man. In fact, you told us that all men were bad and that they couldn't be trusted. You *fell apart* after he left and we had to pick up the pieces. It was heartbreaking.' Her voice trembled at the memory. 'But you did get better... well, you never let it go entirely, but you got on with life. And now... he's here for three days and you're in bed with him?'

Jackie nodded. 'After your dad left, I was ill. I did fall apart. And I am so sorry that you had to take care of yourself and Dawn. You took care of me too, I know. I should have been stronger but I loved this man and he broke my heart. But...' Jackie glanced at her ex husband. 'It was, as you keep saying, a long time ago and seeing him again made me realise that I'm over it.'

'You are?'

'Yes, Camilla. But I also realised that I am still very fond of him and that I fancy him like mad. I haven't... you know... had any lovers since he left.'

'Mum!'

'And it was nice to just let things take their natural course. We had a drink at the pub at lunchtime then came back here and well...' Jackie giggled.

'Camilla, I know it's a bit of a shock but all I can ask of you is that you give us some time.'

'Time for what, Dad?'

'To see where this goes.'

'But you were just basically dumped by your much younger wife. How do you know this isn't a rebound thing?'

Laurence shook his head. 'This isn't. If anything, every relationship I had after your mother was my way of trying to replace her. I never felt I was good enough for her and that one day she might leave me for someone better. I was trying to prove my worth, I guess. And in Benidorm, nothing seemed as real as it does back here in Heatherlea.'

'Your father told me all about his... other two wives and what happened there, Camilla, so you don't need to worry. He's not hiding anything.'

'And what about you?'

'What?'

'Well, Dad didn't tell me exactly but I gathered from what he said that you hid things from us after he left.'

Jackie looked at Laurence and he nodded.

'You mean the cards and letters he sent?'

'And the fact that he phoned. We might not even have wanted to speak to him or to read the cards and letters but the option would have been nice. He left you but he still tried to keep in contact with Dawn and me and you let us believe he didn't want to know us.'

Jackie covered her mouth and her eyes glistened.

'Your mum was upset, love. She was very angry at and she had every right to be—'

'It's OK, Laurence. Camilla's right. It was wrong of me and I'm sorry. I just wanted you to hate him for leaving us. That was so, so wrong of me.' She shook her head.

'Camilla, everyone makes mistakes, some of us more than others. But

I'm back now and I'm not running away again. Please give me a chance. Your mother wants to.'

Jackie got up and stood next to Laurence then wrapped her arms around him. 'I'm not letting you go again.'

'OK…' Camilla released a shaky breath. 'OK. A lot to take in but I get it. At least I want to get it. I can't say it won't be strange having my parents together but you are capable of making up your own minds. Just don't… hurt each other again. And think about Dawnie, won't you? Don't throw this information at her, please, just take it easy and try to handle it sensitively. She's pregnant and… and vulnerable at the best of times. And as for the children, your grandchildren, think of them too.'

'Of course we will, love. Our lips are sealed and as far as they know, your father's just staying here over Christmas until he gets something else sorted. We weren't going to tell you for a while anyway.'

'Then you caught us in flagrante!' Laurence shook his head. 'Apologies for that too.'

'I'm scarred for life now, Dad.' Camilla flashed him a smile to try to diffuse some of the tension in the dining room, even though she didn't really feel like smiling.

'Do you want to stay for dinner, love?' Jackie asked.

'No thanks, Mum. It's Tuesday.'

Laurence frowned. 'What happens on Tuesdays?'

'Camilla, Dawn and their friend Honey all go to The Cosy Cottage Café where the owner Allie makes them food and they put the world to rights.'

'Ahhh. It's good to have friends.'

Camilla nodded. She drained her tea then stood up.

'Right you two. Be careful and don't do anything I wouldn't do.' She grimaced. 'I meant… just be careful.'

She hugged her mother then her father and they walked her to the door, still holding hands.

'See you in the week, but don't worry, I'll ring first. I don't want to see Act two of Fifty Shades Over Fifty.'

She smiled then marched down the path and out into the street. When she was out of sight, she allowed the smile to slip from her face and she slowed her pace. She'd just caught her parents up to goodness knows what and she wasn't sure that either one of them was thinking about how this could go wrong. And it could go very, very wrong indeed. Her mother had been broken when her father left and Camilla couldn't bear to see that happen again. Yet Laurence had told her that he was back for good and that he had feelings for Jackie, so all Camilla could do was hope for the best. She couldn't exactly ban them from seeing each other or make them sleep in separate bedrooms.

Besides, she'd never seen her mother look so young or so happy. Laurence clearly had the ability to make Jackie feel alive and however long that lasted, surely it was a good thing? Although, of course, she preferred not to think that any of it had to do with sex. Who could stand the thought that their parents were doing it? Nope. She would hope that Laurence was making her mum smile again and that he would continue to do so. There was nothing wrong with hoping now, was there?

Chapter Ten

Camilla headed up the path of The Cosy Cottage Café. She was so glad it was Tuesday because she really needed to see her friends, to spend a few hours where she felt comfortable and loved. She wouldn't be able to tell them about what she'd just seen, but at least she could try to put it from her mind for a while.

They would, of course, want to know about how her meeting with her father had gone the previous afternoon at the pub, but she'd already thought about how to deliver that information so as to avoid worrying Dawn. She always considered how best to avoid worrying her little sister, even though Dawn was a grown woman and perfectly capable of dealing with everyday situations. It was, Camilla sometimes thought, more for her own benefit than for Dawn. If she felt that she was looking out for her sister, then she felt useful. So really, if she analysed that objectively, she was well aware that she was relying on Dawn to make her feel needed. She suspected that Dawn knew this too, but they loved each other dearly, so she didn't think Dawn minded being needed too.

She paused for a moment to appreciate the café's exterior. It was such a pretty cottage at any time of year, but with the Christmas tree visible through the window decorated with twinkling lights, the coloured fairy lights draped across the front of the building, the festive wreath hanging on the door and the grey smoke curling up out of the chimney into the dark sky, it was even lovelier than usual. The four front windows glowed invitingly and Camilla felt like she was coming home, something she always felt when she visited The Cosy Cottage Café.

She pushed the door open and went inside, licking her lips as she was greeted by the aromas of freshly baked bread, cinnamon and ginger that were carried on some very welcome warm air.

'Camilla!' Allie greeted her with a kiss on the cheek and a beaming smile.

'Hi, Allie. It's lovely and warm in here.'

'The log burner is wonderful when the weather's like this. It's bitter out, isn't it?'

Camilla nodded.

'Wouldn't be surprised if we have some snow.'

'Really?' Camilla shivered. The last thing she wanted was a big freeze; the idea of being trapped at home alone certainly didn't appeal.

'You never know.' Allie took Camilla's coat then hung it on the stand near the door. 'Now go and take a seat and I'll get you a drink.'

'Thanks.'

Camilla went to the table nearest the log burner, that they always sat at for their Tuesday evenings after Allie had closed the café for the day, and sat next to Dawn. Honey was browsing the bookshelves on the far wall.

'And how are you feeling today, Dawnie?'

Camilla took in her sister's appearance and was pleased to see that she looked well.

'Not too bad, thanks. Rick has made me keep my feet up all day and been very patient whenever I've needed to moan about the *situation*.'

'You mean Dad's return?'

'Who else?'

'It was a bit of a shocker.'
'A bit? I still can't believe he's back. And he seemed so... blasé about it.'
'He did a bit.'
'Have you seen him since Sunday?'
'I popped in on my way back from the station.' Camilla glanced away, worried that Dawn would read something in her eyes about exactly what Camilla had seen earlier.
'And how was he?'
'Oh... uh... all right.'
'And Mum?'
'Yes, she was fine too.'
'Why're you blushing, Camilla?'
'I'm not, am I?' Camilla placed her cool palms against her cheeks and realised they were, in fact, hot. 'It must be the fire. It's so cosy in here after being out in the cold.'
'Did you get any more information about how long Dad's staying around? I haven't been over there yet because I thought they needed some time to talk but I sent Mum a text today to see how she was.'
'What did she say?'
'That she was fine. Nothing more. So I guess I shouldn't worry.'
'No, Dawnie, you definitely shouldn't worry.'
Camilla gazed around at the festive decorations. Allie had made the interior of the café look like a winter wonderland this year with fake snow padding out the bookshelves, sparkling glitter snowflakes dangling from the wooden ceiling beams, silver tealight holders on the tables with snowflake cut outs and twinkling fairylights around the edges of the counter, the inside of the door and windows and on the tree.
'Here you go.' Allie arrived at the table with a bottle of white wine and a bowl of shiny green olives. 'Do you want more lemonade, Dawn?'
'No thanks. I don't want to drink too much because of the bubbles.'
'Shall I get you something else then?'

'No, this is fine for now, thanks.'
'Right I'll go and get the pizzas.'
'I'll give you a hand.' Camilla got up and followed Allie into the café kitchen.
The kitchen was a small space but it was warmly lit with ceiling spotlights, making it extremely inviting, and the smells in there made Camilla's mouth water. On the island in the middle of the kitchen were three large homemade pizzas.
'There's a choice between three cheese, ham, chorizo and mushroom, and spinach, ricotta and mint.'
Camilla eyed the pizzas with their golden crusts and various toppings from the melted cheese to the succulent mushrooms and the bright green herbs freshly sprinkled over the top.
'I can't wait to try them all!'
'Chris made some of his fabulous aioli too, so we'll definitely keep the vampires away tonight. Or should I say the handsome vets?' Allie winked and Camilla shook her head.
'There's no need. Nothing's happened.'
'No? I'm not sure I believe that, Camilla. Come on, help me take these through then you can fill us in with all the wonderful details.'
Camilla picked up a pizza and a small dish of the creamy garlic dip that Chris had made, then followed Allie though to the café. She knew she wouldn't get away with giving them no details at all, but she'd prefer to speak to them about Tom than to have to spend the evening evading discussing her parents and their rekindled romance. Which no one other than her knew about. And which she had to keep to herself. For now at least.
Ten minutes later, the wine had been poured and Camilla was feeling far more relaxed. Honey had regaled them with a tale about the yoga class she'd delivered the previous Sunday that one of the teachers from the local primary school had attended, leaving all the women there open mouthed with surprise.
'There we were, in the freezing cold village hall, me at the front trying to guide my ladies into the downward dog when Dane

Ackerman strode in. I thought he was lost. Not that I'm stereotyping or anything but the only man who's come to my classes up until now is Fred Bennett, and he tends to spend the hour on a chair just doing some upper body stretches. But at eighty-seven, I'm afraid to push him because he hasn't done yoga before. To be honest, I think Fred just likes the company.' She flicked her long multi-coloured hair over her shoulders and smiled.

'So what did you do when Dane walked in?' Camilla asked, glad that the conversation had so far steered clear of her and Tom.

'Smiled and asked him if he needed a mat.'

'He's quite cute isn't he?' Dawn nodded. 'I know him because he teaches year 6. He has quite a following amongst the single mums.'

'I'm not surprised.' A blush spread over Honey's cheeks. 'He's gorgeous. For a primary school teacher anyway.'

'Did he have his own mat?' Camilla was keen to find out.

'No. So I told the rest of my class to carry on with our regular routine then I went over to him, gave him a spare mat and asked what he wanted out of yoga.'

'And?' Allie leaned forwards.

'He said that because he's sustained so many rugby injuries over the years, he's really stiff and gets a lot of aches and pains, and his GP said that yoga might help with flexibility.'

'Ooh! So are you going to help him?'

'Of course. I told him that he could take part in Sunday's session but that he might struggle as they're all quite experienced now. However, I could give him some personal tuition.'

'You didn't?' Dawn giggled.

'I did.'

'When do you start?'

'After Christmas. He's going to come along to group when he can but I said I'll design him a personalised routine to help him loosen up.'

'Do you fancy him?' Camilla sipped her wine.

'Nah... he's over six-foot tall, built like a wall of muscle and has the bluest eyes I've ever seen. Add to that the broken nose and the scar on his lip that I just want to lick and I have no attraction to him what-so-ever.'

Camilla and Dawn rolled their eyes at each other and Allie groaned.

'He sounds horrendous. How come I haven't seen him then?'

'He only started after October half-term when one of the older teachers went off long-term sick. They don't think he'll be back so Mr Ackerman could be round here permanently.' Dawn shifted in her seat. 'I have a foot under my rib today and it's so uncomfortable.'

'I remember that. Jordan was forever kicking my ribs and I swear I was black and blue by the time I gave birth.'

Camilla shivered. 'I don't know how you can stand it. I'd go mad if I had another person in my belly.'

'You might not, you know.' Dawn ran her hands over her rounded stomach. 'Even with swollen ankles, veins in places you didn't know you had them and the over all discomfort, it's still a very special time.'

'I'll take your word for it. I'm just glad I have niece and a nephew and another on the way to dote on.' Camilla picked up the wine bottle and poured more into Allie's glass then Honey's, then her own.

'Anyway, Camilla, weren't you going to tell us about the gorgeous vet?' Allie raised her eyebrows.

'Was I?'

'Yes, what's been going on with you?' Honey asked. 'You never did tell us about the Halloween Party and evaded the questions so many times that I thought perhaps you hadn't even gone but you didn't want to admit it.'

Camilla shook her head. She'd have to tell them something now or this could go on for years.

'Well I told Allie about it the other day when I bumped into her. I've avoided telling you all because it was so embarrassing but basically...'

Five minutes into her story and her sister and friends were laughing so much she thought Dawn might actually pop. Honey had fallen off her chair once and Allie was giggling even though she'd heard the story already.

'Have you seen him since?' Honey asked.

'Yesterday. I bumped into him in the morning and he asked me to meet for a drink. He said he was embarrassed about what had happened.'

'I told you he would be.' Allie nodded. 'My cats are always embarrassing me. Look at what happened with poor deceased Wallace when Luna got hold of him.'

Dawn shuddered. 'Poor Wallace.'

Camilla squeezed her shoulder, knowing that her sister still missed her first little guinea pig, in spite of the fact that Wallace's replacement was absolutely adorable, as were her babies.

'Anyway, we had a drink then I went back to his cottage and had dinner.'

'Ooh! I wish you'd told me about this yesterday, Camilla. It would've take my mind off worrying about Mum and Dad and I could've been wondering what you were doing with Tom Stone instead.'

'Dawn, I know you and it would've given you something else to worry about. Besides, there was nothing to tell. We had dinner, he walked me home, that was it.'

'What no kisses?' Dawn pouted.

'Nope.'

'Camilla, are you blushing?' Allie pointed at her cheeks.

'Well one kiss... a peck that I initiated after he walked me home. But that's it. We're friends and he's very nice and sweet and I fancy him and... oh shit, I really do. I fancy him like mad.' She stared at the other women and they stared back. 'What am I going to do? This isn't supposed to happen to me!'

'Camilla this is a good thing. This is life.' Allie reached across the table and took her hand. 'Remember how you encouraged me when Chris was back in town? You told me to go for it. You said it was high time I enjoyed life and let myself be happy. The same applies to you.'

'No. No, it's different. I mean... he's just so nice. But I'm not.' She hung her head as thoughts swirled through her mind.

'What do you mean you're not nice? Of course you are.' Dawn took

Camilla's other hand. 'You're the loveliest big sister in the world and you have such a warm heart.'
'But I've never let a man get close. In fact, I've pushed them away and even hurt them. What if I hurt Tom? He lives round here and it could be awful... disastrous. I can't allow myself to get close to him.'
'Of course you can. And you won't hurt him.' Dawn squeezed her hand.
Camilla thought of her parents and how her father had run away and how much he had hurt her mother, Dawn and her. But he'd come back and he had reasons for what he'd done, reasons that kind of made sense, even if they didn't completely excuse his behaviour.
'I might. And I don't want to.'
'Camilla, it's OK to be afraid. Love is about taking chances and not all relationships work out but you owe it to yourself to give this a chance if you really like him.' Allie released her hand then raised her wine glass. 'To taking chances on love because let's be honest ladies, it's bloody well worth it!'
They all clinked their glasses then drank.
'It's very early days yet anyway and I don't actually know what Tom wants or if he likes me that much. I'll take it a day at a time.'
'That's all you can do.' Allie nodded. 'That's all any of us can do.'

Chapter Eleven

The next three days flew past as Camilla worked, visited Dawn's to spend time with Laura, James, Lulu, Wallace and Wallace's offspring, and tried to keep herself from texting Tom. Which she failed to resist, of course, but she tried to keep the texts light-hearted and amusing. With her travelling into London and Tom's long hours at the surgery, there was no chance of bumping into him unless she went walking early in the morning, and she was so tired that she convinced herself to stay in bed until a reasonable hour each day. She'd also been trying not to worry too much about her parents and their situation. Hoping she was doing the right thing, she'd kept what she'd seen from Dawn, and she put her faith in her parents to tell Dawn that they were getting back together when they were ready. She knew they were going round to Dawn's for a cuppa that morning but hadn't heard anything, so assumed it all went well and that Dawn wasn't suspicious about their rekindled love affair. Although Camilla now wondered how Dawn would react anyway. She'd been so much happier since Rick had quit his City job to work from home that she didn't seem to get fazed by things anymore. It was as if accepting her third pregnancy, and finding out that her husband loved her as much as when they got together, had released her from anxiety and Camilla loved seeing her far more relaxed. So perhaps Dawn would just take it all in her stride once she did find out. Camilla was also hoping it would work out for Jackie and Laurence, because if it did then life would be easier for all of them. Camilla would feel less responsibility on her own shoulders and that would be very nice indeed.

Friday afternoon arrived and Camilla was itching to see Tom again. She wondered if he felt the same. She'd arranged to meet Allie, Chris and Honey at The Red Fox for the pub quiz that evening, and decided to ask Tom if he'd like to join them. After all, it wasn't really like asking him out on a date, because there would be other people there, but she could ask him if he wanted to be on their team.

She sent a text at four thirty-five then waited.

And waited.

At four fifty-five her mobile buzzed.

Hi Camilla,
Thanks so much for inviting me but I've already agreed to go with Dane. He's new to Heatherlea too and I bumped into him on my run yesterday. We could meet you there though? Two doesn't make a team, after all.
Tom X

She replied.

OK, great. See you around seven. X

Then she sent a text to Honey.

Dane will be at pub with Tom. On our team! X

Her mobile buzzed again.

Yes I know. I'm looking forward to it. Tom X

Camilla groaned. She'd accidentally sent the message as a group text, including Tom and Honey. The darned touch screen buttons were so close together and she didn't always take her time when sending messages.
When her mobile buzzed again, she was afraid to look. But she had to.

Yay! Both our lucky nights then! Honey XX

Another buzz.

Tom X

And another buzz.

Oh no! Is this a group text? Camilla!!!! Read them before you send them. Honey Xx

Camilla placed her mobile on the arm of her sofa and lay back. Oh well, at least there was no danger of Tom being ignorant of how much she liked him. If her behaviour the other evening hadn't given her away, that was.
Now all she had to do was to find something to wear that would say casual and attractive without screaming *I want you in my life. But I don't want to commit. Well at least I don't think I do but, hey, you know some romance would be nice...*
She went upstairs and opened her wardrobe door. At least if she narrowed it down to four or five outfits now, it would save her time later on. She laid a few blouses and jumpers on the bed then opened her drawers and pulled out some of her jeans. The advantage of earning a good income and being single and childless meant that she

had plenty to choose from when it came to clothes, shoes and bags. Her disposable income was hers and her alone, so she could buy herself whatever she wanted. Although sometimes, after a shopping spree, it would have been nice to come home and show someone, to have someone approve of what she'd bought, rather than just doing her own mini fashion show for her plants.

Camilla shook her head. She was getting soft and she blamed her parents and their love revival. She was getting carried away and it would have to stop. Tom probably wasn't even as good looking, intelligent, funny or kind as she thought; she'd probably built him up in her mind since Monday and when she saw him tonight in the pub, she'd be disappointed. Then she'd laugh and get on with her life without giving the vet a second thought.

Yes, that's how it would be.

Wouldn't it?

'Wow!' Camilla's jaw dropped as Honey patted her arm furiously. They were sitting in the corner of the pub near the fireplace with Allie and Chris, and Honey had just drawn her attention to the fact that Tom and Dane had arrived. 'Do you see that, Camilla? They're gorgeous.'

Camilla forced her mouth closed then dragged her eyes from Tom's handsome face.

'I see them.' She met Honey's eyes and they both burst into laughter.

'What're you two giggling about?' Allie asked.

'Look.' Honey nodded at the bar.

'Oh yum.' Allie smiled.

'Excuse me, darling... ahem.' Chris nudged Allie and she turned back to him.

'Sorry, my love. Just approving the girls' choices. I only have eyes for you, of course.'
'You'd better.' Chris kissed Allie softly, his eyes full of her.
'You two are so in love.' Camilla smiled.
'You will be soon, no doubt.' Allie covered her mouth with her hand then muttered, 'They're coming over.'
Camilla straightened in her chair and licked her lips while Honey gathered her colourful hair over one shoulder and played with the ends nonchalantly.
'Evening.' Tom smiled at everyone then his gaze lingered on Camilla. 'Does anyone want a drink?'
'Yes please,' Camilla raised her empty wine glass. 'I'll come and give you a hand.'
'Great.'
Camilla stood up while Tom took a list of drinks then she walked to the bar with him. Dane had taken the seat next to Chris, which meant that he was opposite Honey, and they'd been speaking like old friends as Camilla and Tom walked away.
The quiz turned out to be great fun and Camilla laughed, joked and whispered as her team wrote their answers down to each question in turn. Tom had a broad scientific knowledge, Chris had a wealth of knowledge about the latest bestsellers in the crime fiction chart and Dane knew lots about political history. Allie knew all about baking and maths and Honey answered the art history questions and the sport ones. As for Camilla, she answered when she knew something that no one else did, but on the whole she just enjoyed listening and watching as her friends had a good time.
She was also enjoying being able to sit so close to Tom, to watch him as he thought about the answers and encouraged their teammates. He was kind, caring and attentive and made an effort to include everyone, even trying to coax them into answering questions they found challenging. The more time she spent with him, the more impressed she was.
When the final question had been asked, their answer sheets were

collected in and they were told that the results would be announced in thirty minutes.

'Time for another round then?' Chris asked.

'Oh go on then.' Allie stood up and they took the empties to the bar.

'That was great fun.' Tom turned to Camilla. 'We have a good team here.'

Camilla nodded. 'Might even win.'

He frowned. 'Maybe but I did notice that the team over there,' he gestured at a group of elderly men and women who had whispered furiously throughout the quiz as they debated the answers, 'seemed to know them all.'

'Ah...' Camilla smiled. 'Makes sense. That's Judith Burnley's team. We don't want to challenge their quiz crown.'

'Do they always win?'

'They have whenever I've been here for the quiz.'

'That's right.' Honey leaned over to join in. 'And Judith Burnley is a force to be reckoned with. Don't mess with her whatever you do.'

'Thanks for the warning.' Dane pretended to quiver.

The results came in early with Burnley's Bards winning with nineteen out of twenty correct answers, closely followed by seventeen from Allie's All Stars.

'Do you want another drink or do you want to go?' Tom asked Camilla.

She gazed at him, drinking him in, knowing that she didn't want to leave him and the great evening they'd had but also aware that she was really tired.

'I suppose I should go on home. It's been a tiring week.'

'Come on then, I'll walk you home.'

'There's no need.'

'I'd like to if you don't mind.'

They got their coats and said their goodbyes, earning big knowing smiles from Allie and Honey, and even a wink from Chris, then they made their way out into the December evening.

'Hand?' Tom asked as he held his out.

Camilla stared at it in surprise.

'In case the ground is icy.'

'Oh! Of course.'

She slid her hand into his and heat spread through her at the delight of having his skin against hers. She was glad she'd forgotten her gloves and glad that he wasn't wearing any, even though it was certainly cold enough to justify wearing them.

'What're your plans for the weekend?'

Camilla exhaled, watching her breath curl like smoke into the darkness.

'Nothing much, really. I mean, I suppose I'll need to go to see Mum and Dad.' She shivered. 'Although I'll make sure to give them fair warning before I turn up.'

'Oh?' He glanced at her and she paused for a moment, causing him to stop too.

'It seems that my parents are... very friendly now he's back.'

She watched his face under the glow of the streetlamp, wondering what he would make of this information.

'Very friendly as in... getting on well or as in... hanky-panky?'

'As in the latter.'

'I see.' He nodded. 'And how do you feel about that?'

She sighed then shook her head. 'It's strange. I want them both to be happy, of course I do, but I can't help being concerned too. I mean... at their age and after they've been apart for so long. What if it's not real? What if they wake up after Christmas and look at each other and realise they've made a big mistake? Or what if he does and then he lets her down again? What if... there are so many what ifs.'

Tom took her other hand and stepped closer to her.

'Camilla, I completely understand your concerns here, believe me. But at the end of the day, they're adults. They're old enough to make their own mistakes and to learn from them. You could, of course, try to interfere but where would that get you other than upset? Because I suspect that you would get upset when they didn't listen. It's so difficult trying to advise people, especially your parents and in this case, I think you have to let them get on with it. It might work out and they might be happy. I really hope that's the case. If not… they will deal with it in their own way.'

Camilla ran her eyes over his strong jaw, his cheekbones that were highlighted by the streetlamp and the dark hollows of his eyes. He moved forwards a fraction and she could see the warmth in his gaze. 'You're right. I know you are and it's what I'd already decided to do. I just needed to hear someone else say it.'

'Glad to have helped.' He smiled. 'I do have a question though.'

'Fire away.'

'If you don't have any definite plans tomorrow, do you fancy going somewhere?'

'Like where?' Camilla's heart skipped a beat.

'Like… to a Christmas market perhaps?'

'That sounds like something I might like to do.'

'Fabulous! If you come with me, I'll buy you lunch.'

'Deal.'

He squeezed her hands then released the one and they carried on walking.

When they reached her gate, he squeezed her hand again.

'I'll call for you about nine in the morning. Is that OK?'

'Bright and early?'

'Well I'm always up with HP anyway and we want to be on the road, so to speak, fairly early.'

'I'll be ready.'

'Goodnight, Camilla.'

'Goodnight, Tom.'

He raised her hand and pressed his lips to it, and her heart beat faster as he raised his eyes to meet hers. Then he pulled her towards him, gently lifted her chin with his forefinger and lowered his mouth to hers.

His lips were soft and warm, his breath was sweet and his scent was intoxicating.

When Tom pulled away, Camilla was breathless.

'Now go on in so I know you're safe before I leave.'
'OK…' she squeaked.
'Sweet dreams.'
She nodded then opened her door and went into her home, wondering how she'd ever be able to sleep after that kiss. But she did, and she had the sweetest dreams she'd ever had.

Chapter Twelve

The barren winter landscape whizzed past outside the car window. Dark branches of naked trees pierced the sky and the clusters of houses blocked the light at intervals. But try as she might to focus on the outside world, she was acutely aware that next to her, in the driver's seat, was Tom.
He'd knocked on her door at five minutes to nine and she'd been ready and waiting; her excitement hadn't allowed her to sleep past six-thirty. She'd got up, showered, dressed and tried to force down some breakfast but her stomach had been so fluttery that she'd only managed half a piece of toast.
Tom had refused to tell her where they were going other than that it was a very nice Christmas Market and it was less than an hour away. When she'd locked her front door then walked down the path, she'd gasped when she'd seen his car. A brand new Range Rover Velar, it was sleek, black and so shiny that she could see her reflection in the door as Tom opened it for her to get in. The interior was just as luxurious with smooth leather seats and touchscreen controls. It had that new car smell but the confined space meant that she could also enjoy Tom's scent of sandalwood after-

shave and something lighter that she suspected was a citrus shower gel.

As Tom drove, Camilla allowed herself to relax. It was actually nice to have someone else taking care of things and making the decisions. This was unusual for her, because she liked to control where her life was going and when, but something about Tom made her feel relaxed, and that she could trust him. And this surprised her, even as it pleased her.

'Will HP be all right while you're out?' she asked Tom as they drove through a country lane.

'He'll sleep all morning then use the dog flap if he needs the toilet. He only eats twice a day, and had breakfast before I left, so he'll be fine. Besides, we won't be out late.'

Camilla nodded.

'Did you enjoy the quiz last night?'

'I did. It was a good evening.'

'Me too.' He glanced at her and her stomach flipped as she recalled their goodnight kiss.

'Right we're about ten minutes away so do you want to know where we're going?'

'I think I have an idea...'

'You do?'

'Yes but I don't want to say in case I'm wrong.'

'No harm in guessing, Camilla. It's OK to be wrong about some things. And you probably won't be anyway.'

'OK then... is it Reading?'

He nodded.

'I've been shopping there before but not to the Christmas Market.'

'I did some research and it's meant to be a good one.'

'I'm excited now.'

Camilla gazed at his profile, taking in his strong jaw, dark eyelashes, short brown hair and straight nose. His skin was clear and he was freshly shaven. It made her want to run her hand over his cheek then up through his hair. More than that, being so close to him made her want to hold him close. And that was not something Camilla was used to feeling.

Tom pulled the vehicle into a space in a large open-air car park and cut the engine.

'Do you need to get much today?'

'A few things. Mainly for Dawn and the children. And I suppose I'd better get something for Dad too, now that it looks like he's here for Christmas.'

'No problem.'

'What about you?'

'If I see anything suitable for my parents I'll pick it up.'

'Are you going back to Brighton for Christmas?'

He shook his head. 'Not over Christmas because of work but I am going back next weekend for a few days to drop gifts off and show my face.'

'Is your mum OK with that?'

He shrugged. 'She understands that I needed a fresh start and that my work is here now. She'll be fine. It's a surprise but Dad's whisking her away this year to Paris. He thought that seeing as how I've moved away, it would be a good plan to take her somewhere so she's not moping around. He's always fancied Christmas in France, so now he has the perfect opportunity. He's not a big fan of the festivities anyway.'

'Really?'

Tom shook his head. 'He says it's all a waste of time and money and that we'd be better off scrapping it altogether.'

'I can kind of understand that. I mean, Christmas is about children really isn't it?'

'It is about children but it can also be fun for adults. I'll be on call this year and that's fine, but if I had a family it would be different I suppose.'

'Do you like Christmas?'

'I do. Mum always made it really special when I was growing up and Dad even made the effort to get into the festive spirit.'

'I've always gone along with it all for Mum and Dawn, but more recently it's been about Laura and James. I don't know though... there's just something about Christmas that I like.'

'There is a sense of magic about it.' He smiled. 'Especially when you have good company.'

'Exactly. And the best part is the build up.'

'Days like this.'

'Yes.'

'So let's have some fun, shall we?'

He undid his seatbelt then turned to her and gently stroked her cheek. They gazed at each other for a moment, and the gentle movement of his thumb against her skin made heat course through Camilla. It wasn't just that he was handsome, intelligent and kind. There was more to him and she felt that she had only scratched the surface of who he was and what he could mean to her. Part of her mind cried out that this was wrong, that she didn't do this. Camilla Dix did not develop feelings for men. Ever.

But she quickly squashed the voice and instead turned her head slightly and pressed her lips to Tom's palm. Whatever had happened in her life up to this point, right now, she didn't care. She wanted to enjoy being with Tom today, to lose herself in his company and in just being alive. It might be risky, it might be something she would have scolded herself for just weeks ago. But for today, at least, Camilla was throwing caution to the wind and letting herself have fun.

Camilla slipped her charcoal grey poncho with the faux-fur trim over her head then pulled on her black leather gloves. She'd worn black jeans and a long-sleeved black tunic top with her low-heeled knee-high grey leather boots. It had been cosy in the car but outside, there was a chilly breeze, so she was glad that she'd also brought her black beret, which she now put on before hooking her small cross-body bag over her head and tucking it securely in front of her. When she was ready, she looked up to find Tom smiling at her over the roof of the car. She returned the smile and felt her cheeks glow as she realised he'd been watching her get ready.

She walked around the car and paused as he zipped up his brown leather bomber jacket then tugged a black beanie over his brown hair.

'Do you have gloves?' she asked him.

'No.' He frowned. 'Keep losing them. It's OK though, I have pockets.' He tucked his hands into his jacket to demonstrate and Camilla nodded.

Then he shook his head, brought one hand back out then offered it to Camilla.

'Don't want to risk losing you if it's busy.'

'Please don't.'

She took his hand and he tucked his into his pocket while holding hers firmly, then they made their way towards the Christmas market in Forbury Gardens. Camilla's first thought as they approached the market was how colourful it was. Everywhere she looked she saw red, green, gold and silver. From chalet-style stalls to rides to decorations that hung from lampposts and trees, everything was gorgeously festive.

As they approached a stall, a large Santa plodded past them, rubbing his ample belly as he tucked into a slice of Christmas cake. He smiled as Camilla caught his eye and offered her a *Ho Ho Ho*.

'Think I've got competition there?' Tom nudged her.

'What? From Santa?'

'Well, he does have a fantastic white beard and a sleigh that flies.'

'Good point.' Camilla grinned. 'But he lives in the North Pole and it's a bit far to travel for work.'

'Thank goodness for that.' Tom laughed. 'Although I bet the skiing is amazing there.'

'Have you been skiing?'

'A few times. Have you?'
Camilla nodded.
'And?'
'I enjoyed it. Once I managed to stop, that was.'
'It's great exercise and so invigorating being out in the fresh air, cutting through the snow.'
'I'd like to go again.'
'I'll remember that.'
Camilla smiled inwardly. He made it sound as though there could be a future for them. Then she released a deep breath. She shouldn't get ahead of herself; she didn't even know if she could fall for someone. She'd spent a lifetime erecting emotional barriers, preventing herself from caring for a man. What was different this time?
She knew the answer to that.
It was Tom. He was different. He was… everything she admired in a man and more.
'Penny for them?'
'I was just thinking about how lovely this is but also how hungry I am.'
'Well let's find something to eat first then we can go shopping.'
'Great.'
They approached a colourful stall that looked like it could have blended in at a fairground, where steam poured out of a funnel like chimney in the roof and the aromas of spices and savoury meats filled the air.
'Schnitzel?'
'Sorry?'
'Frites?'
'Pardon?'
Tom pointed at the front of the stall where the words were written. 'It's the German Sausage Company. Fancy something from here?'
Camilla frowned then shook her head. 'I'm in the mood for something sweet. How about crepes?' Camilla nodded at the next stall. 'Now that sounds perfect!'

Tom waited in the queue, still holding Camilla's hand, and when they reached the counter, he ordered for them both, glancing at her twice to check she was in agreement.
Soon, the vendor passed him two large paper plates.
'Let me give you some money.' Camilla released Tom's hand to open her bag but he shook his head. 'My treat.'
'Oh, no. I can't allow that.'
'Please, Camilla, it's just food. You can pay for some drinks or something later on. There'll be plenty of chances for you to spend your money.' He handed her one of the plates.
'OK then.'
They made their way to a bench where they sat down and Tom As they ate, Camilla savoured the perfectly thin crepe that was coated in crunchy sugar and fresh tangy lemon juice.; it seemed even nicer because they were eating alfresco.
When they'd finished, Tom took the tray back to the stall then handed Camilla some paper napkins to wipe her hands.
'Are you thirsty?'
'Yes.'
'How about a hot chocolate?'
'Mmmm.'
This time, Camilla paid, and handed Tom a colourful mug featuring a festive pattern.
They stood near the stall as they drank the sweet creamy drink that was topped with whipped cream and marshmallows. It might have been the sugar hit from the crepe and the drink but Camilla felt full of energy and she couldn't stop smiling.
After they'd returned the mugs, they walked along, peering into the chalets and soaking up the atmosphere. Camilla realised that she'd never done this with a man before, at least she'd never walked along holding a man's hand, comfortable when they were talking as well as when they were silent, and she marvelled at how Tom relaxed her so much that she could enjoy it.
They paused at a chalet selling colourful wooden toys.

'Do you think there might be something in there for your nephew?' Tom asked.
'There might be.'
They went into the cosy space and looked at the toys on offer. There were small red trains, figures, animals and houses.
'What about this?' Tom asked as he held up a car transporter. 'It has four cars with it and looks pretty sturdy.
'That's lovely. I think James would really like it.' Camilla took the box from him. 'Ooh! And there's a car wash. I'll get that too.'
'What about your niece?'
Camilla roamed her eyes over the rest of the toys. 'Well she's not much older than James but sometimes she seems like a teenager.'
'They grow up so quickly these days.' Tom shook his head and pursed his lips. It made his chin dimple more prominent and Camilla had a sudden urge to kiss it. 'Are you OK?'
'What? Why?'
'Your cheeks just went bright red... as if you suddenly got hot.'
Camilla smiled. 'I'm absolutely perfect, thank you. I'll get these for James but keep looking for Laura.'
She paid for the toys then the stallholder wrapped them in tissue paper and put them into a bag, which she handed to Tom.
'Oh it's all right. I can carry them.' Camilla held out her hand but Tom shook his head.
'Allow me. You can keep your hands free for shopping then.'
'But you have shopping to do too.'
'Not as much as you and besides, you need one hand free to do this.' He took her hand as they walked out of the chalet.
'Of course I do.'
Camilla smiled and squeezed his fingers.
They went from chalet to chalet and she bought gifts for her mother, Dawn, Rick, Allie and Honey. When they reached the end of the row, she groaned.
'What's wrong?' Tom leaned closer to look at her.
'I just realised I'll need to get something for my dad. I haven't bought

him anything in years as there was no point, obviously, but now he's here and staying for the foreseeable future, I need to get him something but I have no idea what.'

Tom frowned. 'It's a difficult one but everyone needs something to drink out of, right?'

He pointed at a stall opposite and Camilla saw that it sold kitchenware.

'You could get him a tankard. That's a suitable dad present, right?'

They made their way over to the chalet.

'These carved pewter tankards are nice.' She held one up. It had an elaborate Celtic band around the middle.

'That is nice. Does he have any Celtic roots?'

Camilla chewed her bottom lip. 'I think there was a Welsh great grandfather in the mix somewhere.'

'There you go then! Perfect.'

Camilla paid for the tankard then they went back into the fresh air.

'OK, I think I just need something for Laura. But what about you? You haven't bought a thing yet.' Camilla gazed up at Tom, enjoying the warmth in his soft brown eyes and the way his skin glowed in the cold. He was so handsome that she was breathless just looking at him.

Tom nodded at the bags he was carrying. 'It looks like I've bought plenty though doesn't it?'

'Give me some of the bags.'

'Nope. You need to keep looking for Laura. Don't worry about me, even if I don't get anything today, I'll pick something up next week when I go back to Brighton. They'll be away for Christmas anyway, so if I get them something to take, it'll need to be small enough to fit into their suitcase.'

An hour later, following another stop for roasted chestnuts and a coffee, they came across a bookstall selling beautifully illustrated versions of children's fairytales. Camilla bought two collections for Laura and picked one up for James, explaining to Tom that she couldn't resist buying books for her niece and nephew.

'What time is it?' Tom asked.

Camilla checked her mobile. 'It's one-thirty. I can't believe it. Where did the morning go?'
'Are you tired?'
'Not really. Are you?'
He shook his head. 'Let's walk for a bit then and see what else is here.'
They wandered along, holding hands and enjoying the pretty chalets, the colourful strings of lights that hung from lampposts and food stalls and the Christmas carols that filled the afternoon air as they flowed from speakers positioned around the market.
At the end of the path was a large Christmas tree decorated with hundreds of round white baubles. As the approached, Tom sighed audibly.
'What is it?'
'Look closely.'
Camilla did and she saw that the baubles all had pictures of dogs on them.
'It's a rescue charity that supports dogs.'
'By selling baubles?'
'All sorts of things but this is what they do at Christmas. I've seen them around before.'
He pulled his wallet out of his back pocket.
'Pick one.'
'Oh... Uh...' Camilla gazed at the baubles and saw greyhounds, Yorkshire terriers, labradors, poodles and more.
'How about this one?'
Tom held out a silver bauble with a handsome British bulldog on it. The dog's bottom teeth protruded slightly from his jaw and he wore a red Santa hat on his large head.
'He's gorgeous! Looks just like HP.'
Tom nodded then handed a twenty-pound note to the fairy holding a collection tin.
'Thank you kind sir!' she said. 'We don't have any change though unfortunately, so do you want to give me something smaller?'

Tom waved a hand. 'I don't want change. Hope you raise plenty today for the dogs.'
'Merry Christmas!' the fairy said, offering Tom and Camilla a broad smile.
Tom gave the bauble to Camilla.
'Merry Christmas, Camilla.'
'Don't you want to keep it?'
'No. It's for you. So you can remember today. If you want it of course.'
Camilla slid the bauble into her handbag then zipped it carefully.
'Thank you. I can't wait to put it on my tree.'
As they wandered around, they passed an ice rink and bumper cars, both of which Tom asked Camilla if she wanted to try but she laughed and declined. They had lots of shopping bags and she suspected that the skating needed to be booked in advance. There were teenagers whizzing around on the ice and she didn't fancy getting bumped, plus the queues were building for the stalls and the Christmas market was getting really busy.
'Ready to make a move then?' Tom asked. 'Just thinking that with the drive, it'll be about right then to get back for HP and give him his dinner.'
'Yes, OK.' Camilla nodded as they turned and made their way back to the car park.
'Let's pick up something for lunch on the way back.'
They stopped at the German Sausage factory stall and Camilla bought them a tray of frites to share. They ate as they walked, savouring the hot salty chips.
Once they were inside the car and her shopping bags were safely stowed in the boot, she realised how tired she was. The combination of good food, hours in the fresh air and the emotions that Tom stirred in her, had all combined to make her sleepy. And as Tom pulled out onto the main road and Silent Night flowed from the car radio, Camilla tried to stay awake, but soon found herself drifting into a delicious snooze.

Winter at the Cosy Cottage Café

Camilla pushed open her front door then turned and waved at Tom. He beeped the horn before driving away. As she closed the door behind her then set her bags on the hall floor, she smiled. It had been a wonderful day and she'd enjoyed Tom's company immensely. But she couldn't deny that having to say goodbye just then in the car, was difficult. She'd fallen asleep on the journey home and only woken when they'd reached Heatherlea. Tom had smiled when she'd apologised and told her that he completely understood and planned to have a nap once he'd fed HP. It had made her feel a bit better but she also felt sad that she hadn't made the most of his company in the car. However, yet again, she realised that Tom made her feel incredibly relaxed. So relaxed that she was able to sleep in his company.
Was that a good thing? She wasn't sure. Especially if she'd been dribbling.
She unhooked her handbag from around her body and went to hang it on the banister but then noticed that it was bulging and remembered the bulldog bauble. She took it out of her bag, went into the lounge then hooked it onto a branch of the Christmas tree, right at the front. It was a gift from Tom and she knew she would treasure it, just as she'd treasure the memories of their day out.
Camilla knew that she was acting out of character, she knew that she'd never allowed herself to get this emotionally attached to a man before, and she wanted to stop herself caring about Tom, but she also knew, without a doubt, that it was far too late for that.

Chapter Thirteen

The rest of the weekend passed quietly. Camilla had hoped that Tom might text her to invite her round that evening or the next day, but the text he sent her at ten-thirty Sunday morning said that he'd fed HP after he'd arrived home on Saturday, then lay down on his bed for a nap and hadn't woken until six am on Sunday. He'd had errands to run, like food shopping and cleaning the car, and he said he hoped to see her in the week. She wondered if he was being deliberately cool, if he was really that cool about their relationship, or if he was trying to remain in control of his own feelings.

Camilla had gone to Jackie's for Sunday lunch and enjoyed her time there with Dawn, Rick and the children, and felt some hope that things would work out all right for her parents after all. It was still a bit strange having Laurence around but she knew she could get used to it. And seeing her mother so happy, positively glowing in fact, made Camilla want it to work out with all of her heart.

The week passed in a blur as she was busy meeting clients before the start of the Christmas break. Being self-employed, it was tempting to keep working right up to Christmas Day but for the first time in years, she found that she didn't want to. She wanted to enjoy some time with her family and, if possible, some time with Tom.

On Thursday evening, Tom sent a text to ask her to meet him at The Red Fox on Friday for lunch. He said he was taking a half day in order to travel back to Brighton that evening. Camilla's heart had sunk. She hadn't realised he was going on the Friday but comforted herself with the fact that he'd said he'd be back for Christmas, as the locum vet covering him couldn't do Christmas Eve or Christmas Day. Camilla replied and told him she'd be there at one. And she was, walking into the pub with her heart in her mouth. She hadn't seen Tom since the previous Saturday and she'd missed him. So much so that she had an ache in her chest and worried that she'd become emotional when she laid eyes on him.

Tom was already at the bar and he smiled when he saw her. The pub was warm and cosy and Camilla removed her hat and gloves as she approached Tom.

'Hey there, beautiful.' Tom kissed her cheek. 'I've missed you.'

'You have?' Camilla unbuttoned her coat and shrugged out of it then hooked it over her arm.

'Yes, of course. It's just been a mad week. What with call-outs and emergency surgeries and the like, you'd think every animal in the vicinity was trying to get their ailments out of the way before Christmas.' He ran a hand through his dark hair. 'I'm exhausted. The last thing I feel like on a Friday is travelling back to Brighton. I'd much prefer to spend it in front of the TV with a delightful companion.'

'I'm sure HP would like that too.'

Tom frowned. 'I meant with you.'

Camilla laughed. 'I hoped you did.'

'What can I get you?'

'I'll have a coffee, please.'

Tom paid for two coffees then they took them to a table near the fireplace.

'What have you been up to?' he asked as he hung his coat over the back of a chair.

'Work. Sunday lunch with my parents. You know... the usual.' She huffed. 'Actually, not the usual. It's still really strange saying *my parents* rather than just *my mother*.'

'It will probably take a while to get used to it. How's it going anyway... with your mum and dad?'

'They seem happy.' Camilla worried her bottom lip. 'At least, that's how I think they seem. It's almost like he never went away.'

'That's good, right?'

She nodded.

'Anyway, what time are you leaving?'

'About four. I was thinking later initially, but if I hit traffic, I don't want to be too late arriving. I've already packed what I need for the weekend.'

'What about Christmas presents? You haven't had time to get any have you?'

A grin spread across his face. 'Don't tell them but I ordered from Amazon. I had a delivery yesterday to the surgery, so Mum and Dad are all sorted.'

'I like your thinking.'

'Camilla... I had a great time on Saturday. I didn't want the day to end.'

She swallowed hard. 'Me either.'

'I'd like to do it again some time. If you would?'

'What go to a Christmas market?'

'Not just that. A day out. Wherever you fancy. Before or after Christmas.'

'That would be lovely. Why not both?'

As she gazed into Tom's eyes, his pupils dilated and her stomach fluttered. She could look at him all day long and not get bored.

'What're you doing this weekend?'

'I promised Allie I'd help her pack food parcels for the elderly folks in the village. She does it every year... fills boxes with her cakes, jams and a bottle of something then delivers them to anyone she knows who is in need of a treat.'

'Your weekend will be taken up visiting then?'
Camilla nodded. 'I don't mind. I always end up thinking about how lonely it must be when you don't have anyone around. Lots of people don't, especially if their friends and partners have passed on.'
Tom nodded. 'Life can be lonely whatever age you are but especially if you're elderly and can't get out and about.'
Camilla sipped her coffee as she pondered his comment. She'd never thought of herself as lonely, preferring to see herself as a busy career woman with friends and family to visit and her own pretty little cottage to go back to. However, since she'd spent time with Tom, she found being alone hard. It was as if she missed his gentle presence, his warmth and his smile and she thought about him constantly. She'd never had a man take up so much of her heart and mind before and she wondered if he thought about her too.
But he probably didn't. She knew men liked her looks and that they wanted her company, especially if they wanted an attractive companion for an evening out or a weekend away, but she'd never had a deeper connection with those men, even if they'd slept together. It had been physical and fun and nothing more. But with Tom, they'd kissed but not even had sex, and yet... he was under her skin and there was nothing she could do about it.
'Do you want to go back to mine?' she blurted.
Tom placed his mug on the table and met her gaze.
'Don't you want to eat here?'
Camilla took a deep breath. 'I just thought you might want to be alone.'
'Oh...' He reached across the table and took her hands. 'Camilla... I...'
She stood up and pulled him up quickly, before she could change her mind or allow doubt about how he felt for her to enter hers.
'I have some fabulous coffee there and a cold chicken and ham pie that Allie gave me yesterday. It'll be delicious with potato salad.'
Tom grabbed his coat and helped Camilla into hers then they hurried from the pub and made their way to her cottage, giggling along the way like mischievous Christmas elves.

Rachel Griffiths

Camilla set the table in her small kitchen then went to the fridge and got a bottle of wine out. She held it up for a moment to read the label then paused. Tom had to drive to Brighton later, so giving him wine was not a good idea. Besides, she was so nervous that she realised she might neck a glass or two and that would be wrong. Because she wanted to be fully alert for whatever might happen between them. She put the wine back in the fridge and got the pie out along with a tub of potato salad, also courtesy of Allie, and placed them on the table. Then she filled a jug with water and slices of lemon and put that on the table between the wine glasses.

'Tom?' she called him but he didn't appear, so she went through to the lounge and found him standing in front of her bookshelves.

He smiled at her. 'You really like to read, huh?'

She nodded. 'Always have. I forget that the shelves are so full most of the time as I'm rushing around, but all except for those on the two shelves at the bottom – and they're my to-be-read shelves – have been devoured over the years.'

The bookshelves took up the wall opposite the window and were groaning with the weight of all her books. For Camilla, the books were part of her life story. She'd read some of them more than once as she liked to revisit stories and characters she'd grown attached to on a precious reading, but she also had an addiction to buying more books, so she'd made room for the TBR books too.

'And is this you?' Tom held up a gold frame that held a photograph.

'Yes. Me and Dawnie in the local park. I was eight there and she was six.'

'Did your mum take the photo?'

She shook her head. 'That would've been Dad. After he left, the photographs stopped for a while. Mum just didn't have the heart for it.'

'My mother was the keen photographer in our house. She has boxes and boxes of photos of me. And what for?' He shook his head. 'After she's gone, who's going to want them? I certainly won't. They're of my most embarrassing years.'

'Embarrassing?' Camilla eyed him. She couldn't imagine him looking anything less than gorgeous.

'Oh yes. I wasn't always so... dashing!' He laughed and it lit up his whole face.

'You weren't?'

'Uh uh. First there are the faded baby pictures with me in all sorts of horrendous outfits, closely followed by me as a toddler with a bizarre bowl cut. My mother cut my hair herself for years and boy does it look like it! I have kind of a cowlick going on so a fringe never did sit right. When my adult teeth came in wonky, and it was not a pretty sight, I had a brace fitted. There are about two years of photos of me looking extremely awkward and uncomfortable as I try to smile with my mouth closed. Next up, is young adult me... very thin and with no fashion sense at all, and by that I mean I wore whatever was in fashion even if it didn't suit me and then... I learnt to hide from the camera.'

'I would love to see those photos. I bet they're not half as bad as you think.'

'Perhaps one day I'll show them to you. After I've had a few drinks.'

'Deal!'

'But you've always been beautiful. Just look at you on here with that lovely dark hair and those sparkling emerald eyes. You're stunning, Camilla.'

He placed the frame carefully back on the shelf and turned to her.

'Shall we eat?' she squeaked as his eyes found hers and she saw something in their depths that stirred her heart.

'OK.' He nodded then followed her into the kitchen.

They ate slices of the savoury pie with creamy potato salad and washed it down with the lemon water. It was a simple meal but a good one, and Tom made Camilla laugh as he regaled her with stories of his childhood. She had some that she shared, from before Laurence left, but after she turned ten, there weren't many good memories. Not until she went to university and escaped Heatherlea for a while. But she loved the village and had always known she would come back to live there. So what had she been keen to escape? Certainly not Dawnie, who she had always adored, so had she needed to escape her mother and the shadow of the past?

She took a sip of her water as a bitter taste filled her mouth. Camilla loved her mother, she really did, but Jackie had been difficult to live with. Difficult to be around every day. And Camilla had felt selfish but she had wanted to live, to stretch her wings for a while and going to university had allowed her to do that. She'd come back and settled into her life again, knowing that she'd be there for Jackie whenever she needed her, and in the time she'd been away, her mother had seemed to relax her hold on Camilla and to grow in terms of her own independence. So it had been good for both of them and for Dawnie too, especially when Dawn had gone to university and had her own taste of a life without the shadow of Laurence and what he'd left behind.

Camilla realised that she still blamed her father for leaving but she knew Jackie was to blame for some of what had happened too. And yet... it was all such a long time ago and life had moved on. People moved on and always would do. Camilla might be able to move on herself if something happened between her and Tom. She'd never thought she could care for a man and the one sitting opposite her right now was altering her long held belief by the minute.

'That was a delicious lunch, Camilla. I'll wash the dishes, shall I?'

'No, no. Leave them.' Camilla stood and carried her plate and glass to the sink. 'You'll be going soon and I'd prefer to spend the time enjoying your company than washing up. I'll do them later. Let's have a cup of tea and go and sit in the lounge.'

'If you're sure.'

'I am. Do you want to light the fire?'

Tom nodded and went through to the lounge while Camille made tea. She put two mugs on a tray then filled them with tea from the pot once it was brewed and got a packet of biscuits from the cupboard. She arranged the biscuits on a plate, wishing all the time that Tom wasn't going soon and that they could spend the evening together. When she entered the lounge ten minutes later, the fire was already crackling in the grate, the Christmas tree lights were twinkling and Mariah Carey's Christmas hits flowed from the stereo in the corner. Tom was on the sofa, his left arm stretched over the back of the seats and his eyes were closed as if he'd fallen asleep as soon as he sat down.

Camilla gently placed the tray on the coffee table and sat next to Tom. She turned in her seat so she could look at him then wriggled closer so that his arm was behind her. She breathed in his now familiar scent, enjoying how good he smelt and how comfortable he seemed in her home.

Suddenly, he grabbed her and pulled her closer, causing her to squeal.

'What're you staring at Ms Dix?'

'You had food on your face.'

'What?' He raised his eyebrows. 'That's not true!'

He pulled her over his legs then started tickling her. She writhed as his fingers wriggled over her tummy and hips then under her arms, and tried to tell him to stop but she couldn't because she was laughing so hard.

When he finally stopped and helped her to sit upright, she realised she was sitting on his lap with his arms encircling her. Her heart pounded as he moved his head closer to hers and when their lips met, she moaned softly with delight. They kissed for a while, gently tasting each other and Tom ran his hands over her face and shoulders then up and down her arms. Her whole body responded to him and she slid her arms around his neck and hugged him tight.

'Camilla?' Tom pulled away slowly but didn't release her.

'Yes?'

'We should stop.'

'Why?'
'This wouldn't be right.'
She surfaced from the fog of need and desire as quickly as she would have if he'd thrown a bucket of iced water over her.
'What?'
'Not like this, not when I'm going away for a few days.'
'Oh.'
'Believe me, it's not that I don't want to… because I really, really do. I just don't want to make love to you then have to leave you until next week. If I made love to you now, I would want to hold you all night.'
Camilla wriggled off his lap and swung her legs over the sofa so she was sitting next to him.
'Can you understand that?'
She met his warm chocolate-brown eyes and tried to read them. Was he being honest? Did he really desire her as much as she did him or was he letting her down gently? Had she read the signals wrong and thrown herself at him? Camilla never threw herself at anyone; the men who wanted her did all the chasing and she was the one to pull back or walk away. Always.
She reached for her mug of tea and cradled it between her hands.
'Yes, it's fine. Don't worry about it. I understand.'
Tom touched her cheek then rested his hand on the back of her neck. Emotion bubbled inside her. She wanted him to want her, to care for her and to need her but she was afraid to tell him. He would probably be scared away and she hated to show any weakness. She never wanted to be… like her mum had been.
'Maybe when I come back, we can pick up where we left off. I have some things to sort when I go back to Brighton but next week, I'd love to see you as soon as I'm home. Would that be OK with you?'
Camilla nodded. Although her body was aching with longing and her heart was pounding with insecurity, she knew deep down that Tom was being very sensible and very adult about all of this. It was how Camilla would normally be. Cool, calm and in control. But today she wasn't and that was because of Tom.

A giggle burst from her chest.

'Camilla? What's funny?' Tom frowned in confusion.

'Oh...' She shook her head. 'It's just me and my strange sense of humour.'

She raised her mug to hide her smile. She wanted to explain but surely Tom would think her mad because she was actually delighted that she was feeling everything so vividly around him, and she was in awe of her own emotions. Even though she was apprehensive, she was happy. Tom had awakened emotions in her that she didn't know she had, let alone the scope of their intensity and depth.

So she would wait until he returned and look forward to seeing him again, to seeing if this could go somewhere. She hoped with all of her heart that it would.

Chapter Fourteen

'Put your finger there.'
'Gosh you're bossy, Dawnie.'
'Only when I need to be. Now come on... finger!'
Camilla pressed her finger to the knotted ribbon and held it there while her sister tied a big red bow.
'Lovely. Don't you think?'
Camilla nodded.
'And that's it then, ladies.' Allie stood back and admired the three tables of festive baskets.
'This is really generous of you, Allie.' Camilla stood next to her friend.
'I'm just trying to give a little something back to the village that gives so much to me.'
'Heatherlea is a lovely place to live, isn't it?' Dawn asked as she rubbed her bump.
'I love it here. Especially since Chris came back.' Allie smiled and Camilla groaned.
'Well don't you find it even nicer since Tom moved here?' Allie met Camilla's eyes.

'I've always loved Heatherlea. I'll admit that there have been times when I've been a bit down and have enjoyed the escape of heading into London, or flying away somewhere warm, but I always come back.'

Dawn wrapped an arm around Camilla's waist. 'You always did, Camilla. You always came home to look after me and Mum.'

Camilla smiled then eyed the baskets that Allie had packed for the elderly people of the village. Inside each one was a jar of homemade jam, a bottle of ginger cordial, a Christmas cake, six mince pies, four gingerbread people and a small box of chocolates. The baskets had been packed then wrapped in cellophane that was tied with a red ribbon.

'When are you going to deliver them?' she asked Allie.

'I won't.'

'You won't?'

Allie shook her head. 'Jordan and Max have volunteered. It's so handy having their help. They make a great team.'

'They seem really happy.'

'Yes they are. And to think I had no idea that Jordan was in love with his best friend. It couldn't have worked out better for them.'

Dawn stretched and groaned.

'Right Mrs, get yourself onto that sofa with your feet up and I'll make us some gingerbread hot chocolates.'

'Now you're talking.'

'Camilla, you too.'

'No, I can help you.'

'Nope! Sit! You've helped me enough this morning.'

Camilla and Dawn went over to the comfy leather sofa near the window and sat down. Dawn moaned as she sank into the leather and Camilla helped her to prop her feet up on a cushion that she placed on the coffee table in front of the sofa.

"I know you're tired, Dawn, but you're glowing today.'

'Thanks. I don't feel it though. This baby is sapping all my energy.'

'How are Laura and James?'

'Excited. They finish school on Wednesday, so then it'll be Christmas mayhem.'
'It's lovely though isn't it? The excitement of Christmas. I love seeing their faces when they open their presents.'
'And next year there will be another one to enjoy the fun.'
'I'm excited about that.'
'Camilla...'
'Yes.'
'When were you going to tell me about Mum and Dad?'
'What do you mean?'
'Oh come on... it's obvious.'
'I was waiting until it was more... permanent. I didn't know if they were just getting to know each other again and if it would all go wrong. It still could do and I was afraid that you'd get hurt all over again.'
Dawn nodded. 'I can see why but I am all grown up now, Camilla.'
'I know that.'
'I'm grateful to you for the way you still look out for me but I can take the truth and it's better for me to know about things like this. Otherwise I might... you know... accidentally FaceTime Mum when she's... well, you know.'
'You didn't!' Camilla covered her eyes for a moment.
'I did and she must have forgotten that I could see her. I guess she was caught up in the passion of the moment and she answered when she was naked.'
'With Dad?'
Dawn nodded. 'It wasn't a pretty sight, let me tell you.'
'I caught them at it too.'
'See! If you'd told me then I would have been prepared but as it was, I had to quickly cover the screen of my phone and tell her to get dressed.'
'I'm sorry.'
Dawn took Camilla's hand. 'It's OK. At least it's out in the open now.'

'And how do you feel about it?'

'I'm happy for them. I was a bit surprised. I mean, after all those years of Mum calling him every name under the sun, I didn't expect her to jump into bed with him again. But she's an adult woman and she knows what she wants... or at least her body does.'

'I guess so.'

'Let's just hope it works out for them.'

'Or we'll be picking up the pieces.'

'Exactly. And to be honest with you, much as I love Mum, I'm not going to have the time with two kids and a baby. It's not fair that you should have to spend all your time taking care of her either.'

'Well let's see what happens. Who knows... perhaps there'll be a wedding and we'll be able to let them live happily ever after.'

Dawn laughed. 'Oh I hope so. It would be nice wouldn't it? To have parents who're together. I have missed Dad, even though he was a total bastard for leaving us.'

'I don't think it was quite as clean cut as we thought, Dawnie.'

'No?'

Camilla shook her head. 'More to it. Some of it Mum's fault.'

'Well that's to be expected really, isn't it? It takes two to make a relationship and two to break it. At least, that's what I want to believe. Otherwise it's a bit hard not to still feel mad at him isn't it?'

'It wasn't all his fault. Hopefully, in time, he'll speak to you about it too. He didn't say anything negative about Mum but I know that the blame can't be placed entirely on him.'

'Here we go, ladies. Gingerbread hot chocolates and Christmas cake.'

'You've cut your cake early for us?' Camilla asked.

'Not my own one, no. I made a load for the baskets and there are a few left over, so I thought we could enjoy some now.'

Camilla handed Dawn a china plate with a slice of shiny brown cake on it, then she took a plate for herself. She sniffed the slice of cake and aromas of cinnamon, orange, mixed fruit and marzipan made her mouth water. The cake was packed with sultanas, raisins, dates and cherries. The top and side had a thin layer of yellow marzipan and a slightly thicker one of crisp bright white icing. As she bit into the cake, her mouth was filled with festive cheer.

'Delicious, Allie,' she said once she'd eaten it.

'Thank you. It's the same old recipe I use every year.'

'It's so good. Never change it.' Dawn licked her lips. 'The heartburn will be worth it.'

'Oh no! Do you want some milk?' Allie asked.

'It's fine. I'll have my hot chocolate then see how it goes. I have antacids in my bag anyway. I carry them everywhere.'

'How are things going with Tom?' Allie asked before taking a sip of her hot chocolate.

Camilla shrugged. 'He's busy, I'm busy, so… we're just enjoying each other's company when we can.'

'All right…' Allie nodded.

'I think she loves him.' Dawn bit her lip and giggled.

'Look, little sister, just because you're pregnant doesn't mean I'll let you get away with comments like that.'

'Like what?' Dawn widened her eyes. 'I'm hormonal. I'm allowed to be a bit… emotional about things.'

'Excuses, excuses.' Camilla wagged a finger at her sister.

'But you do love him, don't you?'

'No I don't. It's far too early to be making such sweeping statements.'

'Is it?' Allie met her eyes.

'Well yes. We've only been out together a few times and I do like him but it's nothing more.'

'No?' Allie smiled.

'No.'

'Where is he now?'

'He's gone back to Brighton to see his parents before Christmas but he'll be back early next week.'

'And how do you feel now that's he's away?'

Camilla stared into her mug. How did she feel?

'He only went yesterday.'

'And?' Dawn nudged her.

'I feel terrible. All achy and empty and I just wish I knew I'd be seeing him later.'
'See!' Dawn clapped her hands. 'It's love.'
'No it's not. At least I don't think it is. Oh god... how would I know?' Camilla looked at her sister then at her best friend. 'How the hell do you know when it's love?'
'You just do.' Allie nodded. 'In here, in your heart. You'll know if he's the one you want.'
'But what if I let myself believe that then he doesn't feel the same way?' Panic surged through Camilla at the thought. What if she did let herself love Tom and he didn't reciprocate those feelings?
'That's a chance we take on love but after seeing how he was gazing at you during the pub quiz, I don't think you've got anything to worry about.' Allie sighed. 'In fact, he seemed so smitten that even Chris commented on it.'
'He did?' Heat warmed Camilla's cheeks and a lovely glow spread through her.
'He did. When we got home, he told me that he thought Tom seemed well loved-up.'
Camilla covered her chest with her hands and took a few slow deep breaths. She felt dizzy, elated and confused and had a sense that she was falling, yet she knew she was sitting on the sofa in Allie's café. But perhaps she wasn't actually falling anywhere literal; perhaps she was falling in love.
'The physical effect of all of this is quite... alien to me.'
Allie and Dawn nodded.
'Am I going to be OK?'
'Of course you will.' Dawn patted her hand. 'We've got you. And this is a good thing.'
'A very good thing,' Allie added.
'Oh look... I've finished my hot chocolate.' Dawn pouted as she stared into her empty mug.
'I'll make us all another one, shall I? After all, Camilla's falling in

love, so she needs all the strength she can muster to deal with the emotions.'

Camilla nodded, wondering why her eyes had filled with tears and why she suddenly felt shaky. But as Dawn pulled her into a hug and she rested a hand on her sister's curved belly, she realised that it would all be OK. She had her family and she had her friends and she had the added security of being able to enjoy the comfort of The Cosy Cottage Café.

The emotions swirling inside her were new but they were good. So she was going to enjoy them and embrace them, just as she would embrace Tom when she next saw him. And she couldn't wait for that.

Chapter Fifteen

'Your turn!' Laura nudged Camilla as they sat at Jackie's table that Sunday afternoon.
'Pardon?' Camilla shook herself as she realised she'd been staring into space.
'I said it's your turn, Auntie Camilla.'
'So it is!'
Camilla shook the dice, rolled them, then counted the four spaces along the snakes and ladders board.
'Ha ha! Down the snake!' James clapped his hands. 'You lose!' He held up his left hand making the shape of a backwards L.
'James, that's the wrong hand.' Laura rolled her eyes at Camilla.
'And we told you not to do that didn't we?' Dawn said as she walked into the room to find her son now holding up his right hand and making an L shape at Camilla.
'It's only a bit of fun,' Camilla said as she winked at her nephew.
'You might think that but his teacher doesn't. She rang Rick last week to say that James had done it to her when she couldn't find her glasses.'

Camilla bit her bottom lip to stop herself from laughing. James was an adorable little boy but he definitely had a wicked side.

'Your turn then, James,' Laura said and James shook the dice then moved his small blue figure along the board.

'You want a cuppa?' Dawn asked Camilla.

'That would be lovely, thanks.'

'I win!' James shouted suddenly then jumped up and pulled his t-shirt over his head.

'James, be careful!' Dawn called as he bounced around the room then tripped over a chair leg and landed facedown on the floor.

'I've got him.' Camilla got up and hurried around the table. She gently pulled his t-shirt back down and peered at his face, afraid that he'd be in tears but instead he was grinning up at her. 'Are you all right?'

'Yes thank you, Auntie Camilla. I won!'

She shook her head then helped him to his feet.

'Come on, Dawnie, I need that tea. Or perhaps something stronger.'

Dawn nodded and they went through to the kitchen.

Jackie was standing in front of the sink gazing out into the garden and Laurence was at her side, where he always seemed to be since his return to Heatherlea, and they were crooning along to Ella Fitzgerald's version of *Let it Snow*. As Dawn and Camilla watched, Laurence moved behind his ex-wife and slid his arms around her waist then they rocked gently in time with the music.

Camilla turned to Dawn and they shook their heads at each other then Camilla went to the kettle and switched it on.

'Hello girls.' Jackie slipped out of Laurence's embrace and patted her hair self-consciously.

'Hey Mum.' Dawn smiled. 'Dad.'

'Where's Rick gone?' Camilla asked. 'I thought he was helping with the dishes.'

'He was but now he's outside fixing that new bird feeder to the fence.' Jackie gestured at the window.

'I let him do it,' Laurence said. 'Didn't want to impose seeing as how he brought his drill over.'

'I could have done it, Dad.' Dawn said, resting her hands on her hips.

'What and shake that baby up?' Jackie shook her head. 'Don't be daft, Dawnie. Let your husband crack on with it. He's done a fine job, anyway.'

The kettle clicked as it came to the boil and Camilla dropped teabags into the pot then poured water over them.

'I'll just see how he's getting along.' Dawn slipped out of the back door leaving Camilla alone with their parents.

As Frank Sinatra took over from Ella Fitzgerald, Laurence grabbed Jackie's hand and started waltzing her around the kitchen. Camilla pressed herself against the worktop to keep out of their way. Jackie was soon laughing and breathless and Camilla had a lump in her throat. It was good to see her mother so happy, so relaxed and so... different.

As festive music filled the kitchen, the sounds of drilling came from outside. Her parents giggled like teenagers in front of her and Camilla started to laugh herself. It was wonderful to see the people she loved enjoying themselves, being close as a family and just doing what she classed as *normal* things on a Sunday. In the past, she'd always felt guilty leaving Jackie on a Sunday afternoon, wondering how her mother would fill the lonely hours until she went off to work early on a Monday morning, but now she didn't need to worry. Her mother had someone. Her mother had her father.

It amazed Camilla how people could transform over such a short space of time, but Jackie really had done. She had fallen into a new pattern since Laurence's return and here they were, moving in synch, anticipating each other's dance moves as if it had always been this way. As if the twenty plus years they'd been apart had merely been a glitch in their relationship that sent them in different directions, but now they had found their way back to each other again. But perhaps that was human nature. Perhaps this was how people could repair, restore and progress. Perhaps love really was that powerful.

An urge flooded through Camilla, starting in her belly and spreading out to tingle in her fingertips and toes. She needed to speak to Tom and she needed to speak to him immediately. In fact, she knew she couldn't wait a second longer!
She pulled her mobile out of her back pocket and went through the hall and into the lounge where she scanned her recent contacts until she found Tom's name.
Then she pressed call and waited for him to answer.

Camilla dropped her mobile onto the carpet and stared at it as if it had burnt her fingers.
How could this be?
Her heart pounded and nausea climbed up her throat, threatening to choke her.
She'd been such a fool!
She left her mobile where it was and went into the hallway then pulled on her coat and boots with trembling hands.
'Camilla?' Her father stood in the kitchen doorway frowning. 'Where are you going? I thought we were having tea?'
She stared at him, willing herself to stay strong, not to break down and sob on the stairs as she felt like doing.
'I need to go home.'
'But why? I thought we were having fun, angel.' He tucked his hands into his brown corduroy trouser pockets and tilted his head. 'Hey... you don't look at all well. Eat too much pudding did you?' He laughed. 'Come on, have a cuppa with us and you'll feel better.'
'No I won't!'
Laurence pulled his hands from his pockets and raised them slightly as if to calm her.
'Something else has happened hasn't it? But what? How?' He shook

his head and looked around as if the answer was on the gold tinsel looped around the banister or the mistletoe pinned to the hallway mirror.

'It doesn't matter.' Camilla tugged her hat down over her ears. 'I'll see you in the week.'

Her father stepped closer then glanced into the lounge.

'Is that your mobile on the floor? Let me get it for you, Camilla. At least take that with you.'

He went into the lounge and Camilla turned quickly and let herself out, pulling the front door shut behind her.

Then she ran and ran and ran until her heart felt as if it would burst from her chest and her cheeks were wet and cold.

When she opened her own front door, she locked it behind her and pressed her forehead to the smooth hard wood. She'd been so stupid to let herself get caught up in romantic fantasies. And look at what had happened. Now her heart was broken and Christmas would not be the joyous occasion she'd anticipated.

But she had no one to blame other than herself.

And there was no way she'd ever let herself open up to love again.

Chapter Sixteen

Camilla rolled over on the sofa and gagged. Her head hurt, her mouth was dry and her tongue had a fur coating. She peered from under the throw she must have dragged over herself at some point.
What time was it? The only light that had managed to sneak through the gap in her curtains was grey, so it could be morning or afternoon. She she didn't care.
Her coffee table was a mess. Mugs, wine glasses, used tissues and sweet wrappers littered its surface and as she forced herself to sit up, she realised that the horrible smell making her nauseous was coming from her. She hadn't showered since Sunday and that had to be two or three days ago. Maybe more. The house was cold, the fire in the lounge had long gone out and she hadn't bothered to relight it.
Her landline had rung and rung since Sunday, so she'd unplugged it from the wall. Her mobile was still at her mother's and although someone had, at some point – but she couldn't remember when – been knocking on the front door and calling through the letterbox, she'd shouted at them to go away. She thought it had been Rick, probably keen to put Dawn's mind at rest, but she also believed she recalled her father's voice too.

Camilla pushed the throw to the side and stood up, then wobbled as her head spun. She needed water desperately.

She padded out to the kitchen and groaned as she took in the mess out there too. The clock on the wall told her it was seven-thirty, so it was morning after all. She'd just filled a glass with cold tap water when someone knocked on her door and the letterbox fluttered open.

'Camilla! It's your father. If you don't let me in today, I'm getting the police or the fire brigade out to break your door down.'

Camilla froze. Break her door down? It was cold enough as it was without losing her front door.

She went through the hallway and knelt in front of the door then pressed her lips to the letterbox.

'Go away, I'm fine. I just want to be left alone.'

'You've said that for the past three days since you ran off from your mother's after lunch. Your mobile kept ringing all Sunday night then all day Monday and yesterday the battery must've run out as it finally stopped. We could see from the caller ID that it was that vet, Tom, but we didn't like to answer it.'

Camilla shook her head then winced. So what if it was Tom? She had nothing to say to him. And three days? Her father had been back every day to check on her? The wine haze must've blurred her concept of time.

'Dad... please go away.'

The letterbox creaked open and she saw her father's eyes blinking at her through the narrow gap.

'Please let me in Camilla.'

She sighed. If she didn't, then he'd keep coming back or get her door broken down, so she could just let him in – so he could see that she was all right – then send him on his way.

As she opened the door, Laurence stood there with a tote bag in one hand and a sad smile on his face.

'I brought you some groceries. Figured you might need milk and bread.'

'I guess you better come on in then.'

Camilla led the way to the kitchen and watched as her father unloaded the contents of the tote bag onto her kitchen table.
'Right, love, where's the kettle?'
Soon, he handed her a steaming mug of tea and a plate with two slices of toast covered in thick yellow butter.
'Let's go into the lounge, I'm sure it's warmer in there.' He gestured at her for her to go in front of him.
'It's really not. I haven't lit the fire.'
'No problem.'
He rolled up his sleeves then knelt in front of the log burner as Camilla sat back down and pulled the throw over her legs again. She made herself nibble the toast and washed it down with sips of hot tea. Her stomach churned but she knew it would make her feel better if she could just keep it down.
Once the fire was established, Laurence got up and sat next to Camilla on the sofa.
'Looks like the ghost of Christmas past has visited.' He eyed the mess on the coffee table and the floor then met Camilla's eyes. 'Sweetheart, what is it? Is it me being back? Does it bother you that much?'
She shook her head.
'Is it Tom then? Has he said something to hurt you?'
She shook her head.
'Then what? I want to help.'
Camilla shook her head and to her horror, her bottom lip wobbled and a strangulated sound came from her throat.
Laurence opened his arms. 'Let your old dad give you a hug and try to make it better.'
'You can't,' she squeaked. 'No one can.'
'Maybe I can't but I can try.'
Camilla didn't want to fall into his arms, she didn't want to release her pain and she certainly didn't want to show weakness, but in spite of all that, she found herself sobbing on her father's chest, and as he gently stroked her hair and murmured words of comfort, she was

glad. Glad that he was there. Glad that he cared. Glad that he'd come home. And glad that he was finally holding her and looking out for her the way she'd always wished he would. He couldn't take back the past but he could be here for her now and in the future.

Once she'd stopped crying and her eyes stung and her throat ached, her father lifted her chin. 'Now do you want to tell me about it?'

'OK.'

'Take your time.'

So she told him about Tom and the Halloween party, about how she'd really liked him and how they'd spent time together and how she'd felt herself falling for him. Then she told him about all the years of sadness when Laurence hadn't been there and how much she and Dawn had missed having their dad around and about how angry she'd been with him, but how she'd secretly hoped that one day he'd walk back through the door.

And he had.

'So you like Tom and he likes you? What's the problem then?' Laurence asked finally.

'After I saw you and Mum dancing in the kitchen I realised I really wanted to speak to him. I thought it would be wonderful to hear his voice and to tell him how much I was missing him.'

'But?'

'A woman answered his phone.'

'Oh...' Her father frowned. 'Perhaps it was his mother? He's gone to visit her hasn't he?'

'It wasn't his mother, Dad.'

'How'd you know?'

'When she answered I asked to speak to him and she said he was in the shower. I asked if she was his mother, wanting to say hello to her and tell her I'm a friend of Tom's. You know, I didn't want to say girlfriend or anything similar, in case he hasn't told her anything about me yet. But she said...' She took a deep breath. 'She said she was his wife.'

'Oh...' Laurence sighed. 'I see.'
'So do I. *Now*.'
'There could be a perfectly logical explanation, Camilla. Perhaps she's teasing you or perhaps they're separated or... you know. Something like that.' He shrugged. 'You need to speak to him. I brought this for you.' He placed her mobile on the table in amongst the mess. 'Call him again and find out.'
Camilla shook her head. 'It doesn't matter. Whoever she was, doesn't matter. I've learned a valuable lesson about myself and that is that I need to stay away from love. I was right all along and love just isn't worth the risk!'
'You don't know that for certain, angel. You should give Tom a chance to explain. Look at how differently you might have thought about me if you'd known I tried to stay in contact with you and Dawn.'
'Maybe. Probably.' She did wish she'd known her father had tried to stay in touch, but as for Tom, she couldn't see a way forwards now; he was married, after all.
'Why don't you go and have a hot bath and I'll tidy up a bit.'
'OK but Dad...'
'Yes?'
'You'll still be here when I come down?'
'Of course I will.'
He wriggled on the sofa then reached around behind him and frowned.
'What's this?'
He held up the white bauble Tom had given Camilla and the bulldog swayed from side to side in his fingers.
'It's nothing, Dad. Just an old decoration.'
Camilla took it from him then dropped it into the wastebasket by the fireplace with a handful of tissues that she pulled from up her sleeve.
'Goodbye Tom,' she whispered.
Then she made her way upstairs to run a bath. She intended to wash

away the ghosts of Christmas past and to embrace Christmas present as she looked to the future.

She had so much more than so many other people did and she wasn't going to take it for granted a moment longer. Even if she knew it would take a while to let go of Tom completely. Even if she suspected that letting him go would be very difficult indeed.

Chapter Seventeen

Camilla accepted a mug of mulled wine from Chris as she stood in the front garden of The Cosy Cottage Café. It was a beautiful cold crisp winter evening and the weather was perfect for the carol service.
'Thank you.'
She raised the mug to her nose and sniffed. The combined scents of the ruby wine, cloves, cinnamon, brandy and citrus were beautifully festive. An image of strolling around the Christmas market with Tom flashed into her mind and she gasped with pain and sadness. This year, she'd hoped Christmas would be a time of celebration that she'd enjoy with Tom. But it wasn't meant to be. She closed her eyes and forced the image of his handsome face away then opened them to find Chris gazing curiously at her.
'It's the mulled wine. It smells so good.' She took a sip and shivered with delight as it tingled on her tongue then warmed her throat and belly as it travelled down.
'Might have known you'd be here sampling the wine already!' Dawn nudged her.
'Oh yes, sorry you can't have any, Dawnie.'

'You wait until next year. I'll make up for it.' Dawn giggled.

'It'll be lovely to have another little one around, won't it?'

Dawn's eyes shone. 'I feel so lucky, Camilla. I have everything I've ever wanted. With Rick being around more, our relationship is better than ever. Laura and James are happy, I'm happy, and Rick is like a different man. He's so much more relaxed, you know?'

'I know and I'm so happy for you.'

'And it's just wonderful to have Dad here for Christmas.'

'I can't argue with that.'

Camilla turned and looked around for her father. He was standing at the gate to the café garden with her mother, shaking people's hands as they arrived. Probably letting the locals know he was back, she realised. Since he'd come to her cottage on Wednesday, he'd been her rock. He'd explained to her mother, Dawn and Rick that Camilla had been a bit under the weather, then gone to see Allie and Honey and said the same to them. Of course, they all knew what was wrong with Camilla, but they also knew that she needed some time to deal with her emotions. So they'd visited her, bringing cakes and chocolates, love and laughter, and she'd managed to act as if everything was all right, even though inside she felt as if her heart had frozen and would never thaw.

Each time her visitors had gone, Camilla had sunk onto her sofa with the throw, and her dad had come to her and held her tight as she'd cried. After her mobile had charged, it had rung several times on the Wednesday, but she'd ignored it then turned it off, not wanting to know if Tom was trying to reach her or not. He had a whole life that she wasn't a part of and she had to ensure that she still had her life without him.

He had a wife…

She swallowed hard. The thought still burned her insides like bile and she forced herself to push it from her mind. She was Camilla Dix, strong businesswoman, loved daughter, sister, auntie and friend. She would get over this… *blip*… and move on.

'Hi Camilla.' Rick arrived next to his wife, slightly out of breath.

'What's wrong with you?' Camilla asked.
'Just as we were leaving the house, Mum phoned and started telling me all about her latest Poldark adventure. I thought I'd never get away, so I told Dawn and the kids to go on ahead and I'd catch up. I didn't expect Mum to go on for quite that long though.'
'Poldark at Christmas?' Camilla giggled.
'Yes! Paul has taken Fenella back to Cornwall for Christmas. Just the two of them and they're staying until the New Year.'
'Holed up in a cottage with a sea view.' Rick nodded.
'That's so romantic.' Camilla's heart contracted.
'Isn't it?' Dawn smiled. 'Since he found out how low she was feeling, he's done his best to spoil her. He still has his hobbies but he's devoting more time to his marriage these days.'
'And long may it continue!' Rick said. 'Look, Dawn, there's Honey and Dane. Best go and say hello.'
'Tell Honey I'll catch up with her later.'
'Will do. I'm hoping this will wear Laura and James out to be honest because they're so excited about Santa coming later.'
Camilla kissed Dawn's cheek then watched as Rick led her sister across the garden. She walked around the side of the café and sat down on a bench under the pergola. Thick cushions had been spread over the benches and the pergola had been draped with colourful fairy lights that glowed in the darkness of the cold, crisp December evening. Beyond the lights, the sky was pitch black and the stars twinkled like diamonds. A few soft grey clouds moved slowly across the sky, creating a layered effect that reminded Camilla how much there was beyond Heatherlea, beyond the earth and how much there was still to discover. It was beautiful and uplifting.
In fact, the whole of the café and the garden contributed to the magical festive mood. The garden was illuminated by the lights of the café that glowed warmly from the windows and by the fairy lights that had been draped over the trees, the front of the cottage itself and the pergola. Gas outdoor heaters were dotted around the lawn,

sending warmth into the evening and people gravitated towards them, cradling their mugs of mulled wine or hot chocolate. In the corner of the garden, to the left of the gate, a large Christmas tree stood proudly, dressed with twinkling lights, tinsel and, at the top, a sparkling silver fairy.

As Camilla sat, quietly watching the people she knew gathering for the annual Christmas Eve celebration, Allie appeared at her side.

'Hello you.' Allie sat next to her. 'How are you feeling?'

'I'm OK.' Camilla offered her friend a smile. 'It's been a busy year, hasn't it?'

'Oh yes it has. For all of us.'

'I'm so glad things have worked out so well for you and Dawnie. Hopefully for Honey too if the way Dane is gazing at her is anything to go by.'

'Well, they're just friends at the moment but who knows what the New Year will bring.'

'A baby.' Camilla cradled her mug between her hands.

'What?' Allie turned to face her.

'Oh... not Honey or me, of course! I was referring to Dawn.'

'Of course you were.' Allie shook her head. 'I think I must've sampled too much of that mulled wine as I was making it.'

'You'll have a lovely Christmas with Chris.'

Allie nodded. 'But I'm worried about you.'

'Don't be.' Camilla took Allie's hand. 'I have so much. Look at my family. Reunited at last.'

'It is wonderful to see your mother so happy. Do you think...' Allie bit her bottom lip.

'Think what?'

'Do you think your father will stay?'

'Who knows? I hope so because it is so good to see Mum happy. And he has been amazing this week, almost as if he were trying to make up for lost time.'

'Do you think that's possible then?'

Camilla paused. Could people make up for their mistakes? Could they really put their hurt aside and learn to forgive.

'I do. I wasn't sure if I could forgive him, or if Mum could, but now... perhaps it's the Christmas magic in the air but I feel like I could forgive anything.'

'Perhaps that's a good thing.'

'What?'

'Well I know what happened with Tom. I made your father tell me, even though he didn't want to.'

'Oh.'

'Now remember what you said about forgiveness and Christmas magic?'

'Yes, but why...'

Allie nodded at the Christmas tree across the garden and Camilla followed her gaze.

Her heart froze and her stomach dropped to the frosty grass.

'However you feel right now, just talk to him. Misunderstandings can ruin perfectly good relationships.'

'I didn't think he'd come back. I mean... I did, because he has his business but I didn't expect to see him today.'

'Well he is back and he was only gone just over a week. Not twenty years like your father. See what he has to say and remember, Camilla, we're all here for you and we love you.'

Allie hugged Camilla tight then got up and walked away and Camilla was left gazing at Tom. Hairy Pawter was with him and the dog was wearing what looked like a canine version of a Christmas jumper. Tom wore jeans and heavy boots with a padded black North Face jacket and matching beanie. His face looked pale underneath the hat, and as he turned and looked around, he met her eyes and gave a half wave.

She was overwhelmed by an urge to jump up and run. Anywhere. Just to escape the way her heart was thundering and how her stomach churned. But she knew that she wouldn't, because as much as she'd been hurt by what she'd found out, she had missed him and it was good to see him. Even if it was to say goodbye.

As he walked over to her, she downed the rest of her mulled wine then stood up.

She would face this on her feet like the grown-up that she was. Camilla Dix was not afraid of anything… because her worst fears had already been realised, so there was nothing left to hurt her.

Chapter Eighteen

'Camilla.'
His soft brown eyes roamed her face and her stomach somersaulted in the way she was getting used to whenever Tom was around.
'Hi Tom.'
'It looks amazing here. Is it like this every year?'
She nodded. 'Allie always makes an effort. It's important to her and it's become a festive tradition to have carols at the café on Christmas Eve.'
'All we need now is some snow and it will be perfect.'
Camilla gazed at his handsome face, his broad shoulders and the faint dimple in his chin. The familiar urge to caress it rose but she squashed it immediately. There would be no caressing of chin dimples now or any other day.
'Snow would be good, yes. Laura and James would love that.'
A snuffling at her feet brought her attention to HP and she crouched down to greet him.
'Hello boy!' She rubbed his velvet-soft ears then let him sniff her hand. His little tail wiggled madly.
'He's glad to see you. He's missed you. And so have I."

Camilla planted a kiss on HP's nose then stood up again.

'I missed him too… and you. But—'

'Camilla!' He raised a hand and shook his head. 'I think I know what might have upset you.'

'I'm not upset.' She folded her arms across her chest and took a deep breath.

'Are you sure? You haven't answered one of my calls or texts since I left and I've been worried sick about you.'

'You don't need to worry about me, Tom. I'm absolutely fine.'

His face fell. 'Are you?'

'Yes.'

'Well in that case will you have a mulled wine with me?'

'I don't think that's a very good idea.'

'Why not?'

She bit her lip. She didn't want to sound petty but something inside her was fizzing and she couldn't seem to stop it. 'Perhaps *your wife* wouldn't like it.'

'I knew it!' He sighed. 'That's what I wanted to talk to you about.'

'There's no need. You have a wife back in Brighton and you've been with her, probably enjoying all the festive build up and having all the sex and all the fun…' She sniffed. 'While I was back here waiting for you, thinking that we were somehow, in some way, falling in love. But that's just fine! I am fine! And I wish you and… *your wife* well. Merry Christmas, Tom.'

Camilla made to march past him but he grabbed her hand and stopped her. She wanted to shake him off but her heart was aching and Hairy Pawter was blinking up at her with his big brown eyes, looking so cute and cuddly in his Christmas jumper.

Her anger drained away and she was suddenly afraid that she was going to cry.

'Camilla…' His voice caught and when she met his eyes, she was surprised to find them glistening. 'Please let me explain.'

She nodded and he released her hand.

'I went back to Brighton to see my parents, as you know. But on the

Sunday, early in the morning, Danni turned up. I hadn't arranged to see her but there was always a chance I'd bump into her.'

A sour taste filled Camilla's mouth and she swallowed hard.

'Her turning up at your parents' house isn't exactly bumping into her.'

'No, I know that. Of course I do. But she turned up and...'

'And?'

'Danni asked if we could talk. I hadn't seen her for a while and it was a bit strange and strained but it needed to be done. See... one of the reasons I went back was for an appointment with my solicitor. We're getting divorced and I needed to sign the papers and sort out our finances so that's it's all finished... once and for all.'

Camilla blinked at him, not quite sure what to say.

'So she is still your wife?' she forced out eventually.

'In legal terms but not for long.'

'And you don't want her back?'

He laughed. 'Not at all. A lot happened between us and we drifted apart a long time ago. But her affair was the final straw, the sign that we needed to end our marriage.'

'And she's happy with that too?'

'Extremely. She's still with the guy she left me for and she's seven months pregnant with his child.'

'Wow!' Relief coursed through Camilla.

'Exactly. So I signed the final papers on Monday and wanted to get in to see the bank manager about the house sale that has finally gone through, but I couldn't get an appointment until Thursday. I tried to ring you and text you to let you know but...'

'I didn't even read your texts or answer your calls.'

'I was so worried. I thought about phoning your mother or the café but it seemed too personal and I knew I'd be back soon, so I just gritted my teeth and focused on sorting everything so I could come back to Heatherlea. Back to you.'

'Oh Tom.' Camilla's legs were trembling and she worried that her knees would give way. 'But... why did she say she was your wife?'

'Slip of the tongue? Perhaps because legally she still was? She answered the phone when I was in the shower and told me someone called Camilla had rung. She said she went to correct herself but you'd cut her off.'

'Why were you showering when she was there?'

'She arrived early and my phone was in the kitchen when she went to have a coffee with mum. She answered it automatically, I think.'

Camilla nodded. 'I dropped my phone when she said she was your wife. I was a bit shocked. Then I left it at Mum's.'

'My old life is behind me, Camilla. For good. I'll soon be officially single, although... I'd like to think that I might have a girlfriend.'

Camilla smiled. 'You're rather optimistic.'

'Well it's Christmas Eve and I'm back where I want to be. I'd like to remain in Heatherlea and build a life here now. So would HP.'

The dog pawed her leg then as if he was agreeing with his master.

'What do you think? Could you be my girlfriend?'

'What are we? Fourteen?' Camilla giggled.

'Not for some time but I wouldn't want to be a teenager again. Horrible time.'

'If you'd like me to be your girlfriend, I'd like that too.'

'Well that's settled.'

He reached out and caressed her cheek, sending tiny shivers of desire down her spine then he leaned in and kissed her softly. His mouth was warm, his scent was spicy and intoxicating and his hand on her face was warm and strong. As he kissed her, HP whined.

Tom broke away and smiled at her. 'I think HP is jealous.'

'Because I'm kissing you.'

'He wants all your attention for himself.'

Camilla rubbed the dog's ears again and he nuzzled her hand.

'Shall we get a mulled wine? Looks like the carols are about to start.'

Tom took her hand.

'Yes, come on.'

Chris took Camilla's empty mug then gave them fresh mugs brimming with the festive drink and they walked over to join the locals standing in front of the tree.

Dawn and Allie flashed Camilla smiles and winks and she smiled in return. She'd thought Christmas would be different this year but had no idea exactly how different. Tom was back. He wanted to see more of her. And she'd won HP's affection too.

It all seemed perfect.

The opening chords of *I'll Be Home for Christmas* rang out from Jason Robbin's guitar and the rest of the local band joined in. The drummer, Martina Prestin, had a tambourine, probably not wanting to set up her drumkit in the freezing cold, but the others had acoustic guitars, except for their singer Erica Connelly, who sang the first few lines in her strong and beautiful voice that reminded Camilla of Adele. When they reached the chorus, everyone joined in and goosebumps rose all over Camilla's body.

There was a sudden gasp from the crowd and James shouted, 'It's snowing! Mummy, Daddy, Laura, look!'

People laughed as James ran into the centre of the lawn and stared up at the sky. And sure enough, fat white flakes were drifting down. They came slowly at first but soon, the air was filled with snow and everything around them grew white.

Camilla laughed as she looked at Tom and saw that he had a dusting of snow on his hat, shoulders and boots. Even HP hadn't escaped and he was snapping at the snowflakes, trying to catch them in his mouth.

The song ended and Erica announced the title of the next one, which she said was now very appropriate, and as she sang the old favourite *White Christmas*, Tom leaned down and kissed Camilla, and she felt as if her heart would burst with happiness.

'Merry Christmas, Camilla.'

'Merry Christmas, Tom.'

And they spent their first ever snowy Christmas Eve together, singing carols, drinking mulled wine and smiling, surrounded by friends old and new, at The Cosy Cottage Café.

The End

Spring at The Cosy Cottage Café

Spring at The Cosy Cottage Café

Artist Honey Blackwell is happy with her life. Teacher Dane Ackerman is working hard to secure a job at the village primary school. Will they be able to find a way to be together, or will they have to accept that sometimes love just isn't enough?

Chapter One

'It's all about new beginnings isn't it?' Honey Blackwell smiled at her friend, Camilla Dix.
'What is?'
'Spring. It's such a beautiful time. I love how it chases those dreary winter days away, offering a sense of hope and renewal.'
'Mmm. I love spring too. But then I love summer, autumn and winter.'
'You love any season as long as Tom's around.'
Camilla giggled. 'Am I that transparent?'
'You are, but that's OK. I'm happy for you.'
'I'm happy for me too.'
They strolled along, arm-in-arm, through the pretty village of Heatherlea. It was a beautiful morning, the first Saturday in March, and Honey had suggested they go for a walk to make the most of the sunshine.
The sun glinted on car windows as they passed and birds sang in the trees and from their perches on rooftops. It was as if nature shared Honey's feeling of optimism and anticipation, as if something wonderful could happen at any moment.

'What did you say Tom was doing again?'

'He's gone to see his parents for the weekend. He tries to get back to Brighton at least once every six weeks, although it's not always possible with the surgery... and the fact that he wants to spend time with me.'

Honey nodded. Camilla and the local vet, Tom, had been together since Christmas and although Camilla had told her friends that they were *taking it slowly*, it was evident that they were very much in love.

'And you got to look after Mr Squidgeyface.'

'I did.' Camilla leant forwards and rubbed the head of the large British bulldog. 'HP is a good boy, aren't you?'

The dog glanced over his shoulder at Camilla and Honey, his pink tongue dangling from the side of his mouth.

'It still makes me laugh every time I hear his name.'

'Hairy Pawter?'

Honey nodded. 'It's brilliant.'

As they strolled past the church, Honey admired the architecture of the old stone building. It hinted at the village's history and strong sense of community. She found the worn headstones in the graveyard fascinating because they dated back hundreds of years and some of them belonged to ancestors of people who still lived in the village today.

'HP was named by the man who owned him before Tom adopted him. It suits him and I can't imagine him being called anything else.'

'Is HP all right staying with you when Tom's away?'

Camilla nodded. 'He's happy to snore his head off in front of the fire and the TV while I work, and I have a key to Tom's place, so I can take him home for a bit too.'

'I see... swapping keys now and what...' Honey counted on her fingers, deliberately exaggerating each one, 'you're only around three months in?'

Camilla's cheeks coloured.

'Camilla, I'm teasing. I really am so happy for you. Tom's such a great guy.'

'I know. I just never thought I'd get involved with someone. Let alone end up almost living with him.'
'So you're staying over more often than not?'
'Yes.'
'Why don't you sell your cottage and move in properly?'
Camilla chewed her bottom lip. 'I might, but not just yet. I need to be sure.'
'You have doubts?'
Camilla met Honey's gaze and her bright green eyes shone. 'No. Not at all.'
'Then why wait?'
'He hasn't asked me to move in.'
'Well you could ask him.'
'I could. But I don't want to push him if he's not ready. I figure he'll ask when he feels the time is right.'
Honey shook her head. 'You're such a bright and confident woman, Camilla, but when it comes to affairs of the heart…'
'Tell me about it.'
Camilla squeezed Honey's arm.
'Anyway, what about you and Dane? Any news there? I know you said he's busy today because he has a pile of books to mark, and that he's quite often got things on in the evenings, but how are things going between you?'
Honey pressed her lips together. 'All right, I guess. I mean… we've been seeing each other in a kind of… relaxed manner for a few months now. We've been out for a few meals and joined you all at the pub quiz, but we're—'
Camilla waved a hand. 'I know all that! I've heard that at the café when you're deliberately trying to be vague about how things are going between you, but don't you want more? How do you *feel* about him?'
Honey shrugged. 'I like him. He's smart, handsome, funny and a great cook but for some reason, we're just… more like friends.'

'Friends?' Camilla frowned, a line marring the porcelain skin between her eyebrows.
'Well, yes.'
'Hey, that's OK. Perhaps it's just too early for you to feel anything else... *yet*.'
'Perhaps, but I'm confused about him. A few times, he's walked me home and I've invited him in, and I've gone back to his house but... nothing ever happens. I'm too embarrassed to ask him if he likes me enough to want more.'
'So you're both a bit shy. It could be that.'
'I don't know... maybe. I'm just afraid to push for more in case it ruins what we have. Although, I'm not certain that we have anything at all.' She pushed her light-blue hair with its pink streaks back from her face.
'And how does he feel about it?'
Honey shrugged. 'Dane seems fine. He's never tried to do more than give me a quick kiss and has never asked me to stay over. He seems happy being friends.'
'It could be that he's just taking it slowly and that there are reasons why. Maybe he's been hurt in the past or he doesn't want to push you in case he scares you away.'
'He could be gay.' Honey chewed her bottom lip. Now she'd actually said it out loud to someone, she realised it was a very real possibility. Not that he had to be gay not to fancy her, of course, but there was a very real possibility that she'd misread the early signals she'd thought she was getting from him, and he really didn't fancy her at all.
'Do you think he is?' Camilla's eyes widened. 'I didn't see any signs.'
'It's not like a flashing light above someone's head, you know, Camilla.'
'I know that, Honey.' Camilla shook her head. 'What I meant was that the way he looks at you... it just suggests that he's *into* you.'
'Or he's very short sighted and he's staring really hard.'
Camilla giggled. 'I'm convinced it was the look of a man who's falling for a woman.'

'I'd like to think so. You know, I'm probably just as much to blame for holding back as he is.'

Honey suspected that she knew why she hadn't been able to progress her relationship with Dane, but hadn't admitted it to anyone, not even her closest friends when they met up on Tuesdays at The Cosy Cottage Café for food and drinks. It wasn't that she didn't trust Allie, Dawn and Camilla, because she did; she'd trust them with her life. It was more that she didn't trust herself. Honey was aware that if she started trying to explain why she felt the way she did, why she couldn't let go and fully commit to a relationship with Dane, then she knew she wouldn't stop and her whole life story would come pouring out. Then her friends would wonder why she'd kept it from them for so long and the last thing she wanted to do was to hurt or offend them. They'd been so good to her since she'd moved to Heatherlea; she'd never had friends like them before, and she would be devastated to lose them. So she'd kept her true feelings about Dane and their romance and her past to herself, buried deeply inside. Only now… Camilla was gently probing and Honey had already admitted more than she'd wanted to say.

'Shall we go back to mine and have a drink? I've got some chocolate muffins there and that coffee machine Tom got me for Christmas makes the best lattes. Not better than Allie's at the café, of course, but pretty close.'

'That would be lovely.'

'Come on then.'

They turned and made their way back to Camilla's pretty little cottage, and Camilla chatted as they walked, about the weather, about her latest trip into London to meet a very wealthy and rather famous client, and about anything other than Honey and Dane. And Honey was grateful to her friend for understanding that she needed to change the subject, because it was making her head hurt. Honey needed time to think but she also needed time to take some head space away from it all.

Besides, Dane didn't seem in any rush with their relationship either, and Honey wondered if he had secrets of his own. If only she could ask him openly, and find out. But that would mean opening up to him too, and she didn't know if she was ready for that, or if she ever would be.

Chapter Two

Honey closed her front door behind her and kicked off her shoes then pushed her feet into her battered old slippers. She tucked her shoes under the bench that had sat there for as long as she could remember. The old stone cottage had belonged to her aunt, and when she'd passed away over two years ago, she'd left everything to Honey. Honey's aunt hadn't had any children of her own and Honey was an only child, so she'd inherited everything.
She caught sight of herself in the mirror as she shrugged out of her coat. Sometimes, she wondered what other people thought of her with her blue and pink hair and her tiny sparkling diamond nose stud. The residents of Heatherlea weren't hugely conservative, but apart from the local hairdresser and beautician Jenny Talbot, she was the only person she knew who had hair that would make a unicorn or mermaid proud. But Honey liked her dyed hair; it lifted her, whereas her natural straw-blonde shade had seemed to drain her face of all colour. The nose stud had replaced a hoop that she'd worn for several years and she liked the sparkle of the tiny diamond that caught her eye whenever she looked in the mirror. Dane had told her that he liked it too, and described it as cute. Honey had no idea whether that

meant he fancied her or just thought she was cute like a puppy or a kitten.

She sighed as she hung her coat on the peg and trudged through to the kitchen where she opened the door of the bright red Smeg fridge and gazed at its contents. She didn't feel hungry, as she had eaten two chocolate muffins and drunk three coffees at Camilla's, so she could probably wait until later to eat a proper meal.

'Saturday afternoon,' she said to her kitchen, turning around and gazing at the solid oak units and the granite surfaces. All of it was her aunt's choice of décor – except the fridge, which Honey had ordered to replace the old one when it had conked out last summer – but she didn't mind because her aunt had had great taste and the things she'd bought were quality and meant to last. Even the old fridge had had a good run, but Honey had been glad to have the excuse to buy a new one, as she liked how the red fridge brightened the kitchen. 'Now, what shall I do?'

Movement from outside the kitchen window, that overlooked the back garden caught her eye, so she peered through the glass. It was just her chickens moving around in their enclosure, their heads bobbing as they pecked at the ground, eager to find tasty morsels. She loved her chickens and she'd had the enclosure built in the extensive back garden to provide extra protection from foxes. She could have just had a small pen built and put in a hen house but the thought of her girls being attacked one night was more than she could bear, so she'd sought out a local carpenter and gone for a more secure construction. And so far, so good.

The garden was a combination of neatly mown grass and wildflowers. Either side of the lawn ran hedges and in front of them, the flowerbeds were awash with the colour of spring flowers. The first part of the garden led to a wooden archway abundant with spring-flowering alpine clematis, and beyond that were her raised beds where she grew herbs and vegetables, then her greenhouse where she grew tomatoes and peppers in the summer months. Past this was the third section of the garden where she had her studio. In the studio, she kept her kiln and her easel; it was the sanctuary where she let her creativity flow. Honey sold some of her pottery and paintings locally – under a company name and not her own, because she liked the air of mystery this brought – and some on Etsy, and she even took commissions when she was approached via email. Her aunt had left her a generous inheritance, but Honey liked working and earning her own money from her artwork, her pottery, and the yoga classes she taught. And a percentage of it went to a special charity.

One in four women...

She shook her head. She didn't want to think about that, especially not when she had a whole Saturday afternoon and evening stretching out ahead of her. If she sank into dwelling on that now, then...

No, she would change into her yoga gear and work through her routine. The familiar stretches and poses would soon transport her to a positive mindset and relax her, then she could take a long hot bubble bath and watch some TV.

She headed for the stairs and emptied her mind as she climbed them, focusing instead on her breathing and the way her muscles yearned to form the yoga poses that had become her salvation over the past few years.

'OK, great. See you tomorrow.' Honey ended the call and flopped back on the sofa. When she'd seen Dane's name on the caller ID, she'd hoped he was ringing to invite her over for an impromptu dinner, but no. He was just calling to see how she was and to tell her that he'd finished marking his pupils' maths books but now needed to move on to the history work. However, he had invited her out for Sunday lunch tomorrow, so that was something.

Just as well that she'd put her pyjamas on after her bath and not bothered to get dressed again. She put her mobile on the side table and switched on the lamp that instantly bathed the corner of her lounge in a golden glow. Outside the French doors, the shadows were deepening in the back garden and the beautiful spring day was giving way to twilight. At least the evenings were getting lighter. It could be difficult through the winter months when the nights were so long. Not that Honey allowed herself to wallow in despair, but sometimes she did get lonely and it was always worse in the winter months. That was why meeting Dane and sensing a mutual attraction had been so exciting; it had been years since Honey had even looked at a man but something about Dane had been different. Although as the months had passed, she'd begun to wonder if there was a physical attraction there or if Dane was just lonely too. If he only wanted her companionship, then Honey would be disappointed, yes, but she'd also be happy to have him as a friend. Dane was a great guy and friends were so important. She'd just have to push all thoughts of tearing off his clothes and admiring his rugby-player physique, the physique she'd been up close to when she'd helped him to master some of the more challenging yoga poses at her classes, from her mind...

Pizza!

Pizza would help her to think of something else. She'd picked up a sun-dried tomato and mozzarella pizza when she'd done her weekly shop, so she'd pop that in the oven, throw together a green salad and maybe even open a bottle of wine. It was Saturday, after all.

An hour later, Honey sat cross-legged on her big squishy dark-green sofa, a plate of pizza balanced on her knees and a glass of ice-cold sauvignon blanc on the side table, the droplets of condensation on its surface glowing in the warm lamplight. Honey took a bite of pizza then washed it down with a sip of cool wine, savouring the aroma of apricots and the crisp dry finish. And as the opening music of her new favourite show *Peaky Blinders* filled her lounge, she smiled to herself.

'See Honey, who needs Dane Ackerman when you have Thomas Shelby, pizza and wine? Not you, that's for sure.'

As she took another bite of pizza, she almost believed it.

Chapter Three

The next morning, Honey was pottering around in her kitchen when her mobile buzzed on the counter. She took a deep breath before picking up her mobile, steeling herself in case it was Dane cancelling their lunch date, but when she swiped the screen, she found a brief message from Camilla.

Hey Honey,
Hope you're OK this morning. Saw Dane running past my cottage earlier. He's a hottie! Get in there, girl! Nothing to lose...
Speak soon, C x

Honey sighed as she placed her mobile back on the counter. Camilla was right; Dane was a hottie but he certainly wasn't warming Honey up at the moment. However, that was fine... she could settle for friendship.
Friendship was good, right?
She filled the kettle and switched it on, then slid her feet into the wellies that she kept by the back door and headed out into the slightly

misty morning to check on her chickens. She let herself into the enclosure then did a quick clean around, picking up any mess she'd missed last night and disposing of it.

After refreshing their water dispensers, she filled the feeders with pellets, before lifting the wooden hatch that led into the chicken coop. One by one, her girls made their way out into the daylight, and she watched them carefully to ensure that each one looked fit and healthy. As they bobbed around her ankles, she scanned the enclosure for stray eggs then did a check of the nesting boxes, where she found five fresh eggs that she deposited into the basket she'd brought with her.

The eight Bantam Welsummer chickens always made Honey smile. With their beautiful golden brown feathers – that glowed amber in the sunlight – and their easy-going natures, they laid enough eggs for her, as well as some for the café, and their unique personalities meant that she had named each one accordingly. She ran through their names as she watched them enjoying their breakfast: Princess Lay-a, Hen-solo, Cluck Rogers, Albert Eggstein, Mary Poopins, Maid Marihen, Henifer Aniston and Tyrannosaurus Pecks.

'Looks like it's eggs for breakfast then,' Honey said, as she let herself out of the wire enclosure and made her way back to the cottage.

She left her wellies just outside the backdoor, where she could wash them off later with the garden hose, and took the basket of eggs inside. Initially, she'd decided to get some chickens as a kind of hobby, but their egg laying had been a bonus. She'd done her research and knew that Bantams weren't always the friendliest breed and that they didn't always lay the most eggs, but her *girls* (as she liked to think of them) were as good a reason as any for getting out of bed in the morning. She had time to run through a yoga routine before taking a shower and eating some scrambled eggs, then she could spend the morning reading a good book and looking forward to her lunch at the local pub with Dane.

Honey walked through the village at just after one o'clock and was surprised to find that her stomach was full of butterflies. And why? She'd been out with Dane on several occasions, been to his house and he'd been to hers, but for some reason this felt like a first date all over again. If dating was what they'd been doing… Otherwise, she might have got the wrong end of the stick and would need to adjust her mindset about the handsome teacher. It was possible that she had been wrong about him, wasn't it?

A sudden gust of wind brought goosebumps to her skin, so she pulled her coat together over her chest. She'd dressed simply in a grey long-sleeved top, black skinny jeans and knee-high suede black boots. She'd wound her long blue and pink hair up into a bun that she'd pinned high on her head and her makeup was minimal – tinted moisturiser, mascara and a pale pink lip gloss. Having thought long and hard about Dane and where their relationship was headed, the last thing Honey wanted to do was to seem as if she was making a huge effort to attract him when he could well see her as just a friend.

Honey soon reached The Red Fox and went through the side door. The delicious aroma of cooked dinner made her mouth water. She scanned the bar and smiled at a few locals before spotting Dane at a corner table. He waved her over, so she pointed at the bar, but he held up a bottle of wine.

'Hi Honey, I hope this is OK? I know you like white wine, so I thought seeing as how we're having lunch, we could share a bottle. Probably shouldn't, you know, as I still have marking to do but I can get back to that later.'

'That's lovely, thanks.' Honey removed her coat then sat down and Dane poured two glasses of wine.

'How has your morning been?' Dane asked as he smiled at her. Honey looked at him, taking in how broad his shoulders were in a fitted black t-shirt and how slim his waist was in his low-slung indigo jeans. His bright blue eyes gazed back at her, framed with thick dark lashes, and his black hair was short but stylishly messy, as if he'd just got out of bed. Even the scar on his full upper lip – from a collision with another rugby player's knee – and the widened bridge of his nose, from where he'd broken it in another rugby game, added to his allure. As much as she wanted to deny it, Honey found Dane incredibly attractive and the fantasy of wrapping her arms around his neck and kissing his beautiful mouth played through her mind as it always did whenever she was near him.

'Honey?' A quizzical expression passed over Dane's face. 'I asked how your morning was.'

'Oh! Uh... very relaxing, thanks.' She lifted her wine and took a sip, keen to hide her embarrassment at being caught out staring at him, while thinking about what she'd like to do to him if she ever had the chance. 'I fed the girls, did some yoga, had a nice warm shower... you know...' Why had she told him about her shower? 'And I read some of my book.'

'Sounds good to me. I went for a run then tried to settle to marking again but I must be a bit tired today because I struggled to focus.'

'Well you have been working really hard, Dane.' Honey thought of the numerous times he'd told her he had marking and planning to do and she'd wondered if he did, or if it was just an excuse not to see her. But then teachers did work hard and he probably did have a heavy workload.

'I know.' He nodded. 'It's just that with this being a supply post, I feel... that I have to make a good impression.'

'I'm sure you have done. Dawn said that you've got a fabulous reputation at the school already.'

'That's good to hear but it doesn't make the position permanent, does it?'

'I guess not.'

Dane was currently covering at the local primary school for a teacher who'd been on long-term sick leave. He was renting a cottage in the village and had told Honey that he wanted to move to Heatherlea permanently, but it depended on the work situation.

'I wanted to tell you actually, that I found out on Friday that Mr Brown, the teacher I'm covering for, isn't coming back, so I want the school to know I'm good enough to employ permanently. Not that I want to steal anyone's job, but… well… they're advertising the post externally.'

'That's brilliant news… for you, not for him.'

'Initially, the head teacher told me there would be supply work until the end of the summer term but now there will be a full-time and permanent position. She said there will be a very short turn around, as they want to know they have a teacher in the post for the summer term, and they were just waiting on finalising some figures before advertising it.'

'When are the interviews?'

'Next week.'

'Wow! That is fast.'

'I'm going to apply for it but, of course, I have to face that fact that I might not get it.'

Honey's stomach lurched. 'I'm sure you will.'

'There's no guarantee, is there?'

'I guess not but you deserve it. But… if the worst happened, then you could always commute to another job.' She scanned his face, hoping that her words wouldn't hurt him. She wanted him to get the job and believed he should, but it depended on other factors that they had no control over.

'I could.' Dane sipped his wine. 'But the main reason I rented instead of buying was because the position was temporary, and – aside from the fact that I might not have got a mortgage as a supply teacher – I didn't want to put down roots until I knew how things were looking.'

'Well you have to do what's right for you.'

Dane gazed at her and she felt a flush rising up her chest into her neck.

'Is that how you feel then, Honey?'

'What do you mean?'

'Well... oh it doesn't matter. Let's just have a good meal and some wine and enjoy the afternoon. We could even go for a long walk afterwards and blow the cobwebs off.'

'Sounds good to me.'

But as she perused the Sunday lunch menu, she wondered what he was going to say. He'd asked how she felt. Did he mean about him moving on if he didn't get the job, or something else? Would he consider staying if she told him she wanted him to? And she did want him to, but she just couldn't get the words out, because if she was wrong about his feelings for her, she could make an enormous fool of herself and then their friendship would be ruined.

So she swallowed her doubts and her questions and her desire for the man sitting opposite her, and focused instead on making light conversation about films and books and good places to holiday. *Safe subjects*, as Camilla would describe them.

But deep down, her heart ached, her desire fluttered and her confusion grew. Honey knew that she'd have to decide what to do about Dane one way or the other, and soon, but for this afternoon, she would go with the flow.

Tomorrow would be another day; tomorrow could be when she plucked up the courage to make or break whatever it was that they had between them.

Chapter Four

The following Tuesday, Honey opened the gate to The Cosy Cottage Café, and some of the tension that had settled in her shoulders since the weekend loosened. She loved the evenings she spent at the café with Allie, Camilla and Dawn. The three women were her closest friends in Heatherlea and the closest thing she had to a family.
The sky above the café garden glowed in shades of gold and orange. The air smelt fresh and new, delicately fragranced with spring flowers. In the borders surrounding the green lawn, daffodils, crocuses and tulips waved their colourful heads in the gentle breeze, a beautiful sea of yellow, white, red, purple and pink. The plants that climbed the front of the café were green and strong, and would soon be awash with colourful flowers, bringing a beautiful summer vibrancy to the old stone cottage.
Honey reached the café steps and admired the purple shutters that surrounded the windows, realising that they'd had a recent lick of paint, as had the white front door. Not only was the café a very pretty place, it was also warm and friendly, and the exterior conveyed this, from the garden to the warm glow that emanated from the windows. A sound off to her right made Honey turn and she spotted Luna, one

of Allie's cats, stretching out on the path just behind the wooden specials board. Honey knew that the cats weren't meant to be at the café since Allie had moved in with Chris, but she also knew that Luna, in particular, sneaked back some days to check on her old haunts.

Honey pushed open the door to the café and entered, immediately appreciating the warm interior, as well as savouring the delicious aromas of baking and coffee that always greeted her here.

'Honey!' Allie smiled from behind the counter. 'We thought you'd never get here. Dawn is starving.'

Honey smiled in return. 'Sorry. I don't know what happened. I went out to put the chickens in the coop for the night and got distracted by a few weeds growing in one of my raised beds and when I next checked the clock, it was gone five and I still needed to shower.'

'Well you're here now and didn't make me wait any longer so I'll forgive you,' Dawn said from the table near the log burner. 'But I'm not sure about this little one.' She rubbed her swollen belly that stretched the navy and white striped material of her maternity dress.

'How're you feeling?' Honey asked Dawn as she approached the table and took a seat next to Camilla.

'About to pop. Full yet ravenous. Uncomfortable. In need of a good night's sleep yet I can't sleep, because if I stay in one position for more than twenty minutes I get leg cramps. My boobs have already started leaking and don't get me started on how many times I have to get up to pee.' Dawn shook her head.

'Did you have to ask her?' Camilla frowned at Honey then laughed. 'My poor baby sister is SO ready to get this baby out.'

'It's true.' Dawn nodded. 'I can't wait and then I'm keeping my legs crossed forever.'

'I'm not sure that'll work, Dawn,' Allie said as she set a plate of fresh bread rolls down on the table along with a jug of dark red liquid.

'What're we drinking?' Honey asked, wondering if Allie had made them cocktails to have instead of wine.

'This is cranberry juice for Dawn, but you can have some if you want.'

'I do like cranberry juice but I also like—'

'Wine?' Camilla asked.

'Yes.'

'Wine is on its way.' Allie gestured behind her at the kitchen.

'I cannot wait to have some wine,' Dawn said. 'I also can't wait to be able to see my feet, to paint my toenails and to do a lot of other things.'

'I am never going through that.' Camilla sniffed. 'How you can do it three times I have no idea.'

'Well I didn't exactly choose to go through it this time did I, Camilla?' Dawn filled a glass with cranberry juice.

'I know the pregnancy was an accident but you don't regret it now, do you?' Honey asked.

'Not at all,' Dawn replied. 'And one day, Camilla Dix, you might change your mind. Especially when you see the beautiful baby at the end of all this.'

Camilla shuddered dramatically and Dawn laughed.

'You wait, big sister!'

'Perhaps Tom doesn't want babies.' Camilla leant forwards, resting her arms on the table.

'Have you asked him?'

'We've talked about children.' Camilla looked around the table at her friends. 'Not as something we were planning but just… you know… discussed other people who have children and how they always seem so tired, and about how we're both lucky that we don't have that drain on our energy and resources.'

'Give them a year.' Allie held up a finger. 'And we'll see what they're saying then.'

Camilla sighed. 'I doubt it very much. I've said it before and I'll say it again… not everyone wants to be a mother. Besides, Dawn's done enough procreating for both of us.'

'Honey, could you give me a hand bringing the food through?' Allie asked.

'Of course.'

Honey followed Allie into the kitchen.

'Thought we better give the Dix sisters a chance to get that subject out of their systems. I'm not sure that Camilla will change her mind about children; she's always been so set against it.'

'But then she was set against relationships until Tom came along.' Honey picked up a serving plate of miniature roasted vegetable quiches that sat on a bed of dark green spinach.

'True.'

'Not that everyone has to have children, of course,' Honey added, thinking not just of Camilla but also of herself. 'It doesn't happen for everyone.'

'It certainly doesn't and as long as she and Tom are happy then that's all that matters.'

'And they have HP.'

'That they do.' Allie giggled. 'And he's a handful all right.'

'Speaking of animals, I think I saw Luna outside.'

'Darn her!' Allie tutted. 'She keeps coming back, but then she wanders the village all the time. She always finds her way home but I do worry sometimes that she might go too far, or be picked up by someone.'

'All the villagers know she's yours.'

'They do but Luna does keep pestering poor Mrs Burnley. I think that she encourages Luna by feeding her to be honest, but when Luna takes her a gift... she comes in here to complain.'

'Is Luna still taking mice to Mrs Burnley then?'

'Not just mice, Honey, but anything she can get her jaws around. She took her poor old dead Wallace, and since then she's taken her a squashed frog, a squirrel and a pair of boxer shorts that she must have pulled off someone's washing line.'

'Really? I mean, I knew about Wallace but not about the boxers!' Dawn had been distraught the previous autumn when her children's guinea pig had died then been stolen by Allie's cat and left as a gift on Mrs Burnley's doorstep. The elderly woman had thought it was a giant white rat and Dawn's husband Rick had been forced to retrieve the guinea pig from Judith Burnley's bin then bury it in their garden before their children found out.

'At least they were from Marks and Spencer.'

Honey snorted and they both burst into laughter.

'Come on let's take all this through and feed the pregnant one.'

They carried the serving plates and a bottle of chilled Pinot Grigio through to the café and set them down on the table. As they tucked into the freshly prepared food, Honey enjoyed every mouthful of Allie's wonderful spread, from the mini quiches with their crumbly melt-in-the-mouth pastry and herby roasted peppers, to the home-grown spinach and the crusty rolls spread with locally-made creamy butter. Allie had also provided a plate of skin-on potato wedges with a bowl of garlic mayonnaise and another bowl of coriander and lemon houmous.

'This is so good,' Dawn mumbled as she stuffed another wedge into her mouth. 'So, so good. The heartburn will be worth it.'

'I did wonder about that as I was baking, but thought that if you're anything like I was when I was pregnant with my two, then everything will give you heartburn at this late stage.'

'Oh it does!' Dawn nodded. 'I'll follow up with a pint of milk and I'll be fine.'

The next hour passed in a flurry of chatter, clearing of plates and laughter, as the four friends enjoyed one another's company and Honey's heart brimmed with happiness that she had such good friends. Even though they didn't see one another every day, because they were all busy, she knew that they were there for her just as she was for them.

'Right I need to pee!' Dawn announced as she wiped her hands on a white napkin. 'Help me up, Honey.'

Honey stood then took Dawn's hands and leaned backwards as her pregnant friend hoisted herself up. There was a loud pop then a gush of fluid covered Dawn's shoes.

'Oh my god, Dawn! What was that?' Camilla grimaced.

Honey and Dawn looked down at the puddle on the floor then back at each other.

'I think you might have left it too long before going to the toilet,' Honey whispered, even though Camilla and Allie were right there with them and could hear every word.

'It's not her bladder that's emptied, Honey.' Allie stood up and pushed her chair back.

'It's my waters…' Dawn's eyes were wide as she gazed around the table in shock. 'And… ouch!' She hunched over and grabbed the edge of the table. 'I think the baby's on its way.'

Chapter Five

'What?' Camilla shrieked. 'How can the baby be on its way? It's too soon.'
Honey and Allie helped Dawn over to the leather sofa in the corner of the café and she sat down, cradling her bump.
'Not really, Camilla.' Dawn shook her head. 'I'm thirty-eight weeks along.'
'Noooooo!' Camilla was shaking her head vigorously as if she couldn't believe what she was hearing. 'It should be forty.'
'That's not strictly true, Camilla.' Allie placed a hand on Camilla's arm. 'Anything from thirty-eight to forty weeks... sometimes up to forty-two weeks, is considered acceptable.'
'Nope.' Camilla had paled and her green eyes seemed huge in her pretty face.
'What do you mean, nope?' Dawn scowled at her sister from the sofa where Honey was holding her hand. 'You don't have power over this, Camilla. Your niece is on the way... Ouch!'
Dawn started to pant and Camilla stumbled forwards but Allie caught her.

'It's all right, Camilla. Dawn will be fine but we do need to call Rick and probably an ambulance.'
'No time!' Dawn squeezed Honey's hand as she panted. Honey bit down on her own lip to prevent herself from crying out as her knuckles were squashed together. 'But call Rick... and tell him to hurry.'
Allie helped Camilla to sit down opposite Dawn, then ran to the counter and grabbed her mobile from behind the till. Honey heard her mutter into the mobile, clearly telling Rick to get there immediately.
'Oh... oh...' Dawn panted and squeezed Honey's hand tighter. 'I'd forgotten how much this hurts. The stinging! The awful stinging...'
'Are you sure the baby is coming now?' Honey tried to keep her voice calm, but the pain in her hand and the fluid that ran down Dawn's legs every time her belly tightened to a point under her fitted dress, were all making her own panic rise.
'Have a look!' Dawn said as she spread her legs and pulled her skirt up to her thighs.
'I can't look!' Honey replied. 'I don't know what I'm looking for.'
'Camilla?' Dawn asked her sister but Camilla buried her face in her palms.
'I can't, Dawnie. I feel faint.'
'It's all right, I've got this.' Allie pushed the coffee table out of the way. 'Honey, you keep holding her hand and Camilla... CAMILLA!'
'What?' Camilla raised her head but kept her eyes averted from her sister. 'Go through to the cottage and get some clean towels. Jordan and Max should have some in the kitchen but if not, check upstairs.'
'Can Jordan help with this?' Camilla asked hopefully.
'He's not here. Max has taken him into London for a night out.'
'Oh... OK.'
'Hurry up!'
Camilla nodded then disappeared through to the living quarters that formed the rear of the cottage. Allie had lived there with her son,

until Chris returned to the village and had asked Allie to move in with him. Since then, Jordan's boyfriend Max had moved in.

'Right, Dawnie, Rick is on his way. He's going to drop the children with your mum and dad then come straight here.'

'OK.' Dawn nodded then closed her eyes, squeezing Honey's hand again as another pain overwhelmed her body.

'I'm going to remove your underwear and have a look now. Is that OK?'

'Yes.' Dawn's lips blanched as she pressed them together.

'Can I do anything else?' Honey asked, feeling utterly helpless as she watched her friend in pain.

'Just hold her hand and say comforting things,' Allie said.

What classed as comforting to a woman in labour?

'There, there, Dawnie. It'll all be fine.' Honey grimaced as the words sounded so weak in the face of what Dawn was going through. 'You've done this twice, so third time'll be a doddle.'

Dawn opened her eyes and guffawed. 'A doddle? Shit, Honey, you can tell you haven't done this. Childbirth is never *a doddle.*'

'Sorry.' Honey's cheeks burned. 'I just didn't know what to say.'

'Ouch!' Dawn jolted on the sofa.

'Oh god, Dawnie, I can see the head!'

Honey leaned forwards and gasped. 'Is that the baby's hair?'

Allie pursed her lips but her shoulders shook.

'No, that's not the baby's hair...' She gestured at the place where Honey was looking, and Honey realised that what she'd seen was in fact hair that belonged to Dawn. 'Come around a bit and look... there.'

Honey peered at where Allie was pointing.

'Oh... I see it! I can see the baby's head. You're having a baby, Dawnie!'

'Gaaaahhhhh!' Dawn groaned and Honey quickly looked away as the baby's head stretched parts of her friend that she'd never wanted to see.

'Arghhh!' Honey cried as Dawn crunched her fingers together.

'Hurry up, Camilla!' Allie shouted.
Camilla appeared, clutching a pile of multi-coloured towels and threw them down in front of Allie, who quickly tucked some under her friend then draped one over her arm.
'Here. We. Go.' Dawn pressed her chin to her chest and emitted a sound that Honey could only describe as raw animal pain. The noise was echoed by Camilla as she swooned to the floor, while the door to the café swung open and Rick appeared, his eyes wide and his face coated in a sheen of sweat.
'Dawnie!' he cried as he dashed to his wife's side.
'Rick... You made it.' Dawn's voice was full of relief.
'You have a beautiful baby girl.'
A cry filled the room as the newborn took her first breath, and something inside Honey fluttered like the wings of a moth about to take flight. She swallowed it down, refusing to acknowledge the surge of emotion and deep sense of loss.
Allie carefully wrapped the baby in a towel then placed her on Dawn's stomach, and Honey slumped against the wall as the pain in her hand subsided now that Dawn had released it.
'Where's Camilla?' Allie asked.
'Over here.' Camilla emerged from behind the coffee table rubbing her forehead.
'Are you all right?'
'I think so. I just can't stand to see Dawnie in pain and I must've fainted.'
'We'd better get you checked out,' Allie said as she helped Camilla to sit on a chair.
'Me too,' Honey said as she held out her squashed hand.
'Welcome to The Cosy Cottage Café little one,' Dawn said as she gazed into the face of her tiny baby. 'Say hello to your daddy and three aunties.'
Honey smiled in response, but she couldn't see a thing because her eyes were filled with tears.

Dawn's midwife made it to the café before the paramedics. She'd been in the area seeing her own pregnant daughter, and Rick had called her straight after Allie had spoken to him.

Once she'd checked Dawn and the baby over, cut the cord and ensured that the placenta had come away, she accepted a cup of tea from Allie and sat opposite Dawn and Rick who were cuddled up on the sofa with their new baby.

Honey was on the chair next to the midwife, nursing her own cup of tea and wondering when she'd be able to talk properly again. She was so overwhelmed that she kept choking up. Dawn had just given birth to her third child in Allie's café and everyone was fine. It was all fine. Sometimes things did work out the way they were supposed to.

Honey turned to the midwife, a rosy-cheeked woman in her early fifties who seemed to have a permanent smile on her lovely face.

'Will...' She cleared her throat. 'Will they both be OK?'

'Yes, dear, of course they will. That was a very straightforward labour. Dawn's done it twice before so third time was a charm.'

'They don't need to go to hospital?'

'Not at all. Many women have successful home births, and although this is a café, she had no problems in her labour and the baby is feeding well.'

Honey nodded and returned her gaze to Dawn, who was cradling her daughter in her arms as she took her first feed. Allie had replaced the wet and bloodied towels with clean dry ones and fetched a soft blanket from the café cottage to wrap around Dawn. Rick had brought Dawn's delivery bag along, so Dawn would be able to change into fresh pyjamas before they made their way home.

'Hello!' Chris, Allie's partner, entered the café and grinned at everyone. 'I hear there's a new baby in the village?'

'Hi love.' Honey watched as Chris's eyes lit up when they roamed Allie's face.

'I've brought a little something to celebrate.' Chris held up two bottles of champagne. 'We had them in the fridge at home ready for a special occasion and this is evidently the right time.'

'I'll get some glasses,' Allie said.

'I think you'd better change too, Allie.' Chris pulled a face as he pointed at her jeans.

'I hadn't even noticed.' Allie looked down at the dark damp patches on her legs.

Honey suspected that they'd need to give the sofa and café a thorough clean the next day before opening, but knew that big-hearted Allie wouldn't mind. Her best friend's baby had just made its way into the world in her café; there was nothing negative in that at all. Honey had to blink hard again as tears flooded her eyes. She wasn't usually so emotional but this... this was incredible and, of course, it brought some of her suppressed emotions to the surface. How could it not? But right now she was extremely happy for her friends. She also realised that she wished Dane was there to share this perfect moment.

'Right lovelies, the paramedics are here,' the midwife peered through the window, 'so I'll have a quick chat with them before they check you over, then we'll leave you to it.'

'Thank you so much,' Rick said.

Twenty minutes later, the midwife and the paramedics had gone and Allie and Dawn had both changed; Dawn into the pyjamas from her delivery bag and Allie into one of Jordan's large hoodies and a pair of his jogging bottoms that she'd retrieved from upstairs.

Chris had popped the cork on one of the bottles of champagne and poured the bubbly liquid into glasses that Honey had fetched from the kitchen while Allie and Dawn changed.

Chris handed everyone a glass, except for Dawn, who shook her head, then raised his own.

'Congratulations to Dawn and Rick on the birth of little... uh...' He frowned. 'Do you have a name yet?'

Dawn and Rick looked at each other then back at Chris.

'Alison.' Dawn stroked her baby's cheek. 'For Allie because she helped me deliver this beautiful girl.'

'You don't have to do that, Dawn. ' Allie shook her head.

'We want to. If we call her Allie, it'll be too confusing, so we'll go with Alison.'

'In fact,' Rick said, 'her full name will be Alison Camilla Honey Dix-Beaumont.'

'Really?' Honey squealed then covered her mouth. 'Oh my goodness. I can't take any more emotion! It's all just too lovely.'

'So,' Chris said, raising his glass once more, 'congratulations to Dawn, Rick and little Alison Camilla Honey!'

They all clinked glasses then drank the cool, crisp champagne and Honey gazed around the café at her friends, old and new. Moments like these were so precious and she took a mental snapshot, intending to treasure it, and hoping she'd get the chance to tell Dane all about it soon.

Chapter Six

The two glasses of champagne had made Honey lightheaded and as she made her way home, she had the sensation of walking on air. It made her want to continue the evening, to make the most of such a wonderful feeling. She could pop to Dane's and tell him what had happened. Even if he was working, she hoped he'd have ten minutes to spare for a chat.

On the way there, she stopped three times and almost turned back and made for home, but her desire to see him was strong so she surrendered to it and let her feet carry her to Dane's rented cottage. She paused outside the front door. Honey had not always been sensible and thought things through before acting, but time and experience had made her cautious and what she was about to do was, in her opinion, a bit... reckless. But then, she was only popping to see a friend for a cuppa. What harm could it do?

She knocked on the door before she could change her mind again.

'Honey!' Dane looked genuinely pleased as he opened the door.

'Hi Dane. Um... I hope it's OK to just turn up. I know we didn't have plans but I... uh... wanted to see you to let you know what happened this evening. I hope that's OK? Oh gosh, I doubt it is, is it? I should go. You're probably really busy and I don't want to intrude on your evening. Ok... uh... I'll be off.'

She turned to go but Dane placed his hand on her shoulder. She paused, not wanting to pull away as that could be seen as rude, but she knew that if she turned around he would see that her face was scarlet with embarrassment.

'Honey?'

'Yes?'

'Please look at me.'

'OK.'

She turned slowly and he removed his hand from her shoulder.

'I'm delighted to see you. It's a lovely surprise and to be honest... I was thinking about you this evening. I thought you'd be at the café with your friends though. I know it's your designated girls' night in with them.' He smiled. 'I've been struggling to concentrate on my marking and it would be nice to have a break. Come in and I'll put the kettle on.'

Honey was suddenly conscious of his close proximity, of how his blue eyes held hers and of how good he smelt, like sandalwood with a hint of woodsmoke from the fire.

It might have been the champagne, or it might have been months of longing, but she threw all of her caution to the wind. She pushed her concerns, worries and insecurities aside, flung herself towards him, then wrapped her arms around his neck. He froze for a moment, then slid his arms around her waist. And they were kissing. Gently at first, then with growing need, as if they'd both waited too long for this moment and needed to make up for lost time.

Then he carried Honey through the door, pushed it closed with his foot and shut out the world.

They were alone.

At last.

Honey blinked several times, trying to make sense of her surroundings.
She sat up with a jolt and pulled the covers to her chest as realisation dawned.
Had that really happened last night?
Had she gone to Dane's and thrown herself at him and…
A rustling made her turn. Yes. It was true. Dane was lying next to her, over six foot of muscular man, his chest bare for her to admire. And admire it she did, before forcing herself to do a reality check. She had spent the night with Dane!
They had… done things… and she'd thoroughly enjoyed herself, but she had no right to allow herself to have so much fun, to feel so alive and to surrender to her emotions. Honey was good at being sensible and holding back. But last night she'd let her barriers down and made love to this beautiful man. And now, as she watched him sleep, his dark eyelashes fluttering gently and his full lips slightly parted, fear crawled over her, digging its icy fingers into her heart. She couldn't do this. She'd held back for so long, doubting that Dane could want her and worrying about what might happen if he did.
But Dane had been holding back too; that was evident from the outpouring of passion he'd shown last night and the sweet things he'd whispered as he'd held her and kissed her. Honey had pressed her lips together, not wanting to make promises she couldn't keep and fearing telling him anything in case everything came pouring out, but it had been so, so difficult. Sealing their relationship by making love to him was the worst thing she could have done, because now her heart was laid bare and they were both vulnerable.
Dane had told her as much last night and the thought of hurting him made her stomach churn. But if she left now, sneaked away and kept her distance, Dane might well be all right. He'd soon recover and see

it as a one-night stand. Wouldn't he? A one-night stand that had got the passion out of their systems in order to enable them to both move on.

Honey hoped Dane would be able to move on, even as she hated the thought of him being with another woman. She would have to harden her heart to her feelings for him because she didn't deserve to love and be loved. It was too risky, too dangerous; for her and for him. As much as they had seemed to know each other last night when their limbs had been tangled in Dane's sheets and they'd been as close as two humans could be, the problem was that Dane didn't really know Honey at all. He didn't know what she'd done in the past and what had happened to her. She hadn't told him the whole truth and she didn't know if she ever could. She couldn't bear to see the disappointment in his eyes, to watch as the light faded as he realised what she was really like. As it became clear that she had omitted to share the whole truth.

Honey slipped from under the covers then rooted around on the floor for her clothes. Once she'd found them, she left the bedroom as quietly as she could and descended the stairs, her heart pounding in her chest with each step in case Dane came chasing after her. But he didn't. He was fast asleep and for that she was grateful.

She dressed in the semi-darkness of his hallway, pushed her feet into her boots, and grabbed her coat from the bottom of the banister. She paused for a moment, almost wishing that Dane would appear at the top of the stairs and ask where she was going, but the house stayed quiet.

So she let herself out of his cottage, closed the door gently behind her, and hurried home, hoping that it was early enough that none of the villagers would see her walking home in the grey light of dawn.

Hoping that she could go home and get into bed and wake up to find that this had all been a dream.

But Honey had a terrible feeling that this would be there for the rest of her life, taunting her and reminding her that she let people down. Even the people she should be holding dear.

Chapter Seven

Honey turned her mobile off as soon as she got home then went straight to bed. She crawled beneath the cool duvet, shivering with cold and sadness, and tried not to think about how warm and solid Dane's body had felt in bed next to her.
It just wasn't meant to be.
It couldn't be.
She closed her eyes and tried to focus on her breathing, to allow the oblivion of sleep to claim her, but it just wouldn't come. She tossed and turned, wondering if Dane was all right and if he'd got up and gone to school as usual. Was he wondering why she'd disappeared? Was he angry or confused, sad or hurt? She hoped he was none of those things and that he'd gone off to work to spend a day educating the local children and that he would secure the job next week at interview. At least then he could make some decisions about his future and know if he'd need to move on or if he could settle in the village.
Not that Dane settling in the village would be a good thing for Honey, now. Knowing he was here every day, in Heatherlea, living his life while she lived hers would be so hard.

She pushed the covers back and sat up. Did she really need to do this? Had she acted rashly in a moment of panic? Perhaps pushing him away wasn't necessary. They evidently cared about each other, so couldn't she find a way to tell him the truth about her past, then see if he wanted to try to make a go of things with her?

Trying to sleep wasn't going to work. Besides, she needed to see to the chickens, so she pulled on her clothes and trudged down the stairs. Whatever happened, the chickens needed her. When she opened the coop, they trotted out happily, oblivious to everything except the physical need for food, water and fresh air. If only life could be as simple for humans, if only she didn't have needs and desires that went beyond food, water and shelter.

Honey could run through as many renditions of *if only* as she liked, but she couldn't escape the truth.

She had some things to sort out and she knew where she needed to start.

'That's it...' Honey walked around the village hall. 'Don't forget to breathe, Mrs Braithwaite. Yes, Mrs Hall... and elongate your spine.' She forced herself to focus on teaching her Wednesday evening yoga session, pushing her worries about Dane from her mind. The women in her class had every right to her full attention and Honey intended to ensure that they had it.

Until the door opened and Dane walked in.

Honey's heart pounded and she tried to swallow, but her tongue stuck to the roof of her mouth. Her eyes followed Dane as he walked to the mini stage at the front of the hall, dropped his rucksack then unzipped his grey hoodie and dropped it onto a chair. In his fitted blue T-shirt and jogging bottoms, he looked so big and muscular, yet so vulnerable. There was hurt and confusion etched on his face and it made Honey's stomach clench. She had hurt this lovely man and she hated herself for it.

But he was here and that was a positive thing. If he hated her, he wouldn't have come. It wasn't as if it was compulsory to attend her yoga sessions, but he always did, without fail, even when his workload was heavy. When he hadn't arrived ten minutes early as he usually did, Honey had assumed that he wasn't coming. Yet here he was, ten minutes late, but here nonetheless.

'Dane.' She smiled as she reached his side. 'Are you... all right?'

'I'm fine.' His jaw clenched and Honey decided to back off, not wanting to make him even more annoyed.

'OK. Well we haven't long started so you can join in when you're ready.'

He nodded but didn't meet her eyes, keeping his gaze fixed on a spot in the distance as if he couldn't bear to look at her.

'Right,' she said, steeling herself then taking a deep breath. 'Here we go...'

Honey encouraged class members to stretch, telling them to breathe deeply and trying to ignore the usual occurrences like Mrs Gregory farting and the muttering of innuendos from Miss Peterson. Normally, Honey would smile at the farting and the innuendos, but today her heart was heavy and nothing held the usual amusement. She gently helped eighty-seven-year-old Fred Bennett to perform some stretches on his chair. He never achieved a lot but she suspected that he attended the classes for company and that was fine with her. Yoga was about improving all aspects of health and that included the mind and heart.

She avoided looking directly at Dane, though she could see him from the corner of her eye as she walked around the hall, and it took all of her strength not to go over to him and hold him.

When the hour had passed, yoga mats had been rolled and goodbyes said, the hall emptied and Honey found herself alone with Dane. Her chest tightened and her head felt light, but she couldn't leave before him; she had to speak to him. They weren't children and she owed him civility at the very least.

She approached him cautiously.

'Dane?'

He kept rolling his mat.

'Dane? Can we talk?'

He stopped rolling and threw the mat to the floor making her wince.

'What about, Honey? I can't imagine why you'd need to speak to me.' His eyes were hard, not at all like the eyes Honey had gazed into for months, the eyes she had melted into and that had made her heart grow.

'Well...' she licked her lips 'about us.'

'Us?' He frowned. 'There's an us? I woke up alone this morning after one of the best nights of my life to find you gone. You didn't answer my calls or texts or even leave a note. How do you think I feel?'

'I'm so sorry.'

'Are you?'

She nodded.

'I feel used. Cheap. Unworthy. I thought we had a... a connection but you left after we made love and didn't even say goodbye. Was it a mistake for you?'

'No.' She shook her head. 'Well, yes. Kind of. Not in that way. Oh gosh... I don't know how to explain it.'

'Well don't bother. I guess I know where I stand now. Goodbye, Honey.'

He left his mat on the floor, grabbed his bag then marched to the door. Honey watched him, her heart pounding out his name.

'Please don't go.' Her voice was high with panic.

'Why not? Give me one good reason why I shouldn't walk out of here right now.'

Honey took a deep breath. The words were on the tip of her tongue, teasing her but not emerging. She tried to articulate them, to push them into the air but her voice remained trapped in her throat.

Then Dane was gone and an icy draft blew through the front door and into the hall, circling her ankles and chilling her flesh so that goosebumps rose on her skin.

'Because I have things to deal with before I can move on. Because I need you to trust me while I sort them out. And... because I think I love you,' she whispered into the emptiness as a lone tear trickled down her cheek.

Chapter Eight

Saturday morning, Honey hooked the pink gift bag containing a present for baby Alison over her arm, locked her door then set off for Dawn and Rick's house. They were having a few friends around and Honey was looking forward to seeing everyone, although she was hoping that none of them would ask about Dane.

The air was heavy with the threat of rain and grey clouds hung low in the sky, creating a claustrophobic effect and making Honey long for clear blue skies and the heat of summer.

When she got to Dawn's house, she took a deep breath before knocking the door and ran through the answer she had prepared in case anyone did ask about Dane: *He's very busy this weekend marking books.* It was a perfectly plausible excuse, as he was, very often, marking books.

She knocked on the door with her free hand then waited until it swung open and Rick stood in front of her.

'Honey! How are you?'

'Oh, you know...' she smiled, taking in the dark shadows under his eyes, his stubbly jaw, stained black T-shirt and odd socks. 'Not bad at all.'

He ran a hand through his hair. 'Well excuse the state of me but a new baby means that everything else – sleep included – has to take a back seat.'
'So it seems.' She nodded. 'But you're all doing well?'
'Yes, wonderfully!' He peered behind her. 'Dane not with you?'
Honey bristled. 'No. Should he be?'
'Oh... uh... he's been invited too and as you are...' Rick scanned her face. 'Oh... maybe you're not quite uh... what I meant was.' He sighed. 'You know what? I'm sleep deprived and I'm being rude keeping you on the doorstep. Come on in.'
Honey stepped into the hallway then removed her boots and tucked them under the shoe rack with the others.
'I really am sorry, Honey. I thought you and Dane were a couple now.'
'Not exactly. But don't be sorry.' She shrugged out of her jacket. 'It's fine, honestly.'
But she didn't feel fine. In fact, her heart ached. Rick had said that Dane was invited this morning too, so that meant he could turn up while she was here and that would be very awkward indeed.
'Go on through to the lounge and I'll put the kettle on.'
'Where are Laura and James? It seems very quiet.'
'Dawn's parents took them out for the day to spoil them. We're keen to ensure that they don't feel at all put out now that little Alison is here. It's such a juggling act making sure everyone feels happy and included.'
'I can only imagine.'
In the lounge, Dawn was on the sofa surrounded by pillows, with her feet on a large pouffe. She looked tired but she grinned when she saw Honey.
'Hello, love!'
Honey leant forwards and kissed her cheek then handed her the pink gift bag.
'There was no need for this,' Dawn held the bag aloft. 'But thank you anyway.'

'It's just a little something.'
'Hi Honey,' Camilla said as she emerged from the kitchen carrying a tray laden with mugs. Tom followed her holding a plate of biscuits.
'Hi Camilla, hi Tom.'
'Oh Honey!' Dawn said as she unwrapped the gold tissue from around the unicorn ornament that Honey had made. 'It's beautiful.'
'It has hair a bit like yours,' Tom said.
Honey nodded. The small white unicorn had a mane of pink and blue hair to match its colourful horn.
'Can I see it?' Camilla asked.
She got up and took the unicorn from Dawn and held it up to the light. 'It's so pretty. It's exactly like the...' She paused and looked at Honey. 'Honey... Have you been keeping a secret from us?'
Honey's skin prickled and she looked away, feigning interest in the cards on the windowsill.
'You have, haven't you?' Camilla pushed her. 'You've been hiding something.'
Honey dug her fingernails into her palms, trying to work out how to explain her awful secret to her friends, to explain why she had kept it from them for so long.
'What are you talking about Camilla?' Dawn asked, shaking her head.
'I think Honey has been modest about her sculpting and painting. This is so much like the Purple Hen range, that I'm convinced it is one.'
Honey looked from Camilla to Dawn and back again. She was talking about her designs not the other thing...
'Oh! Yes... I'm behind Purple Hen designs.' She smiled as relief seeped through her.
'Why didn't you say anything? This brand has really taken off lately. I've seen it in several shops and online but I had no idea it was you.'
'Well, it started as a bit of a hobby when I arrived in Heatherlea and I didn't think anything would come of it. In fact, I didn't think anyone

would be interested but lately I've been getting more orders and I'm actually struggling to meet the demand.'
'Well that's fantastic!' Dawn said. 'Good for you.'
Honey's cheeks glowed at the praise.
'I didn't say anything because I didn't want to seem like I was boasting.'
Camilla shook her head. 'Honey, it's not boasting to tell your friends about your business success, you know.'
'Actually, Camilla, now that it's out in the open, I think I might need some help.'
Camilla held up her hands. 'I'm not at all creative.'
'No, I meant with the accounts.'
'Anytime, lovely. Get everything together and we can arrange a day for me to come and take a look.'
'Wonderful, thank you.'
'I wish you'd told us before. There's never a need to keep secrets from us.'
Dawn smiled at her and guilt gushed through Honey. Now the fact that she had another secret, a far worse one, seemed dreadful. How could she tell them that her business wasn't the only thing she'd been keeping quiet?
'There's a box of fresh eggs in there too, Dawn, to keep your strength up.'
'Believe me I need all the nutrients I can get the way this little one is feeding.'
'That's what I thought.' Honey peered into the crib next to the sofa.
'You can hold her if you like,' Dawn said.
'Oh...' Honey stepped backwards. 'It's OK, she's sleeping.'
'That's fine. Have a cuddle.'
'No. Not yet.'
Confusion passed over Dawn's face so Honey turned away and went to the chair in the corner, picking up a mug of tea from the table as she passed it. The thought of holding the tiny baby made something inside her wobble, and she worried that whatever it was

would burst to the surface if she so much as stroked the baby's soft pink cheek.

'Well I'll have a hold if you won't.' Camilla gently lifted her niece then sat next to her sister while Tom took the other chair. 'She's gorgeous.'

'What do the children think of her?' Honey asked, keen to move on from her apparent distaste for cuddling little Alison.

'They're besotted.' Dawn smiled as she picked up a mug of tea. 'They can't do enough to help me and Rick at the moment; they're taking their roles as older siblings very seriously. That's why I was so happy that Mum and Dad offered to take them out today. I wanted them to have some attention focused on them and I'm not quite up to a day out just yet.'

'No and we need to get some sleep in before we do make any plans,' Rick said as he entered the room.

'So true.' Dawn just about managed to stifle her yawn with her hand. 'I'd forgotten how difficult the sleep deprivation is.'

'Well Tom and I will happily babysit anytime you like,' Camilla said as she gazed down at her niece.

'Yes, of course we will.' Tom got up and crouched next to Camilla. 'She's perfect.'

Honey felt a bit strange sitting across from the display of adoration. It wasn't that she didn't think tiny Alison was one of the most beautiful things she had ever seen, because she did, but she was afraid to become too involved in case certain emotions resurfaced. Emotions that she'd been very good at hiding for a long time.

Instead, she looked around the lounge at the chaos. There were piles of gifts as yet unwrapped, pink cards and vases of flowers on every available surface. On the coffee table were rings from mugs, toast crumbs and two empty biscuit packets. Dawn and Rick had evidently been too busy to clean or even open all the baby's gifts, but they were happy; they had each other and their beautiful family.

From where she was sitting, Tom and Camilla looked as though they could be the adoring parents of the baby and she realised that she could well be seeing a vision of their future. It might not happen, of course, but the way Camilla's face had softened as she looked at the baby and the way she sighed when the tiny fingers curled around her thumb made her somehow... different. Camilla had always insisted that she'd never be a wife or a mother but now she had Tom and perhaps being in love had changed her perspective on things. Life did take people on unexpected journeys, and it was highly possible that Camilla was heading along a route she'd had no idea she would ever go.

'I'm in love with her, Dawnie,' Camilla said. 'Can we keep her, Tom?' She looked up at her boyfriend from under her lashes and Honey saw the flush that rose in Tom's cheeks. He certainly didn't look afraid or repulsed by the idea.

'Well, not Alison, as I don't think Dawn and Rick would be too happy about that but you know... we can always consider trying for one of our own.'

A silence fell over the room as they all digested Tom's words then Dawn burst into laughter.

'I suspected this would happen when you fell in love, Camilla.' Camilla's cheeks glowed as she glanced around the room. 'I'm just feeling a bit broody now that this beautiful little one is here. I didn't feel like it before, granted, when Laura and James were babies but it wasn't the right time. I don't know though... perhaps my biological clock has started ticking. It's certainly got new batteries.' She giggled and they all joined in.

A knock at the door silenced their laughter and Rick got up to answer it. Honey held her breath and listened, and her heart skipped a beat at the familiar voice. What was she going to do now? Camilla and Dawn glanced at her but Honey broke eye contact and stared into her drink.

'Morning everyone.' Dane entered the room, bringing with him the scent of fresh air, flowers and his sandalwood cologne. Honey tried not to look at him but her eyes wrenched themselves from her mug and sought him out.

He handed a bouquet of flowers and a small gift bag to Dawn and a bottle of bubbly to Rick, then he stood awkwardly by the sofa staring down at the baby.
'Take a seat.' Rick gestured at the chair he'd recently vacated. 'Tea or coffee?'
'Coffee, please. Milk no sugar.'
Rick nodded then took the bouquet from Dawn. 'I'll try to find a spare vase for these.'
Dane looked around the room. 'Sorry, looks like a florist's in here already.'
'Never say sorry for bringing flowers, Dane. And they're beautiful, thank you so much. As is this.' Dawn held up a lilac baby grow with a matching bib.
'I got three to six months because I wasn't sure what size she is now.'
'That's fabulous, believe me. It always helps to have things for them to grow into. I'm very impressed with your selection.'
Dane cleared his throat. 'I had a bit of help from a kind lady in Tesco. She was buying clothes for her grandchildren and suggested lilac as a nice change from pink. She said you'd probably have lots of pink.'
'We have.' Dawn nodded. 'But she suits lilac and pink so we're lucky.'
'We bought her blue things,' Camilla said. 'Jeans, dungarees, hats and socks, so she doesn't fall into a girly stereotype before she's even turned one.'
'I'm sure that wouldn't happen, Camilla. She has an older sister and a brother to help bring her up and James has already said he's going to teach her to play football and rugby.'
'Yes that's right,' Rick said as he handed Dane a mug of coffee. 'Our children are going to form their own rugby team apparently.'
'If you keep on having children you'll soon have enough for a rugby team.' Camilla snorted.
'Ha! Yes, funny.' Rick pulled a face at his sister-in-law. 'If we don't get some sleep soon, there'll be no energy for making more.'
'No more for the foreseeable future.' Dawn smiled at Rick. 'We have enough children to focus on now.'

Honey glanced at Dane and found him gazing at her, but when she met his eyes, he looked away. She wanted to speak to him so badly but she'd caught the hurt in his eyes and knew that this wasn't the right time or place. In fact, the last thing she wanted to do was to make him feel uncomfortable. These were his friends too.

'Oh!' she exclaimed. 'I've just realized that I left the gate to the chicken enclosure unlocked. If I'm not careful the chickens will destroy my raised beds. I'd better hurry back and lock it.'

'I hope they haven't noticed yet,' Camilla said, her eyes wide to convey that she knew what Honey was doing, but was going to play along anyway.

'Me too. I love those girls but they will eat anything.'

Honey stood up. 'Sorry to love you and leave you but I'd better get back.'

'Of course.' Dawn accepted her hug. 'Come see us soon. I won't be at the café next week so come here instead if you like.'

'When you're not busy, Dawnie. You've got your hands full at the moment.'

Honey went out into the hallway and Rick followed her.

'Don't be a stranger, Honey. Dawn loves to see you and will be glad of the company. She'll be glad to talk about things other than nappies and breastfeeding.'

'I bet.' Honey accepted a brief hug from Rick. 'See you soon. Have a lovely weekend.'

'Thanks. Don't think we'll be straying far from the sofa though.' He rolled his eyes but he looked so happy and contented that Honey knew he was joking.

She made her way back to her cottage, thinking about how happy her friends were now and how happy she was for them that they'd found love and contentment. Neither were to be underestimated or taken for granted. Sure, Rick and Dawn had had their fair share of problems, and at one point last year it had seemed as though they might split up, but they'd come through it all stronger and more in love than ever.

But Dane… he'd looked sad and tired and she was devastated that it was because of her. She wanted to run back there and hug him but she couldn't do that and she wasn't big on public displays of affection at the best of times, so the thought that he might push her away was enough to keep her feet moving forwards.

When she got home, she walked through to the kitchen then out into her back garden. She checked the chicken enclosure and it was locked, just as she'd known it was. But she couldn't have stayed any longer knowing that Dane was as uncomfortable as she was. She'd also been afraid that someone might mention Purple Hen designs and Dane would feel even more betrayed, because she hadn't told him about its growing success either. He was always so busy with work and striving to succeed, so telling him that her hobby had blossomed into a successful business seemed almost cruel. She'd never been one to show off, preferring to keep any successes to herself, but she realised now that it also meant that she never really opened up to anyone. Not her friends, not her boyfriend…

It was time to be positive and to make a plan for her future. She was still only in her twenties but life had a habit of passing quickly and there were things she wanted to achieve before thirty. She still wanted to continue to grow her business and she wanted to learn how to make pastry that didn't shrink when she put it in the oven and she wanted to do lots of other things too. Life was for living, right?

A few hours later, there was a knock at the door. Hope sparked in Honey's gut as she wondered if it was Dane. Had he come to talk to her now? Did he need to see her as much as she longed to see him? But what good would it do them when her past was still clinging to her like clay clung to her fingers.

Still, there was no sense in standing in the garden wondering who it was, so she'd just as well go and find out…

Chapter Nine

'Hello, you!' Camilla smiled at Honey from her doorstep. Her short black hair shone and her green eyes sparkled.
'Hi Camilla.'
'Oh... what's wrong? Disappointed it's me?'
'No, of course not. I just wasn't expecting you, that's all. Come on in.'
Camilla followed Honey through to the kitchen, the tote bags she was holding clinking as she walked.
'What've you got in there?'
Camilla placed the two bulging bags on the kitchen table. 'I've been shopping. I thought you needed a girls' night in.'
'But we haven't had one of those in—'
'Ages! I know. We've had our Tuesdays at the café but not a good old night in wearing pyjamas and eating ice cream and cake. Allie's coming over too once she's closed the café... as long as you're up for it.'
'Well, yes. It sounds great, but what about Tom?'
'He can take care of himself.'
'I don't like to take you away from him though.'

Camilla walked around the table then wrapped her arms around Honey, who felt tears pricking at her eyes.
'Don't be so daft, woman! We're friends and we all need to make time for one another. Obviously, Dawnie can't make it, but I think we've been a bit neglectful of our group lately and Allie agrees. So I hope you've got ice in the freezer.'
'I have but I don't have much food in.'
Camilla waved a hand. 'Not a problem at all because Allie said she's got that covered and I brought the drinks.'
Camilla opened the bags and started pulling out bottles.
'Bloody hell, Camilla.'
Camilla wiggled her eyebrows.
'I brought a selection because I didn't know what you'd fancy. There's elderflower gin, plenty of tonic and some lemons. Then there's white rum, soda water and limes in case you fancy mojitos. Ah...' She chewed her lip. 'I forgot the mint.'
'There's plenty of mint in the garden.'
'Wonderful!'
Camilla rolled up the tote bags and stuffed them into her Marc Jacobs handbag.
'And I bought plenty of tortilla chips and two boxes of chocolates, because... well, I think you need them.'
Honey gazed at the bottles and snacks on the table then at Camilla.
'Hey, love, what is it? Did something happen between you and Dane?'
Honey nodded.
'I take it things progressed but not as you'd hoped?'
'Kind of...' Honey squeaked.
'Say no more! Camilla's here now.' She released Honey and handed her a tissue from the box on the table. 'What are we going to do with you? I know! We'll make some cocktails then you can relax and let it all out.'
'OK. Sounds good.' She blew her nose. 'I'll go and pick some mint.'
'Mojitos it is!' Camilla declared.

When Honey returned from the garden, where she'd picked plenty of fresh dark green mint and pondered the wisdom of drinking cocktails mid-afternoon, Camilla was using the cocktail shaker from Honey's cupboard while dancing round the kitchen to Abba.
'Hope you don't mind my music? It's a feel-good playlist I put together. All sorts of great songs on there like Abba, Queen, Whitney Houston, Journey, Christina Perri, the Bee Gees and so on... Always gets me smiling, even on my lowest days.'
'You have low days?'
Camilla stopped dancing. 'Of course! Doesn't everyone?'
Honey nodded. 'Especially at certain times of the month.'
'I know. It's a rollercoaster sometimes being a woman but then you see my gorgeous nieces and nephew and it's just...'
'All worth it?'
'Absolutely!'
Honey got two long thin glasses from the cupboard and took them to Camilla, then she washed the freshly picked mint and tore it up onto a piece of kitchen roll.
'Right, let's get changed then enjoy some drinks!'
'Changed?' Honey asked.
Camilla nodded then opened her large handbag and pulled out two rolled up garments.
Honey's mouth fell open as she stared at them. 'Really?'
'It's what you need. Come on!'
Camilla dragged Honey upstairs by the hand then gave her one of the garments. 'See you in a minute... I need the loo.'
Honey stripped to her underwear then held the garment up. Was she really going to put it on? She shrugged; she had nothing to lose.
'Wow... You look fabulous!' Camilla exclaimed as she entered the bedroom ten minutes later.
'I do? Where did you get it?'
'I had them for Christmas from my mother but haven't worn either of them yet. I was waiting for the right occasion.'
'I guess that romantic nights in with Tom don't call for these?'

'Not exactly.' Camilla giggled. 'But tonight's the perfect night to wear them.'

They stood in front of the mirrored cupboard doors and grinned at their reflections. Camilla was wearing a grey elephant onesie with a trunk and floppy ears on the hood and Honey had on a unicorn onesie that was white with rainbow stripes up the sides, a rainbow mane and glittery white horn on the hood. Both onesies had chunky feet – Honey's resembled hooves – and padded fronts that made Honey feel a bit like she'd eaten too much. She turned sideways and admired her bulging tummy.

'Oh don't you start.' Camilla shook her head and her trunk wobbled from side to side.

'I thought I looked full rather than pregnant,' Honey explained.

'OK, I'll believe you. In light of your business success, I thought it was particularly appropriate for you.'

'I am sorry I didn't tell you all about it. To be honest, it's all happened so quickly.'

Camilla hugged her. 'Not a problem, sweetie. We're all delighted for you.'

'All?'

'I hope you don't mind but I told Allie when I spoke to her earlier and she's over the moon.'

'She is? She's not... disappointed that I didn't say anything.'

'Of course not. We're friends and we understand why you kept it quiet.'

Honey chewed the inside of her cheek. She could tell Camilla everything now, unburden and have no more secrets from her friends. It would feel good, surely, to get it all off her chest...

'Anyway, it's mojito time!' Camilla said, breaking into Honey's thoughts. 'Let's go have some fun.'

Back in the kitchen, drinks in hand, they danced around the kitchen to Whitney, Christina and Journey until they were both breathless and getting rather warm in their onesies.

'Another drink?' Camilla asked after she'd drained her glass.

'Go on then. That was delicious.'
'Open the tortilla chips, will you? I'm getting peckish.'
Honey opened the bag and tipped the chips into a bowl then placed it on the table before sitting down. Camilla returned with more drinks and started to disco dance when the Bee Gees high voices filled the kitchen. Honey clapped and laughed as Camilla gave a performance that could have won her a role in *Saturday Night Fever*.
'I didn't know you could dance like that.'
'Neither did I.' Camilla snorted. 'But it's nice to let go once in while. I'm such a sensible accountant most of the time, you know.'
'I do know and I promise not to tell anyone that you discoed around my kitchen dressed as an elephant.'
'Thank you. Between us right?'
Honey nodded.
'So... now you have something on me, would you like to tell me anything else? You don't have to, of course. There's no pressure but I sense that there's something you've never told me... and I'm not referring to Purple Hen designs this time. If it would help you to get it off your chest, then I'm here to listen. I might even be able to help.'
Camilla sat opposite Honey and pushed her hood down. Her hair was slightly damp with perspiration and her cheeks were flushed. Honey realised that Camilla had been trying to relax her, to get her to forget about her worries for a while and to have some fun. Silly fun, but fun all the same. And Honey did feel lighter because of it. But now... Camilla was offering her the chance to talk, to really talk and get all of her worries out in a safe environment.
The mojitos had relaxed her, warming her from the inside, and she was tired of carrying around her secrets. If she could tell her friend about her past, it could help. Camilla might be able to offer her some advice. It had been so long since Honey had felt light and free; she gave the appearance of being blithe, but inside, her heart was heavy and her conscience was soiled.
'I do have... things that I've never told anyone. Nothing terrible, you know, like murder... but things I've carried my whole adult life. I

should have told you and the girls before but I just couldn't seem to do it, then it seemed too late to suddenly admit to having secrets from you all. The growth of Purple Hen was bad enough but that's such a recent thing and the other thing is worse...'

Camilla reached across the table and covered Honey's hand with her own, stilling her tapping fingers.

'Don't apologise. Everyone has secrets; families are hives for secrets and lies. Some things we can tell and some are perhaps, best left unsaid, but usually, sharing can lighten the burden. I know you don't have any close family to lean on and that's why I want to help. Allie, Dawn and I... we're here for you. Trust us.'

'I do trust you. I just worried that if I suddenly told you about what happened to me, then you'd wonder why I hadn't said anything before.'

Camilla shook her head. 'Some things emerge when the time is right. No one knows anyone inside out, Honey.'

'True.'

Honey sipped her drink, savouring the fresh minty aroma, the sweetness of the sugar and the warmth of the rum as it slipped down her throat and into her stomach. She could drink mojitos all day and not get tired of the taste.

'OK. I'll try to start at the right point but I may end up moving around a bit.'

'I've got all day and all night, Honey. You take your time.'

'Right...' Honey took a deep breath then released it slowly. 'Before I came to Heatherlea...'

Chapter Ten

'And I guess that's why I've kind of drifted along for the past nine years. After what happened ... I couldn't seem to apply myself to anything with the same vigour as before. Growing up, I'd had dreams of studying art at university and travelling the world to gain inspiration for my own work, but none of that held the same allure.'
'I'm so sorry, Honey. You've had a lot to deal with over the years and...' Camilla shook her head, 'no wonder you found it difficult at Dawnie's this morning being around the baby.'
'Please don't think I'm not delighted for her and Rick.'
'I don't, not at all. I feel sorry for you having gone through such pain. Yet you've been so strong.'
'I'm not strong. I went through what millions of other women do every day.'
'That doesn't mean it's any less painful.'
'I'm OK though.'
'You are?'
Honey nodded. 'But Dane doesn't know any of this either and it's the kind of thing I should tell him. But when's the right time? Not on the first few dates, yet not on our first anniversary either.'

'It is difficult, Honey, but not impossible. After all, Dane has likely got his own secrets too. I found out that Tom was still married, remember, and that was a huge shock. It's better to be honest as soon as you can be, I think. Misunderstandings can cause their own problems.'

'I agree, but I also want to sort a few things out first, so I feel I can move on properly.'

'Of course.'

'Shall we have another drink?'

'Absolutely.' Camilla smiled then looked at the clock on the wall. 'Allie should be here soon.'

'I'll tell her too.'

'Allie is always great with advice.'

'I know. She's been through so much herself.'

Camilla picked up their glasses. 'I think, dear Honey, that life puts us all through the mill and that we're all stronger because of it.'

There was a knock at the front door then, so Honey went to answer it while Camilla made more drinks. Allie stood on the doorstep holding a large cardboard box. Her face creased up as she looked at Honey.

'Is it fancy dress then? Dammit! I don't have a costume.'

'What?'

'You're a unicorn.'

'Oh, right.' Honey stood back to let Allie in. 'It's Camilla's. She said we needed to wear onesies.'

'And what's Camilla come as?' Allie asked as she kicked off her shoes in the hallway while balancing the box on one knee.

'She's an elephant.'

Allie grimaced. 'Of course. An elephant and a unicorn!'

They went through to the kitchen and found Camilla pouring mojitos into three glasses.

'Love the onesies, Camilla.' Allie put the box on the worktop.

'Thanks. Shame I didn't have a third one.'

'I'm good, thanks. I can't wear the things because they make me feel panicky.'

'Panicky?' Camilla frowned. 'How can a onesie make you feel anything other than happy?'
'It's the being confined thing. I prefer pyjamas, where the bottoms are separate. That whole being enclosed in one garment experience is just...' Allie shivered. 'Not for me.'
'Each to her own.' Camilla shrugged. 'Right then ladies, here's to friendship.'
They clinked their glasses together then drank.
'Mmmm. Good job, Camilla,' Allie said, raising her glass to admire the drink.
'Thank you. I'm rather proud of my mojito-making skills.'
'They've gone to my head already,' Honey said, pulling a face at her friends. 'I'm a bit tipsy.'
'I've catching up to do then.' Allie took another sip.
'No rush, Allie, we have all night.'
'I've brought some goodies from the café.' Allie opened the box and showed them the contents. 'There's all sorts of savouries and some cakes too.'
'Yum! I'm quite hungry now.'
'Well let's eat.' Allie carried foil trays and dishes over to the table while Honey got knives, forks and plates. Delicious aromas filled her kitchen as the light outside changed from afternoon brightness to dusk. They drank more mojitos, enjoyed the food from the café then opened the chocolates Camilla had brought. By the time Honey had to switch the lights on, she was fit to burst.
'So, Allie. What do you think?' Honey asked, now that she'd told Allie everything too.
'That you have nothing to worry about. I understand why you want to be open with Dane and why you want to deal with certain things before you do that. Don't feel bad at all. No one has a flawless past, you know?'
'That's what I told her,' Camilla said then popped a hazelnut whirl into her mouth.

'Thanks so much.' Honey smiled at her friends. 'I'm so grateful to you for listening and not… judging.'

'Why would we judge you?' Allie asked.

'I didn't think you would… but as I didn't tell you before, I worried you might think less of me for keeping it in.'

'All I wish is that I could go back in time and give the younger you a big hug and tell you that everything would work out. There is nothing for you to feel guilty about, you know.'

'Thank you so much. Shall we go through to the lounge?'

'Good idea.' Camilla stood up then picked up the boxes of chocolates.

'I need to put the chickens to bed, first.' Honey glanced at the clock. 'Poor loves. I've been distracted.'

'You go do that then and Allie you can help me with the next batch of mojitos.'

'Will do.' Allie saluted Camilla.

'The night is young!' Camilla sang, as Honey stepped out into the cool darkness of the garden and made her way to the chicken enclosure.

The moon was full overhead, so she could see enough without needing a torch, but the corners of her garden lay in shadow. The chickens had already gone into the coop, so she locked the hatch, then the enclosure before gazing around the garden. The air was laced with woodsmoke from a nearby cottage and a dog barked in the distance. She wondered what Dane was doing, then she shook the thought away.

Tonight was about spending quality time with Camilla and Allie and putting the past to bed. She felt so lucky to have such close friends and she silently thanked The Cosy Cottage Café for bringing them all together. If it hadn't been for her going in there when she moved to Heatherlea, then she might never have found such kind and supportive friends. Honey had so much to be grateful for and she felt much better now that she'd finally spoken about her past. No one was judging her; in fact, they were more supportive than she could have imagined.

'Psst!'

Honey looked up to see Camilla standing in the kitchen doorway.

'Stop daydreaming in the garden and come and have a dance.'

'Another one?'

'It's good for you. Think of the endorphins.'

'OK, coming.'

Honey smiled as she returned to the cottage. Whatever else happened in life, as long as she had her friends, she knew she'd be OK.

Chapter Eleven

Honey wrinkled her nose the next morning when she entered the kitchen. A glance at the clock informed her that it was eight-thirty, much later than she usually rose. She filled the kettle and switched it on then wandered around picking up glasses and chocolate wrappers. How many mojitos had she drunk yesterday? Bottles cluttered the kitchen worktop and she winced as she saw that they'd drunk most of the bottle of white rum. She didn't drink a lot of alcohol and when she did, it was normally a nice wine and she tended to stop at two glasses, three maximum, because she hated hangovers.

However, it looked as if she was stuck with a hangover for today. The morning sunlight warmed the kitchen tiles and she stood still for a moment, enjoying the heat on her naked toes. Hangover or not, she needed to go and sort the chickens out, so she stepped into her wellies and went outside.

The garden was fresh and bright and she inhaled the sweetly fragranced air. Once she'd opened the coop and seen to the chickens' food and water, she locked the enclosure and stood there for a moment watching as they emerged and helped themselves to breakfast.

Honey knew that she probably needed to eat too, to help her body to recover after all the rum. She should also rehydrate her system, so lots of water was essential today.

She'd eaten two pieces of toast, drunk three cups of tea and a pint of water when the door went. She frowned. It was Sunday morning and still early. Two reasons why she wasn't expecting visitors. It could be Ethan, the little boy from next door, asking if his ball was stuck in her apple tree again. He was only six and loved playing in his large back garden. Of course, he often kicked the ball too high and Honey had returned it over the fence many times, but the last time it had been stuck in the branches of her tree and it had taken Honey some time, and a lot of laughter, to shake the ball from the branches. Ethan also liked to see the chickens and had been round several times to help Honey collect the eggs, which he loved doing, especially when he got a box of fresh eggs to take home for his breakfast.

Another sharp rap at the door, made her hurry through the hallway.

'I'm coming, I'm coming!'

She swung the door open, about to greet little Ethan, but when she saw who was standing there, her mouth fell open.

'Hello, Honey.'

She swallowed hard. 'Bloody hell, what're you doing here?'

'I needed to see you.'

She stared at the tall, slim man standing on her doorstep. His long wavy hair glowed in the sunlight, the red brighter than she remembered, and he roamed his olive-green eyes over her face.

'But I haven't seen you in... about eight years.'

'I know.' He stuffed his hands into his pockets and looked around self-consciously.

'How did you even... know I was here?'

'I asked around and, to be honest, you can find out most things on Facebook these days. Look, Honey, do you think I could come in?'

'Oh... of course, Elliott.' She gazed at him for a moment, confused by the emotions surging through her, then she flung her arms around his neck. 'It's good to see you.'

He hugged her back, his long arms easily encircling her waist. It was strange holding him after such a long time, yet he smelt familiar, as if beneath the aftershave and fabric softener that fragranced his clothes, his scent was the same; unchangeable. But some things did change, like her feelings towards him.

He released her and she looked up at him again.

'Come on in.'

'Thank you.'

He entered the hallway, and as Honey was about to close the door, she spotted Dane on the opposite side of the road wearing his running gear. His cheeks were pink and his hands rested on his hips as he stared at her.

'Dane!' She waved at him.

What had he seen? Her hugging Elliott on her doorstep on a Sunday morning. How would that look to him? She hadn't even told him anything about Elliott. It was easy to imagine how this could be misconstrued.

She hurried down her path, meaning to speak to Dane but he shook his head then jogged away. Honey watched him go. What else could she do right now?

This.

This was what she needed to do before she could be open with Dane. She wished he hadn't seen what he had, as she'd wanted to speak to him and explain everything, but sometimes, plans went awry, so she'd have to hope that Dane was all right for the time being and deal with Elliott first.

'Everything OK?' he asked from the hallway as she entered.

'Yes. Everything's fine.'

'You sure? You have that worry line between your eyebrows that you always used to get.'

'Some things don't change, huh?'

'They certainly don't.'

'Let's have a coffee and a chat.'

'Great, thanks. But can I ask you something?'

'Sure.'
'Why are you dressed as a unicorn?'

Honey wrapped her hands around her mug of coffee and waited for Elliott to return from the toilet. She couldn't believe he was here. She'd been talking about him just last night with Camilla and Allie and it was as if some kind of magic had brought him to her doorstep, so she didn't even need to try to track him down.
'This is a lovely cottage, Honey.'
Elliott entered the kitchen and she took a good look at him. His ginger hair still brushed his shoulders but he'd grown thick sideburns that sat like lamb chops on his cheeks. He still had the smattering of light-brown freckles on his nose and a few on his forehead. He was as slim as he'd been as a teenager and wearing clothes that would have fitted him back then too: jeans and a long sleeved tie-dye top that made Honey's eyes hurt with the effects of her hangover. In fact, Elliott could have come straight from Woodstock.
'Thanks. I haven't changed it since I moved in so the décor is mostly my aunt's.'
'Sorry for your loss, by the way.'
'Sadly, I didn't know her that well, but when I came here to see the cottage, I knew I couldn't sell it. It was kind of like coming home.'
'It's very homely.'
He smiled and her cheeks warmed slightly. There was a familiarity between them, certainly, but also a kind of awkwardness, developed from years apart.
'So, Elliott, it is good to see you but why have you turned up on my doorstep on a Sunday morning... out of the blue...'
'I had to speak to you, and I wanted to do it in person. An email or a text... if I'd even had your number still, which I didn't... well they

didn't seem right. And a Facebook message might have been missed, plus it's not the right way to go about this; I didn't want to do that to you.' He frowned. 'Shit, perhaps I've been too presumptuous. I mean, maybe you wouldn't even have cared. Look at you… beautiful, successful, living in a chocolate-box pretty village. You're obviously doing really well so why would you care what your ex was up to?'

'I do care. Of course I care. We have… quite a history and for a long time you were my best friend, Elliott. Don't forget that.'

'I haven't and that's why I came in person. And, if I'm honest, I wanted to see you once more.'

'Once more? That sounds very final.'

'Well, yes, because you see… I'm—'

Honey held up a hand. 'Hold that thought!'

She jumped up and hurried to the kitchen door where a chicken was bobbing its way towards her vegetable stand.

'Is that a chicken?'

'No, it's a dog.' She rolled her eyes at Elliott and he laughed.

'What's it doing in here?'

'Hennifer Aniston shouldn't be in here. I must've left the enclosure unlocked. Fancy giving me a hand? They'll be all round the garden by now.'

'Sure. I'm always up for a challenge.'

They went out into the garden, Honey shooing Hennfier Aniston ahead of her towards the enclosure.

'Well I didn't expect to be doing this today,' Elliott said, once they'd managed to get the three chickens that had escaped back into the enclosure.

'Me either. At least not with you. I usually lock the enclosure properly but I must've been lax with my hangover.'

'You're hungover?'

'A bit. I had a few friends round last night.'

'Good for you. I forget what it's like to have a good drink. Of course, we haven't been drinking much recently but that's because I'm trying to be a supportive partner and to be in good shape for when the b—'

Honey froze.

'The b...? You're going to be a dad?'

Elliott pressed his lips together as he nodded.

'That's why I needed to speak to you. Well, why I *wanted* to speak to you.'

'I see.' Honey headed back towards the house. 'I uh... I need my coffee.'

As she pushed the door open and entered the kitchen, Honey suspected that she'd need more than one coffee if Elliott's news was of the baby kind.

Chapter Twelve

Coffee in hand, Honey sat opposite Elliott again, waiting for him to begin. The kitchen was so quiet that she could hear the clock ticking and the birds singing outside. But she was waiting for Elliott to speak first, because he was the one with the news.

'Honey…' He licked his lips then sighed. 'We were so close for so long weren't we?'

She nodded. 'Best friends.'

'Looking back, it all seems such a long time ago but I remember it as if it were yesterday.'

Honey and Elliott had grown up as next-door neighbours in Basingstoke. They'd been friends through primary school, fallen out in the first year of high school, then become good friends again at sixteen when they'd both gone to college to study art. Elliott had been her slightly geeky, lanky friend. She hadn't known she had any romantic feelings for him until they'd gone to a house party, the summer after their first year at college, and ended up kissing. The transition from being friends to being a couple had been almost seamless, and as they'd already known each other so well, it had been a relationship free of the usual awkwardness of first dates or finding out something that put them off each other. Honey had also recently lost her father – just after her sixteenth birthday – and Elliott had helped her to come to terms with her grief. She'd been shocked, lost and broken and Elliott had been her much-needed rock, while her mother had turned to yoga to deal with her own loss.

Then, when Honey and Elliott had come towards the end of their time at college and been considering university courses, everything as they'd known it had changed again.

'The good and the bad?'

He nodded.

'I'm sorry I haven't been in touch before, Honey, but I just felt that you were better off without me.'

'I thought the same about you. I wanted to speak to you so many times but it didn't seem right and I thought that seeing as how you were off enjoying university, you wouldn't want me spoiling your fun.'

'My fun? Honey, I thought about you every day and wondered how you were coping. I wished you would go to university yourself and do something with your talent.'

'I have done things.' She lifted her chin.

'I hope so.'

'I paint and I have a kiln in my workshop at the bottom of the garden. I sell some of my work on.' She didn't elaborate, not wanting to seem as if she had something to prove to him.

'I'm glad to hear it.'

'What about you?'

'I design T-shirts for a few different firms.'

'Like that one?' She gestured at what he was wearing.

'Yeah and some with slogans or sketches. Quite dystopian stuff some of it.'

'But that was your style, wasn't it?'

'I also do some prints. I have a website.'

'I'll have to check it out.'

'I'd like that.'

They drank their coffee and Honey ran her fingers over the side of her olive-green mug. It was one she'd made when she'd first come to Heatherlea; simple yet solid and that was what she'd craved from life at that time. Wasn't it what she still craved?

Elliott drained his mug then put it down on a coaster.

'I've been seeing someone for a while. She's not an artist. In fact, she works at the local chip shop.'

'The one down the street from your mum's house?'

'That's right.'

Honey's mother had sold their house years ago and as she'd travelled around with her yoga – to retreats and clients – Honey had travelled with her, essentially running away from her pain. She'd finally settled in a rented flat in Reading when she turned twenty-one. She'd got a job in a supermarket and drifted through her days, occasionally visiting her mother, and her aunt in Heatherlea, but never really feeling connected to anyone. Then her aunt had died and left her everything and life had changed. She'd finally had something solid; a home, friends and a sense of purpose.

'Anyone I know?'

He shook his head. 'She's lovely. Her name is Yvette and she's been good for me.'

'I'm happy for you.'

'The thing is... we're getting married in the summer. After the baby comes.'

Honey's mouth went dry. Elliott was going to be a husband *and* a father. She'd known it would probably happen one day but hadn't expected to know about it.

'That's wonderful. Congratulations.'

'Thank you.'

'But why did you need to see me?'

He shook his head. 'I don't know exactly how to explain it, but after everything we went through and because we were so close, I wanted you to hear it from me and not from anyone else.'

She nodded.

'Do you still think about...' He tilted his head.
'Sometimes. It's not as raw as it was but I do think about what we lost.'
'We might still be together if it hadn't happened.'
'Perhaps.'
He smiled but his eyes were sad. 'It would have all been very different.'
'Very different indeed.'
'It wasn't your fault you know.'
'I can't help thinking that if I hadn't been so negative about things at the start then maybe...' She folded her arms over her chest.
He shook his head. 'It wouldn't have changed anything.'
'I was eighteen, young and healthy. If I'd just...'
Even as she spoke the words, Honey knew that sometimes, there was no explanation for what had happened.
'Honey, you can't keep blaming yourself. Yes, it wasn't planned, and yes, it was a dreadful loss, especially after we'd decided we would make a go of things, but it's so common and so many couples go through it.'
'It doesn't make it any less painful.'
'No it doesn't.'
'I'm sorry, Elliott. I wish things had been different.'
He reached over the table and took her hand. 'Me too.'
A tear trickled down Honey's cheek and she wiped it away.
'I also need to apologise for how I behaved afterwards. You were grieving too and I pushed you away.'
'But I never blamed you, Honey. I did want to hold you and for us to comfort each other, but your grief was unfathomable and when you broke away from me, I knew you needed some space.'
'I should have been there for you instead of shutting down then running away.'
He sighed. 'We all react differently in different circumstances. Grief is unpredictable.'
'I was so full of self blame that I didn't have time for anyone else.'

'We were young and neither of us knew how to deal with what happened.'
'Does anyone know how to deal with that?'
He shook his head. 'How's your mother?'
Honey shrugged. 'Fine, I guess. Off teaching yoga to some celebrity somewhere hot. She texts now and then and emails, but she's busy and we've never really been close.'
Elliott nodded. 'I know and it's a shame. I had hoped that you'd become closer when you went travelling with her.'
'That didn't happen. She threw herself into the life and I spent a lot of time in hotel rooms and walking on beaches alone.'
'I'm sorry.'
'Don't be. It certainly wasn't your fault. Besides, I've made some really close friends here and things are much better now.'
'I'm glad to hear it. Are we… are we good then?'
'Of course, and I appreciate you coming here to tell me your news. You'll be a wonderful father.'
'I'll try. Are you… seeing someone?'
'Kind of, but it's complicated.'
'Like in a Facebook way?'
'Ha! Yes, I suppose so.'
'Do you think you'll ever want to try again?' He held up his hands. 'That's none of my business. Forget I asked.'
'I have no idea. Right now, the thought terrifies me and I know it could go wrong again… if it ever happens. Afterwards, with the infection… they said there was a chance of scarring.'
'You're still young.'
'And I'm not ready for all that right now, but I also have to accept that it might not happen.'
'I'm so sorry, Honey.'
She squeezed his hand.
'What will be, will be.'
'Always so philosophical.'

'Not always and deep down I'm a terrible worrier but keep that between you and me.'
'I'll take it to my grave.'
'Are you hungry?'
'I could eat.'
'Still got hollow legs then?'
Elliott laughed. 'I do have a big appetite, yes, and seem to be able to get away with eating a lot.'
'Then let's have some brunch, shall we? That's the thing with hangovers, they make me hungry.'
Honey went to the fridge and got out some peppers and mushrooms then broke some eggs into a bowl. She made them a hearty vegetable omelette and more coffee. Speaking to Elliott had made her feel better, although it had left her drained and she hoped she'd have a chance to take a nap that afternoon.
Clearing the air could be therapeutic; Allie and Camilla were right about that. She couldn't change the past, no one could, but she could learn from it and try to embrace the present and look towards the future.
And as for that future, who knew? For now, she would have brunch with Elliott then consider how to explain everything to Dane. She owed him that much and hoped that he would understand.

Chapter Thirteen

'Thanks for coming, Elliott.'
'I'm glad I did. I feel... better for clearing the air.'
'Me too. I'd been thinking about it for a while, only I didn't realise quite how much it was getting to me.'
They smiled at each other then Elliott opened his arms and Honey hugged him. They stood there for a few minutes, and the remaining tension seeped out of Honey as she let go of the past. There was definitely an air of sadness about the situation but it was also a good thing, because now she could move on. Hopefully, she could really be herself with Dane.
'Goodbye then.'
Elliott kissed her cheek.
'Goodbye and good luck! I hope it all goes well for you. Text me and let me know...'
Elliott nodded but Honey suspected that he'd be far too busy to think about her once his baby arrived; his heart and mind would be full of his wife and child, and that was exactly how it should be.
As she waved Elliott off, her thoughts returned to Dane. He'd seen Elliott entering her cottage and hadn't looked happy about it. She'd

shower and dress – because she didn't want to head over there dressed as a unicorn – then go to see him this afternoon.
Honey padded up the stairs with a smile on her face, feeling better than she had done in a while, because now she felt able to fully commit to her future.

Honey knocked on Dane's door then turned to look at the pretty front garden. In the borders, tulips and daffodils created a sea of colour, and on the neighbouring roof, a blackbird sang, creating the perfect springtime scene.
Footsteps inside alerted her to Dane's presence and when the door swung open, she smiled, anticipating seeing Dane's handsome face. But the frown that sat heavy on his brow made her stomach lurch.
'Oh,' he said. 'It's you.'
'Hi.' She licked her lips nervously. 'Uh… I wanted to speak to you.'
'What about?'
'I saw you earlier and I wanted to explain.'
He stared at her, a tiny muscle in his jaw twitching, then he sighed.
'Come in.'
He led her through to the lounge.
'Take a seat. Can I get you anything?'
She thought about asking for a coffee, as her hangover still lingered uncomfortably, but she couldn't bear to wait any longer to speak to him.
'No, I'm fine, thanks.'
Dane sat on a chair, not next to her on the sofa, and her heart plummeted. She allowed her eyes to roam over him, taking in his freshly washed hair, the grey T-shirt that clung to his muscular arms and chest and his loose jogging bottoms. He'd clearly showered recently and slung on his comfy clothes.

'Dane… that was my ex that you saw me with earlier. I haven't seen him in ages and that's why I was hugging him.'
Dane shrugged. 'You don't need to explain anything to me.'
'Well I do… because if I saw you hugging a woman, I'd want to know why. It wasn't how it might have looked.'
'OK. Thanks for telling me.'
'We had a good talk… me and Elliott, and I feel able to… I'd really like—'
Dane shook his head.
'Honey, I'm sorry. I appreciate you coming here but I've got a lot to do.'
'But I'd like to tell you about what happened to me before. About why I've been scared.'
He nodded.
'I have things I'd like to tell you too. Like… this week I have a job interview.'
'You do? I'm so sorry, I meant to ask but got side-tracked…'
'It's OK. Anyway, I was shortlisted.'
'Well that's great!'
'It is and it isn't.'
'It's in the bag, surely?'
'I can't be certain of that.' He dropped his gaze to the wooden floor and she noticed that he couldn't keep his hands still. 'It's a big deal for me as I love the school and I'd love to settle in Heatherlea.'
'Of course it is and I really hope you get it, Dane.'
'Thank you.' He smiled and the coldness in the room thawed slightly. 'I've got a lot of work to do today though. I have to prepare a lesson, prepare for the interview, then if I'm shortlisted again on Wednesday, I'll have to go through another day of it on Thursday.'
'Two days?' Honey gasped.
'Well they had a lot of interest, even at such short notice, but I guess there are lots of teachers looking for a great position in a beautiful village school. There are some strong candidates in the running,

apparently. The head teacher's PA told me... unofficially, of course. The selection process is going to be tough.'

Honey's stomach clenched at the thought of Dane having to go through so much.

'Are any of the candidates newly qualified teachers?' She asked the question, as she knew that new teachers sometimes had the edge over more experienced colleagues because they were cheaper to pay.

Dane shook his head. 'I wouldn't have thought so because the school is also offering a teaching and learning responsibility with the job... for coordinating science. That's why there were so many applicants, as well as the fact that it's a fabulous school to work at in a great location.'

'Wow! You'd be great at that.'

Dane gave a small laugh. 'I'd give it my best shot. I'm enthusiastic about delivering science to the pupils because we're creating our next generation of scientists, doctors, nurses and more. But there could be a candidate with better experience or someone who interviews better than I do. I hate to admit it, Honey, but I'm really nervous and when I'm anxious I don't always come across very well.'

His cheeks flushed and Honey saw how difficult this was for him. He really wanted this job, and to stay in Heatherlea, and she knew that she didn't want to complicate this week any further for him.

'You'll be amazing, Dane. Look... we can talk another time.'

'No.' He shook his head. 'You had something you needed to tell me.'

'I do, but it can wait. You have enough on your mind right now. Is there anything I can do to help?'

'Not unless you have the interview questions and fancy teaching the lesson for me?' He rubbed his hands over his face then pushed them back through his hair.

'I would if I could.'

Honey stood up.

'I'm going to go now and let you get on with your planning. If you need anything at all, just give me a shout. I'm not going far today.'

Dane walked her to the door.

'Thanks, Honey.'

She smiled then gently pecked him on the lips and walked out into the bright afternoon. When she turned to wave, Dane was standing in the doorway, the blue of his eyes darker than she'd seen it before and his shoulders slightly slumped, as if he was weighed down by the thought of the week ahead.

Honey wanted to run back to him and hold him tight, to make all of his nerves subside and to help him prepare for the interview, but she knew that she'd probably be more hindrance than help. So she made her way home, her heart heavy and her mind racing. Her feelings for Dane ran deeper than she'd realised; her urge to see him succeed in his chosen career and to see him happy, really mattered to her.

He really mattered to her.

Chapter Fourteen

Wednesday morning dawned and Honey was a bag of nerves. She'd barely slept, watching the numbers on the digital clock on her bedside table change, taunting her as she tossed and turned. Finally, at just gone five, she'd got up and pulled on her yoga pants and vest top and run through her routine, enjoying how the familiar stretches and controlled breathing helped her to zone out, if just for a short while.

After seeing to the chickens, she'd picked at a piece of toast and drunk two mugs of green tea before deciding that a day at home would not be good for her at all. She needed to get out and to keep her mind busy, so she'd go to the café to see Allie. She had heard from Dane, via text message, several time since Sunday, and it sounded as though he'd been working every spare minute he had. Honey could only hope – for his sake – that if he secured the job, then he'd be able to relax a bit and enjoy some time out. Working so hard all the time would not be good for him long term; it was a sure fire way to burn out.

Once she'd showered and dressed, she made her way to the café, arriving at the same time as Allie.

'Good morning.'
'Hi, Honey.' Allie frowned. 'Am I late opening or are you just up and about very early?'
'It's still early. I couldn't sleep.'
'You OK?' Allie asked.
'Yes, just a bit anxious about today.'
Allie let them into the café then took her bag and the keys and tucked them behind the counter.
'What's today?'
'Dane's interview.'
'Oh, yes!' Allie tucked her blonde hair behind her ears then pulled a red apron over her head. 'When we don't have our Tuesday meet ups, I forget what day it is.'
Honey nodded. They hadn't got together at the café last night, as they usually did on a Tuesday, because Dawn wouldn't have been able to make it. Camilla had wanted to go to see her sister and the baby, so Allie had suggested to Honey that they leave it until next week.
'Do you want to come through to the kitchen while I get ready for the day?' Allie asked.
'Yes, of course.'
While Allie chopped and stirred, Honey got stuck in peeling potatoes and vegetables, and soon an hour had passed with them chatting about Dawn and the new baby, as well as about the egg hunt that Allie and Chris were planning for Easter Sunday.
'Time for a coffee, I think.' Allie washed her hands then they went through to the café.
'Make mine a strong one, please.'
'You need the caffeine?'
'I was worrying about Dane so much last night that I couldn't rest.'
'That's understandable. Interviews can be so gruelling.'
'He's not supposed to know but the head teacher's PA told him there are some strong candidates.'

'But Dane's so good at what he does, isn't he? I remember Dawn telling us that local parents approved of him.'
'Yes and he's dedicated and energetic and he really wants this.'
'Here you go... one latte with a double shot of espresso.'
'Thank you so much.'
'Let's have a sit down, shall we? I have ten minutes before I officially open.'
They settled onto the leather sofa.
'Try not to worry. I'm sure Dane has as good a chance of getting the job as any of the others. Besides, he's been doing the job, so he probably has a *better* chance.'
'I hope so but nothing's guaranteed.'
Allie cocked her head.
'What's wrong?'
'I can hear my mobile ringing.' Allie patted her pockets through the apron then stood up and peered at the counter. 'I'm not sure what I did with it.'
She hurried through to the kitchen and the ringing stopped.
Honey sipped her coffee and tried to relax. Usually, the lovely interior of the café with its shabby-chic furniture and groaning bookshelves, as well as the delicious aromas coming from the kitchen, made her feel better. It was a safe haven; a place where troubles could be put aside and she could find comfort in a warm drink, a good meal and the company of her best friends. But this morning, even the café's ambience was failing to raise her spirits.
Allie appeared in the doorway, her face pale.
'What is it?' Honey put her mug on the coffee table in front of the sofa. 'Has something happened?'
Allie slumped onto the sofa and turned her mobile over in her hands. 'It's Mandy. I'm so worried about her.'
Allie's daughter worked in London and rarely returned to Heatherlea. She'd been devastated by her father's death over six years ago and had told her mother that there were too many painful memories in the village. Allie had admitted that she missed her daughter enor-

mously, and she got up to London whenever she could, but it wasn't as often as she'd have liked because she had the café to run.

'What did she say?'

'Oh...' Allie blinked hard then leant her head back on the sofa. 'She was crying again. She doesn't feel very well, which I suspect is due to stress, and she wants to come home. Actually wants to come home for a break... but she's torn because of work and doesn't want to miss any time.'

'Couldn't she take some leave?'

'Maybe. But she's not very good at listening to my suggestions. I said that she should come back and have a rest but she started spouting reasons why she couldn't. I think she's exhausted to be honest.'

'If she's working as hard as you said she is, then I'd say definitely.'

'She loves her job so much but there have been... complications.'

'Oh.'

Allie sighed. 'There's a man and from what she's said... or not said... I think she's in love. Problem is that she doesn't know how he feels and doesn't want to push things.'

'That sounds familiar.'

Allie gave a wry laugh then squeezed Honey's hand. 'It's not easy this life, is it?'

'Not at all. I'm sure Mandy will be fine though. She's her mother's daughter.'

'I think that's why she's finding this relationship so difficult. She's having trouble letting go of her independence.'

'Do you think it will last?'

'I have no idea. As long as she's OK though, that's all that matters.'

'I'm sure she will be.'

'Do you know what I need?'

'What?'

'Cake.'

'At this time?'

'Breakfast muffins, Honey. As good an excuse to eat cake before nine as I can think of. Want one?'

'Go on then.'
Allie got two freshly baked blueberry muffins and handed one to Honey. It was light and sweet and the blueberries slightly tart as they popped in Honey's mouth. It was the perfect combination and she savoured every mouthful.
'I needed that.' Honey wiped her fingers on a napkin. 'Comfort food.'
'The best kind. Time for another coffee?'
'I have all the time in the world.'
'Wonderful.'
And as Allie made two coffees, Honey carried their plates out to the kitchen and put them in the dishwasher. Allie was right; life wasn't easy, but good friends, cake and coffee helped, and Honey was lucky enough to be able to enjoy all three.

Chapter Fifteen

Stomach fluttering, Honey stood outside Dane's front door and paused. Was she doing the right thing? She was desperate to know how his day had gone, to find out if the interview had been a success. When he came to the door, he was wearing suit trousers and a white shirt that was open at the throat, revealing an enticing triangle of skin. She fought her desire to step forwards and press her mouth to that skin, to kiss him and wrap her arms around his waist. It was a hard fight.
'Honey.' He smiled, his eyes appraising her, and she was glad she'd made the effort to wear one of her pretty dresses. She'd also pinned her hair up the way he liked, in a loose bun high on her head with some tendrils hanging down either side of her face. She liked the way it showed off the contrast of the blue and pink in her hair and how her neck felt cool and free.
'I brought you a treat!' She held out the purple cake box from the café.
'Thank you. That's really kind. Come in.'
She followed him through to the kitchen where he placed the box on the worktop and switched the kettle on.

'Tea?'
'Yes please.'
He took two mugs from the cupboard then dropped tea bags into them. Honey had to bite her lip to prevent herself asking how his day had been; she was sure he'd tell her when he was ready.
When the tea was made, they took their mugs to the table and sat opposite each other.
'How's your day been?' Dane asked.
'Fine. Stressful. Oh, Dane, I've been worried about you. How did you get on? I have to ask.'
He nodded.
'It went well. At least I think it did. My lesson was successful, in terms of how well the children behaved and how they clearly made progress, and I think I gave good answers to the questions in the preliminary interview. There were five candidates in total, as two dropped out this morning, and at the end of the day, two were thanked for their time and the three of us remaining were asked to return tomorrow.
'That's brilliant news!'
He sighed and rubbed his eyes. 'Yes it is, but the other two candidates are very strong. I had a chance to talk to them both and they have plenty of experience and can spout all the current educational jargon. I'm just afraid that they're better than me.'
'I'm sure they're not.' She reached over the table and took his hand. 'You're amazing, Dane, and you can do this.'
'I'm really tired though. Today was draining and I have to go through another round tomorrow. We have to do something they call the goldfish bowl, where they'll give us some teaching and learning scenarios and we have to discuss them while the interview panel observe us.'
'The three of you will have to talk while people watch?' Honey shuddered, horrified at the thought of having to hold a formal discussion while being observed.
Dane nodded. 'The head teacher, deputy head and three of the governors. And that's not me, Honey. I'm not good in that type of

situation. Put me in front of the pupils or other staff when there's a purpose and I'm fine, but this seems so unnatural. What if I clam up completely?'

Honey gazed at his handsome face and his bright blue eyes, so earnest and clear, and her heart went out to him.

'Dane… you are an intelligent and capable man and I am convinced that you will be absolutely fine. You can do this.'

He squeezed her hand. 'And you're a lovely person, Honey. Sorry if I seem a bit… weak—'

'You're not being weak! You care about this job and the village and the school and the pupils. You're only tense because you care and this is a challenging situation to be in but you will get through it.'

He raised her hand and pressed it to his lips. His breath tickled her fingertips and the hairs on her nape rose.

'Thank you, Honey. I appreciate you coming here, and the cakes and the pep talk.'

'I wouldn't want to be anywhere else.'

He held her gaze and she drank him in, wishing she could hold him and soothe away his concerns, but she knew he'd need to prepare for the next day.

She drained her tea then stood up. 'I'm going now because I know you have things to do but please let me know how you get on tomorrow… as soon as you can.'

Back in the hallway as she opened the front door, he stroked the side of her neck, so she turned to him.

'I'll ring you tomorrow afternoon.'

'Please do.'

When he reached out and cupped her cheek then leant forwards and kissed her gently, a soft moan escaped from deep inside her, and before she could think, she slid her arms around his waist and held him tight. They stood that way for a while, taking strength from each other, and when they finally broke apart, he kissed her once more.

'Good luck, Dane. You show them what a catch you are.'

He laughed. 'I'll try. Speak tomorrow.'

Rachel Griffiths

Honey walked down the path with a spring in her step, because she knew Dane would be all right. He was clever, talented and dedicated and she was sure that the head teacher and the governors would see that and make sure they kept him on at the school. And she'd meant what she said about him being a catch, in more ways than one.

Chapter Sixteen

The next day, Honey went through all of her usual routines, but not even yoga could soothe her nerves. This would be such a big day for Dane, a make or break day, and she hoped he wasn't feeling as nervous as she was.

Four o'clock came and went and she still hadn't heard anything. Surely, it would be over by now? She checked her mobile every five minutes just in case she'd missed his call, even taking it into the downstairs toilet with her in case he rang then.

At four thirty-five, her mobile buzzed. Honey took a deep breath then swiped the screen.

'Hello?'

'Honey?'

'Yes?'

'Great news!'

She punched the air with her free hand.

'You got the job.'

'I did! I can't believe it, I really can't. One of the candidates dropped out this morning. In fact, he didn't even bother to turn up, so that left two of us – me and the woman who's been teaching for two years

longer than I have. I thought she was onto a winner, to be honest, because she was so articulate and confident and the goldfish bowl thing was hellish. However, I don't know how, but something inside me clicked and I thought, right I'm going to give it all I've got. It was a bit awkward at first but I soon got into the swing of it. I pretended that we weren't being observed and focused on the points I wanted to make and it worked.' He laughed.
'Dane, I am delighted for you! Come over and we can celebrate.'
'Hold on. I'm just outside the school and the head is waving at me from the window. They want me back inside.'
'OK, well you'd better get back in there.'
'Stay on the line and I'll check what she wants.'
Honey heard his footsteps as he walked back into the school's reception then he must have covered the mouthpiece as his voice became muffled. She gazed out of the window at her back garden where the chickens were bobbing around in their enclosure and where the leaves on the trees swayed in the afternoon breeze.
'Honey?'
'Yes.'
'Look, uh... I would've loved to come over but the head has just asked me to stay and meet the full governing body. She said that the governors who interviewed me were very impressed. They're putting on a buffet and some of the PTA are coming too. I didn't know they'd do this and I was so focused on the interviews, that what happened if I got the job just didn't cross my mind. Sorry about this. I would say I'd come round later but who knows how long this is going to take?'
'Don't be sorry, Dane. This is wonderful and I'm delighted for you. Besides, I bet you're shattered after all that. Look... you go and meet them all. Perhaps we could celebrate tomorrow?'
'I'm working in the day, as my supply contract runs until the end of this term, then my new contract begins after Easter. How about we meet up at the pub around seven tomorrow?'
'Wonderful. Shall I invite anyone else?'
'That's up to you. Surprise me.' His voice was full of excitement and

Honey wished she could see his face, because she felt certain his eyes would be sparkling.

'All right I will. Have a fabulous time and well done again.'

'Thank you. I'm still in shock.'

'Go enjoy!' Honey swallowed hard. Emotion was bubbling inside her and she didn't want to start crying on the phone.

'See you tomorrow.'

He cut the call and Honey pictured him being led to a conference room where he'd be fussed over by the governing body and able to enjoy his success. She was so happy for him and happy for herself, because now Dane would be staying in the village and that was exactly what they'd both wanted.

She opened the contacts on her mobile and located Allie's number in her favourites. It was time to plan a proper celebration for Dane, to show him exactly how happy she was that he'd secured his dream job. And exactly how much he meant to her.

At Jenny Talbot's small village salon the next morning, Honey tried to relax. She hadn't had her hair cut in a while, although Jenny had done the colour for her a few times.

'How short are we going, Honey?' Jenny met her eyes in the mirror. Honey paused, watching as Jenny's hand moved up and down the length of her hair.

'Just a good trim I think.'

'Two inches? It'll still be long.'

'You know what? I think I'll have it shorter than that. It's been years since I've had anything above my shoulders, so today I'm going to be brave.'

'Are you sure? Once I cut it, it'll be too late to go back.'

'Just above my shoulders then. Go on… go for it.' Honey took a deep breath. Whether it was seeing Elliott and putting their past behind her or the fact that she felt ready to move forwards with Dane, she suddenly believed it was time for a change.

'The colour will still show but there'll be less of the pink.'

'That's fine. The ends need to go anyway.'

As Jenny parted Honey's hair with clips then started to cut the back, Honey tried not to wince. It was hard making changes but sometimes it needed to be done. Soon, the chair she sat on was surrounded by colourful hair, and she was the proud owner of a much shorter hairstyle.

'How about if I touch up the colour and when we dry it, I put in some waves?'

'Go for it!' Honey waved a hand. 'I trust you, Jenny.'

The hairdresser smiled at her in the mirror and Honey thought, as she always did, that Jenny was a beautiful woman. With her waist-length hair – that regularly changed colour and was currently bright red – her svelte figure and flawless makeup, she could have been a celebrity. But more important than her looks was her radiance; she was such a kind and friendly person and made everyone feel welcome at her salon. Back last summer, she'd given Allie a makeover and it had renewed the lovely café owner's confidence. Honey knew that looks weren't the be all and end all but feeling good about yourself could be tied in with your appearance. Jenny knew how to give people a boost by helping them make the most of themselves.

An hour and a half later, Honey nodded as Jenny showed her the back of her hair in a smaller mirror. The transformation was stunning. Jenny had given her hair a good cut, put in more colour, so that it was now a blend of purple, blue, pink and silver, and curled it with a heated wand.

'That wand really is magical.' Honey giggled as she patted her soft waves.

'Bit of spray now to hold it, then you're good to go.'

Honey held her breath as Jenny sprayed around her head.

'Perfect. It really suits you, Honey.'

'Thank you so much. Are you coming tonight?'
Honey had invited Jenny to The Red Fox that evening to help celebrate Dane's news.
'I would love to, and might make it, but I'm waiting on a text message to find out if I have a date of the uniformed kind.' Jenny waggled her eyebrows.
'That's a shame. It would've been lovely to see you there. Although, of course, if you have a hot date then that's no bad thing.'
'Be a shame to miss having the opportunity to kiss Dane's cheek when I congratulate him.' Jenny squeezed Honey's shoulder but Honey's heart had plummeted to the hair-covered floor. 'Hey... I'm joking. I know he only has eyes for you and when he sees your new hairstyle, he's definitely not going to look at anyone else.'
'I hope not. I'm... very fond of him.'
'Fond?' Jenny pursed her full lips. 'I bet it's a lot more than that. You know... when he was in here the other week having his hair cut, he was talking about you.'
'He was?'
Jenny nodded.
'What did he say?'
'It wasn't so much *what* he said but *how* he said it that made me wonder.'
'Oh...' Honey wanted to ask for more details but didn't want to seem desperate. She didn't think Jenny would judge her but she would judge herself.
'I asked him if he was dating anyone... of course, I knew you'd been seeing him but I played a bit dim... and he named you. Said you were the sweetest person he'd ever met and that he hoped he'd be able to stay in Heatherlea.'
Honey nodded.
'Thing is... it was obvious that he wants to stay here because of you. He's got it bad. When he said your name, his expression softened and... he blushed.'
'It did? He did?'

'He did indeed. So... now that he's staying here... perhaps you two can get on with whatever it is that you've started. I do love a good wedding.'
'Wedding?' Honey gasped. 'I think that's a bit... premature.'
'We'll see. I've got one of my feelings about this.' Jenny frowned. 'At least... I've got a feeling that you two will end up together, and... that there will be a wedding in Heatherlea this summer. You mark my words.'
'A summer wedding would be nice.' Honey watched the smile that spread across Jenny's face. 'No! Not for me but for someone. A lovely summer wedding at The Cosy Cottage Café.'
'Shall we do your nails to match your hair?' Jenny gestured at the nail bar on the other side of the salon.
'Yes please! I haven't had a manicure in ages.'
'Come on then. I have some beautiful new shades I've been itching to try out and they'll go perfectly with your mermaid look.'
Honey sat in the chair then let Jenny guide her through the lovely array of colours. She had to agree with Jenny that a summer wedding would be nice but she knew it wouldn't be hers. However, even though she wasn't up for the idea of getting married, it didn't mean that she wouldn't consider the prospect of falling hopelessly and irrevocably in love.

Chapter Seventeen

'Well don't you look gorgeous!' Allie said that evening as Honey entered The Cosy Cottage Café.
'Do you like it?' Honey patted her hair.
'Like it? I love it! You must have had lots cut off though.' Allie came around the counter and gently touched Honey's hair.
'I did have a good cut. It felt like the right time to do it.'
'And the colour's so lovely; it seems like it's shimmering.'
'Jenny put in some silver and purple streaks and freshened up the pink and blue. I'm really pleased with it.'
'It frames your pretty face. Jenny's so talented.'
'Plus my nails match!'
'So they do.' Allie smiled. 'And I love your dress.'
'I don't wear dresses very often, as you know, but this one's been sitting in the wardrobe since I bought it and I thought, why not wear it tonight?'
Honey had fallen for the black silk tunic dress, with lavender embroidered along the knee-length hem, the moment she'd seen it in an online boutique. And with the fifty percent discount too, she knew

she had to have it. Worn with black tights and knee-high suede boots, she was comfortable but smart.

'Great news about Dane, anyway, and thanks for inviting us this evening.'

'I thought it would be nice to have everyone there to help him celebrate... make him feel like a proper part of the community.'

'Good plan. Chris said he'd meet us there, as he's finishing his copyedits on the latest book and he doesn't want to stop until they're done.'

'Another bestseller?'

Allie crossed her fingers. 'I hope so. He's very successful but always tells me that an author is only as successful as their last book, so he keeps the pressure on himself to write well and to please his readers.'

'Admirable.' Honey nodded, wondering how Chris could concentrate for such long periods of time on his writing. She admired his talent but didn't think she'd ever be able to write a book.

'I know. I love reading but I don't think I could ever write a novel.'

'Me either. But you could write a cook book.'

'Perhaps. In fact, I quite like that idea. OK, everything's off, so I just need to get my bag and we can go.'

Allie locked up the café then they walked arm-in-arm to The Red Fox. Camilla and Tom were meeting them there, as was Dane.

'Have you heard from Mandy today?'

Allie nodded. 'A brief text this morning to say she was fine but I don't believe her. What can I do though, Honey? She's a grown woman so I can hardly go to London and force her to come back to Heatherlea can I? She's so independent anyway that she'd be furious with me if I even tried.' Allie laughed. 'I love being a mum but it comes with a lot of worries and overwhelming guilt. I wonder all the time if I've done a good enough job, if I'm doing the right thing for them and if I could be better.'

'You're a wonderful mum to Jordan and Mandy. They're very lucky.'

'Thanks, sweetie, I hope so. Chris tells me not to worry but I'm afraid it's part of motherhood.'

Honey winced.

'Oh Honey, I'm so sorry. That was insensitive of me.'

'Not at all. Don't worry about it.' Honey squeezed Allie's arm.

When they reached the pub, Allie went in first and Honey followed her, scanning the bar for their friends. She spotted them at a table near the fireplace, so she waved.

'Shall we get some drinks in?' Allie asked.

'I asked Derek to put two bottles of champagne behind the bar, so we can take those over.'

'I bet he was delighted!' Allie giggled.

Derek and Gail Connelly were the owners of The Red Fox and Derek loved a celebration at his pub because it was good for his bank balance.

Allie went over to Camilla and Tom while Honey got the champagne and glasses.

'Hello.'

She turned to find Dane standing next to her.

'Hello yourself. Congratulations!' She offered her cheek as she was holding a tray. Dane kissed her then took the tray from her.

'Are we celebrating something?' He cocked an eyebrow and Honey laughed.

'Nah… just a regular Friday evening. Did I forget to tell you that I always drink champagne on Friday?'

'You did. That could be expensive.'

'I'm worth it.' She grimaced but Dane nodded.

'You certainly are.'

Dane placed the tray on the table and accepted congratulations from Camilla, Tom and Allie then Honey poured them all a glass of champagne.

'No Dawn and Rick?' Dane asked.

'No, they're so sleep deprived they'd be snoring under the table after one glass.' Camilla shook her head. 'It's not easy having a new baby and two young children.'

'I bet,' Dane said.

Honey raised her glass. 'Shall we get this party underway then? Well done, Dane, on getting your dream job. We're all delighted for you!'

'Thank you.' Dane clinked glasses with everyone. 'I'm so relieved. I love the school, the village and teaching and I didn't want to have to move and start over again. I've just got settled.'

'Will you buy a house in Heatherlea now?' Camilla asked, her black eyebrows slightly raised.

'Uh... possibly.' Dane cleared his throat. 'I haven't thought much beyond getting the job and preparing for the next term. I suppose I should start thinking about that though... renting can be costly and it's good to invest in a property.'

'Ignore Camilla,' Honey said. 'There are lots of factors that go into deciding to buy... including having a hefty deposit. The days of getting a mortgage easy peasy are long gone. I was lucky that I didn't have to try to get one because I inherited the cottage, but not everyone has generous relatives.'

'That's sad but true,' Tom said. 'However, some people leave their houses to animal charities these days.'

'Tom loves that idea,' Camilla explained. 'He's even got posters up in the surgery telling people how they can go about leaving everything to dogs and cats.'

'And donkeys, rabbits and hedgehogs.' Tom nodded. 'It's a win-win if you ask me and animals need love and support too.'

'They do,' Camilla agreed. 'But it's not for everyone.'

'Especially not if you have children.' Allie frowned. 'Mandy and Jordan will get anything I leave behind... and Chris of course.'

'They'll get Chris?' Dane chuckled.

'No!' Allie smiled. 'Chris will get a share of my estate. Although they might well want to inherit him as he can keep their children entertained with plenty of stories.'

'Ah have I arrived during a morbid conversation?' Chris smiled down at them. 'I thought this was meant to be a celebration.'

'It is!' Honey stood up. 'Take a seat and I'll pour you some champagne. Tom was just trying to persuade us to leave all our money to animal charities.'

'Guilty as charged.' Tom held up his hands.

'Did you finish your edits?' Honey asked Chris.

'Yes, thank goodness. I loved the story when I started but after three rounds of edits and copyedits, I'm glad to see that book go off to my publisher.'

They all laughed.

'It's really good though.' Allie beamed with pride. 'I read it and I think it's even better than the last one.'

'You always say that.' Chris hugged Allie and she gazed at him, her eyes full of love.

'Honey, you look incredible this evening. That dress is beautiful and your hair... just wow!' Dane spoke quietly to her.

'Really?' Heat rushed into Honey's cheeks.

'I love the new length. You could pull any hairstyle off.' He reached out and ran a finger over the curl that caressed her cheek and she shivered with delight.

'I'm glad you like it. Having it cut was nerve-wracking but I'm glad I did. Jenny's a great stylist.'

'She certainly is.'

'More champagne?' Honey asked.

'Go on then. You shouldn't have done this... gone to all this trouble, I mean.'

'I wanted to. I...' She paused and met his gaze. 'I'm so happy for you.'

'I can't stop smiling.'

'Did the meeting with the governors go well last night?'

He nodded. 'But after two hours of polite chat, I was ready to drop.'

'I bet. And how did today go?'

'I got through it, let's put it that way. The pupils were really well behaved, even though they could sense that I was exhausted. The head teacher gave an assembly this morning to officially welcome me to the school, which was nice, and lots of my class made me cards to say congratulations.'

Rachel Griffiths

'That's so sweet.'

'One of the bonuses of teaching... I'm privileged to work with the next generation of Heatherlea. It's amazing, Honey, wondering who will go on to be lawyers, writers, scientists, doctors and nurses, teachers and artists...' He smiled as he gazed into the distance, and Honey experienced a surge of affection. He really cared about what he did and she knew that any children he taught would be very lucky indeed.

Chapter Eighteen

'See you soon!' Honey waved at her friends as she left the pub with Dane.

Outside, the sky was clear and stars twinkled like tiny diamonds set in ebony silk. The air was cool and fresh and after the bustle of The Red Fox, the peace and quiet was a relief.

'I'll walk you home, shall I?' Dane asked.

'OK.' She'd hoped he would anyway, or that he'd invite her to his cottage, but she had tried not to lead him; she wanted him to decide for himself.

They walked side by side and Dane talked about what a great time he'd had and how excited he was about the coming term. When they reached Honey's street, he walked her up her path and waited while she unlocked the front door.

The heat rushed out as she swung the door open; it was cosy and inviting inside.

'Are you coming in?' she asked, trying not to meet his eyes in case he felt pressurised in any way.

'Uh... I have to be honest, Honey, I'm completely beat. It's been a tough week.'

She swallowed her disappointment.
'Of course it has. You need to rest this weekend.'
'I wish! I have so much to do now... preparing for the new term and all that, plus...' He sighed. 'Honey, I have to go away over Easter. I was hoping to spend some time with you but I've been offered an opportunity... There's a pioneering school in Wales that has developed new teaching and learning strategies and the head teacher asked me to go on the residential course they're running.'
'On your own?'
'No, with some of the other staff.'
'For two whole weeks?'
He nodded.
'Some of my colleagues can't go for the full course as they have families, but as I... uh... don't have any commitments as such, and seeing as how I've just got the job, I didn't like to say no. Besides, it's a fantastic opportunity to check out what other schools are doing and to share good practice.'
Honey held his gaze, and seeing the excitement there, she knew that she couldn't ruin it for him.
'It sounds amazing, Dane, and you should go for it.'
'We could spend some time together this week if you like?'
'Aren't you working?'
'Well, yes, but in the evenings.'
'Right... yes, OK. Now go and get some rest.'
She leant forwards and kissed him on the cheek before turning and heading inside.
'Good night, Dane. Good luck getting your work done over the weekend. I'll see you at some point in the week.'
He stared at her for a few moments in silence, and Honey wondered what he was thinking. Had she blown it by pulling away from him before? Even though Dane would be staying in the village now, it seemed that just weren't destined to spend more time together. Hard as it might be, perhaps she needed to put this behind her and move on. Dane was going to be very busy over the next few

months and perhaps there was no room in his life for Honey or for love.

Keeping busy over the next week kept Honey from going over what had gone wrong between her and Dane. She'd definitely developed feelings for him but gone through a variety of ups and downs as she'd tried to understand how to deal with those feelings. Yes, she physically desired Dane and she enjoyed his company, but she knew she'd held back because of old fears that she'd never really dealt with. Add to that Dane's workload, and his desire to secure a teaching position in Heatherlea, and things between them had just seemed to fizzle out. It was possible that her own lack of certainty about what she could offer to a relationship had dampened Dane's desire for her but it could also be that he hadn't actually liked her enough to fight for her in the first place.

Whatever it was, she had to get on with her life and spending long days in her studio painting and making unicorns, mermaids and pretty pots had helped her. She'd played her music loud, drunk plenty of herbal tea and focused on her art in its various forms. When her muscles had ached and her stomach grumbled, she'd gone inside and spent time on yoga and in the bath, as well as eating plenty of chocolate, and tried to ignore the messages that made her mobile buzz.

Tuesday at the café had been a quiet affair with just her, Allie and Camilla, and they'd spent most of the evening discussing possibilities for the Easter Sunday party at The Cosy Cottage Café. When Honey had allowed herself to read Dane's messages, they'd been polite enquiries about how her week was going and nothing more, so she'd sent one reply, telling him she was deep into an art project and would speak to him soon.

On the Saturday morning, when she knew he was leaving for Wales, she considered popping round to his cottage but then thought it would be better if she didn't. He would be busy getting ready and she didn't want to get in the way, so she donned her old dungarees and flip-flops and headed down to her studio, where she turned her music up loud and carried on with her work in progress.

Two hours later, she was singing along to eighties hits when a loud knock at the studio door made her jump.

She turned the volume on the music down and shouted, 'Come in!'

Dane's large frame filled the doorway. His indigo jeans and light grey shirt emphasised his broad shoulders and muscular arms. He was clean-shaven and his dark hair was shorter than usual. 'Sorry if I startled you but I tried ringing and I kept getting your voicemail. I didn't want to leave without saying goodbye.'

'Oh...' Honey was suddenly conscious of the state of her dungarees with their paint splatters and torn knees, and her unwashed hair that she'd pushed behind her ears. 'Uh... excuse the state of me. I wasn't expecting company.'

'You look amazing.' He smiled cautiously but his eyes twinkled.

'Ha ha! Yes, I bet I smell amazing too.' She clamped her arms to her sides, not wanting him to catch a whiff of her sweat. The studio got warm through the day and Honey hadn't showered that morning, intending on having a long hot bath when she'd finished.

'Even the paint on your cheek suits you.' He stepped closer and brushed the spot with his thumb. Her nerve endings fired at his proximity and his touch, but she kept her arms pressed to her sides, afraid now that she would throw herself into his embrace if he touched her again.

'Well, have a good time. I hope it's a great course.'

She held out a hand awkwardly and Dane stared down at it.

'You want to shake hands?' He frowned.

She nodded, so he took her hand and shook it woodenly, as if they were nothing more than acquaintances.

'Look...' He met her eyes and something burned in his. 'I know that we had something between us and I also know that I might have blown a bit hot and cold towards you, and for that I'm really sorry. I've had… it's no excuse, but I've had a lot on my mind. Add to that the fact that I wasn't always sure what it was that you wanted from me, and it's been a bit of a rocky time emotionally. However… I like you… I more than like you, and I'd like to think that you have feelings for me that stem beyond shaking hands.' When Honey didn't respond, he continued, 'Do you?'

'I do.' Her voice was croaky, her mouth and throat suddenly dry.

'OK. That's good. It's a starting point.' He offered a shy smile. 'I have to go now but when I return, I think we need to talk. Properly. No holds barred, about what it is we want. If we left things like this and never spoke about it then I'd have regrets.'

'So would I.'

He opened his arms and Honey stepped into them, pressing her face against his hard chest. He smelt so good, like ginger and citrus, and underneath it was the scent of man that made Honey's heart pound against her ribs.

'I'll keep in touch but I should be back two weeks today. Have a think about how you feel and what you want, Honey. We've both been to blame for not being open about our feelings. Relationships aren't straightforward and people come with baggage, but I'm hoping we can work through ours… together.'

'Dane, I—'

'No… please, don't tell me now. It'll be too much of a rush and make it harder to leave than it already is. Let's talk when I get back. I have to go or I'll miss the bus and make the head teacher mad if I'm late.' He grimaced.

'That wouldn't be a good start.'

'No.' He raised her chin and pressed his lips to hers. It was a gentle kiss but one that made Honey's heart lift because she felt a connection in his touch, as if a kiss could convey what words couldn't.

'Before I go…'

'Yes?'

'I love the work you've been doing here.' He gestured at the rows of unicorns and mermaids set out on the shelving units and workbench in various stages of production. 'It looks like you're working on a large order.'

She smiled. 'Something like that.'

'Good for you. You're very talented and it's wonderful to see that the public will be able to appreciate your work.'

'Thanks. It's quite a recent development but also very exciting.'

'Why didn't you say anything?'

'You were busy and I was busy and it never seemed to be the right time.'

He shook his head. 'I should always have made time for you. I am here for you, Honey.'

She nodded. 'Thank you.'

'Speak to you soon.'

He walked to the door and Honey raised a hand in farewell. She hated to see him go, but would cling to the fact that he'd be back. Two weeks would feel like a lifetime, but she had her work, her chickens, her friends and the Easter party to help with, so she'd be busy, as would Dane. Then he'd return to Heatherlea and they would talk. The thought made her anxious, as opening up like that was a huge risk, but if she didn't, she would likely lose Dane forever.

So she would tell him everything; it was a risk she was willing to take.

Chapter Nineteen

Before Honey knew it, a week had passed and she'd barely had time to wallow in missing Dane at all. Her friends had kept her busy, she'd spent time in her studio working on her orders, and Allie had requested her help at the café the previous two days as she was baking ready for Easter Sunday.
The day of the party dawned fresh and sunny, the sky was forget-me-not blue without a cloud in sight and daffodils and tulips poked their colourful heads up in pots and borders, basking in the rays of the spring sunshine.
As she walked to The Cosy Cottage Café, the air was filled with the sweet scent of flowers and newly mown grass, as everything awoke properly after the bleak winter months. It lifted Honey's spirits and filled her with hope and yearning for things yet to come.
The white gazebo was already set up in the front garden of the café and the pink, lilac and yellow bunting that Jordan had draped around the front of the cottage and looped between the trees, flapped in the breeze. Honey set the box she was carrying down on a trestle table under the gazebo and waved at Allie through the window.
It was going to be a good day and she was looking forward to it.

'I can't wear this, Allie.' Honey frowned at her reflection in the full-length mirror of the café toilet. 'I look like some kind of—'
'Easter Bunny?'
'Yes.'
'Well that's what you're supposed to look like. Anyway, look at me!' Allie held out her arms and the fluffy yellow wings attached to them bounced.
'You're a chick.'
'Exactly. Come on, it's all part of the fun.' Allie straightened the hood of her costume with its bright red beak that sat like a sun visor above her eyes.
'I guess I could get used to it.'
Honey eyed her reflection, from the satin white onesie to the big white feet that fit over her shoes, to the tall white ears that sat on the headband. Beneath it, her colourful hair sprang out in waves. She turned slightly to give the bobble tail sitting above her bottom a flick.
'You're a gorgeous bunny, Honey.' Allie laughed. 'Honey bunny.'
'Ha ha!'
'Come on, let's go and see how the boys look.'
'You're making Chris wear a costume too?'
'Of course. Jordan and Maxwell helped me choose it.'
'Poor Chris.'
In the café, Honey bit her lip when she saw the costume Chris had been allocated. From the waist up, he was normal Chris, but his legs dangled over the shoulders of a bunny. Until Honey looked more closely and saw that the bunny's legs were, in fact, his, and the ones hanging over the bunny's shoulders were fake.
'Hello ladies,' Chris said as he smiled at them. 'I'm going to have a lazy day being carried around by this bunny, aren't I?'

'It looks so real,' Honey said as she lifted one of the fake legs. 'Except for the tiny feet on the end of the legs.'

'Chris doesn't have tiny feet at all do you, love?' Allie kissed him and he sniggered, so Honey feigned interest in her nails, pretending she didn't understand the intimate joke.

'Time to get the food out and the music on?' Jordan asked as he emerged from the kitchen, closely followed by his boyfriend, Maxwell. The young men were dressed as giant Easter eggs in colourful costumes decorated with glitter and bows. Their straw cowboy hats had painted eggshells dangling from string around the edges.

'Absolutely...' Allie clapped her hands. 'Jump to it crew!'

Once the food and drink was set up on the trestle tables under the gazebo, and the local band had set up in the corner, the Easter party got underway.

Children arrived with their families, and drinks were poured. The band played a range of covers from Fleetwood Mac to Whitney Houston to Ed Sheeran, and soon the café garden was full. Honey smiled as she strolled around speaking to villagers and offering them refreshments. Allie's café was the heart of the community and people of all ages had gathered for the party and the annual Easter Egg hunt.

'Honey!'

She turned to see Dawn and Rick walking up the path. Rick was pushing a very trendy looking pram with the hood up and behind them came their older children, Laura and James. Laura was dressed like she'd just stepped off *Strictly Come Dancing* and James seemed to be some sort of spaceman in white trousers and shirt with a wide brown belt and what seemed to be a brown towel pinned to his shoulders.

'Great costumes, guys.' Honey said as she crouched in front of Laura and James.

'They spent a lot of time deciding what to wear,' Dawn explained when Honey stood up.

'I'm James Skytalker.' James patted his chest then pulled a plastic light sabre from his belt.

'Of course, I could see that straight away.'

He reached behind and gave his towel a flutter.

'And Laura is a mingo dancer.' James pointed at his sister.

'A mingo dancer?' Honey frowned at Dawn and saw that her friend was biting her lip.

'He means she's a flamenco dancer.'

'Ah...' Honey snorted. 'Comedy gold out of the mouths of babes, right?'

'All the time,' Rick said. 'You should hear the questions we've had about where the baby came from and about breast feeding.'

'Oh no!'

Dawn nodded. 'He shouted when he first saw me nursing Alison because he thought she was eating me. When I explained that I was feeding her, he asked how I get milk out of my armpits.'

'Mummy, can we go and see Jordan and Max?' Laura interrupted.

'Yes of course. Keep an eye on your brother.'

Laura nodded then grabbed James's hand and they ran over to Jordan.

'And how is the little one?' Honey asked.

Dawn smiled. 'She's beautiful. Keeping us awake until all hours but with Rick working from home now, I don't have to do it all myself. Although I do tell him to stay in bed as he can't exactly breastfeed her.'

'I could give her a bottle if you'd express.' Rick gazed down at his daughter.

'I know and I will in time. I'm just afraid that she'll like the bottle more than me.' Dawn shrugged and cast an apologetic smile at her husband.

'I only want to help as much as possible.' Rick kissed Dawn's head. 'I wasn't there as often when Laura and James were babies and I want to be hands on this time around.'

Honey leant forwards to peer into the pram and she gasped.

'She's so perfect, such an angel.'

'Thank you. We think so too, especially now that her cheeks have filled out a bit. When she was first born she had that slightly squashed look but now she looks more baby than butternut squash.' Dawn laughed then pushed the hood of the pram down. 'Would you like to hold her?'

'Oh... uh...' Honey dragged her gaze from the baby and glanced around them. 'Uh... perhaps later? It's just quite busy and I'd be nervous about dropping her and the egg hunt is about to start and uh...'

Dawn placed a cool hand on Honey's arm. 'It's OK. No pressure. As and when you're ready. I know babies can be scary things.'

'Thank you.' Honey did want to hold the tiny baby but was also terrified of doing so in case she lost control and burst into tears. A sobbing bunny was not what the children of Heatherlea needed to see when they were about to embark upon their egg hunt.

'I'd better go and give Allie a hand, so I'll see you in a bit.'

She gave the baby one more longing glance then crossed the lawn to find Camilla and Tom talking to Allie and Chris. Tom had HP with him and the dog's eyes widened when he spotted Honey.

'Wow! The chick, the strong bunny and the pretty Easter Bunny.' Camilla grinned. 'You three look fabulous. It's like spring has well and truly sprung.'

'Ha ha!' Honey shook her head. 'I guess if you'd worn your cat costume you'd be chasing us round by now.'

Camilla grimaced. 'I can't wear that costume when I'm near HP... it must remind him of the night we met.'

They all laughed. When Camilla had gone to Tom's Halloween fancy dress party in a very sexy cat costume, she'd gone outside for some fresh air and bumped into Hairy Pawter. The bulldog had pounced on her and she'd been mortified when Tom had found her pinned to the decking by his dog.

'Anyway, he seems to like your bunny outfit too.'

Honey looked down at HP. His mouth was hanging open and his stubby tail was wagging madly.

'Is he all right?' she asked Tom. 'He's not going to pounce?'

Just as she asked that, HP moved closer to her large white feet and cocked a leg.

Tom shouted, 'NO!' but it was too late and Honey's right foot was instantly warm and wet.

She stared at the spreading yellow stain on her bunny foot then met Tom's eyes.

'I'm so sorry, Honey. He never does that.'

'He must just get excited around costumes.' Camilla snorted.

'It's not funny.' Honey shook her head. 'It's not even my costume.'

'Ah don't worry about it,' Allie said as she waved a hand dismissively. Her face was red and tears trickled down her cheeks as she laughed.

Honey started to laugh too; it was just her luck that a dog had decided to water her rabbit feet!

'Right let's get this Easter egg hunt going.' Allie strode over to the corner where the band had set up.

'Good morning egg hunters!' she said over the microphone.

The villagers responded with cheers.

'Are we ready for the annual egg hunt?'

'Yes we are!' the children sang.

'All children taking part, go and grab a basket from Jordan and Max then make your way to the front gate.'

When every child had a basket and they were all gathered at the front of the lawn, Chris went and stood in front of them.

'On your marks... get set... GO!'

Children streamed around him, racing in all directions around the café garden. There were squeals of delight and laughter as the small foil-wrapped eggs were located and deposited in baskets. The egg hunt led them around the sides of the café, under benches and tables and even rooting around in planters and hedges.

When children started to return to their parents, their baskets full and their faces hot and sweaty, Allie tapped on the microphone again.

'Well done, everyone! OK… does anyone have a purple egg?'

A hush fell over the garden as children searched through their baskets.

'I do!'

All heads turned to James who was holding the small purple egg aloft.

'Congratulations, James Dix-Beaumont! Bring the egg here, lovely.'

James marched up to Allie and handed her the egg.

'Right, you have won a special prize, James.'

'Have I?' His face lit up. 'What is it?'

Honey met Dawn's eyes and she shook her head. Every year there was a different prize for finding the purple egg, and Allie refused to tell anyone what it would be prior to the egg hunt.

Jordan arrived at his mother's side, carrying a large box wrapped in shiny silver paper.

'Wow!' James exclaimed, making everyone laugh.

'You don't know what's inside it yet,' Allie said, as Jordan set the box down in front of James.

'But it's huge…'

James' eyes were wide as he knelt next to the box and tore off the paper. When he lifted the lid, his mouth fell open and he scanned the crowd.

'Mummy? Daddy?'

'Yes?' Dawn and Rick waved at him.

'It's lots and lots of books.'

'Wonderful!' Rick said.

'Thank you so much, Allie. Me and the mingo dancer will read all of them.'

'It's *flamenco* dancer, James!' Laura flounced over to him and peered into the box. 'But yes we will. They're all the new ones from the book charts.'

'That's right.' Allie nodded. 'I had some help from Mandy.'

'OK, everyone please help yourselves to refreshments and afterwards there will be games for the children and more music from Erica and the Heatherlea band.'

Honey filled her plate with an array of delicious foods. The buffet was, as always, incredible. She helped herself to asparagus, spring onion and mint tart, mini salmon and dill en-croutes, scotch eggs, rosemary and sea-salt brioche rolls and peppers stuffed with couscous, courgette and mozzarella. When she'd eaten her fill of savoury delights, dessert included chocolate and spice hot cross buns, chocolate Battenberg, chai-spiced carrot cake and lemon-curd ice cream. Underneath her bunny costume, her belly groaned, but she consoled herself that she wouldn't need to eat again until the next day.

'How's the food?' Allie asked as she appeared at Honey's side with another tray of cakes.

'I'm so full, I think I need to sit down before I keel over.' Honey patted her belly.

'I had help from Chris, Jordan and Maxwell, so I can't take all the credit, and a few people brought some of the side dishes too.'

'It was all delicious. It's a shame Dane isn't here to enjoy it.' Honey suppressed a sigh. She was missing him more today than she had all week.

'Why don't you try a Cosy Cottage Café spring spritzer?' Allie nodded at the drinks table where Jordan was dancing round with a cocktail shaker, the eggs on his hat bobbing in time to the music from the band.

'What's in a spring spritzer?'

'Lavender syrup, lemon juice, Lillet rose vermouth and prosecco.'

'Sounds delicious.'

Honey headed over to Jordan and watched as he made her drink then she thanked him and looked around. The café garden was still busy but she fancied a sit down, so she went around the side to the pergola, where it was quiet.

She sat on a bench and closed her eyes, enjoying the music from the band, the murmur of conversation from the villagers and the pretty

birdsong from the hedge that bordered the garden. The spring sun was warm on her face and the sweet scent of freesias from the pots on the table teased her nostrils. Everything was perfect. Except for…
'Honey?'
She started but kept her eyes closed.
Was she hearing things? She must be. That had sounded like Dane. She must be missing him so badly that she was imagining the sound of his voice.
'Honey? Are you awake.'
She blinked.
'Dane? What are you… how are you…'
He sat next to her.
'Honey, you look great. I wasn't even sure if it was you for a moment until I got closer.'
'Oh… this old thing.'
'You like dressing up then?'
'What?'
'Well… unicorns… bunnies.' He smiled but he had dark shadows under his eyes.
'I do like getting into the spirit of things, yes and this was for the sake of the village children, so…' She shrugged. 'Got to make an effort, right?'
He nodded.
'You're home early.'
'Yeah… the course runs until Friday. Some of the teachers with children and family commitments came back early and I couldn't face staying away for another day.'
'What about the head teacher? Won't she be disappointed?'
'I explained that although I'm thoroughly committed to the job, I do have things in my life to sort out too. She seemed to take it quite well, better than expected really. Said that I needed my head in the right place to start the summer term, so to go home and sort things out.'
'Do you think she meant it?'
He nodded. 'She just wants to know that her staff members are

committed to the children of the school and that's fair enough. I'd want the same for my own children.'
Honey sipped her drink.
'This is delicious. Want me to get you one?'
'In a bit. I need to talk to you first.'
He took one of her hands in his. His palms were warm, his fingers long and lean and her heart fluttered as she recalled how it felt to have those hands on her face, in her hair and roaming over her skin.
'Honey... I had to know where we stand. If you don't want to be with me then I will have to accept that and move on but I can't stop thinking about you. You have such a generous heart, a sweet nature and you're loyal to your friends. I've never met anyone like you. You're also very independent, but sometimes... that independence means that you push people away.'
She nodded. 'I know. I'm sorry. But it's more than that. See... I really like you. In fact, I care for you deeply but I'm afraid.'
He caressed her palm with his thumb.
'I'm afraid too. Nothing worth having comes without risk, you know?'
'I know. But, Dane, you pushed me away too.'
'I did. With my busy schedule. I was terrified I wouldn't get the job and I'd have to move away and the thought of not seeing you and being around you hurt me. But the irony is that I missed so much time that I could have spent with you because I was working so hard.'
'I know you have to work hard but you also need—'
'Balance.'
'Yes, balance.'
'That was one of the reasons I decided to take up yoga, wasn't it? Plus I needed to try to loosen these old rugby tensions.'
'Did I help with that at all?'
'You did. But I think I need a live-in yoga teacher.'
'You what?'
His eyes widened. 'Did I say the wrong thing?'
'Uh... no... but...'

'Move in with me, Honey. Let's give this a go. I'd love to see you every morning and hold you every night.'
'Wow.'
His face dropped. 'I've scared you.'
'No... no, you haven't scared me but you have surprised me.' She swallowed hard. 'In a good way.'
'What do you think, then?'
'Dane, I need to tell you something. The reason I ran away after our night together wasn't because I didn't want to be there but because I hadn't told you everything about my past.'
He shook his head. 'You don't need to tell me everything.'
'OK, not absolutely everything, but there are things… like when I was with Elliott, we had a… I had a…'
He squeezed her hand, gently encouraging her to continue.
'I lost a baby,' she whispered, her heart contracting as she vocalized the words, releasing them onto the breeze.
'You lost a child?'
She nodded, her vision blurring.
'I'm so sorry, Honey.'
'The pregnancy wasn't planned and I was young, but just as I started to accept the idea of being a mum, it was over.'
He took her drink and placed it on the table then opened his arms and embraced her. She pressed her face against his neck, breathing him in and a sense of calm and security filled her. Dane had her back; he wouldn't hurt her or leave her, he was in this for the long run.
She leant back and gazed up at his face.
'I've stayed away from relationships and intimacy because I was terrified of it happening again. The idea of losing another baby was too much for me and I was filled with guilt because I always believed it was my initial lack of enthusiasm for the pregnancy that led to me miscarrying. Kind of like a punishment.'
'Honey,' he lifted her chin and met her eyes, 'it wasn't your fault.'
'I know. I spoke to Elliott about it and I've read about it. I've spoken

to other women in online support groups. I know that I'm not to blame but there's a lot of guilt attached to losing a baby.'

He nodded. 'Women often blame themselves. My mum lost a baby after she had me. She told me about it when I was older and said that she was filled with guilt. If only she'd eaten better, rested more... the list went on. But it wasn't her fault and it wasn't your fault.'

'I also... I shut down and pushed Elliott away. I couldn't bear for him to touch me, kiss me, even be near me. It was as if I was punishing him for what happened.'

'I'm sure he understood.'

'He does now but back then, we were so young and it was all so raw. I know I was cruel to him when he needed comfort too. It's why I find it so hard to open up... why I've struggled to tell you how much I care. I never want to be the reason why you hurt, Dane.'

'I care about you too. A lot.'

'Dane, you said something earlier about children. I don't know if I'll be able to...'

'Look, we'll be together in everything as a team and make decisions together. We've plenty of time. I want to be with you... get to know *you* better.'

'I had a D and C after the miscarriage and developed an infection. There could be scarring of my womb and that could make conception difficult.'

'Honey, didn't you hear me? I said I want you. If, one day, years down the line, we decide we'd like to start a family then we'll deal with any challenges together.'

'Are you sure?'

He leant forwards and kissed her. His lips were soft and warm, his scent was deliciously familiar, and as he slid his arms around her, she felt his strength enveloping her and keeping her safe.

'Look! Mr Ackerman is kissing the Easter Bunny!'

Honey pulled away from Dane to see three small children with chocolate-covered faces gawking at them.

'Hello, Sir.' One of the boys grinned. 'Did she bring you a nice egg?'

'Sorry?' Dane frowned.
'Well you were kissing the bunny to say thank you, weren't you?'
'Oh! Yes, that's right.' Dane glanced at Honey then cleared his throat. 'Why don't you kids run along now? Go and ask the band to play a special song. In fact... come here a minute.'
He stood up and whispered into the boy's ear then they shook hands.
'What was all that about?' Honey asked, pushing herself to her feet.
'Special request.' Dane frowned at her. 'What happened there?' He pointed at the yellow stain on her foot.
'HP.'
'Ah, right, say no more!'
'Exactly.'
Dane reached for her hand as the band started to play.
'I think I know this,' Honey said.
'It's *You Make My Dreams Come True* by Hall and Oates. By request. Dance with me?'
'To this?'
'Why not?'
'It's quite... funky.'
'And appropriate.'
Honey let him pull her close and they moved in time with the music. Dane twirled her under his arm then back to him and round again, but Honey started laughing.
'What is it?'
'You keep stepping on my big feet.'
He smiled. 'They are rather large. I don't know how you ever find shoes to fit.'
'Thank you.'
'What for? Laughing at your feet?'
'For being you.'
'Ditto.'
He cupped her face then kissed her. Honey slid her arms around his neck and felt his hands roam over her bunny tail before giving it a tweak.

'Hey!' she murmured against his lips.

'You know, I'll have to behave myself in public from now on. I can't have the pupils seeing me kissing the Easter Bunny again, so I was making the most of it.'

'Mandy?' A shout from the front lawn made them freeze.

'MUM!'

Honey and Dane hurried around to the front of the café as the music stopped. Everyone was staring at the young woman standing at the gate in a red satin ball-gown. Her blonde hair was a windswept mess and mascara was smudged down her cheeks making her look as though she'd just completed a military assault course. She pushed the gate open then ran into Allie's arms.

'It's all gone so wrong, Mum!' she wailed.

'Come on, love, let's get you inside.' Allie led her daughter into the café, followed by Chris and Jordan, then they closed the door behind them.

'What happened there?' Dane asked.

'I'm not sure but I know Mandy hasn't been very happy lately. Looks like she needs her mum.'

'Allie will sort her out.'

'If anyone can, Allie can.' Honey nodded.

The music started again and Maxwell called people to the drinks table, obviously keen to distract the villagers from the dramatic scene they'd just witnessed.

'Should I go and see if I can help?' Honey asked Dane.

'Probably best to leave them to it. I'm sure Allie will call if she needs you.'

'I guess you're right. What shall we do then?'

'How about we go back to mine and discuss this moving in together idea in a bit more detail?' Dane stroked her cheek and goosebumps rose on her skin.

'Actually, how about we go back to mine and see if there's enough room in my wardrobe for your things?'

'Really?'

'Well, I own my cottage but you rent, so it makes more sense. Besides, I have the chickens and my studio and one of the spare rooms would probably make a great study for you.'

'Sounds like a plan.'

'Come on then. If you play your cards right I might even take these bunny feet off.'

'Now you're talking.'

They said goodbye to their friends, then walked through the gate and onto the street. Honey was worried about Allie and her family but she knew her friend would call if she needed her, and that she had the support of Chris and Jordan.

Before walking away, Honey cast one more glance behind her. It really had been an eventful start to spring at The Cosy Cottage Café, and for the first time in a long while, she was looking forward to embracing the present and anticipating the future. With Dane at her side.

The End

Spring Spritzer Cocktail

Ingredients: (*NB – 1 shot = approximately 30ml / 1 oz*)
1 shot lavender syrup
1 shot Lillet rose vermouth
1 shot freshly-squeezed lemon juice
2 shots prosecco
Directions: Fill a cocktail shaker halfway with ice then add the lavender syrup, Lillet rose vermouth and lemon juice. Shake well.
Strain into a glass then top up with the prosecco.
Garnish with a slice of lemon and a sprig of lavender.

A Wedding at The Cosy Cottage Café

A Wedding at The Cosy Cottage Café

Someone has been planning a proposal…
Join Allie and her friends this summer as cakes are baked, secrets are shared and surprises bring smiles and tears at The Cosy Cottage Café.

Chapter 1

Allie

'OK, Mandy... sit there.' Allie Jones gestured at the battered old leather sofa in the corner of the café but her daughter didn't release her hand. 'Mandy?'
'Yes?'
'Sit there for a moment and I'll be right back.'
'Allie, tell me what you need and you can stay with Mandy.' Chris Monroe, Allie's boyfriend, placed a cool hand on her shoulder.
'Thank you. Can you get the brandy from the kitchen? It's in the top right cupboard above—'
'I know where it is.' He squeezed her shoulder. 'I'll be right back.'
She nodded as he padded away in his rabbit feet, still wearing the costume he'd put on for the Easter party at the café. From the waist up, he was normal Chris, but his legs dangled over the shoulders of a giant rabbit. Well, they were fake legs meant to resemble his, while his real legs looked like they belonged to the rabbit that was supposedly carrying him around. She was also conscious of the fact that she was still dressed as a fluffy yellow chick, something that had been great fun for the party, but now felt rather ridiculous.

Allie sat down next to her daughter. Mandy immediately buried her face in her hands, her shoulders shaking as she cried softly.

'What can I do, Mum?' Jordan, Allie's son, was still standing in the doorway, his face pale and his blue eyes wide.

'Sit down, love.'

Panic crossed his face.

'Or go help Max keep an eye on things outside.'

'Yes... good plan. But... uh... will Mandy be OK?'

Allie nodded, her heart aching, because even though Jordan was twenty-three — and now lived at the cottage attached to The Cosy Cottage Café with his boyfriend Maxwell Wilson — he was still her little boy.

'Yes, Mandy will be OK; she's home now. I'll have a chat with her, then come and find you.'

'Thanks Mum. See you later, Mandy.'

Jordan let himself out of the café then closed the door gently behind him, shutting out the sounds of the villagers of Heatherlea enjoying their Easter celebrations, just as Allie had been doing just ten minutes ago, before Mandy had arrived. Her twenty-four-year-old daughter — who had a successful career in publishing at a big London firm — turning up on her doorstep in a ball gown, her hair a bird's nest and her face streaked with tears, was something Allie had never wanted to see. In fact, it broke her heart.

'Mandy, are you going to tell me what's happened?' Allie rubbed her daughter's slender shoulders, exposed by the beautiful strapless damask dress.

Mandy let out a sound like one of Allie's cats might make. It was a pitiful squeak-come-sniffle.

'Here you are.' Chris was back and he handed Allie a glass of brandy. She looked at it, took a gulp, then patted Mandy's shoulder.

'I think you better drink this. It'll warm you up if nothing else. You're freezing, Mandy. Have you been out all night?' Panic rose in her throat at the thought that her beautiful daughter had indeed been out all night, alone and vulnerable.

Mandy didn't answer; instead she accepted the glass and sipped the spirit, wincing as she swallowed. But she kept drinking until she'd drained the glass.

'More?' Chris was hovering at Allie's side.

'Please.' She met his eyes and gratitude surged through her that he was there, that he'd returned to the village of Heatherlea last summer and that he loved her. Still. Even after all the years they'd been apart. Even after she'd married their mutual friend, Roger, and had two children by him.

Chris gently stroked her cheek then took the glass and went back through to the café kitchen. Allie turned back to Mandy and found her staring into space, her shoulders hunched, her eyes red and puffy. But at least the awful crying had stopped. For now.

'Mandy...'

'It's OK, Mum. Sorry to turn up like that but I didn't know what else to do.'

'How did you get here?'

'Early train.'

'Did you come straight from a party?'

Mandy nodded. 'It was an awards celebration for bestselling authors at a posh hotel with champagne, a sit-down meal and dancing.'

'Sounds lovely. But I take it that it wasn't lovely?' Allie watched Mandy closely. Since she'd last seen her daughter, her features were sharper, her arms more toned, as if she'd been working out and eating differently. Mandy had always been slim but she now had that gym-toned appearance that a lot of celebrities promoted.

'It was... at first. Then it all went wrong.' Mandy's lip trembled and a fat tear escaped from her right eye, ran down her cheek then plopped into her lap, staining her dress.

'How, love?' Allie took her hand.

'He's been lying to me all along, Mum. So many lies and I... I loved him so much.' Mandy's eyes brimmed with fresh tears. 'I really loved him!' She flung herself at Allie and sobbed in her arms, and Allie held her tight, wondering who she had to hunt down and punish for what he'd done to her baby girl.

Chapter 2

Dawn

'Do you think they're OK in there?' Dawn Dix-Beaumont asked her husband, Rick.

He glanced at the café then shook his head.

'You don't?' Dawn's voice rose with concern, so she coughed then made an effort to speak quieter as she asked, 'Really?'

'I didn't mean that they're not all right. What I meant was that Mandy did look quite upset but she's in the best place. So we shouldn't go interfering.'

'What? I had no intention of interfering.' She frowned at Rick but he smiled.

'I know that, angel. We have enough to deal with as it is.' He smiled down at their baby daughter who was fast asleep in her pram. 'We need to give them some space and I know how close you, Allie, Camilla and Honey are. You'll all want to rush to help Allie fix her daughter.'

Dawn nodded. 'You know me too well.'

He was right; her sister, Camilla Dix, and friend, Honey Blackwell, certainly would want to help in any way they could. They were close friends and always there for one another. But Rick was right; this was something Allie needed some space for and besides, Chris was with her.

'It might be a good time to head for home though.' He pointed at the café lawn where their young children Laura and James were racing around, their faces red, sweaty and chocolate covered.

'Oh goodness, yes. They both need a shower.' She smiled, her love for her children filling her chest. She felt so lucky to have such a wonderful husband and three beautiful children. Just the previous autumn, she'd been worried that it was all slipping away from her, as Rick had seemed distant and she'd suspected him of having an affair. He hadn't been, and had, in fact, been trying to protect her from his own worries, but now things were better than ever and they had a new baby too. Precious little Alison. She gazed at her baby's peaches and cream complexion and a familiar tingling spread through her as the let-down reflex kicked in.

'What is it?' Rick wrapped an arm around her shoulder. 'You've gone a bit flushed.'

'It's time for Alison to have a feed. Either that or I need to express.'

'No problem, my love. I'll round up the terrors and we can get going.' He headed across the lawn in the direction of Laura and James, and Dawn watched as James shook his head and stamped his foot, then giggled as Rick hoisted him onto his shoulder and tickled him. Laura skipped towards her, looking exactly like a mini Spanish flamenco dancer in her Easter costume, except for the chocolate around her mouth, that was.

'Mummy!' James gasped as Rick tickled him again when they arrived at her side. 'Daddy... says...' He squirmed. 'Daddy... stop!'

'Not until you say sorry for stamping.'

'I... wasn't... stamping!' James squeaked between breaths.

'I saw you stamp, James.' Dawn said, then she reached under his arm pit and wriggled her fingers.

'No, Mummy, no! Not you too!'

When Dawn and Rick stopped tickling James, and Rick set him down on his feet on the grass, James caught his breath.

'I wasn't stamping, Mummy, I promise. I was showing Daddy how Laura's supposed to do her mingo dancing.'

'I'm not a mingo dancer, James, it's flamenco!' Laura scowled at her younger brother, suddenly eighteen not eight, and Rick met Dawn's eyes.

'Looks like it could be a long afternoon.'

'Indeed. For you at least.'

'What's that supposed to mean?' Rick kissed her cheek.

'Well I need to feed the baby then take a nap. All the fresh air has worn me out.'

Rick sighed then kissed her again. 'You don't think your mother will want them for a few hours do you?'

'I have no idea… however…' Dawn waved her sister, Camilla over.

'Hey best big sister ever, I have a favour to ask.'

Camilla smiled. 'Anything.'

'You think you could watch Laura and James for a bit.'

'Pleeeassse, Aunty Camilla!' Laura took her aunt's hand. 'We'll be so good.'

'Can I play with Hairy Pawter?' James asked, pointing at the large British bulldog currently snoring at his owner, Tom Stone's, feet.

Camilla looked at her boyfriend, Tom, who was also the village vet, then back at her niece and nephew. 'I don't see why not. We didn't have anything else planned.'

'Yay!' James ran over to Tom and Laura soon followed.

'Are you sure?' Dawn asked her sister.

'Of course. You two look like you need a sleep. I'll take them back, make them wash that chocolate off then give them some tea before bringing them back.'

'Thank you so much.'

'What are big sisters for?' Camilla wiggled her perfectly shaped black eyebrows. 'You think they're all right in there?' She nodded at the café.

'I hope so,' Dawn replied.

'Like I told my wife, Camilla, you need to give them some space.'

Camilla's eyebrows rose slightly as she evaluated what Rick had just said.

Rick held up a hand. 'I also told her that I didn't mean to sound patronizing. I just meant that Allie has Chris and they probably need some time alone with Mandy. If we all go rushing in there, it'll likely be too much for Mandy and right now, she needs her mum.'

'You're right, Rick. It's hard to take a step back though.' Camilla shrugged. 'I'll text Allie later and see if we can help at all.'

'I'll just grab the box of books the children won.'

Rick went over to the band, who were set up in the corner of the café lawn, and picked up the box of books that James had won in the Easter egg hunt.

'Are we ready to go?' he asked when he returned to Dawn's side.

'Yes, let's get some sleep.' Dawn hugged Camilla. 'Thanks, sis, and any problems, let me know straight away.'

'We'll be fine. Besides, Tom's a vet so he knows first aid.'

'What?' Dawn blurted before she could stop herself.

Camilla giggled. 'Just teasing. Your children will be safe with us and I promise no first aid will be required. Now go and get some rest!'

Dawn pushed the pram down the path and through the café gate, then out onto the street. She glanced back at her children, who were stroking Hairy Pawter as he lifted his front paws in turn, then at the café.

'They'll be fine.' Rick hoisted the box of books onto his hip, then slid his free hand around her waist. 'All of them.'

'I hope so, Rick. I really do.'

Then they made their way home to catch up on some much-needed rest.

Chapter 3

Camilla

'Aunty Camilla?'

'Yes, James?'

Camilla smiled down at her nephew as he tugged at her hand.

'Is Hairy Pawter our cousin now?'

Camilla glanced at Tom and he shrugged, clearly as puzzled as she was by James's question. 'Because Laura said that Tom's our new uncle.'

Camilla stopped walking and took a deep breath.

'Tom is my...'

What? Boyfriend? Partner? Lover? BAE?

'We are a couple now, James.' Tom jumped in and saved Camilla from her quandary. 'So seeing as how HP is my... BFF, then I guess he's now your cousin. If that's how you want to think about him.' Tom flashed a grin at Camilla and she smiled in return.

'Yay!' James hopped on the spot causing the brown towel pinned to his shoulders as a cape, to float behind him. 'We have a cousin, Laura. James Skytalker has a cousin!'

'Don't be silly, James, HP can't be our cousin. He's just a dog. And you're James Dix-Beaumont not Skytalker. That's just your costume.'

HP gazed up at them, his fat pink tongue dangling out the side of his mouth, then he lifted a paw and offered it to Laura.
'I think he's trying to tell you something,' Tom said.
Laura crouched down next to HP. 'What is it boy?'
'He doesn't like being called *just a dog*, Laura, you silly billy.' James blew a raspberry. 'He wants to be our cousin.'
Laura kissed HP's paw then released him and stood up. She looked at Camilla and at Tom then rolled her eyes in James's direction.
'OK, James, HP is our cousin. Whatever.'
As Laura and James ran on ahead, Camilla tucked her arm into Tom's.
'Well that was interesting.'
'Which bit? The part where you didn't know what to call me, or the part where HP became an official family member?'
'Uh... all of it really. I mean... I think of HP as my family now and I couldn't imagine if he wasn't around, just as I couldn't imagine not seeing you every...' She bit her lip.
'Go on... finish what you were going to say.' Tom raised her hand and kissed it.
'Sorry, I'm still getting used to this. What I was going to say is that I couldn't bear not seeing you every day, Tom. Well, except for when you go back to Brighton and see your family and when you go on vet courses and... gosh, I know there will be times when I don't see you every day, but I know I will see you again, so it's OK... But if I wasn't going to see you again, I don't know what I'd do.'
Tom stopped walking and turned to her.
'Camilla, it's OK.' He smiled then glanced left to check on the children, who were currently studying a beetle that was making its way along the dry-stone wall outside the village church. He gave Camilla a quick kiss that sent warmth flooding through her. 'I need to see you every day too. You, beautiful lady, have become my whole world.'
'You're my world, Tom. I'm so glad you came to live in Heatherlea.' She gazed into his soft brown eyes, knowing she would never tire of looking at him.

'Me too.' He kissed her again. 'But I do think we need to decide upon an appropriate term.'
'A term?'
'You need to know what to call me if people ask.'
'What do you call me?'
'Camilla.'
She gave his arm a mock punch. 'No, how do you describe me to people?'
'I'll be honest; I've skirted labels by saying that I'm dating you, or in a relationship with you, or that we're a couple. Calling you my girlfriend feels a bit… young, I guess, and calling you my partner feels quite formal.'
Camilla nodded.
'Perhaps…' Tom's brown eyes seemed to sparkle with mischief as he held her gaze.
'Perhaps what?'
'Perhaps we need to have a new way to refer to each other.'
'A new way?'
He inclined his head. 'Yes. You know… a more permanent way.'
Camilla frowned as she tried to work out what he meant. What other names were there for the person you were in a relationship with?
Tom squeezed her hand. 'Camilla what I'm trying to say is—'
'Aunty Camilla!' Laura's scream cut him off.
Camilla tugged her hand from Tom's and ran towards her niece.
'Oh my god, Laura, what's wrong?'
She looked at her eight-year-old niece, who she swore resembled Dawn more every day, and winced at the tears brimming in her pretty eyes.
'A wasp stung me.'
'What? Where?' Camilla stroked her niece's soft hair as Laura lifted the hem of her flamenco costume and showed Camilla her ankle.
'Oh, sweetheart.'
Camilla knelt next to Laura and gave her a hug just as Tom and HP arrived at their side.

'I have some cream at the surgery that will take the pain away, and I'm pretty certain Auntie Camilla has some ice cream at her cottage that will make you feel better.'
'James, what's wrong?' Camilla realized that her nephew was standing behind Laura and that he had tears running down his cheeks too.
He sniffed, his small shoulders shaking.
'I should have protected Laura.'
'How, sweetheart?'
'With my powers.' He gestured at his costume. 'But I didn't see the wasp and now she's sad and hurt and... I'm a bad brother.'
Camilla reached out and pulled him into their hug. 'James, you are not a bad brother. Wasps sting people all the time and no amount of super powers will change that. Isn't that right, Tom?'
'Indeed it is.' Tom was holding HP on a tight lead because he was trying to get to the children, no doubt to shower them with slobbery doggy kisses to make them feel better.
'HP is worried about you both.'
James turned and rubbed the bulldog's silky ears. 'We're OK, HP. Don't worry.'
Camilla got up, and with a child holding each hand, they made their way to Tom's veterinary surgery. She'd only had her sister's children for twenty minutes and already they were both in tears. She might be their loving auntie but she needed to make sure that they both had smiles on their faces when they returned to their parents later. Dawn and Rick were worn out and she wanted to help them as much as she could, but they'd never let her look after Laura and James if they returned home with horror stories of being stung and crying in the street.
Dawn had told her numerous times that parenting was wonderful but really hard work. Camilla hadn't always believed it, wondering how such tiny human beings could cause a problem for anyone, but the more time she spent with Laura and James, the more she admired her younger sister.

Thank goodness that she and Tom hadn't had a serious discussion about having children of their own. They'd cooed over baby Alison, and hinted that it could be something they'd consider in the future — likely testing the water with each other — but no concrete plans had been made. Which was just as well, because Camilla was inclined to believe that she'd be a disaster at the whole thing.

Better to be a favourite auntie and leave it at that.

When they arrived at the surgery and Tom unlocked the door then ushered them all inside, Camilla realized that he hadn't had a chance to finish what he was about to say. That conversation would have to wait, because Laura had a wasp sting that needed treating and James needed ice cream to put the smile back on his sweet little face.

Chapter 4

Honey

Honey stretched out her arms and legs, enjoying the delicious sensations that coursed through her limbs. Nothing like a Bank Holiday Monday to make a woman feel relaxed. The bedroom was golden with the early morning sunlight that was filtering through the curtains and whispering of a beautiful day ahead.

The duvet next to her moved and dark hair appeared first, followed by Dane's handsome face and bright blue eyes framed with thick black lashes.

'Good morning, roomie.' He grinned lazily at her, his left cheek featuring a pillow crease and his stubble already casting a dark shadow over his strong jaw.

Honey leant towards him and kissed the bridge of his nose, widened by a break in a rugby game, then she kissed his full lips, the top one with its thin white scar where someone in the opposing team had caught him with their knee. She loved his scars, his small imperfections that made him who he was. To her, he was perfect in every way. He pulled her into his arms and kissed her back, and she breathed him in, the warm male scent laced with yesterday's citrus-ginger cologne, a combination that made her stomach flip.

'Mmmm. Good morning, to you too, roomie.'

They lay back on the pillows, holding hands, enjoying the birdsong from outside that seeped through the open window. Honey always left the bedroom window open a crack, even in winter, because she liked to have fresh air in her room.

'What shall we do today?' Dane asked as he played with the fingers of her left hand, straightening each one out in turn then planting kisses on the tips.

'I don't mind.' She turned to peer at his profile and her heart fluttered. She couldn't believe her luck. This beautiful man with his sapphire eyes, his short thick dark hair and his strong broad shoulders was hers. Her lover. Her friend. Her partner in crime. Dane had agreed to move in with her, now that he was staying in the village — after securing his teaching post at the local primary school — and she was beyond delighted.

'I can tell you one thing, Honey.'

'You can?'

He nodded. 'I'm not doing any school work today.'

'You're not?'

'Nope. Today is reserved.'

'Ooh! Reserved for what?'

'You and me.'

'Dane, that's so good to hear.'

She rolled onto her side and snuggled up to him, winding her arm over his chest, her leg over his. Dane had worked so hard to secure a permanent position at the local primary school that Honey had been worried about him. In fact, he had recently admitted to being aware that he'd neglected everything else. But now he'd established himself, Honey hoped he'd be able to find more of a work-life balance.

'And in that case... how about if we start moving your things in here?' She ran her fingers over his chest, stroking the dusting of black hair on his chest then slowly following the line that ran down to his navel and beyond.

'Hey!' He lifted her chin with his forefinger.

'What?'
'I asked you a question. Didn't you hear me?'
'No... I, uh, was thinking about something.'
'Were you now?'
He laughed then rolled her onto her back and leant over her, his blue eyes scanning her face.
'I think I know what you were thinking about but I'll have to test the theory.'
Honey smiled as he gently ran a finger over her cheeks then over her lips and down over her chin to the hollow of her throat, where he pressed a soft kiss.
'I asked you, Honey, if we should have a good breakfast first, as moving requires a lot of energy.'
'Definitely. I have lots of eggs, so I'm sure I can whip something up.'
'No you don't. I'll make breakfast.'
'Are you sure?'
He nodded. 'Absolutely.'
'Before you go...' She smiled at him.
'Before I go?'
'One more kiss?'
'Just one more.'
She rolled onto her side again then he kissed her, and all thoughts of making breakfast temporarily slipped from their minds.

Chapter 5

Allie

Allie walked into the kitchen of the cottage she shared with Chris and shivered. It wasn't cold in there, but she felt cold because she'd barely slept a wink. All night long, thoughts about Mandy and how upset she was had raced through Allie's mind and she'd wondered if this could have been avoided in some way.
'Morning.' Chris looked up from his iPad. He was sitting at the kitchen table near the window.
'Is that coffee fresh?'
'It is indeed.'
She sat down as he poured the dark brown steaming beverage into a large mug then handed it to her.
'Thank you. What time did you get up?'
'About half an hour ago.'
She glanced at the clock.
'You were up at six?'
'Yeah, I didn't sleep that well to be honest.'
'I'm surprised I didn't hear you get up.'
'I was as quiet as I could be because I didn't want to disturb you after the awful night you had.'

'I know... I tossed and turned. I'm just so worried about Mandy.'
Chris reached out and squeezed her hand. His touch was warm and reassuring and she sent out a silent thank you that he'd come back to her. He made her feel safe but also that she could achieve anything. He saw her in the way she'd always wanted to see herself and she loved him for it.
'Mandy will be OK. You know that don't you? She has you and Jordan, and now, she also has me.'
'Thank you.'
'Hey, don't thank me. I'm your partner, remember, and I love you more than anything, Allie. You're my everything.'
'Do you love me more than writing?' She used their favourite joke, trying to lighten the heaviness that had weighed her down since Mandy had turned up at the café yesterday.
Chris frowned, pouted, then met her eyes.
'You know... I think I do. But only just.'
They smiled at each other and she took comfort from his familiar handsome features, her very own George Clooney lookalike. But without the baby twins that Mr Clooney had, thankfully. In her early forties and with two grown up children, Allie did not fancy adding to her brood, and seeing as how Chris had agreed that he was happy to continue as they were, there would be no tiny feet pattering around in the cottage. It had formerly belonged to Chris's mother, and even now, Allie sometimes thought of it as *Mrs Monroe's cottage*. Not that it mattered, because Allie was happily settled there with Chris. Knowing that she would fall asleep in his arms every night and wake to find him next to her was the best feeling in the world.
'Allie, I've been thinking.'
She sipped her drink, savouring the delicious aroma of the good quality coffee Chris insisted they buy.
'I...' He ran a hand through his salt and pepper hair. 'I think that we should... now that we're together and have been for a while, I was thinking it might be a good idea if we...'
Allie peered at him over her mug.

His cheeks were flushed and he was worrying his bottom lip.

'What is it? You look worried. Chris, is everything OK?'

He nodded. 'It is. Absolutely. I'm just trying to find the right way to say this. But perhaps here and now isn't the right time. It should be more... special. Yes.' He nodded as if listening to an internal voice.

A creak from above their heads made them both look up.

'More special? What should be *more special*?'

Another creak from above.

Allie put her mug down on the table and stood up. Chris held up a hand. 'She might just be using the bathroom. Don't go up just yet in case she goes back to bed.'

'But what if she needs me?'

'Then she'll come down. She probably needs to catch up on some sleep too.'

Allie sat down again. 'You're right. I'm like one of those space shuttle mums.'

'A what?'

'You know... the ones who hover around their children nervously all the time, waiting to hug them at the first sign of a frown or a wobbly lip.'

Chris's lips twitched.

'What's amusing you?'

'I think you mean helicopter.'

'Helicopter what?'

'Helicopter mums. They're the ones who hover round their children.' Allie waved a hand. 'Yes, that's what I meant. Then again, if I was more attentive and if I had gone to London more often then I'd probably have spotted that something wasn't right in my daughter's life. I could have saved her from this.'

'No, you couldn't. Mandy is an adult now, Allie, and she has her own life in London. She wouldn't have appreciated you popping in every five minutes and even if you had, you couldn't have controlled her social circle or who she dated.'

Allie drained her coffee then wrapped both hands around the empty mug.

'I know. You're right. I just feel so guilty. Even though she is a grown woman, she'll still always be my baby and all I want is to see her happy. Jordan is happy here in Heatherlea with Max and they're such a perfect match. But Mandy has always been such a go-getter, so determined and driven. I never thought she'd be the one to end up destroyed by love.'

'Did she tell you any more about what happened?'

Allie shook her head. After they'd brought Mandy back from the café, Chris had made himself scarce by going out to see a friend, while Allie had tried to talk to her daughter. But Mandy had been too upset to explain properly and in the end, Allie had thought a long hot bubble bath and a very early night would be of more benefit to Mandy than trying to talk it all through. Sometimes it was better to sleep on something and return to it with a fresh mind and heart. Allie had ended up falling asleep on the sofa, only waking when Chris had come home and led her up to bed.

'She needed to wash the day away and to rest. Perhaps she'll tell me today. Perhaps she won't. But either way, I'm hoping she'll agree to stay for a while to get herself together.'

'I'm sure she will.'

Allie got up and went around the table to Chris then wrapped her arms around his shoulders and buried her face in his hair. He slid his strong arms around her waist and held her tight. They stayed that way for a while, as the boards above their head creaked, signalling Mandy's return to bed, and outside a lawnmower started up as someone made the most of the bank holiday sunshine.

'I don't know what I'd do without you, Chris.' Allie spoke into his hair, breathing in his sandalwood shampoo and his own very special scent.

'You, my love, will never have to find out.'

Chris turned her around so she sat on his lap then kissed her softly.

And although he'd never be able to stop her worrying completely, with him at her side, Allie knew she would be able to deal with whatever came her way.

Chapter 6

Dawn

Dawn pushed the pram along the pavement, taking deep breaths of the cool fresh air. It was a beautiful April morning and she was glad to be outside. She'd left Rick and the children in bed, believing that after an exciting party at the café then an afternoon spent with Camilla and Tom, Laura and James could do with a lie-in. Rick had been up with her in the night when she'd seen to Alison, so she thought he deserved some more sleep, and Dawn had had to get up anyway to feed and change the baby at six.

When she'd opened the curtains downstairs to find such a glorious morning, she'd decided to pop Alison in the pram and make the most of it. She had an ulterior motive, of course, hoping it would make Alison sleep through the morning so she could spend some time with Laura and James, but a walk would also help get her fitness up and get her back in shape after her pregnancy. She'd need to be fit and healthy to run around after three children, after all.

She walked briskly, imagining the toning effect upon her legs and belly, and almost ran straight over a squashed black shape on the pavement at the end of her street.

'What the hell is that?' She peered around the pram, wondering if someone had lost a jumper or a scarf on their way home from the Easter party at The Cosy Cottage Café. But no… It was something else, something far more distressing than an item of clothing.

'Oh, Alison, what are we going to do?' She looked beneath the hood of the pram at her tiny daughter and Alison blinked her grey eyes, as if she was giving the matter some serious consideration. 'I can't really do much about it can I, as I have you with me and I don't want to go back yet, because if I do, then I'll wake everyone up. We'll have to come up with an alternative plan.'

She put the brake on the pram, then looked around. She spotted a long stick in the grass that edged the pavement. After she'd picked it up, she gingerly poked at the black shape. It moved with a squelch and she grimaced. Not good, not good at all. No sign of life there. The poor thing must have crawled from the road, or been struck with such a force that it had ended up on the pavement. With a flick of her wrist, she moved the shape across to the grass. At least it was out of the way and if anyone came along, they wouldn't step on it. Hopefully, no one else would even see it.

That would have to do for now.

'Come on then, Alison. Let's go see Auntie Honey and ask what she thinks we should do.'

Honey's house was the closest and she hoped that her friend would probably be up doing yoga or feeding her chickens, so she'd head there first.

She clicked off the pram brake then walked in the direction of Honey's cottage. The day hadn't exactly got off to the positive start she'd expected, but that was life, and if she could spare someone from the upset of seeing what she just had, then that was what she would do.

Chapter 7

Camilla

'How about we do something special today?' Tom asked as he poured boiling water into the teapot and swirled it around.
'Like what?' Camilla carried the plate of toast to the table then sat down. The French doors were open and outside, HP was sniffing around the decking. Mild spring air drifted into the kitchen, carrying the heavenly scents of sweet peas and the sharp floral aroma of lavender from Tom's pots. Camilla stifled a yawn, not wanting to put a dampener on Tom's plans. The previous day, with the Easter party at the café, as well as taking care of Laura and James until the evening, had been tiring and she'd imagined a relaxing day with Tom and HP at his cottage, possibly with a pub lunch at The Red Fox then an afternoon nap.
Tom brought the teapot and mugs to the table and sat opposite her. 'We could go somewhere. Perhaps for a walk at a park or—'
'Aren't you supposed to be on call?'
Camilla spread some of Allie's homemade strawberry jam onto a piece of toast. The sweet fruity conserve was like summer in a jar, and this morning, the smell of the strawberries seemed to be stronger than usual.

'I am but I wasn't thinking of going too far. It's just nice to get out and about sometimes. And it is a bank holiday.'
'And you feel that you should be doing something?'
He smiled and his soft brown eyes crinkled at the corners.
'We don't have to.'
'I like the idea, but let's have breakfast and shower first then decide what to do.'
Tom glanced at the clock on the kitchen wall. 'It is still early, I guess.'
Breakfast eaten, washed down with three mugs of tea, dishwasher loaded and switched on, Camilla headed upstairs for a shower. She loved being at Tom's cottage, with the personal touches like the paintings by local artists — including Honey — and neutral rugs and furnishings, with the scents of his washing powder and shower gel that hung about his towels and bathroom, and with the whisper of his aftershave in the bedroom. It all combined to make her realise how much she cared about him and how far they'd come as a couple. She'd been so keen to stay single before she'd met Tom, convinced that she'd never meet a man who would change that. Years of her mother ranting about her father — who'd walked out when Camilla and Dawn were children, leaving their mother to struggle alone — had made Camilla harden her heart to love. Then Tom had come to the village with HP and bit-by-bit, they'd both stolen her heart.

Life was so different to how she'd once thought it would be and her father's return to Heatherlea in the autumn, followed by his reunion with her mother, had been a big part of that. Laurence Beaumont was now happily living with his ex wife and had morphed from the fun-loving party guy Camilla had been brought up to believe he was, into a loving partner and doting grandfather. The best thing about it all for Camilla was seeing her mum and Dawn so happy at his return. It was as if he'd never been away and yet... the past could never be undone or forgotten. She shrugged. Perhaps it was meant to be that way so that when he came back to Heatherlea, his relationship with his family would be all the better for it.

Camilla had maintained her independence by keeping her cottage while Tom had his, but they spent most nights together. She still experienced moments of fear, when she'd worry that Tom might change his mind about her and that he'd walk away, but they were becoming less frequent the more time they spent together. Tom had won her trust and confidence in a way no man ever had done before and she hoped with all her heart that nothing would spoil their relationship.

When they'd first become close, she'd found out that Tom was still married —although he'd been separated from his wife for some time — and it thrown her into a sea of doubt about their relationship. But the divorce had been finalised just after Christmas, his ex was heavily pregnant by her new partner at the time, and Tom had reassured Camilla that his marriage had been over long ago in every way except on paper.

She walked into the bathroom and caught sight of her reflection in the mirrored cabinet above the sink. Her face was so pale, and were those dark shadows under her eyes? Perhaps yesterday had worn her out more than she'd realised. Nothing a long hot shower and a coat of concealer wouldn't sort out.

She opened the cubicle door and turned on the shower then undressed while the water heated up. Camilla never liked to get straight under the spray, as being chilled wasn't something she enjoyed. Tom said a quick blast under the cold water was invigorating but she couldn't agree with that at all. Once the cubicle was nice and steamy, she opened the door, stepped in and let the hot water wash her thoughts away.

'Camilla?'
Tom was standing outside the shower cubicle when Camilla opened

the door. He opened up a large fluffy towel and she stepped into it, smiling as he wrapped it around her then hugged her tight.
'Mmmm. That's lovely, thank you.'
'Can't have you getting cold, can we?'
He lifted the corner of the towel and gently wiped her face.
'I was thinking that we could just take it easy this morning if you like, then perhaps head out later. What do you think? You look a bit peaky and I hope you're not coming down with something.'
'So do I. If I am, it's likely something Laura and James passed on to me.'
'Well perhaps you'll feel better later. Do you need me to go and get some paracetamol or something?'
Camilla took in the baggy grey lounge pants that sat on his slim hips and the soft white surf brand T-shirt that emphasised his broad shoulders and muscular arms. His light brown hair was still sleep-mussed and he needed a shave. He'd never looked better.
'No, I'm fine, really. I probably need a strong coffee and a read. That'll sort me out.'
Tom nodded then planted a kiss on the top of her short damp hair.
'OK, beautiful, as long as you're sure. Think I'll jump in the shower.'
Camilla walked to the door as he turned the shower on, then she turned back, unable to resist admiring his lean frame as he shed his clothes.
Yes, a day lounging around at home with her man sounded pretty perfect, and as for going out later, well they could see how they felt after lunch.

Chapter 8

Allie

Allie was stuffing clothes into the washing machine when she heard footsteps on the stairs. She turned to Chris and he mouthed, *I'll be in the garden.*
This was it then.
Mandy was coming downstairs and Allie would finally find out what had gone wrong.
'Morning, Mum.'
Allie stood up as Mandy entered the kitchen. 'Morning, love. Cup of tea?'
Mandy nodded then shuffled to the table where she sat down and pulled Allie's spare dressing gown around Allie's borrowed pyjamas. Mandy had arrived with just the clothes she was wearing, so Allie had quickly rooted through her things last night to find some garments that would fit her rather slimmed-down daughter.
'Something to eat?' Allie poured milk into two mugs and carried them to the table then went back for the teapot.
'I couldn't face a thing.'
'Are you sure? You need to keep your strength up.'
'Maybe later.'

Allie poured tea into the mugs then passed one to Mandy.

'Thanks.' Mandy raised her puffy red eyes to meet Allie's. 'Sorry, Mum, I didn't mean to be any trouble.'

'You've never been any trouble, love. Just the opposite, in fact. You're so strong and independent that sometimes I wonder if you need me at all. But I'm very proud of you and all that you've achieved.'

Mandy smiled but it didn't reach her eyes. She wrapped her hands around her mug then raised it to her lips and sipped her drink.

'That's good tea.'

'Earl Grey, just how you like it. You do still like it with a splash of skimmed milk don't you?'

'I do. It's good to be home, Mum, even if this isn't the home I grew up in.'

'You always have a place with me. Wherever I am.'

Allie sipped her own tea, wishing her palpitations would stop. Her heart was thrumming so hard, she wondered if it was going to burst through her chest and fly off through the open door. She meant what she'd said; Mandy would always have a place with her but she hoped for Mandy's sake that this man, whoever he was, wouldn't ruin the life Mandy had worked so hard to build. The life that she loved and always spoke about so enthusiastically whenever Allie rang her. Mandy was always getting up early for a meeting or dashing off to another author lunch or book launch. She raved about the latest bestseller to climb the charts — something that author Chris completely understood — and she had dreams of climbing the ladder in publishing; she had such ambitious plans. So many plans. But now... it seemed as though one man might have ruined all of that.

'I'll be OK, Mum. I just need some time to... compose myself, I guess.' Mandy moved her neck from side to side as if trying to loosen the knots that had formed there.

'Do you feel ready to talk me about it yet?'

'I do.' Mandy drained her mug. 'But can I have another mug of tea first, please?'

'Of course you can.'

Rachel Griffiths

'And actually, perhaps a piece of toast.'
'I have some blueberry muffins that I made yesterday.'
'Your blueberry muffins? Now, Mum, you know I can't resist those.'
Allie set about making more tea then placed a fresh mug and a muffin in front of Mandy. When she sat down again, her stomach was clenched and her mouth dry. She knew she wouldn't be able to eat a morsel until she knew what had happened to her daughter and if it could be sorted, but she'd be glad to see Mandy get some food inside her.

Motherhood was a rollercoaster indeed, and with such love came an open chasm of vulnerability. She'd felt that way the first time she'd held Mandy in her arms and gazed at her perfect tiny features and the soft downy head. The same had happened when she'd held Jordan for the first time too. She'd known she'd do anything for the pair of them, anything at all, and that if anything or anyone ever hurt them, she would become a tigress ready to protect her offspring. That time had come and she was trying hard not to growl or sharpen her claws...

Chapter 9

Dawn

Dawn pushed the pram up Honey's path then put the brake on and knocked on the door. It was still early and the bedroom curtains were closed, so she hoped she wasn't about to wake Honey and Dane up because she knew Dane needed to rest on his days off. Not that he had many days off according to Honey because he was always doing schoolwork.

Dawn knew how it was to have a busy partner. Rick had worked in the City until last autumn, and most nights, because of the commute as well as long hours, he hadn't got home until after the children had gone to bed. It had been difficult, especially when Dawn got pregnant with Alison. But things had come to a head and Rick had admitted to feeling that he needed to make a big change in his life, and him quitting his City job to work from home was the best decision they had ever made. Yes, money was tighter, especially with three children but they managed and were all happier for it.

She knocked the door again, knowing that now she was here she'd just as well wait until Honey got up, because going back home for what she needed would mean waking her family and then she'd have to explain to Rick what she'd found. The children might overhear and the situation would become a lot worse than it already was. And it really was bad enough.

Her stomach lurched. She had no idea how she was going to explain it.

The door opened a crack and Dane peered out.

'Good morning, Dane.'

'Dawn?' he opened the door wider and squinted at her. 'Is something wrong?'

'No... no, nothing's wrong,' she replied automatically. 'Well, actually something's wrong but it's nothing to worry about. Well... it is, but I'll deal with it.'

'OK...' He frowned at her and she realised that she sounded absolutely bonkers. Here she was, bright and early on a Bank Holiday Monday, with her newborn baby in her pram, knocking on her friend's door because she didn't want to go home and wake her family.

'Look... could I come in? I promise I won't be long but I need something.'

'You do?'

'Yes. From the shed.'

'From the shed?'

He rubbed his eyes and a wave of sympathy washed over Dawn. It seemed like she actually had woken him up. In fact, he was wearing a pink and purple T-shirt that was riding up his belly and pinching his upper arms.

'Are you wearing one of Honey's T-shirts?' she asked.

He looked down at himself and tugged at the hem but it bounced back up, revealing his flat stomach. Dawn made a point of turning her head and gazing at the Bay tree that stood in a pot next to the door.

'So I am!' He laughed. 'Must've pulled it on by mistake.'

'I'm so sorry if I woke you.'

'It's fine. I wasn't actually sleeping... Anyway, uh, come on in.'

Dane stepped out and helped her lift the pram up the step and into the hallway.

'I'll just call Honey.' He nodded at the stairs.

'Thanks. And... uh... sorry. If I'd had a choice, I wouldn't have disturbed you.'

'No problem.'

Dawn watched as he climbed the stairs two at a time, wondering what it was about him that didn't look right and then she realised. He was wearing white pyjama bottoms with pink hearts printed on them, and they also had to belong to Honey. She winced as it hit her that she actually had disturbed them and Dane had grabbed the first items of clothing he could find.

Alison murmured in her pram, so Dawn leant forwards and checked on her. Big grey eyes blinked up at her then the tiny mouth contorted and Alison let out a squawk. She was hungry. Again. Already. Dawn lifted her from the pram then carried her through to the lounge and got comfy on the sofa. She knew Honey wouldn't mind and it would be better than subjecting Honey and Dane to Alison's full dawn chorus of *I'm starving, mother, feed me quick!*

As Alison fed, Dawn relaxed on the comfortable old sofa and gazed at her surroundings. Honey had a lovely home and although a lot of the furniture had belonged to her aunt, and she'd kept it when she'd inherited the cottage, she had also made it her own. Honey was a talented artist who also made sculptures and other crafts, and she'd made Alison a pretty unicorn ornament to celebrate her arrival. It was then that Camilla had recognised the design of the unicorn and they'd found out that Honey was, in fact, behind Purple Hen designs. She'd been quiet about it in her typically unassuming and modest way. However, she'd then admitted that she was doing quite well and had more orders coming in than she could keep up with. Camilla had agreed to take over her accounts to free up some of her time and Dawn had been thinking that once Alison was a bit older, she might be able to help out too, even if it was just driving deliveries around for Honey.

It was an idea for the future anyway, and Dawn wasn't in any rush to see her youngest daughter grow up. She knew how quickly they became independent and she wanted to make the most of having Alison as a baby, because she didn't think they'd try for another. Three children kept them busy enough. As well as the guinea pigs, of course.

'Hello, Dawnie.'

Honey entered the room, her face bright with youth and happiness and her pretty bobbed hair – in shades of blue, pink, purple and silver – pushed behind her ears. The tiny stud in her nose twinkled in the light as she came to sit by Dawn.

'Hi Honey, so sorry to wake you. I was hoping to get in and out quickly but Alison had other ideas.'

'Awww, is she feeding?' Honey sat next to Dawn and gazed at the baby.

'Yes. She's always feeding! My boobs are like balloons because I have so much milk. I saw the health visitor on Friday and she said I have enough milk for five babies and a rice pudding.'

Honey wrinkled her nose. 'Not sure I'd fancy a breast milk rice pudding.'

'Me either, but she did make me giggle.'

'Is everything all right though?' Honey's expression changed to one of concern. 'I mean... not that it's not great to see you but I'm a bit surprised to see you so early.'

'I know and I'm sorry. Poor Dane seemed shocked.'

Honey nodded. 'I think he was more embarrassed about the fact that he only realised he'd pulled my pyjamas on when he was talking to you. We're both half asleep.'

'Did he? I hardly noticed.' Dawn giggled. 'Pink suits him anyway.'

'Just don't tell the kids at school, whatever you do.'

'My lips are sealed.'

'Do you want a cuppa?'

'I will do, if you don't mind, but first let me tell you what I need and why.'

'That sounds ominous.'

'It's pretty awful and it's something that needs sorting before someone else sees it. Otherwise, it could cause a lot of distress.'

Dawn swallowed as she thought about what she'd seen and how it had turned her stomach. Goodness only knew the impact it could have on those she cared about if she didn't get it cleaned up as soon as possible.

Dawn closed Honey's door behind her and set off back in the direction of her home. After she fed, burped and changed Alison, she'd settled her back in her pram and reassured Honey that Alison would likely sleep for forty-five minutes to an hour. That should give her enough time to do what she needed to do. Dane and Honey had offered to go and deal with the matter but Dawn had declined their help. She'd seen the terrible thing and wanted as few people as possible to see it too. That's what friends were for; sparing one another from upsetting times, as far as was possible anyway.

Honey had seemed nervous at the prospect of looking after Alison, but Dawn had faith in her friend and her ability to care for her daughter. Besides, she wouldn't be long…

When she reached the spot where she'd come across the awful sight, she looked around. It was still early and thankfully quiet, so she should be able to deal with this before anyone else saw it. She pulled the black bin bag Honey had given her from her pocket and shook it out then walked over to the grass and peered around.

Ah… there it was…

Her stomach churned. She could, of course, go and get Rick, but that would defeat the whole purpose of her going to Honey's and waking her and Dane up, so she had to do this herself.

She placed the bag on the ground, edged the spade closer to the black shape, then slid it underneath. It was heavier than she'd anticipated — having only flicked it a small distance earlier on — and when she went to put it inside the black bag, it stuck to the spade, so she had to shake the spade over the bag, all the time trying not to look too closely at what she was doing.

Object bagged — and she had to think of it as an object or she'd get too upset — she tied the handles at the top, wiped the spade on the grass then set off towards Honey's again. But when she got there, she carried on walking. She wasn't taking this to Honey's, she was heading for Tom's surgery. After all, if anyone would know what to do about this, or with this, it would be Tom.

Chapter 10

Camilla

Camilla lowered her book.
'Was that the door?' she asked Tom.
He lowered his book and frowned. They'd just settled for some reading time and now it seemed that it was about to be disturbed.
'Could be an emergency callout.' He grimaced.
'I knew a whole day of relaxing together was too good to be true.' Camilla accepted his kiss then watched as he left the room and went to the door. When he returned, Dawn was with him. She was pale, her green eyes wide in her pretty face. Her dark hair was pushed behind her ears and she was dressed as though she was about to go for a run.
Camilla stood up.
'God, Dawnie, what's wrong?'
Dawn frowned and Camilla realised she was carrying a black bag and a spade.
'What've you been doing? Clearing up dog poop?'
'No... not exactly. More like road kill.'
'Road kill? Have you gone mad? Get it out of here.' Camilla waved her hands at her sister.

'Actually, I was hoping Tom would take a look at it.'
'You want him to look at a dead animal? Bloody hell, Dawn, it's Bank Holiday Monday and we're trying to chill out together.' She remembered herself. 'And where's Alison?'
Camilla had read about mothers suffering from post-natal issues and acting strangely, walking off and leaving their babies when something distracted them. But picking up road kill? That, she hadn't read about.
'I think that it's...' Dawn bit her lip and Camilla saw that she was actually quite distressed.
'That it's what?'
'I think it's Ebony.'
Camilla's hand shot to her mouth and she met Tom's eyes.
Ebony was one of Allie's beloved cats and she'd be devastated if anything happened to them.
'Let's take it through to the surgery and I can have a look.' Tom took the bag from Dawn then raised it higher as HP came to have a sniff. 'No, HP, nothing in here for you, buddy.'
Dawn turned to Camilla. 'Alison's fine. I left her with Honey after I borrowed the bag and spade.'
'Why didn't you get Rick to do it?'
'He's still in bed. As are the children. I was taking Alison for an early morning stroll to try to get some fresh air and hopefully to make her sleep this morning so I could spend some time with Laura and James, but at the end of our road, I found this cat.'
'Oh, Dawn, that's so sad. And poor Allie. She has enough on her plate right now, what with Mandy turning up in such a state.'
'Exactly.'
They followed Tom out of the door and around to the vet surgery that was attached to his cottage. Inside, it was cool and dark, the light blue vertical blinds still drawn. The familiar scents of cleaning fluid and animals hung heavy in the air and Camilla's stomach rolled. The surgery was kept spotlessly clean, but the smells could never be fully erased. This was a place where animals were treated and cured. A

place where they were born. And a place where, sometimes, they said their final goodbyes to the owners who had loved them.

Tom turned on the lights then went through to the consultation room and placed the bag on the examination table.

'Do you two want to wait outside?'

'No, it's OK. I need to know if it's Ebony.'

Dawn stepped closer to the table but Camilla stayed by the door. The smells and the thought that her friend's cat might be in the bag were making her feel a bit funny.

Tom undid the knotted handles then gently opened the bag and exposed the contents.

Dawn gasped, Tom sighed and Camilla threw up all over the floor.

Chapter 11

Honey

'You don't have to watch her every second you know.' Dane nudged Honey as she stood next to Alison's pram.

She looked up and found him smiling at her.

'I know. I'm just afraid she might wake up and panic.'

'If she does and she sees you staring at her with that goofy smile on your face, she probably will panic.'

Honey touched her mouth. 'Was I goofy?'

He nodded. 'And very, very cute.' He reached out and stroked her hair then ran his fingers down her cheek and her neck until his big hand rested on her shoulder.

'She's just perfect, isn't she?'

He nodded. 'And so are you.'

'I'll get bigheaded if you keep saying such nice things.'

'You deserve to have nice things said to you.' He took her hands. 'Are you OK though?'

'Why wouldn't I be?'

'Well... you know...' He nodded at the pram. 'Having a baby here.'

'Oh...' She chewed her bottom lip. 'I can see why you'd wonder but yes, I'm actually really good.'

She'd recently told Dane all about her past and a miscarriage she'd suffered when she was younger. It had resulted in an infection that meant she didn't know if she'd be able to have children. She'd thought it might put Dane off her, especially as she'd felt to blame for the miscarriage for such a long time, but he had been very understanding, kind and reassuring. He'd told her that he was in no rush to have a family and as long as she wasn't either, then they should be happy getting to know each other and enjoying their time together, and that if one day they wanted to try for a baby, they would deal with any issues then.

'It's lovely having little Alison here and I don't feel under any pressure because no one's watching me. Well, you are but… you know what I mean.'

'I do.' He kissed her softly. 'So you carry on watching her and I'll go and release the hens, shall I?'

'You can if you want. Do you know what to do?'

'I think I can manage a few chickens, Honey. I mean… I'm not exactly going to struggle am I?' He flexed his muscles like some sort of bodybuilder and Honey laughed. She knew he was just teasing.

'You look like you need the toilet when you do that.'

'That's how they do it at the gym. It's the *I'm constipated from all the protein shakes* face.'

'Urgh! OK, you go and get the eggs. But be careful.'

'I will.'

He left her standing there in her lounge, where Dawn had parked the pram, watching the sleeping baby. Ten minutes passed and Dane still hadn't returned.

'You know… I think I need to see how he's getting on, Alison. Some of my girls can be a bit temperamental, so let's go check up on him shall we?'

She took the brake off then pushed Alison through to the kitchen before clicking the brake on again. What she saw when she looked out of the window made her laugh out loud. Dane needed rescuing already!

'Dane? Are you OK?' she called from the back door. There was no answer, so she gave Alison a quick glance to check she was still sleeping, then hurried out into the garden.

Dane was standing in the chicken enclosure, his hands pressed to his chest, as her chickens bobbed around him. She ran through their names to check that they were all there: Princess Lay-a, Hen-solo, Cluck Rogers, Albert Eggstein, Mary Poopins, Maid Marihen, and Tyrannosaurus Pecks.

Where was...

'Honey!' Dane's voice was strangled as he muttered it through gritted teeth.

'Yes?' She reached the enclosure.

'It... she, rather, keeps coming at me every time I move and pecking my toes.'

'Why have you got flip flops on?'

He shrugged his broad shoulders. 'I thought it would be OK and I haven't moved my wellies in yet.'

'Come on, it's OK... you can get out of there. Just move slowly.'

He lifted his left leg as if he was moving in slow motion and an angry squawk pierced the air, then Henifer Aniston came hurrying around from behind the henhouse. Her head bobbed furiously and she pounced at Dane, pecking at his legs and making him hop from foot to foot as he cried out, then she ran off to assume her hiding position again.

'Oh Dane, I don't think Henifer Aniston likes you.'

'No kidding?' His eyes were wide and he held himself stiffly, as if he was terrified to move again. 'She's like a sniper. Every time I try to leave, she strikes.'

'Uh... right... I know, I'll distract her with some food and you can make your escape.'

'Please be quick!'

Honey went back to the house to fetch some pellets and giggled softly to herself. Big burly Dane, a man who'd been injured in rugby games, a man who'd been through the horrendous goldfish bowl interviews that teachers were subjected to now, and emerged unscathed, was being bullied by a little brown hen. However, Honey knew that Henifer Aniston could be quite territorial and surprisingly fierce when she wanted to be. It must be the Hollywood diva in her. Honey grabbed the bag of pellets, checked on Alison again, then hurried back out to the garden to rescue the man she loved.

Chapter 12

Allie

Muffin and tea consumed, Mandy had a bit more colour in her cheeks.
'OK, love?' Allie stroked Mandy's hair back from her face in the way she used to when her daughter was a little girl. At least back then, she'd been able to protect Mandy, but now, it was impossible to do so in the same way.
'Yes, that was good, thanks, Mum.'
Allie nodded and took Mandy's plate and mug to the dishwasher.
'Mum?'
'Yes.'
'Am I a bad person?'
'Oh god, no. Of course you're not. Why'd you ask that?'
Mandy crumpled the tissue she'd been holding, passing it from one hand to the other. Allie noted the crimson nail polish on Mandy's nails that matched that on her toenails. The colour would have been perfect with the beautiful ball gown she'd been wearing when she'd arrived the previous day.
'It's just that... I'm so ashamed of myself.'
'Why, love?' Allie sat down next to Mandy and braced herself.

'Because of what happened.'

Allie nodded, not wanting to interrupt Mandy now she'd finally started to talk.

'See... I fell in love with him. With Michael Bloom.'

'Michael Bloom?'

Mandy nodded. 'He's in publishing too. He's a bit older than me.'

'How old?'

'Thirty-three.'

Allie nodded. Nine years or so but what did that matter? Love didn't always care about age.

'He seemed so knowledgeable about the business, so suave and sophisticated.'

Allie swallowed hard, she had a feeling she knew where this was going.

'We met through work and he asked me out. We dated... he'd come to mine but I never went to his. He said he shared his flat with a group of guys, some of whom were doctors and who worked shifts, so it was unfair to take company back. I believed him. That is... I wanted to believe him but I'm not sure I ever really did. Not fully. Something was niggling at the back of my mind.'

'Sometimes we kid ourselves because we want to.'

Mandy nodded. 'Like you did with Dad?'

'What?' Allie's heart plummeted. She'd thought she'd kept Roger's infidelity from her children. When he'd died in the car crash, she hadn't seen the point in hurting them further. Why make them suffer for his behaviour? She'd done her best to maintain their perception of him as a good husband and father.

'I know you tried to protect us, Mum, but things emerged. I put two and two together and... well... he did what he did.'

'But he loved you and Jordan, Mandy. He loved you both so much.'

'I know. I also think he loved you too... as much as he could love anyone. However, he's gone, so we'll never know exactly why he did what he did, will we?'

Allie shook her head. 'I'm sorry, love.'

'Don't be sorry. You're the best mum we could wish for.' Mandy squeezed her hand. 'But Michael did know what he was doing. He took advantage of my naivety; my desire for him – and it was so powerful, Mum, I'd never felt anything like it before – and he played me. I would've done anything for him.'

'Was he... married?'

Mandy nodded. 'With three young children.'

A clattering came from outside and Chris popped his head around the back door. 'Sorry, dropped the watering can.' Then his head disappeared from view again.

'How did you find out?'

'At the party. He'd tried to encourage me not to go, said it would be full of stuffy types and that he thought I'd be better off staying home.'

'He did what?'

'I know, right? Besides which, it was a really big event and everyone who's anyone was going. I didn't want to miss it. Of course, him trying to persuade me not to go raised my suspicions even higher. He said he wasn't going and that he'd come round to mine. I'd already decided to go though, because I'd had enough of him breaking dates, cancelling weekend plans and enough of crying in front of Saturday night TV.'

'Oh Mandy, you should have come home sooner.'

'I needed to live my life, Mum, and I couldn't keep coming home because I was sad about my boyfriend. If that's what he ever actually was.'

'Of course not.' Allie felt her lips turn upwards a fraction. She was so damned proud of her daughter.

'Anyway, I called his bluff and told him I wouldn't go. But I did. I bought a beautiful dress, had my hair and nails done and strolled into that hotel with a smile on my face and my head held high. It started as an amazing evening and it was wonderful to see so many of our authors receiving awards for their incredible sales and for their achievements. The champagne flowed and I was having fun. Until he walked in with a woman on his arm.'

'His wife?'

Mandy stared at her hands as they fidgeted in her lap, pulling the tissue apart.

'She was so beautiful. Slim and elegant with dark brown hair that fell to her shoulders and big brown eyes. She looked like she took really good care of herself, even with young children. I felt so bad, really guilty as they circulated and she hung on his every word, quite obviously adoring him.'

'It's often the way.'

'I was disgusted with myself and with him and I knew I couldn't stay and watch them, so I told my colleagues I had a migraine coming then I grabbed my things and headed for the door.'

Allie took Mandy's left hand and held it tight. The thought of her baby girl enduring such heartache and humiliation was unbearable and she wished she could go back in time and stop her daughter getting hurt. But that wasn't possible and Mandy had to live her life her way.

'I'd reached the door when I felt a hand on my shoulder. I turned around and found her… his wife… staring at me. She didn't look angry, just sad, and then she said… she said… 'Michael might play around away from home but you're not the first and you won't be the last.' She said that he loved her and the children and he loved her money. That he'd never leave her.'

'How did she knew about you?'

'Apparently he wasn't as good at covering his tracks as he thought. But it was weird because she was so cold, like a robot as she spoke. Almost as if she'd rehearsed the words or said them before.'

'Oh dear.'

'She also said that as long as I didn't force the issue with him, I was welcome to carry on seeing him. But there's no way I would after finding out he was married. What would that make me, Mum? I'm not a cheat and a bitch and I would never want to hurt another woman or her children.'

'I know, love, I know.'

'I told her I had no idea he was married and that if I had, I'd never have had anything to do with him. She just stared at me in that same detached away then told me she pitied me and walked away. Right into his arms. You know... the worst thing was that he watched her speaking to me from across the room, then when she rejoined him, he met my eyes and gave a small nod. As if he thought we would carry on now with his wife's approval. I ran outside and threw up all down the hotel steps then grabbed a taxi to the station.'

'What a complete shit!' Allie muttered.

Mandy gave a wry laugh.

'Yeah... but I guess I had a lucky escape. Imagine being with a man who loved your money more than you. I just feel sorry for her and their children.'

'Children grow up and where will they be then? That poor woman.'

'She knows what she's got though, doesn't she? I didn't know what I was getting into. I made a big mistake and it's one I certainly won't be repeating.'

'What about your job? I know how much you love it.'

'I don't have to see him very often and he was talking about a promotion to a different department anyway. He said he'd delayed it so he could still see me but I suspect he'll be keen to avoid me now.'

'Oh, sweetheart, I'm sorry you went through all that.'

'Life eh, Mum. And you know what... Speaking to you about it and being back in Heatherlea really helps.'

'Do you need to ring work to tell them you're sick?'

'Not today as it's a Bank Holiday but I'll ring in tomorrow and say I'll be back on Wednesday, perhaps even next week. I need to catch my breath and I'm owed some holiday.'

'You can stay here as long as you like.'

'Thanks, Mum.'

'Don't thank me. That's what I'm here for.'

As Allie hugged her daughter tight, she sent out a silent thank you that Mandy was a survivor, that she was strong enough to pull through this. Better now than later when she could have children of her own. Better that she could walk away from this man and his deceit and start again.

Chris appeared in the back doorway. 'Did you hear knocking? I think someone's at the front door.'

He pulled off his gardening gloves and strode through the kitchen and into the hallway. Allie and Mandy listened as he opened the door.

When he returned to the kitchen, Dawn and Camilla were with him.

'Hi ladies.' Allie stood up. 'To what do we owe this pleasure?'

They both looked at Mandy then back at Allie.

'What is it? You both look like you woke up to find someone stole the milk from your doorsteps.'

'Everything OK?' Dawn asked, as she nodded in Mandy's direction.

'I'm fine thank you, Dawn. Well, I will be anyway.' Mandy smiled.

'Ah... good. Glad to hear it. Could... uh... could Camilla and I have a word, Allie?'

'Of course. Do you want a cuppa?'

Camilla shook her head. 'No, thanks. Better to get this over and done with.'

Allie placed the kettle back on its stand and looked at her friends.

'You're scaring me now. What on earth is wrong?'

'It's... it's Ebony.'

'Ebony?'

'Yes...' Dawn released a long sigh then rubbed her cheeks. You see... this morning I... I found something terrible. And I'm so sorry to have to deliver this bad news now but...'

Dawn's jaw dropped and she stared at the open back door where the sunlight was warming the tiles of the kitchen floor.

'Oh. My. God!'

Chapter 13

Dawn

'I don't believe it.' Dawn's hand flew out and tapped Camilla's arm.
'Ouch! Careful, Dawn!'
'But it's...'
'I can bloody well see what it is. It's Ebony. And she's here.'
'Of course it's Ebony.' Allie frowned. 'Where else would she be?'
'At Tom's surgery...' Camilla offered, her raised eyebrows suggesting she didn't believe that for one minute.
'What would she be doing there?' Allie asked.
'Oh no!' Dawn covered her mouth. 'I've only gone and picked up someone else's cat.'
'Indeed you have.' Camilla folded her arms across her chest and shook her head. 'Why didn't you check properly?'
'Tom checked the cat over and he couldn't tell that it wasn't Ebony. Besides which, you saw the state it was in; there wasn't much to check. Although...' Dawn turned to her sister. 'It seems there was enough to make you vomit. I never thought of you as being squeamish.'
Allie was staring at them, her eyes wide, and Mandy was watching their exchange with a matching bemused expression.

'Camilla was sick when Tom got the cat out of the bag.'
'The bag?'
'Yes, see, I found a squashed cat this morning and I went to Honey's for a spade and a bag then I scooped it up and took it to the vet.'
'Why?' Allie was shaking her head.
'I thought it was Ebony and I didn't want you to see her like that.'
'Oh, Dawn, you softy.'
'She is a softy.' Camilla nodded.
'You could have called me, Dawn. I would've come to get her.' Chris went to the kettle and switched it on.
'I couldn't do that. You had Mandy here and I knew you'd be busy.'
'Well thank goodness it isn't Ebony.' Allie sighed. 'I don't think I could have coped with that on top of everything else.'
They all looked at the black cat currently lying on her side in the patch of sunlight, legs stretched out and tail gently flicking back and forth. As if on cue, Ebony started purring.
'Yes, thank goodness.' Dawn nodded.
'So whose cat is it?' Mandy asked.
'No idea but I'd better go back and let Tom know.' Camilla licked her lips. 'Could I have a glass of water first though, please? I have such a dry mouth this morning.'
'Of course.'
Allie filled a glass from the tap and handed it to Camilla.
'I'd better get going too. I left Alison with Honey.' Dawn pushed her hair back from her forehead.
'Why? Where's Rick?' Allie asked.
'It's a long story but basically he's still in bed, as are Laura and James. Anyway, I'll catch up with you later.'
Camilla handed Allie the empty glass then they walked to the front door and Allie waved them off.
'I can't believe that just happened.' Dawn tutted as they walked along the street.
'Me either. But you did the right thing.'

'I guess so. You go and tell Tom and I'll let Honey and Dane know about the mistaken identity of the black cat.'
'The cat you let out of the bag?'
'Ha! Ha!'
'OK, ring you later.'
'Bye!'
Dawn headed back towards Honey's cottage, feeling a lot lighter than she had done half an hour ago. So she'd cleaned up someone's dead cat but thankfully it wasn't Ebony. So much for good deeds.
Although it was very sad that a poor cat had suffered that awful fate. Still, it would make an interesting anecdote to share with Rick when she got home, that she went around picking up squashed cats.
The positive thing about the morning though, was that Mandy had looked all right when they'd walked into Allie's kitchen, so hopefully her situation wasn't as bad as it had seemed yesterday.
Things were looking up.
Weren't they?

Chapter 14

Camilla

Camilla was walking back to the surgery, running the events of that morning through her head, when she stopped suddenly. Dawn was right; she wasn't usually that squeamish. But something about the situation: the smell and the thought of what was in the bag and how upset Allie would be had combined to make her head spin, causing her to throw up.

She decided to take a quick detour and pop into her cottage, as she wanted to use some mouthwash and Tom hadn't had any at his cottage. She let herself in and closed the door behind her then went straight up the stairs to the bathroom. She filled the cap of the bottle with peppermint mouthwash then swilled it around her mouth before spitting it into the sink.

As she placed it back in the cabinet, something caught her eye. She reached for the small cardboard packet full of small blue pills and turned it over in her hands.

Then she did a quick calculation.

She'd been so busy lately with Tom, work and caught up with Dawn and her new baby, as well as her recently reunited parents, that she'd not been as careful with her contraceptive pill as she used to be. She'd

taken it at different times of the day, sometimes the following day if she'd stayed the night at Tom's and forgotten to take the pills with her, but she'd just assumed she'd be fine.
Hadn't she?
Or had she been deliberately lax?
She shook her head at her reflection. Camilla was sensible, reliable, a career woman.
Her reflection stared back at her: huge green eyes, porcelain skin and short dark hair. There was something different about her eyes, for sure. They'd always been large but now they seemed positively luminescent, even though, apart from that, she didn't look well; a bit peaky, as her mum would say.
She couldn't be... could she?
There was that one night when she was at the end of her packet and she'd left it at home, and the next day, she thought it wouldn't matter as it was the end of the three weeks and she was due her pill-free week. She needed to speak to Dawn, see what her sister thought of the situation. Dawn had experience in these matters, having been pregnant three times, the third pregnancy being an accident, if a very happy one. If Camilla was pregnant, then what a pair of sisters they were, getting caught out and at their ages!
She shrugged. What would be would be. And it was highly likely that this was all in her mind and her period would arrive tomorrow. She padded down the stairs and back out into the sunlight then made her way to Dawn's. When she got there she knocked gently on the door. No answer.
Wasn't Dawn back yet then? She had needed to collect Alison from Honey's, so perhaps she'd stopped for a cuppa.
She heard a noise inside then Rick appeared at the door in a pair of blue and grey striped pyjama bottoms with a white T-shirt on top. He frowned at her then ran a hand over his face.
'Morning, Camilla. I don't suppose you've seen my wife, have you?'
'I have actually. Can I come in.'
'Of course.' He stepped back. 'Is she all right?'

'She's fine.'
'OK... Cup of tea?'
'Please.'
She followed him through to the kitchen and took a chair at the kitchen table while he filled the kettle and switched it on.
'Dawn went out for walk earlier with Alison. She said she didn't want to wake you and hoped the fresh air might help the baby sleep this morning.'
'Ah... thought it might be something like that.' Rick nodded. 'Where is she now though and how did you bump into her? You doing the walk of shame or something?'
'What?'
'You know; sneaking home early in the morning in the clothes you wore the night before.'
'Ha! No, not at all. Dawn came to Tom's because she'd found a dead cat and thought it was Ebony.'
'Allie's cat?'
'Yes.'
'Was it?'
'No, thank goodness. Allie would have been devastated. We went to tell Allie that we thought it was Ebony and the cat was sunning herself in the kitchen.'
'So Tom now has a dead cat and you don't know whose it is?'
Camilla nodded, swallowing hard as that strange feeling crawled over her again at the thought of that poor squashed creature.
'Fancy a bacon sandwich?' Rick asked.
Camilla shook her head. 'No. No thanks. Got to... use the bathroom.'
'The downstairs loo's not working. James broke the flush. Better go upstairs!'
She rushed to the stairs, hurried up them then locked herself in the cool white space that smelt of lemons and toothpaste. She knelt in front of the toilet and took some slow breaths until the churning stopped then she sat back on her haunches and looked around. Her sister's bathroom was a perfect family space with its clean white bath-

room suite and large walk-in shower cubicle. Along the side of the bath, Laura and James's toys were lined up, from toy dinosaurs to a Barbie wearing a bright pink swimming costume. Along the windowsill were bottles of baby shampoo, bubble bath and conditioner. The lemon aroma was the result of the bathroom cleaner that sat high up on top of the cabinet, out of the children's reach. Camilla wondered what she would be like as a mother, if it ever happened for her. She'd tried to imagine it in the past but it just wasn't a role she could picture herself in easily. She'd probably forget to put the bleach and spray up out of reach or use normal shampoo on the baby and make its eyes sting. Some women, like Dawn, were natural mothers but Camilla hadn't experienced that powerful maternal instinct and didn't think she'd know what to do.
And what on earth would Tom think?
She shuddered, then stood up and opened the bathroom cabinet, hoping she'd find some paracetamol as her head had started to throb. She moved a few things and came across a long thin white box with blue writing. She pulled it out and read the side then she shook her head. There was no need for that. Overreaction or what? But her hand just wouldn't let go of the box, so in the end she closed the cupboard and leant against the sink, staring at the blue writing as if it could tell her what to do for the best.
This would clear things up, wouldn't it? If she used one of these, she'd know one way or the other for sure. She was about to open the box when there was a frantic hammering at the door.
'Mummy? Is that you?'
'No, it's me.'
'Auntie Camilla?'
'Yes.'
'Oh. What're you doing here?'
'I came to visit.' Camilla stuffed the box into the back of the waistband of her jeans then tucked her shirt over it.
'Where's Mummy?'
'Gone for a walk. She won't be long.'

'Auntie Camilla?'
'Yes?'
'Can I use the toilet? I'm bursting.'
'Oh! Of course.'
Camilla opened the door and smiled at her pretty niece, but the smell of bacon cooking hit her full force so she turned on her heel and rushed to the toilet, emptying her stomach for the second time that morning.

Chapter 15
Honey

'It's not funny you two.' Dane frowned at Honey and Dawn as they giggled together at the kitchen table. Dawn had arrived just after Honey had succeeded in rescuing Dane from Henifer Aniston. He'd been visibly shaken at his encounter with the bossy hen.
'Oh Dane but it was very amusing. You have to see the funny side of it.' Honey wiped her eyes on her sleeve then sipped her tea.
'For you maybe but you didn't have your legs and toes pecked.'
'He really is henpecked and he's only just moved in.' Dawn snorted and Honey joined her in a fresh fit of giggles.
'Well I think it's roast chicken for dinner.' Dane folded his arms across his broad chest.
'Don't you dare. None of my hens are ever going to end up on a plate.' Honey nudged him. 'They're my girls and anyway, you wait and see. They'll come round and warm to you.'
'When he comes out of his shell a bit.' Dawn's eyes widened at her own joke.
'And conquers his fear of the poultrygeist.'
'Right that's it! I'm going to make some more tea.' Dane stood up then picked up their mugs. 'Actually... I've just thought of one.'

'Go on then...' Honey watched him. 'If you're up to it after your hen-counter.'

Dane's lips twitched. 'Right, here goes... How do baby chickens dance?'

Honey and Dawn shook their heads.

'Chick-to-chick.' He smiled. 'Actually, Honey, after that attack, I think I need you to do a thorough eggsamination of me.'

Dawn and Honey laughed until Honey's sides ached.

A murmur from the pram at Dawn's side made her peer into the pram.

'Ah, I'd better get going. I didn't mean to stay this long anyway and Rick's probably up by now.'

'I'll see you out.'

Honey walked Dawn and Alison to the door.

'Hope she sleeps for you today.'

'Yeah, me too. Still, at least Rick's had a lie-in, so he'll be there if I need to grab a nap.'

'I still can't believe you went to all that trouble only to find it wasn't even Ebony.'

'I know, but I couldn't leave the cat there, could I?'

Honey shook her head. 'At least it wasn't Ebony.'

'There is that.'

'What will Tom do with the cat now?'

'Probably cremation, I suppose. If no one claims it. It could well be feral.'

Honey shivered. 'Poor thing.'

'I know.'

'Anyway, thanks for watching Alison.'

'It was a pleasure. She's beautiful.'

Honey closed the door then went back through to the kitchen. Dane was standing at the backdoor peering out into the garden.

'You OK?' She slid her arms around his waist and buried her face in his back, breathing in his wonderful scent and enjoying the feel of his hard body against hers.

Rachel Griffiths

'Yeah. As long as you don't think I'm a wimp for being bullied by your chicken.'

He turned in her arms and hugged her back.

'I think you're amazing, Dane.'

His eyes lit up as he smiled at her. 'Well that feeling is mutual.'

'Do you fancy getting out for a bit? Perhaps go to the café?'

'Sure, why not? But first I need that eggsamination you promised me.'

'I promised you one did I?'

He nodded, then pulled her closer.

Chapter 16

Allie

'Right, love, why don't you take a long hot bath?' Allie had loaded the dishwasher and she switched it on. 'Everything's done here and you look like you need to relax.'
'That sounds like a wonderful idea, Mum. What about you? Do you and Chris have plans today?'
'I think Chris wanted to spend some time sorting the garden out but I said I'll spend a few hours at the café. Jordan's opening up but I'd better be there to help him in case we have a lunchtime rush.'
'On a Bank Holiday?'
Allie nodded. 'Might get some people passing through as well as the local regulars. The café has been doing really well.'
'I'm so happy for you, Mum. You know... with how things have worked out with the café and with Chris. He's a keeper.'
'I heard that!' Chris called from outside.
'It was all good.'
'Thank you!'
Allie smiled. To have her daughter and Chris in the same house on a sunny morning was wonderful. It had been a long time since Mandy had been in Heatherlea and Allie hoped that she might stay for a bit.

She wanted Mandy to go back to her London and to her career, of course, but not just yet.

'I think I will take that bath.'

'There's some jasmine bubble bath in the cupboard and it smells divine. Help yourself.'

'Thanks, Mum.'

Allie hugged her daughter tight, hoping that Mandy knew how special she was and that one idiotic man wouldn't taint her views of herself and of love. Allie knew how it was to have a man break her heart, but then Chris had come along and helped her to heal. She hoped Mandy would heal too and one day, perhaps learn to trust again.

Chapter 17

Dawn

Dawn reached the end of her street again and slowed down. It had been a busy morning and had certainly turned out differently than she could have imagined. She'd thought to have a nice walk then get back to bed, even to the sofa and grab more sleep, but fate had apparently had other plans for her.
Fate? She shook her head. Sometimes she thought it was fate, sometimes she believed she made her own luck. But that poor cat had certainly not seen the car that had squished it coming.
She swerved to avoid the dark patch where the cat had been, and paused.
What was that sound?
Meowing? Faint but there nonetheless.
She looked around. Nothing on the road or the street. She pushed the brake on the pram down then walked towards the long grass just off the pavement. She moved it aside and peered under the hedge. And her heart broke, because there, in what looked like some kind of nest, were two small kittens.
The mewled pitifully, sending Dawn's maternal instincts soaring.
The cat she'd found must have been their mother and they'd lost her.

How would they manage? They probably wouldn't. They were moving around but they looked so small and lost. They wanted their mum.

Dawn knew she couldn't leave them there, so she leant forwards and gently picked them both up. They cried out so she tucked them into her loose T-shirt, making a kind of hammock out of the front, then she kicked off the brake on the pram and slowly walked towards home, pushing the pram with one hand with cradling the kittens with the other.

Goodness only knew what Rick would say when he found out what she'd been up to that morning, but some days were like this. Unpredictable. Unexpected. And as far as Dawn was concerned, she had been in the right place at the right time as far as the kittens were concerned.

Outside the front door she pushed down the brake on the pram again then knocked gently, not wanting to have to try to search in her bag for her key.

The door opened and Rick smiled at her. 'Morning walkies, eh? You should have woken me.'

'You were out cold and I wanted you to get more sleep.'

'Well come on in and you can grab a nap while I give the children breakfast.'

'Ok. But, Rick...'

He was already lifting the pram over the front doorstep.

'Yeah?'

'I... I have something to tell you.'

'It's OK,' he said from inside, 'Camilla told me about the cat. Trust you to feel the need to move it.'

'I couldn't exactly leave it there, could I? And how did Camilla tell you?'

'I'm here, Dawnie.'

Camilla came down the stairs just as Dawn stepped inside.

'Oh, hi. What're you? Why did you...'

'I came to ask you something but you weren't back so Rick made me tea.'

'I also offered her breakfast but apparently the thought of my cooking made her sick.'

'You were sick again?' Dawn winced. 'I hope it's not a bug.'

'Yeah, me too.' Camilla's eyes widened and she shook her head a fraction, just enough to let Dawn know that she had something she wanted to speak to her about. 'Why's your T-shirt moving?' Camilla gestured at Dawn's belly.

'That's what I was trying to explain to Rick. On my way back, I heard a noise in the bushes and found these two.' She opened her T-shirt to show her husband and Camilla.

'Oh my goodness!' Camilla lifted one of the tiny kittens and held it to her chest. 'How sweet.'

'You found them where?' Rick asked.

'Under the hedge at the end of the street.'

'Probably feral and crawling with fleas then.' Rick grimaced and Camilla immediately held the kitten away from her body.

'Maybe but I couldn't leave them there. And what if they're not wild and the mother was somebody's pet that went missing?' Dawn asked.

'We'd better take them to Tom so he can check them over,' Rick said.

'They look about seven weeks old, possibly eight.'

'So that means they still need milk, doesn't it?' Dawn smoothed the soft gently domed head of the kitten she was holding.

'I'm no cat expert but possibly.' Rick scratched his head. 'Let me grab a box from the garage for them and we can give Tom a ring.'

Ten minutes later, the kittens were sleeping, curled up together on a soft wool blanket that Rick had tucked into the box. They'd seemed exhausted and she wondered if they'd been up all night waiting for their mother. Rick had taken them through to the kitchen and put the box in the corner away from drafts. Thankfully, they hadn't seemed to have fleas when Rick had checked them over but she knew Tom would need to see them to give them a proper examination.

'Don't disturb them, mind.' Dawn whispered to Laura and James as they sat in front of the box watching the kittens. Her children had come downstairs to find their mother and auntie cradling the orphaned kittens and immediately asked if they could keep them. Rick had stepped in to say that they were too young to be pets yet and that they weren't to get attached. As if that was going to happen. Dawn was already smitten herself, imagining that the two cats would make a lovely addition to their family. After all, they had the guinea pig family out in the garden, so why not adopt two family cats as well?

'I'll take them back to the surgery, shall I, and see what Tom thinks?' Camilla asked as she peered over Laura and James's heads at the kittens.

'I'll come with you.' Dawn nodded, deciding that she'd just as well be there for that too. 'I need to feed Alison first though.'

'No problem.'

'Dawn, I'll take them and you can stay here and rest,' Rick said.

'Really?' Dawn looked at their three children in turn. 'I would but I'm not sure I'll be able to relax until I know that the kittens are OK. It's so sad that they were orphaned like that.'

Camilla nodded then a sob escaped her and she buried her face in her hands.

'Camilla?' Dawn reached out and squeezed her sister's shoulder. It wasn't like Camilla to show emotion. She'd been a bit softer since she'd got together with Tom, for certain, but bursting into tears?

'It's just... they lost their mum.'

'I know...' Dawn rubbed Camilla's shoulder and made a face at Rick. 'We'll look after them, don't you worry.'

Camilla nodded. 'Sorry. I don't know what's got into me.' She met Dawn's eyes and her cheeks flushed.

Dawn felt her mouth drop open as realisation washed over her.

Pale.

Vomiting.

Emotional.

Oh Camilla...

Chapter 18

Camilla

Camilla and Dawn had taken the kittens to the surgery and Tom had checked them over then declared that they seemed fit and well. He'd said he could keep them in for a few days for observation, as they were still a bit young to be away from their mother, and that he had some weaning milk he could make up for them, as well as some kitten food. Camilla had then made her excuses to leave with Dawn, stating that they'd agreed to meet Allie at the café for an hour but she'd promised not to be long.

Truth be told, she needed to be away from Tom while she did what she needed to do. The small box with the blue writing was still tucked into her waistband and she pressed a hand to it, feeling its reassuring presence.

'Camilla, do you want to talk about it?'

'About what?'

Dawn put a hand in front of Camilla to stop her, then glanced around them but the tree-lined street was quiet.

'About the way you've been feeling. The nausea. The emotional reactions that are not exactly characteristic of you, no offence, sis.'

Camilla met her sister's green eyes and the emotion Dawn had referred to surged within her again.
'Not really.' She bit the inside of her cheek. 'I can't.'
Dawn squeezed her shoulder. 'You can, you know? I love you and I'm here for you.'
Camilla nodded and Dawn pulled her into a hug. She rocked her gently, as she would one of her children and Camilla had to take slow deep breaths to stop herself from crying. Dawn rubbed her back then paused and Camilla realised that her sister had brushed her hand over the box stuffed into the back of her jeans.
'Camilla?'
'Yes?'
'Are you wearing a wire?'
'What?' In spite of her distress, Camilla snorted at the question.
Dawn leant back and smiled at her. 'You know, like on reality TV shows where they have the electronic pack or whatever it is stuffed into their trousers or the back of their dress.'
'It's not a wire and we're not on TV.'
'Thank goodness for that!' Dawn laughed.
Camilla reached under her shirt and pulled out the box, then watched as understanding filled Dawn's face.
'I took it from your bathroom. I was looking for tablets for my headache and I saw this and thought it might be a good idea to try it. Or to do it, or whatever...'
'So you do think you could be...' Dawn let the unfinished question hang in the air.
'I'm not sure. I mean... it's a long shot but I don't feel right and if it's not that then it could be something else.'
'Like what?' Dawn frowned.
'I don't know. Like early menopause or... cancer or some other horrid illness I suppose.'
Dawn shook her head. 'I know you and I've been in your shoes, just about, and I'm pretty certain that you're pregnant.'

'Oh god!' Camilla gasped. 'Don't say that! Don't say those words! I'm not ready for this. I don't think I ever will be.'
'Look, there's no point stressing about it until you know for sure. Worst case scenario, it's some sort of bug that will pass in a few days.'
'That's the worst-case scenario? What's the best case?'
'I'm going to be an auntie!' Dawn hugged her tight and Camilla exhaled shakily. 'This is a good thing, sweetheart. Try not to worry. Now let's go get a drink at the café and you can pee on that stick.'
'OK. Not words I expected to hear today, but I'll try to go with the flow.'
'The flow!' Dawn giggled. 'Yes you need to pop the test stick under the flow. Sorry. This is a serious matter.'
'Indeed it is. But I don't know whether to laugh or cry.'
Camilla let Dawn take her hand and lead her towards her destiny. Whatever that might be…

Chapter 19

Honey

'MMM. This is so good.' Honey took another bite of the fresh buttery croissant and chewed. Neither of them had fancied eggs following Henifer Aniston's attack.

'We worked up quite an appetite didn't we?' Dane grinned at her across the table that was next to the front window of The Cosy Cottage Café.

'We certainly did, you especially what with all that running away from Henifer Aniston.'

Dane shook his head. 'That wasn't what I meant.'

'I know. I'm teasing you.' Honey reached out and stroked his hand where it rested on the table next to his mug of coffee.

'I'm actually quite upset that she doesn't seem to like me.' Dane licked a finger then dabbed at some croissant crumbs on his plate and put them into his mouth. 'I mean... how are we going to manage if I can't help with the chickens?'

'We'll manage, Dane. I've been taking care of them alone for some time.'

Dane frowned.

'What is it?'

'I don't want you doing everything alone, Honey. We're partners and I want us to share the responsibility of running the home and looking after the animals.'

Honey slid her hand into his. He really was a good man and she felt very lucky to have him in her life.

'I'm sure we'll work it out. Perhaps once Henifer gets to know you, she'll be less… aggressive.'

'I hope so.'

Dane raised her hand and kissed it.

'Breakfast all right?' Allie asked as she appeared at their table.

'Lovely, thanks. The croissants were perfect.'

Allie smiled. 'Good. At least I got something right.'

'What do you mean?' Honey asked.

Allie looked around at the other customers in the café then pulled out a chair and sat down.

'I've tried to help Mandy since she came home in that awful state but I can't help feeling as though I failed her in some way.'

'You haven't failed her.' Honey looked at Allie's hands where they sat on the table, wringing a tea towel between them. 'You're a great mum.'

Allie grimaced. 'I wonder if I am though. Didn't I make her strong enough to deal with whatever life might throw at her? Could I have made her more resilient and less inclined to fall for someone who would shred her confidence? It could be that I didn't compensate for Roger's death enough and that left her needing something, craving something from a man that made her vulnerable.'

Honey shook her head. Allie had briefly filled them in on Mandy's situation when they'd arrived at the café. 'Allie, Roger's death was not your fault and you have done everything you could to show your children that they are loved and supported. Look at how happy Jordan is. Mandy is just going through what many people do. Lots of us have our hearts broken along the way.'

'I know that's true.' Allie smiled. 'It's hard being a mum. I just want to wrap them up in a soft blanket like I did when they were babies and protect them from the world.'

'Well you can't do that,' Dane said. 'But you are there for them and your love and support is more than a lot of children get from their parents, believe me.'

'He's right, Allie. You can't protect them from life but you can be there to help ease them over the hurdles.'

'Thank you.' Allie stood up. 'You're both very kind. More coffee?'

'That would be lovely.'

Chapter 20

Allie

Allie was trying to focus on making coffees for Honey and Dane but her thoughts were firmly planted at home with her daughter. Mandy would come through this and hopefully go on to have a great life but if Allie had been able to have her way, she'd protect Mandy from any upset at all. That was the difficult thing with parenting; your children grew up and you couldn't protect them from life and love; you had to let them make their own mistakes.

After all, hadn't her own parents worried about her over the years? Her mother had told her that they'd had to bite their tongues hundreds of times to avoid interfering in Allie's life. But when they'd felt compelled to try to advise her, Allie had often brushed their concerns away, convinced that she was following the right path. It was surely natural to rebel against whatever your parents thought was for the best...

She picked up the coffees and was about to take them over to Honey and Dane when the door opened and Dawn and Camilla entered. The sisters were so alike that it sometimes made her do a double take. With their dark hair, pale skin and those clear green eyes, they were like Elizabeth Taylor in her heyday.

'Hi Allie!' Dawn waved but Camilla scanned the café before following her sister over to the counter.

'Hello both. How are you now?'

'Good thanks.' Dawn smiled. 'What about you?'

Allie gave a small shrug. 'We just have to get on with things, don't we? I keep telling myself that Mandy will be fine and hoping I'm right.'

Concern flashed through her when she looked closely at Camilla. Her skin was so pale it was almost translucent.

'Are you all right, Camilla?'

'What? Oh... yes, I'm fine. I just need the loo.'

'You know where it is!' Allie used the well-worn phrase but Camilla just blinked.

'Yes. OK. Uh... I'm going to go to the loo now.'

Dawn rubbed her shoulder. 'You want me to come with you?'

Allie put the coffees back down on the counter. Since when did Camilla need her sister to take her to the toilet?

'No, thanks. It's fine. It'll all be fine.' Camilla nodded then headed for the door that led to the café toilets.

'Is she OK?' Allie asked Dawn.

'Yeah... she's fine. How many times have we all used that word this morning?' She shook her head. 'Camilla is just a bit tired I think.'

Dawn's cheeks coloured and Allie wondered what was going on. If the sisters had a secret then that was fine, but they were both acting strangely and she felt sure there must be more to it than the whole dead cat debacle of that morning.

'Do you want a coffee?' Allie asked.

'Better not as I'm breastfeeding, and I don't want to mess with Alison's sleep via a milky caffeine infusion if I can help it. I'll have a glass of something cold, though, please.'

'What about Camilla? Shall I make her a drink?'

'Uh... yes please, she'll have a cold drink too.'

'Any preference?'

'Surprise us. Shall I take those to the customers?'

'They're for Honey and Dane.'
'OK, I'll pop them over then come back for ours.'
'Thanks.'
Allie went through to the kitchen and opened the large fridge then brought out a bottle of sparkling elderflower juice. She'd make the sisters a refreshing mocktail and hopefully find out what was going on with them, but only if they wanted her to know.

Chapter 21

Dawn

'There you are. Two coffees.'
Dawn set the mugs down on the table in front of Dane and Honey.
'Thanks, Dawn. How are you feeling after your busy morning?'
'Ah you know... Relieved that Ebony was fine but a bit sad that those kittens ended up without their mum.' Dawn had sent a text to Honey to tell her about the kittens, hoping it was something positive to come out of the sad situation with the squashed cat.
'Yes so sad.' Honey shook her head. 'Hope they find homes.'
'I'm sure they will. They are so cute! Tom's keeping them in for a while but once he's run some blood tests and fed them up a bit, they'll be looking for homes.' Dawn grinned. 'I'm hoping Rick will let me keep them to be honest. I don't want to split them up and they're just adorable. The children would love them.'
'Well if Rick doesn't agree, let us know and I'm sure we can come up with a plan.' Dane smiled as he took Honey's hand.
'Oh we can, can we?' Honey tilted her head. 'And what will that be?'
'I've always wanted to have a cat.'
'Really?'

He nodded. 'But if Dawn takes the kittens on, then perhaps we should visit a rehoming centre.'
'That sounds like a rather big commitment to me, Mr Ackerman.' Honey waggled her eyebrows.
'I'm up for that.'
Honey blushed with pleasure then met Dawn's eyes and smiled.
'I'll keep you posted on them.' Dawn glanced over at the counter. 'I think our drinks are ready.'
'Come join us if you want?' Honey patted the chair next to her.
'What and cramp your style? Ruin your romantic brunch, or is it lunch now... for two?'
'It's fine, really.' Dane gestured at the empty chairs. 'Please join us.'
'Back in a bit then.'
Dawn went over to the counter and accepted the drinks from Allie.
'Ooh! These look nice. What are they?'
'Mocktails. Sparkling elderflower, lemon juice and some fresh mint. Nice and refreshing.'
'Sounds yummy.'
'Is Camilla still in the toilet?'
Dawn nodded.
'She must have quite an upset stomach...'
Dawn frowned. 'I'd better go and check on her.'
She walked towards the toilets but when she reached the door, it opened and Camilla came out. Her skin was waxy and dark shadows sat beneath her eyes like bruises. She stopped when she saw Dawn and her bottom lip wobbled.
'Oh god... try to be strong, sweetheart.' Dawn muttered under her breath. She took hold of Camilla's hand and led her to the counter. 'Look at these lovely drinks Allie made for us. Shall we go and sit down and enjoy them?' She was aware that her voice sounded too bright, that her smile was too wide.
'OK.'
Just then, the door opened and Tom entered, turning to close the door

behind him. Camilla gasped then shot behind the counter and through the door that led to the kitchen, while Allie and Dawn stared at each other, their mouths gaping and their eyes wide.

Dawn knew what must be wrong but Allie didn't, so Camilla's behaviour must seem very strange to their friend.

Chapter 22

Camilla

In the kitchen, Camilla scanned the room for somewhere to hide the white stick that she'd tucked into the waistband of her jeans. She'd followed the directions and peed on the stick then been unable to look at it. She couldn't deal with this now, so she'd have to find out what the result was later. Although the directions said that you had to read the results as soon as possible for accuracy.
Accuracy…
Damn that word. As an accountant she usually loved accuracy but today she felt differently. If she'd been accurate with taking her pill and so on, then she wouldn't even be worried at all now.
She pulled the stick out of her waistband and held it out.
Her hand was shaking.
Turning the stick over slowly, she brought it closer to her face.
She took a deep breath.
Here goes…
'Oh…' She stared at the two blue lines sitting side by side. 'Oh… dear.'
Her legs were trembling so badly, she thought she'd keel over if she didn't take a seat soon. But she also couldn't take the stick with her so she needed somewhere to leave it.

Voices in the café carried through and she recognised Tom's.
What if he came looking for her? She scanned the kitchen and her gaze fell on Allie's bag tucked under the island in one of the baskets. That would do for now! She dropped the test into it and tucked it back in the basket. She'd explain to Allie when she got five minutes, but for now she'd better go back out and act normal. Well, as normal as she could do knowing that Tom's baby was growing in her womb.
Baby?
Womb?
GAAAAHHHH!
What would he think? Would he hate her and blame her for getting pregnant? Would he be horrified? Shocked? Was there a chance that he'd be happy about it all?
Nausea swirled in her belly and she took a few slow deep breaths. She could remember hearing that morning sickness was a sign of a strong pregnancy, but the idea of feeling like this for any length of time scared her. She could barely think straight let alone carry on as normal. But she'd have to until she decided what to do or Tom would know something was up.
She pinched her cheeks, licked her lips then pushed her shoulders back and headed for the door. She was a strong and confident woman and she'd dealt with plenty of difficult situations over the years.
She could deal with this.
Of course she could.
Couldn't she?

Chapter 23

Honey

Over Dane's shoulder, Honey had seen Camilla shoot into the kitchen when Tom entered the café, as well as Dawn and Allie's bewildered faces. There was definitely something strange going on and she wanted to find out what it was to see if she could help. However, just as she was about to excuse herself and go to the counter, Camilla emerged from the kitchen.

Camilla smiled briefly at Tom and he nodded, then they walked over and joined Honey and Dane at the table.

'Are we crashing your romantic meal?' Tom asked, looking a bit sheepish.

'No, not at all. We said you should join us.'

'How are the kittens?' Dawn asked as she joined them too.

'Snuggled up in one of the crates in the surgery. They took a feed, along with some kitten formula, then I settled them in one of the warmest crates along with a big fluffy blanket. They'll be fine now but it's a good job you found them.'

'I can't bear to think of them being out there all alone all night.'

'Well perhaps it wasn't all night. It might only have been a few hours,' Tom suggested.

'I hope it wasn't long but even so, what if they came out and saw their mum?' Dawn grimaced.
'They'll be fine.' Tom nodded. 'Absolutely fine.'
'I'm going to encourage Rick to adopt them. I don't know if it's my hormones with Alison being so young but I feel the need to look out for the kittens too.'
'You'll be a fabulous cat mum.' Tom smiled. 'Camilla? Are you all right, angel?'
All heads turned to Camilla who was chewing at a nail and staring out the window.
'Sorry?'
'I asked if you're OK.'
'Yes. I am, thanks. Just a bit tired.'
Honey took in how pale Camilla was, how tired she seemed, and how she also looked as though she'd been crying. She hoped everything was all right between Camilla and Tom. It would be dreadful to see them split up now.
Allie came over to the table with a tray of cold drinks. 'Everything all right? I brought some more mocktails and Jordan is going to take over so I can have a break. After last night's emotional rollercoaster, I'm exhausted.'
Allie pulled a chair over from the closest table and sat down.
She looked from face to face then frowned.
'What's up? You all look troubled.'
'Do you know what?' Honey decided to try to change the subject.
'I've been thinking about adding a wedding range to Purple Hen designs. It's an area of the market I haven't tapped into yet and I'm sure there are some products I could create that would appeal to bridal parties.'
Camilla flashed her a grateful look and Honey winked.
'That's a fabulous idea.' Allie nodded. 'You could make wedding favours, wedding gifts and table decorations and... ooh, all sorts!'
'We can come up with some ideas together.' Dane smiled. 'I'd love to help you.'

'Thank you.' Honey touched his hand. 'But you'll have too much marking and planning to do, Mr Ackerman.'

Dane rolled his eyes and sighed dramatically. 'Don't remind me. But I will help as much as I can during the holidays.'

'Did I hear something about weddings?'

'Chris!' Allie stood up. 'I didn't see you come in.'

'I know, you were gazing intently at Camilla.'

'Was I?'

Chris nodded.

'Take my chair and I'll get you a drink.'

'No you won't. I'm sure you've been on your feet since you got here. Anyway, I'm not stopping, I just came for the car keys.'

'Why where are you going?'

'I have some errands to run.' Chris waved a hand dismissively. 'Just need to get some more printer paper and a few other bits.'

'OK, love. The keys are in my bag in the kitchen.'

'Great.'

Chris went through to the kitchen and Camilla's eyes widened.

'What is it?' Honey asked, reaching under the table to take her hand. 'You look like you've seen a ghost.'

'No... it's not that... I... I think I left the iron on at your house, Tom.'

Tom frowned. 'Did you even use the iron this morning?'

'I did. I'm sure I did.' Camilla covered her mouth with her hand. 'Yes... oh, now I'm not sure but I won't be able to rest until I check. I'd better go.' She stood up then glanced at the door to the kitchen. 'Now!'

'I'll come with you, Camilla.' Tom drained his glass then stood up. 'Thanks for the drinks, Allie. See you all later.' He flashed a smile but it was obvious that he was worried by Camilla's odd behaviour.

As they left the café, Chris emerged from the kitchen, and now it was his face that had turned pale.

Chapter 24

Allie

Allie shared frowns and shrugs with Dawn, Honey and Tom. It was turning out to be one of the strangest days she'd experienced in a long time and Camilla's behaviour was quite troubling.

'I've got the keys.' Chris appeared at her side. His voice sounded different, quieter and strained, as if he was speaking over the phone on a bad connection. He stood there, his one hand dangling the keys and his other hand clenching and unclenching.

'What's up?' Allie tapped his hand. 'Have you got cramp?'

'No.' He shook his head then took a deep breath. 'No, I'm great. Everything's... great.'

'Okaaaay...' Allie stood up then walked him to the door. 'Are you sure you're all right?'

'Yeah.' He rubbed his hands over his face then through his hair. 'Allie, you would tell me if you were worried about something wouldn't you?'

'What like about Mandy?'

'Yes. But... I meant if there was anything else you'd found out and you wanted to tell me but were a bit worried about how I'd react.'

Allie blinked. What on earth was he talking about?

'Of course.'
Chris cupped her chin in his hands and gently stroked her cheeks. 'You don't need to keep anything from me, you know? I'm with you in all of this and I love you. Anything that ...arises... we can deal with it together.'
'I know.' She closed her eyes as he kissed her.
'I won't be long but if you need me, call me. I'll keep an eye on my mobile. Perhaps we can have a good chat later on?'
'Yep, no problem.'
He opened the door and Allie watched him until he was out on the road.
It really was a very strange day indeed, almost as if aliens had come to earth and taken over the bodies of her friends and loved ones.

'Hello?' Allie called as she entered the cottage and closed the door behind her. 'Chris?'
There was no answer, so she swapped her shoes for her slippers in the hallway then padded through to the kitchen. Mandy was at the table drinking coffee and flicking through a magazine.
'Hiya, love, how are you feeling?'
Allie was glad to see that Mandy had dressed and even had a pair of Allie's trainers on.
'I'm OK, thanks, Mum. Tired but more with it than I was this morning.'
'I'm so happy to hear that. Are you hungry?'
'Not really but I'm going to have pizza with Jordan and Max this evening and watch a movie.'
'Oh!' Allie went to the fridge and looked inside, keen to hide her delight. 'That's nice.'
'You don't mind, do you?'

Allie closed the fridge. 'Why would I mind?'
'Well, I know you like having me home.'
'Oh, love, I do but that's not to say you can't go and spend the evening with your brother. It will do you good. Jordan and Max are fabulous company.'
Mandy nodded.
'I don't suppose I could... uh...'
'You need some cash?'
'This is so embarrassing but I don't have any money left in my purse and there's no cashpoint in the village.'
'It's no problem.' Allie went through to the hall and located her bag then pulled some notes from her purse. Back in the kitchen, she handed them to her daughter. 'Just have fun.'
'I feel like a teenager again.' Mandy chewed her bottom lip.
'Come here my little girl.' Allie hugged Mandy tight, stroking her soft blonde hair and breathing in her sweet floral scent. She'd do anything for her children and even though they were both in their twenties, they'd always be her babies. 'Now go have some fun.'
'Jordan said that if it's late, I can stay over to save walking back.'
'Just text me so I know what you're doing.'
Mandy nodded. 'Will do.'
Mandy left the kitchen and Allie leant against the unit, listening to the familiar sounds of the cottage, from the clock in the hallway to the floorboards upstairs as they settled, and the swishing of the trees outside the kitchen window as the evening breeze picked up. Her whole body ached and the idea of sinking into a hot bath was very appealing. But first she wanted to know where Chris was.
She checked her mobile but he hadn't sent any texts or tried to ring so she went to her favourites and pressed call.
'Hello?'
'Chris? Where are you?'
'Just pulled up outside. Be right in.'
Allie ended the call and placed her mobile on the worktop. She heard

the front door open and Chris walked in carrying several bags of shopping and a box of printer paper.

'You went food shopping?'

'Yeah... thought we needed a few bits and bobs.'

'Lovely.'

He put the bags on the worktop then shrugged out of his jacket.

'Is that why you were gone for so long?'

Allie did trust Chris but old fears and doubts from her past made her wary, even when she thought she'd managed to push them aside. Chris did everything he could to make her feel loved, but her first husband, Roger, had done a lot of damage, and she wondered sometimes if she'd ever fully escape his shadow, and what it would take to feel fully confident about her relationship.

Chris came to her and slid his strong arms around her waist. She rested her head against his chest and listened to his strong regular heartbeat. She loved him so much and losing him would break her.

'Allie?'

She looked up and met his brown eyes. They searched her face and he opened his mouth as if to speak, then he sighed instead.

'Why don't you go and have a nice bath and I'll make us some dinner?'

'That's an offer I can't refuse.'

'Good.' He smiled but there was something in his eyes that made her heart flutter; he was worried about something. 'Just... don't have the water too hot.'

As she accepted a long kiss then slipped from his embrace, she couldn't help but wonder what was on his mind. And since when had he ever worried about the temperature of her bath water?

The delicious aromas of steak, mushrooms and garlic, sizzling in the frying pan met Allie as she entered the kitchen. The table in the corner was laid with pretty vintage style flower-patterned napkins, stainless steel cutlery and crystal wine glasses. A thick ivory candle burned in the centre, its light casting a warm glow on the ceiling above the table.
'Wow! What did I do to deserve this?' Allie went to Chris and hugged him from behind. He squeezed her hands then turned in her embrace.
'You're a very special lady and I love you. Do I need another reason to make you dinner?'
'Well... no. But this is just lovely.'
It wasn't the first time Chris had made her dinner but usually she knew about it in advance, as they discussed their dinner plans and did the weekly food shop together.
'I think the steaks are ready, Allie.'
Chris kissed her head then turned back to the frying pan. Allie went to the table and sat down, noting the olive-wood salad bowl full of dark green spinach, juicy red vine tomatoes, fat green olives and thick slices of cucumber.
Chris set the steaks and mushrooms on two plates and brought them to the table then he went to the fridge and brought out a bottle. When he placed it in front of her, Allie read the label, expecting a Pinot Grigio or a Sauvignon Blanc. She wasn't sure why he'd gone for white, as they had plenty of reds in the wine wrack that would go well with steak, but the label told her it was non-alcoholic wine.
'Are we cutting down?' She pointed at the bottle.
Chris nodded. 'Think it's best.'
'Right.'
What is going on?
Chris poured the sparkling drink into the glasses then handed one to her.
'To us.'
'To us.'
They clinked glasses then drank.

'I feel a bit underdressed now to be honest.' Allie looked down at her fluffy pink pyjamas and her beige slipper boots.

'You look beautiful, as always, and I would prefer you to be comfy. Besides, I love you in those soft pjs.' He winked at her and the familiar warm glow of love and desire for him flickered in her belly.

'Before we eat...' Chris took another sip of his drink. 'I need to ask you something.'

'OK.'

Allie put her cutlery down and rested her hands in her lap.

'Allie... for a while now, I've been trying to ask you something but we always get interrupted or I feel that it's not quite the right time.'

She watched him carefully, running her gaze over the familiar lines of his strong jaw, his straight nose, his salt and pepper hair and his deep dark eyes. It was a face she'd known since childhood and one she had missed when he'd disappeared from her life. When he'd walked back into her world last summer, everything had changed except her feelings for him; they were back and more powerful than ever. Chris had become a part of her life that she couldn't bear to lose.

'Yes... see... I'm going to ask now but I don't want you to think it's because of what I found out today. If you thought that, I'd be devastated. Because it's *not* about what I discovered today; it's about how much I love you and because I want to spend the rest of my life with you. I want you always, Allie, do you understand that?'

She nodded, her throat tightening with emotion. She was torn between wondering what he wanted to ask her and wanting to know what he'd found out today. Oh god! He wasn't ill was he? Was she going to lose him to some horrid illness or had he been asked to go abroad to work on a movie adaptation of one of his books, so she wouldn't see him for months, even years, at a time?

'Chris... you're kind of scaring me a bit here.'

He shook his head.

'No, my angel. Don't be scared. I love and adore you and you are my world. See, that's why...' He got up and pushed his chair back then pulled something from his pocket. When he dropped to his knees, then took her left hand, Allie gasped.

'Allie, will you be my wife?'

She held his gaze, her heart reaching out to him and enveloping him with love.

'Of course I will!'

Chris smiled, his eyes shining, then he slid a beautiful platinum band with a large square diamond onto her ring finger.

'Thank you.' He kissed her hand.

'Thank you for asking.' She leant forwards and kissed him, running her hands over his face, through his hair and over his broad shoulders. When she leant back to look at him, he was frowning.

'What is it?'

'I know this isn't very romantic but my knee has locked.' He grimaced.

'Oh no!'

Allie got up and took his hands and helped him to stand.

'You're not that old, Chris.'

'I know but it's my old footy injury plus the hours I spend sitting at a desk writing. It's not conducive to spending any length of time kneeling.'

'We'll have to get you to Honey's yoga classes. Keep you supple.'

He sat on his chair again and smiled. 'Oh, so you want me more flexible do you?'

Allie laughed.

'It's meant to be good anyway, isn't it? You know for...' He pressed his lips together.

'For what?'

'That's the other thing I wanted to speak to you about.'

Allie waited, wondering what he meant.

'Today, when I came to the café to get the car keys, I found something in your bag.'

Allie frowned. Had she left an open bar of chocolate in there again? The last time she'd done that, Chris had thought one of the cats had used her bag as a litter tray. Or had he found her bag of old pound coins that she'd been carrying round for ages? Pound coins that were no longer legal tender and that she kept forgetting about.

'I was going to propose before I found it and when I did, it didn't affect my intention, except maybe to strengthen it… because I love you and would love you whatever happened. Even if it was really unexpected. As this was.'

Why was he speaking in such a stilted way? As if he was having trouble processing his thoughts into words that wouldn't offend her.

'Allie, I found the test.'

'Test?'

He nodded.

'What test?' Allie was trying to think about what he could be referring to.

'The pregnancy test.'

Allie giggled. 'I haven't done a pregnancy test.'

Chris pulled his chair closer to the table and took her hands. 'You don't have to hide it from me, Allie. I know that you're pregnant and I'm happy about it. Honestly. We'll do this together.'

'I'm not pregnant.' She broke eye contact and stared at the steak on her plate, the mushrooms fat and gleaming, and cooling rapidly in front of her.

'But why did you have a positive test in your bag?'

She shook her head. 'I have no idea. It's the strangest thing. You're not having me on are you?'

'No. I wouldn't joke about something this serious.'

'Of course not.'

'I'll show you.'

Chris got up and went out into the hall. When he came back, he was brandishing a small white stick.

'This isn't yours?' he asked as he sat down.

Allie took the stick and stared at the twin blue lines.

'It's not mine.' She looked up at him. 'Oh no… are you disappointed?

It's just you said you were happy about it and now you know I'm not and... did you want a baby then, Chris?'
He took the stick from her and shook his head.
'No, I really didn't. It's not that we're both in our forties, because that doesn't matter these days, but your children are grown up and you have the café and I have my writing and... well... there are things we want to do. If you had been expecting then I would have been happy and we would have managed, adapted our lives, but knowing that you're not is actually a relief.'
'Thank goodness for that. I wouldn't want to disappoint you.'
'You never could.'
'So where did this come from?'
'I have no idea and that's why we both really need to wash our hands. Someone peed on that stick and we don't know who it was.'
He laughed then helped her to her feet, took the stick from her and placed it on the windowsill then led her to the sink where they both gave their hands a thorough washing.
'Right then my beautiful fiancée,' Chris said as he handed her a towel, 'Shall we eat our first meal as an engaged couple before it gets really cold?'
'Yes, I can't wait.'
And they sat down together, clinked glasses once more, then ate the meal that Chris had prepared. The candlelight flickered, the bubbles in the non-alcoholic wine winked at the brims of the glasses, the diamond sparkled on Allie's left hand, and she fell even deeper in love with Chris
He would have been happy if she was expecting their baby, even though it hadn't been in their plans. He was, however, glad that she wasn't, and that was a relief for Allie. She wanted Chris all to herself and to enjoy the things they had planned, like holidaying in hot destinations, driving across America and drinking champagne in New York.
The difference was, that now she would be able to do it as Chris's wife.

Chapter 25

Dawn

Dawn hurried up the path to the café. It was early morning and she was quite tired after the events of the previous day, but Allie had sent a text late last night asking to meet her and Camilla first thing. Allie had said it was urgent, but she couldn't tell them anything else until they were face to face.

It was another beautiful morning, the air fragrant with spring flowers and the garden of the café was an array of bright colours, with forget-me-nots, tulips and crocuses in the borders and the tree to the left of the cafe was heavy with pale pink blossom that drifted gently to the grass in the light morning breeze.

Dawn pushed open the door and went inside then closed it behind her. Allie was sitting on the leather sofa to the right of the entrance and Camilla was next to her. The familiar smells of coffee and baking met her nostrils and her mouth watered.

'Morning.' Dawn took one of the chairs opposite the sofa. 'What's this about then?'

She met Allie's eyes.

'Would you like a drink first?'

Dawn shook her head. 'Better not. Alison is due a feed soon, so I can't

stay long. Thought I'd get here asap then head back before she wakes.' She crossed her fingers. 'Hopefully! Or Rick'll have an early-morning earful and boy can she make a racket when she wants something. Wilful little thing she is. Just like her auntie.'
'Ha ha!' Camilla poked out her tongue.
'This won't take long.' Allie picked up her bag from the floor next to the sofa and opened it. 'I just wanted to find out if either of you know anything about this.'
She pulled out a small clear plastic bag with something inside it.
'What is it?' Dawn peered at the bag.
'Take a closer look.'
Allie handed her the bag and Dawn blew out her cheeks. 'Ah...' She passed the bag to Camilla and her sister's face crumpled.
'It's mine.' Camilla sniffed. 'Sorry, Allie. I did the test here yesterday then dropped it into your bag when Tom came in because I couldn't face telling him.'
'You're pregnant?' Allie asked and Camilla and Dawn nodded, as Allie wrapped an arm around Camilla. 'Well that's a good thing, surely?'
'Is it? It certainly wasn't planned.'
'Well sometimes that's how it happens.'
'Look at Alison.' Dawn nodded. 'And what a lovely surprise she was.'
'I'm not sure Tom is ready for this though.'
'He loves you.' Allie rubbed Camilla's arm. 'He'll be happy.'
'You think?' Camilla raised red eyes to meet Allie's, so she nodded.
'He will. He's a good man and he loves you.'
Camilla accepted a tissue from Dawn and wiped her eyes then blew her nose.
'Sorry you found that in your bag. I meant to let you know but I was so distracted last night. When we got back, Tom had brought the kittens into the house to keep an eye on them and I was busy trying to act as though I wasn't worried about anything, then I fell asleep on the sofa... I'm just so tired at the moment... and before I knew it, Tom was waking me to go up to bed and that was that.'

'I didn't find it.' Allie grimaced.
'Who did?' Camilla asked.
'Chris.'
'Oh no!' Dawn gasped.
'He thought it was mine.'
'What did you tell him?' Camilla sat up straight. 'Does he know it's mine?'
'Well, no, because I wasn't sure whose it was. I had an idea but thought I'd find out first.'
'Thank goodness for that.'
'It made for an interesting evening.' Allie laughed. 'When are you going to tell Tom?'
Camilla stared at her jeans and splayed her fingers over her legs as if they had the answer to her worries.
'Camilla?' Dawn prompted.
'Today. I have to, don't I? Things like this have a way of getting out and I don't want him finding out from anyone else.'
'Good.'
They sat in silence for a few minutes, mulling over what had happened and what was to come. The café had seen so many important moments in their lives, including revelations and confessions, laughter and tears, hopes and dreams. It had even seen the recent arrival of little Alison and that had been an eventful day indeed!
'Allie?'
'Yes, Dawn.'
'Do you have something to tell us?'
'Uh... like what?' Allie smiled at Dawn.
'Well I'm surprised you can even lift your left hand today.'
'What? Why?'
'Wow!' Camilla grabbed Allie's hand and held it up then turned it from side to side. 'Look at the size of that diamond.'
'Are you...'
'Engaged?' Allie nodded. 'Yes!'
'EEEK! Congratulations!' Dawn and Camilla enveloped Allie in a

group hug then the three of them laughed and cried as Allie filled them in on the details.

'What wonderful news,' Dawn said when she sat back in her seat. 'I'm going to be an auntie and my best friend is getting married. It's going to be an exciting year.'

'Indeed it is.' Allie nodded.

'Oh shit,' Camilla buried her head in her hands. 'I can't believe I'm going to be a mum.'

Chapter 26
Camilla

Back at Tom's cottage, Camilla sat on the floor in front of the sofa with HP's head in her lap. He was snoring gently, his pink tongue sticking out the side of his mouth and Camilla was absently stroking his velvety ears. The kittens were snuggled up in a cardboard box on her other side, enjoying the luxury of full bellies and their fleecy blanket.
When Camilla had returned from the café, Tom had told her he had an emergency appointment coming in and he'd rushed off to the surgery, but he'd promised to be back as soon as he could. Camilla had been glad of the time alone to get her thoughts in order. Allie and Dawn had helped her to prepare for telling Tom and she knew she had to get it done, but every time she thought about saying the words, her stomach rolled. She was so afraid of ruining what they had, of taking the shine off their lovely relationship by bringing another dimension to it. Even if it was their own child.
What if the news came between them and Tom drifted away from her? It had taken her so long to trust him with her heart and to let her guard down that the idea of going back to how she used to be was abhorrent. Camilla didn't want to be that woman anymore, to be

afraid and hesitant; she wanted to be the woman she had started to become: happy, confident and trusting.

She heard the front door creak open and she pulled air deep into her lungs.

This was it then.

It was make or break time; the moment when she'd find out if Tom wanted her and their baby.

Tom appeared in the doorway, his cheeks flushed and his eyes bright. He always looked like this after he'd helped an animal; it was happiness and pride and Camilla knew that he loved his job. His joy in it was one of the things she loved about him. He was straightforward, uncomplicated, decent and honest. And absolutely gorgeous, of course.

'Everything all right?' he asked as he came over and kissed her, being careful not to disturb HP.

'Yes they've all been out cold since you left.'

He sat next to HP and the dog's nose twitched then he opened his eyes a fraction, showing he was aware that his master had returned home.

'It's OK, HP, don't get up to greet me or anything.'

HP's little tail wiggled but he stayed where he was.

'He loves you as much as I do.' Tom rubbed HP's back. 'You're his mum now.'

'His mum?' Camilla coughed, the word almost choking her.

What a word to choose...

'Yes, of course. You're part of his pack.'

'Right.'

'That's OK isn't it? You're happy to be here with us?'

'I am, Tom. I love you both dearly.' She reached out and took his hand. 'Was everything OK at the surgery?'

'Yes, and it wasn't exactly life or death, more a case of blocked anus glands.'

'Whose?'

'Mrs Gilchrist's poodle.'

A Wedding at The Cosy Cottage Café

'Ah. So you squeezed them?'
'Yep. Apparently she thought the way Penelope was dragging her behind around on the best rug was down to something far more serious.'
'I expect it was for the rug.'
'Ha! Ha! Yes.'
'Tom?'
'Hey, what's up, Camilla? Why the frown?' He stroked her cheek. 'And don't worry these hands have been thoroughly scrubbed.'
'I need to tell you something.'
'You can tell me anything.'
'I hope so because this is kind of a big something and I'm terrified it's going to come between us.'
Tom squeezed her hand. 'Nothing could ruin what we have unless you tell me you've cheated on me or are in love with someone else. And then it would be pistols at dawn. For me and him, not you, obviously.'
Camilla ran her eyes over his handsome face, taking a mental snapshot of his happy relaxed expression and burning it into her mind, just in case she never saw it again. In case what she was about to tell him changed the way he looked at life and the way he looked at her.
'Tom... I'm... I'm... I'm pregnant.'
She closed her eyes and held her breath, but the world didn't crash down around her ears and Tom didn't jump up and run for the door leaving burn marks on the wooden floorboards. Instead, when she opened her eyes, he was still there holding her hand and smiling at her, but now his eyes were glistening.
'I'm so sorry.' She scanned his face, trying to read him.
He blinked but didn't reply.
'Tom? I said I'm sorry. It was an accident and I'm not fully sure how it happened but I've done a test and it was positive and I suppose I really should do another one just to be sure, but I was afraid to and I only found out yesterday and I've been trying to think of a way to tell you and... and...'

Tom gently moved HP off her lap then pulled her to him. He wrapped his arms around her and held her tight. She breathed in his scent, felt his love and his strength enveloping her and knew that it was OK. Everything was going to be just fine.

'Best news ever.' Tom said as he ran soft kisses down her neck. 'We're going to be parents.'

'We are. Are you sure you're OK with that?'

He got up and helped her up too.

'You've made me a very happy man, Camilla. Now let's leave HP to kitten sit while we take some time out upstairs.'

'Will the kittens be OK?'

'Did you see him with them this morning? I swear HP thinks he's their dad.'

So Camilla allowed Tom to lead her up to his bedroom, where he showed her exactly how tenderly he could love her and how much he treasured her — with his whole heart.

The next morning, Camilla woke to find the bedroom at Tom's cottage turned the colour of warm honey with early morning sunlight. He had opened the curtains and the window that overlooked his pretty back garden, and the air that whispered into the bedroom was filled with birdsong and the scent of spring flowers from the hanging baskets and pots on his decking. She stretched out and turned over to greet him but he wasn't there.

She sat up and listened.

From downstairs came the sound of Tom singing a song she thought she recognised. But he was doing it badly. She giggled. He was many things, but a great singer was not one of them.

Swinging her legs over the edge of the bed, she grabbed Tom's big T-shirt from the floor and pulled it on. She went to the bathroom,

swilled her face then padded across the landing to the top of the stairs.
'I thought I heard you up and about. Get back to bed!' Tom said from the bottom of the staircase.
'What? Why?'
'Go on and you'll see.' He smiled up at her, looking early-morning cute in his stripy pyjama bottoms and pale blue T-shirt with his dark hair sticking up.
'OK then.'
She went back to the bedroom, climbed into bed and pulled the covers up. The bed was still warm, smelling of lavender fabric softener and of them. It was comforting, this shared space where they made love and slept and she wished she never had to leave.
Thinking back to last night, her stomach fluttered. Confessing to Tom about the accidental pregnancy had been tough but he'd been so accepting, so calm and wonderfully happy about it, as if it was all fine and would be even better. Camilla wanted to believe that it would be; she loved Tom and wanted to think that they could be a family but she was still scared that bringing a baby into the equation would disturb the lovely balance they'd created.
Time would tell.
She heard Tom padding up the stairs, then the sound of panting as HP plodded across the landing and up to the bed. He had a good sniff around then came to her, licking her outstretched hand and grinning up at her. His big brown eyes were so warm and kind and she realized that she really did love the soft old bulldog too.
'Morning HP.'
'He said he wanted to come say hello.'
'Are the kittens OK?'
Tom nodded. 'Fed and gone back to sleep. After a thorough washing from HP, that was. He's a really good mum.'
They both laughed at that and HP's little tail wagged.
'Is he coming up?'
'Bunkup, HP?' Tom asked and the dog placed his two front paws on

the bed then Tom pushed him up. Once in bed, he sniffed around again before sitting next to Camilla.

'Looks like I'm redundant then.' Tom raised his eyebrows.

Camilla wrapped an arm around HP. 'You just go and get us some breakfast.'

'Actually, that's exactly what I was doing.'

'Ooh, don't let me stop you. I'm eating for two now after all.' They both froze. 'I still can't believe it, Tom.'

'Me either but you know what?'

She shook her head.

'I am over-the-moon, Camilla!'

He kissed her then headed back downstairs.

Ten minutes later, she was snuggled up to HP, thinking about the small life just beginning inside her when Tom returned, carrying a tray that he placed on the bedside table.

'For madam, we have freshly made pancakes with fresh fruit salad and maple syrup. I wasn't sure if you could face bacon.'

'That looks delicious.'

HP sat up and peered over her shoulder.

'HP thinks so too.'

'Don't let him eat your share,' Tom said. 'I'll be back in a moment with the drinks.'

Camilla lifted a plate and started to eat, enjoying the light fluffy pancakes with the sweet fresh strawberries, grapes, raspberries and blueberries. Along with the maple syrup, they were a heavenly combination. She shared a few plain pieces of pancake with HP and had almost finished when Tom returned.

'Good?'

'Amazing. Thank you! I didn't know I was so hungry.'

'No nausea this morning?' he asked as he placed a large mug of tea on the bedside table along with a glass of orange juice.

'Not so far. It's strange really. I don't feel right but I haven't felt queasy yet. As long as I relax and think pleasant thoughts, it seems to stave it off.'

'That's good.' He sighed as he walked around the bed and placed his own drinks on his bedside table.
'What?'
'It might get worse though... before it gets better.'
'I know. I've seen Dawn go through it three times.'
'Budge up HP.' Tom sat on the bed and encouraged HP to move over so he was squashed in between them. He started to pant almost immediately.
'He's too hot.' Camilla rubbed HP's velvety ears.
'I knew he would be. Come on HP.' Tom stood up and helped HP off the bed then the dog wandered into the hallway and dramatically collapsed onto the wooden boards.
'It still makes me jump when he does that.' Camilla watched HP as he stretched his short muscular legs out then settled for a snooze.
'He's a bit dramatic isn't he? Likes us to know he's there.' Tom got back into bed.
'Thank you for this delicious breakfast in bed. I should get pregnant more often.' She flashed him a smile.
'It's good news, Camilla. Really good news.'
'Did I tell you Allie's news?'
'I don't think you did.'
'My head was full of how to tell you about the baby yesterday, so it slipped my mind. She's only gone and got engaged.'
Tom's mouth slowly opened then he covered his face with his hands.
'What? What's wrong?' Camilla placed her empty glass on the table then shuffled around to face Tom.
'That's great news but lousy timing.'
'Why?'
'Because... oh Camilla, there's something I've been trying to do for ages and every time I try, something interrupts us or I have to wait. I was going to do it yesterday, then you seemed unwell and so tired, so I planned on doing it this morning... but now you've told me that and...' He blew air out of his mouth and shook his head.
'Blast it.'

'Tom,' Camilla put her hand on his arm. 'Whatever it is, you can do it. I love you. We're... going to be parents. Together.'
'And that's the other issue. I don't want you to think I'm doing it because of that either. I want to do it because I wanted to anyway, and was going to and then... you know what? I'm going to do it anyway.'
He stood up and opened the drawer of his bedside table then pulled something out. He walked around the bed and stood next to Camilla. She gazed up at him, her heart pounding with realization.
Tom lowered to his knees then took her hand.
She waited.
HP started to snore in the hallway. The birds sang in the trees outside. A plane passed overhead, the whine of its engine cutting through the peace of the morning.
'Tom? What is it?'
He shook his head but kept his eyes fixed on the wooden floor.
'Tom?'
Camilla reached out and gently raised his chin then sighed. His eyes were shining and he was biting his lower lip.
'Tom, come here.' She opened her arms and he moved into them then she hugged him tight. 'What is it? Too soon? Too much? Change of heart?' Her stomach lurched at the last question but she had to give him an out if he needed it.
'No. Course not.' His voice sounded strangled, as if the effort of speaking hurt.
'Then what?'
'Just... a lot... of emotion.' He leant back and met her eyes. 'I was, as you know, married before. But it didn't feel like this.'
'Well that's good.'
'And now... now there's a baby too.' He placed his hand on her stomach, and his palm was warm, his proximity comforting, his scent intoxicating as always.
'Yes there is. We can do this, can't we?'
He nodded.

'OK then.' Camilla raised his hand and kissed it, then slid off the bed and knelt in front of him. Holding hands, they gazed into each other's eyes, learning more about each other by the second, knowing that they were in this for the long haul, that they both wanted this more than anything.

Camilla took a deep breath.

'Tom Stone, I love and adore you. I have done since we first met, but it took me a while to accept that. I now know it with every fibre of my being. Therefore, I would be delighted if you would do me the honour of becoming my husband.'

His eyes widened. 'I was going to ask you.'

'But I got there first.' She smiled. 'That's OK, right?'

'Of course it is.'

'So...' She squeezed his hands.

'So?'

'Is there a ring?'

'Yes!' He looked around him then pulled a small black box from underneath his leg. He opened it and there, on a white satin pillow, sat a platinum ring. At the centre was a round emerald with a sparkling diamond either side of it.

'It's beautiful.'

'The emerald is to match your beautiful eyes and to remind you that I love gazing into them.'

Tom took the ring from the box then slid it onto Camilla's finger.

'How did you know the size?'

'I measured it when you were sleeping.'

'Really?'

'No!' He laughed. 'I had a look at your other rings in your jewellery box then gaged it from them.'

'It's perfect.'

'Just like you.'

They got back into bed and Tom slid his arm around her shoulders as they sipped their tea.

'I guess we have to celebrate with tea now?' Camilla held up her mug and Tom gently tapped his against it.
'I guess so.'
'That's fine by me.'
'Me too.'
'Love you.'
'Love you more.'
And they sat that way for some time, as the sun climbed in the sky, HP snored and the kittens slept soundly in their box downstairs. It was such a perfect moment that neither of them wanted to leave it until they had to.
So they didn't.

EPILOGUE - ONE SATURDAY IN JULY

The atmosphere in Jenny Talbot's small salon was electric. It was hot because of the surprise springtime heat wave that had swept across the country, and the four fans that Jenny had placed around the salon just seemed to be moving the warm air around. Jenny had also propped the front door open but the warm July morning meant that little air was coming in to help cool the place down.

There were women everywhere and Honey's head was buzzing. Even though she was a bridesmaid, Jenny had roped her in to help and she'd done everything from making coffee to plucking eyebrows to holding clips as Jenny pinned them into hair.

However, Honey had to admit that it was an exciting morning. One of her best friends in the entire world was getting married and every time she looked at the bride, her heart squeezed.

'Honey?' She resisted the urge to sigh as Jenny called her name yet again.

'Yes, Jenny.'

'I think we're just about ready to open the champagne now, don't you?'

EPILOGUE - ONE SATURDAY IN JULY

'What, you mean we're all done?'

'Yes, sweetie!' Jenny waved a hand in front of her face. 'It's so warm in here. Think we should have the bubbly on the terrace. Come on everyone, outside!'

As Jenny ushered her friends and clients outside, their heels click clacking in unison as they went, Honey got the two bottles of champagne from the fridge in the small kitchen. She stood in front of the open fridge and let the cold air drift out over her legs and toes. Her toes looked really pretty with their pearly-pink nail polish that complimented her strappy white high-heeled sandals. Honey wasn't much of a one for wearing heels, but these were so pretty that they made it worth the discomfort. The sandals had been chosen to match her pale pink bridesmaid's dress. It was made of silk and chiffon, in a Jane Austen style with short sleeves, a fitted bust and a skirt that fell from below the bust to the floor. It had two knee-high side slits so her sandals could be seen when she moved or sat down. She had a necklace of tiny freshwater pearls and matching dropper earrings, revealed today by her hairstyle, with some of her bobbed hair clipped back from her face and the rest falling in soft sausage curls. Jenny had put in more purple and pink streaks before styling her hair, so it now complimented the dress perfectly.

She'd left Dane at their cottage two hours earlier and wouldn't see him again until they met at the café for the ceremony, so he hadn't seen her dress or her hair yet and she couldn't wait to find out what he thought. She was getting used to enjoying his compliments and the way he looked at her, as if she was the most beautiful woman he'd ever seen, and she knew she'd always appreciate it. This was the first wedding they'd attended together and it was going to be a very special day.

She carried the bottles outside and placed them on the table that Jenny had set up outside the village salon. Dawn had already brought the glasses out, so Honey popped one of the corks then started to pour, assisted by Allie's mum, Connie, who was positively radiant in a light blue dress and matching jacket.

EPILOGUE – ONE SATURDAY IN JULY

Dawn looked around at her friends and family. Seeing her daughter, Laura, in her bridesmaid's dress and her mum, Jackie, sporting a cream and gold outfit with a matching hat that would've made the Queen proud, was making her emotional enough, but seeing Honey, Allie and Camilla all dressed up too was enough to tip her over the edge of the emotional precipice. If she tumbled over, she didn't think she'd ever come back. Seeing as how she didn't want to ruin her makeup, she picked up a flute of champagne and took a swig. Even though she was still breastfeeding, Dawn thought a sip of bubbly would be OK on this special occasion, then she'd stick to soft drinks for the rest of the day.

The champagne was cool and crisp and it fizzed in her belly, increasing her feeling of euphoria. She'd left Rick and James at home that morning, taking Laura and Alison with her to the salon. Her daughters were both wearing pretty gowns that matched those of the older bridesmaids, but with fuller skirts. It had been hard work getting Laura and James away from the cats they had adopted back in the spring, as her children adored Meowly Cyrus and William Shakespaw. Camilla and Tom had helped them to choose names for the then kittens, and Dawn found them highly amusing whenever she had to call the cats in for their dinner.

Alison was currently napping in her pram just inside the door of the salon, which was a good thing as Dawn knew she'd be ready for the ceremony at noon. Rick and James would meet them at the café because James was a pageboy and Rick was best man. He'd been delighted to be asked and was taking his role seriously. He had looked so handsome in his light grey suit with the silver tie and Dawn had given him a long tender kiss before leaving home.

Honey finished filling glasses then raised her own.

'Ladies!' She cleared her throat. 'I would like to make a toast to the

EPILOGUE - ONE SATURDAY IN JULY

bride. When I came to Heatherlea, my life was very different. I was lonely, directionless and had never really known what true friendship was. Then one day, I went to the café and met three wonderful women. Now my life is so full of love and happiness that I count my blessings every day. Thank you my dear friends for your love and support. Thank you Jenny for making us all look rather fancy. Here's to the beautiful bride and to her lifetime of happiness! You deserve it, sweetheart!'

They raised their glasses: 'To the bride and to a lifetime of happiness.' They took it in turns to say a few words, and Dawn smiled at the warmth of this circle of women. Laura came and stood next to her then gave her a hug, and Dawn's throat tightened even more.

This was a beautiful start to what would hopefully be a beautiful day, a day when she'd see two people she adored agreeing to spend the rest of their lives together.

Camilla held her skirts up with one hand and her bouquet in the other. The dress was so beautiful and she didn't want to get the hem dusty or to snag it on any stones. She was a combination of excited and nervous, a strange feeling but it was such a special day. She hadn't been sure that the silk and chiffon dress would suit her but when she'd gone for the final fitting, and saw how it fell from her bust to her feet, she'd known that it was a perfect dress for her baby bump. She was nearly five months along now and everything was going well. The horrid morning sickness had disappeared at around fourteen weeks and she'd had two scans to confirm that everything was OK with the baby. She and Tom had agreed that they didn't want to find out the gender of the baby but at the second scan it had been impossible to ignore the fact that they were having a son. Tom had grinned

EPILOGUE - ONE SATURDAY IN JULY

at her when they'd seen the evidence on the monitor then he'd kissed her and told her how happy he was. His happiness matched her own. The pregnancy might have been a shock but Camilla wouldn't change a thing now. She was getting more and more excited about the prospect of motherhood every day and had started to prepare one of the bedrooms as a nursery after she'd rented out her cottage and moved in with Tom.

When they neared the street of The Cosy Cottage Café, the women slowed down and Jenny did a quick check of dresses, hair and makeup.

'Time for us to go and join everyone else,' Jackie said, as she hugged her daughters and granddaughter, while Connie hugged Allie.

The older women headed to the café, then the remaining women got into the order in which they were going to enter the café garden to walk along the aisle that Jordan and Max had created.

'You all look so perfect,' Jenny said. She took some photographs on her mobile phone, including a selfie with her in, then she hugged them all quickly. It had been agreed that guests would take lots of photo on their mobiles or with their own cameras then send them to the bride and groom, and the money that would have been spent on a photographer would go to a local charity instead. 'Right, ladies, are we ready?

'Yes,' they said in unison.

'I'll go and let them know you're ready.'

Jenny gave a wave then hurried off along the road, going as fast as her gold platform heels and tight red satin dress would allow her to move. This was it then... the wedding was about to begin...

Allie breathed deeply, trying to fill her lungs with the warm

EPILOGUE - ONE SATURDAY IN JULY

fragranced July air. She couldn't believe the day had arrived. This wedding had taken quite a lot of planning and preparation, in spite of it being a relatively small affair, with friends and close family as guests and the rest of the village invited to join in the celebrations at the café afterwards.

'Do I look all right?' she asked.

'Mum, you look amazing. Everyone does.' Mandy smiled. She was looking so much better herself, Allie thought, as she took in her daughter's glossy hair and rosy cheeks. Her heartbreak had knocked her down but just as Allie had hoped, Mandy had got back up and was almost back to her best. Almost. She'd returned to London and her job after a week but had come home every other weekend since Easter, something that had delighted Allie, Chris and Jordan. They hadn't seen so much of Mandy in years, but it was as if running to her family when she was at her lowest ebb, had reminded her how much she loved and needed them, and it had definitely brought them all much closer. Allie wouldn't have seen Mandy hurt for all the world but she couldn't deny that seeing more of her daughter again was absolutely wonderful.

She took Mandy's hand and they walked along the pavement to the café then slowed before they reached the gate. Allie opened her arms and hugged her daughter then hugged Dawn, Camilla and Honey. Their shared friendship and the love and support they offered one another had carried them all through some tough times and that made the good times all the more special.

And now, there was to be a wedding at The Cosy Cottage Café.

Allie watched as her friends took their places in front of her, starting with Dawn and her two daughters, with baby Alison in her pram, the

EPILOGUE - ONE SATURDAY IN JULY

hood of which had been decorated with white roses, sweet peas and ribbons. Next was Camilla, then Honey. The three of them were like beautiful angels in their pale pink gowns with their happy smiles and sparkling eyes.

Mandy took her arm and as if by magic, Jordan appeared at her other side. Her children had agreed to walk her along the aisle. Her father could have done it, but as Mandy and Jordan were older now, they'd decided that this would be their way of showing that they trusted Chris to love and care for their mum.

'Ready?' Jordan asked.

She met his eyes and nodded. 'I'm ready.'

'Ladies.' He gestured at the café.

The gate to the café was open ready, and the murmur of conversation in the garden faded as the enchanting melody of a harp floated through the air, playing an instrumental version of Christina Perri's *A Thousand Years*.

The bridesmaids made their way along the aisle first, and from either side of the path, the guests smiled and nodded their approval. Jordan and Mandy led Allie to the gate and she looked up to find all eyes on her. She smiled at her mum and dad and at her friends, then her gaze was drawn to the door of the café, where under an arch of cream roses and purple lavender, Chris was waiting.

And from that moment, she saw nothing except for Chris.

As she walked towards him, with Jordan whispering under his breath: 'Right together, left together,' the years fell away and memories of time spent with Chris flashed before her eyes. Laughing as he handed her an ice cream from the van, then when he turned with his own, the top scoop of vanilla falling from his cone and landing on his black T-shirt. Giggling hard after they'd been caught in a summer thunderstorm in the park, their clothes soaked through. Baking together in the café kitchen, then Chris sliding his arms around her waist and kissing her neck, flour everywhere as she turned in his arms and held him tight.

EPILOGUE - ONE SATURDAY IN JULY

When she reached his side, Mandy and Jordan kissed her and Mandy took her simple lavender bouquet, then they went and sat next to their grandparents.

Chris took her hand and kissed it.

'You're so beautiful, Allie.'

She was glad that she'd chosen the simple silver gown made of silk and chiffon. It was light and floaty and cut in the same style as the bridesmaids' dresses. Her blonde hair had been gently curled and she wore a silver headband set with grey and cream freshwater pearls.

'You look pretty good too, Chris.'

And he did, in his white shirt, lavender waistcoat, light-grey jacket and matching trousers. His salt and pepper hair was cropped short and his brown eyes were warm and familiar as they roamed over Allie, making her tummy flip with love and happiness.

The majority of the ceremony took place in the café garden under the flowered arch, but Allie, Chris and their chosen witnesses, Camilla and Tom, had to go inside the café, along with the registrar and her assistant, for the contracting and declaratory words.

When they emerged from the café as husband and wife, they were met with cheers and applause, and handfuls of rose petal confetti. Chris led Allie across the lawn to the area they'd had set up as a dancefloor and there, before their family and friends, he lifted her and twirled her round then lowered her, cupped her face in his smooth hands and kissed her.

It had taken them half a lifetime to get to this moment and to be married, but now they were joined together for the rest of their lives and Allie wouldn't have it any other way.

The dancing went on all afternoon, and guests enjoyed a summery buffet made up of local produce. Allie and Chris had worked hard

EPILOGUE - ONE SATURDAY IN JULY

through the week to prepare the food for the buffet. Savoury dishes included lemon, asparagus and ricotta tart, herby salmon and couscous parcels and the local butcher had brought a large mustard-roasted beef fillet as a wedding present. For dessert there were mini lemon meringue pies, red cherry bakewell tarts and white chocolate berry cheesecakes. Mandy had insisted on having the wedding cake made by a friend of hers in London. It was a beautiful three-tiered chocolate cake with rich shiny chocolate frosting and juicy red strawberries dotted around the sides.

Jordan and Max served the drinks, including pink champagne, rum punch with slices of lemon, lime and orange, and there was freshly-made cloudy lemonade or virgin mojitos for the children and those adults not drinking alcohol.

As the sky darkened and stars appeared like diamond pinpricks set in ebony silk, Chris and Allie wandered away from the dance floor and over to the pergola, which was fragrant with honeysuckle and roses. Tea lights flickered in colourful jars on the tables under the pergola and the fairy lights draped around the pergola and the trees twinkled. The air was intoxicating and Allie couldn't tell if it was the champagne she'd drunk, the heady scent from the flowers or the fact that she was so happy making her feel lightheaded.

Chris slid his arms around her waist and gazed into her eyes.

'Thank you for making me the happiest man alive, Allie.'

'You've made me happier than I could ever have imagined, Chris.'

'You're my wife,' he whispered, his eyes shining as they reflected the candlelight.

'You're my husband.'

'It's how it should always have been. I love you, Allie.'

'I love you too.'

Chris lowered his head and kissed her softly, and the world around them dimmed, until it was just them and their love for each other. When they finally broke apart, Chris took her hand. 'Shall we dance?'

'I'd like that.'

EPILOGUE - ONE SATURDAY IN JULY

And they headed back to their family and friends, to the warmth and love that the community of Heatherlea offered.

It truly had been a wonderful wedding at The Cosy Cottage Café.

The End

Dear Reader,

Thank you so much for reading **A Year at The Cosy Cottage Café**. I hope you enjoyed reading it as much as I enjoyed writing it.

Did the story make you smile, laugh or even cry? Did you care about the characters?

I would be so grateful if you would leave a rating and a short review.

Stay safe and well!

With love,

Rachel X

Acknowledgments

Firstly, thanks to my gorgeous family. I love you so much! XXX

To my friends, for your support, advice and encouragement and to everyone who has interacted with me on social media, huge heartfelt thanks.

Special thanks to Daniela Colleo of StunningBookCovers.com for the beautiful cover.

To everyone who buys, reads and reviews this book, thank you.

About the Author

Rachel Griffiths is an author, wife, mother, Earl Grey tea drinker, gin enthusiast, dog walker and fan of the afternoon nap. She loves to read, write and spend time with her family.

WANT MORE?

Visit my website here - https://rachelgriffithsauthor.com to subscribe to my newsletter, to download free short stories and find out what's next.

Take a look at ***Also by Rachel Griffiths*** for plenty more delightfully uplifting stories!

Also by Rachel Griffiths

Cwtch Cove Series

Christmas at Cwtch Cove

Winter Wishes at Cwtch Cove

Mistletoe Kisses at Cwtch Cove

The Cottage at Cwtch Cove

The Café at Cwtch Cove

Cake And Confetti at Cwtch Cove

A New Arrival at Cwtch Cove

A Cwtch Cove Christmas (A collection of books 1-3)

The Cosy Cottage Café Series

Summer at The Cosy Cottage Café

Autumn at The Cosy Cottage Café

Winter at The Cosy Cottage Café

Spring at The Cosy Cottage Café

A Wedding at The Cosy Cottage Café

A Year at The Cosy Cottage Café (The Complete Series)

The Little Cornish Gift Shop Series

Christmas at The Little Cornish Gift Shop

Spring at The Little Cornish Gift Shop

Summer at The Little Cornish Gift Shop

The Little Cornish Gift Shop (The Complete Series)

Sunflower Street Series

Spring Shoots on Sunflower Street

Summer Days on Sunflower Street

Autumn Spice on Sunflower Street

Christmas Wishes on Sunflower Street

A Wedding on Sunflower Street

A New Baby on Sunflower Street

New Beginnings on Sunflower Street

Snowflakes and Christmas Cakes on Sunflower Street

The Cosy Cottage on Sunflower Street

Snowed in on Sunflower Street

Springtime Surprises on Sunflower Street

Autumn Dreams on Sunflower Street

A Christmas to Remember on Sunflower Street

Secret Santa on Sunflower Street

Starting Over on Sunflower Street

The Dog Sitter on Sunflower Street

Autumn Skies Over Sunflower Street

A Christmas to Remember on Sunflower Street

A Year on Sunflower Street (Sunflower Street Books 1-4)

Standalone Stories

Christmas at The Little Cottage by The Sea

The Wedding

The Cornish Garden Café Series

Spring at the Cornish Garden Café
Summer at the Cornish Garden Café
Autumn at the Cornish Garden Café
Winter at the Cornish Garden Café

Printed in Great Britain
by Amazon